P9-DOF-424

The stranger reached the wood and looked around for a place to make a temporary nest, but each paw prickled with restlessness, and none of the hollows or the spaces under the tree roots seemed quite suitable.

As the day began to fade, the cat left the trees behind and reached the crest of a hill covered in tough moorland grass. Below, a scarlet sunset was reflected in the lake, transforming the water to the color of blood. Above the stranger's head, the first warriors of StarClan were glimmering in the sky.

The traveling cat took a deep breath. *I have returned. Let vengeance begin.*

WARRIORS

THE PROPHECIES BEGIN

THE NEW PROPHECY

POWER OF THREE

OMEN OF THE STARS

DAWN OF THE CLANS

explore the WARRIORS world

MANGA

The Lost Warrior

Warrior's Refuge

Warrior's Return

The Rise of Scourge

Tigerstar and Sasha #1: Into the Woods

Tigerstar and Sasha #2: Escape from the Forest

Tigerstar and Sasha #3: Return to the Clans

Ravenpaw's Path #1: Shattered Peace

Ravenpaw's Path #2: A Clan in Need

Ravenpaw's Path #3: The Heart of a Warrior

SkyClan and the Stranger #1: The Rescue

SkyClan and the Stranger #2: Beyond the Code

SkyClan and the Stranger #3: After the Flood

NOVELLAS

Hollyleaf's Story

Mistystar's Omen

Cloudstar's Journey

Tigerclaw's Fury

Leafpool's Wish

Dovewing's Silence

Mapleshade's Vengeance

Goosefeather's Curse

Also by Erin Hunter

SEEKERS

RETURN TO THE WILD

MANGA

SURVIVORS

OMEN OF THE STARS

WARRIORS

THE FORGOTTEN WARRIOR

ERIN HUNTER

HARPER

An Imprint of HarperCollinsPublishers

The Forgotten Warrior
Copyright © 2011 by Working Partners Limited
Warriors Adventure Game © 2011 by Working Partners Limited
"Training Day" © 2011 by Working Partners Limited
Series created by Working Partners Limited
Map art © 2015 by Dave Stevenson
Interior art © 2015 by Allen Douglas
All rights reserved. Printed in the United States of America. No part of
this book may be used or reproduced in any manner whatsoever without
written permission except in the case of brief quotations embodied in
critical articles and reviews. For information address HarperCollins
Children's Books, a division of HarperCollins Publishers, 195 Broadway,
New York, NY 10007.
www.harpercollinschildrens.com

Library of Congress Cataloging-in-Publication Data
The forgotten warrior / Erin Hunter. — 1st ed.
　　p.　　cm. — (Warriors, omen of the stars ; #5)
Summary: When an outsider appears in ThunderClan's midst, it
drives the Clans further apart and as tension mounts they must decide
who they can trust before it is too late.
ISBN 978-0-06-238262-7 (pbk.)
[1. Cats—Fiction.　2. Prophecies—Fiction.　3. Clans—Fiction.
4. Courage—Fiction.　5. Loyalty—Fiction.　6. Forests—Fiction.
7. Secrets—Fiction.　8. Adventure and adventurers—Fiction.
9. Fantasy.]　I. Title.
PZ7.H916625 For　2011　　　　　　　　　　　2011534106
[Fic]—dc22　　　　　　　　　　　　　　　　　　　　CIP
　　　　　　　　　　　　　　　　　　　　　　　　　AC

Typography by Ellice M. Lee
19　20　　CG/BRR　　20　19　18　17　16　15　14
❖
Revised paperback edition, 2015

Special thanks to Cherith Baldry

ALLEGIANGES

THUNDERCLAN

LEADER
FIRESTAR—ginger tom with a flame-colored pelt

DEPUTY
BRAMBLECLAW—dark brown tabby tom with amber eyes

MEDIGINE GAT
JAYFEATHER—gray tabby tom with blind blue eyes

WARRIORS
(toms and she-cats without kits)

GRAYSTRIPE—long-haired gray tom

DUSTPELT—dark brown tabby tom

SANDSTORM—pale ginger she-cat with green eyes

BRACKENFUR—golden brown tabby tom

SORRELTAIL—tortoiseshell-and-white she-cat with amber eyes

CLOUDTAIL—long-haired white tom with blue eyes

BRIGHTHEART—white she-cat with ginger patches

MILLIE—striped gray tabby she-cat with blue eyes

THORNCLAW—golden brown tabby tom

SQUIRRELFLIGHT—dark ginger she-cat with green eyes

LEAFPOOL—light brown tabby she-cat with amber eyes, former medicine cat

SPIDERLEG—long-limbed black tom with brown underbelly and amber eyes

BIRCHFALL—light brown tabby tom

WHITEWING—white she-cat with green eyes

BERRYNOSE—cream-colored tom

HAZELTAIL—small gray-and-white she-cat

MOUSEWHISKER—gray-and-white tom

CINDERHEART—gray tabby she-cat

LIONBLAZE—golden tabby tom with amber eyes

FOXLEAP—reddish tabby tom

ICECLOUD—white she-cat

TOADSTEP—black-and-white tom

ROSEPETAL—dark cream she-cat

BRIARLIGHT—dark brown she-cat

BLOSSOMFALL—tortoiseshell-and-white she-cat

BUMBLESTRIPE—very pale gray tom with black stripes

DOVEWING—pale gray she-cat with blue eyes

IVYPOOL—silver-and-white tabby she-cat with dark blue eyes

QUEENS   (she-cats expecting or nursing kits)

FERNCLOUD—pale gray (with darker flecks) she-cat with green eyes

DAISY—cream long-furred cat from the horseplace

POPPYFROST—tortoiseshell she-cat (mother to Cherrykit, a ginger she-cat, and Molekit, a brown-and-cream tom)

ELDERS (former warriors and queens, now retired)

MOUSEFUR—small dusky brown she-cat

PURDY—plump tabby former loner with a gray muzzle

SHADOWCLAN

LEADER **BLACKSTAR**—large white tom with jet-black paws

DEPUTY **ROWANCLAW**—ginger tom

MEDICINE CAT **LITTLECLOUD**—very small tabby tom

WARRIORS **OAKFUR**—small brown tom
APPRENTICE, FERRETPAW (cream-and-gray tom)

SMOKEFOOT—black tom

TOADFOOT—dark brown tom

APPLEFUR—mottled brown she-cat

CROWFROST—black-and-white tom

RATSCAR—brown tom with long scar across his back
APPRENTICE, PINEPAW (black she-cat)

SNOWBIRD—pure white she-cat

TAWNYPELT—tortoiseshell she-cat with green eyes
APPRENTICE, STARLINGPAW (ginger tom)

OLIVENOSE—tortoiseshell she-cat

OWLCLAW—light brown tabby tom

SHREWFOOT—gray she-cat with black feet

SCORCHFUR—dark gray tom

REDWILLOW—mottled brown-and-ginger tom

TIGERHEART—dark brown tabby tom

DAWNPELT—cream-furred she-cat

QUEENS　　**KINKFUR**—tabby she-cat, with long fur that sticks out at all angles

IVYTAIL—black, white, and tortoiseshell she-cat

ELDERS　　**CEDARHEART**—dark gray tom

TALLPOPPY—long-legged light brown tabby she-cat

SNAKETAIL—dark brown tom with tabby-striped tail

WHITEWATER—white she-cat with long fur, blind in one eye

WINDCLAN

LEADER　　**ONESTAR**—brown tabby tom

DEPUTY　　**ASHFOOT**—gray she-cat

MEDICINE CAT　**KESTRELFLIGHT**—mottled gray tom

WARRIORS　　**CROWFEATHER**—dark gray tom

OWLWHISKER—light brown tabby tom

WHITETAIL—small white she-cat

NIGHTCLOUD—black she-cat

GORSETAIL—very pale gray-and-white tom with blue eyes

WEASELFUR—ginger tom with white paws

HARESPRING—brown-and-white tom

LEAFTAIL—dark tabby tom with amber eyes

EMBERFOOT—gray tom with two dark paws

HEATHERTAIL—light brown tabby she-cat with blue eyes

    APPRENTICE, FURZEPAW (gray-and-white she-cat)

BREEZEPELT—black tom with amber eyes

    APPRENTICE, BOULDERPAW (large pale gray tom)

SEDGEWHISKER—light brown tabby she-cat

SWALLOWTAIL—dark gray she-cat

SUNSTRIKE—tortoiseshell she-cat with large white mark on her forehead

WHISKERNOSE—light brown tom

ELDERS   **WEBFOOT**—dark gray tabby tom

    TORNEAR—tabby tom

RIVERCLAN

LEADER   **MISTYSTAR**—gray she-cat with blue eyes

DEPUTY   **REEDWHISKER**—black tom

    APPRENTICE, HOLLOWPAW (dark brown tabby tom)

MEDICINE CAT   **MOTHWING**—dappled golden she-cat

    APPRENTICE, WILLOWSHINE (gray tabby she-cat)

WARRIORS   **GRAYMIST**—pale gray tabby she-cat

    MINTFUR—light gray tabby tom

    ICEWING—white she-cat with blue eyes

    MINNOWTAIL—dark gray she-cat

    APPRENTICE, MOSSYPAW (brown-and-white she-cat)

PEBBLEFOOT—mottled gray tom

MALLOWNOSE—light brown tabby tom

ROBINWING—tortoiseshell-and-white tom

BEETLEWHISKER—brown-and-white tabby tom

PETALFUR—gray-and-white she-cat

GRASSPELT—light brown tom

TROUTSTREAM—pale gray tabby she-cat

RUSHTAIL—light brown tabby she-cat

QUEENS

DUSKFUR—brown tabby she-cat

MOSSPELT—tortoiseshell she-cat with blue eyes

ELDERS

DAPPLENOSE—mottled gray she-cat

POUNCETAIL—ginger-and-white tom

CATS OUTSIDE THE CLANS

SMOKY—muscular gray-and-white tom who lives in a barn at the horseplace

FLOSS—small gray-and-white she-cat who lives at the horseplace

OTHER ANIMALS

MIDNIGHT—a star-gazing badger who lives by the sea

GREENLEAF
TWOLEGPLACE

TWOLEG NEST

TWOLEG PATH

TWOLEG PATH

CLEARING

SHADOWCLAN
CAMP

HALFBRIDGE

SMALL
THUNDERPATH

GREENLEAF
TWOLEGPLACE

HALFBRIDGE

CAT VIEW

ISLAND

STREAM

RIVERCLAN
CAMP

HORSEPLACE

ABANDONED
TWOLEG NEST

MOONPOOL

OLD THUNDERPATH

THUNDERCLAN
CAMP

ANCIENT OAK

LAKE

WINDCLAN
CAMP

BROKEN
HALFBRIDGE

TWOLEGPLACE

THUNDERPATH

KEY
To The
CLANS

THUNDERCLAN

RIVERCLAN

SHADOWCLAN

WINDCLAN

STARCLAN

NORTH

SANCTUARY
COTTAGE

HAREVIEW
CAMPSITE

SADLER WOODS

LITTLEPINE
SAILING
CENTER

LITTLEPINE ROAD

TWOLEG VIE

LITTLEPINE
ISLAND

RIVER ALBA

WHITECHURCH ROAD

KNIGHT'S
COPSE

ABANDONED
WORKMAN'S
HOUSE

QUARRY ROAD (disused)

QUARRY

CRYSTAL
POOL

HARE HILL
WOODS

SANCTUARY
LAKE

HARE HILL

HARE HILL
RIDING STABLES

HARE HILL ROAD

KEY
To The
TERRAIN

DECIDUOUS WOODLAND

PINE FOREST

MARSH

LAKE

FOOTPATHS

NORTH

PROLOGUE

Brambles rustled at the edge of a wood as a cat emerged into the open. Watchful eyes flicked to each side; then the cat strode out across a wide stretch of meadow grass, heading toward another belt of trees in the distance. Bright newleaf sun shone down on a landscape patched with fields and hedges. Twoleg dens clustered together beside a Thunderpath.

Even so early in the season, the sun was hot, and the cat's ears flicked in irritation as flies buzzed around them. *It will be cooler under the trees,* the traveler thought, pausing for a moment to flex tired paws. *And there's not much farther to go. Just beyond that range of hills . . .*

But before the cat reached the inviting shade of the wood, a loud hiss sounded and a second cat leaped out from under a nearby hedge: a tough, lean tom with a gray pelt and one bitten ear.

"What are you doing here?" the tom demanded. "If you're looking for somewhere to rest, keep looking. This is *my* place. And the prey around here is mine."

The traveling cat halted and looked the tom up and down

with narrowed eyes. "Your *place*? You mean, you live in this hedge?"

"No, I'm from the farm over there." The tom waved his tail in the direction of a large Twoleg den just visible above the thorns. "And I don't like strangers. Keep going, or I'll make you." He bared his teeth and slid out his claws, his mangy cloud-colored fur fluffing up in anger.

The traveler rocked back on its haunches. *It's been a while since I used my fighting skills . . . but I'm not going to let this mange-pelt scare me.* "I'm just passing through. I'm no threat to your precious prey."

The farm cat let out a disbelieving snort and tilted his head to one side. "Are you one of those cats from the lake?"

The journeying cat's tone was wary. "Why do you ask?"

"Because I've seen them coming this way before," the gray tom replied. "Oh, they haven't seen me, I've made sure of that. But I've heard them talking about the mountains." He rolled his eyes. "Who'd want to go all that way? Can't they find enough food where they live?"

"Maybe they're not looking for food." The first cat's voice was tinged with scorn. "There are other things in life, you know."

The farm cat sat down and scratched his ear with one hind-paw. "Like what?" he mewed contemptuously. "Gazing at the stars and imagining your ancestors are looking back at you?" At the traveler's start of surprise, he added, "I've listened to plenty of tales about what happens on the other side of those hills. As long as they don't trouble me, I don't care what those cats get up to. They can—"

"Right," the traveler interrupted, pushing past the farm cat and padding on. "As long as they don't steal your prey."

The gray tom sprang to his paws and followed. "You're one of them, aren't you?" he asked as he caught up. "I think I've seen you before."

"Maybe." The journeying cat's whiskers twitched. "A long time ago."

"Where have you been?" The farm cat's voice was curious. "Did you get lost?"

"Oh, no." The stranger sounded faintly amused. "I always knew where I was."

The farm cat fell back, watching the stranger pad toward the trees. Then he shook his head and bounded back to the farm, vanishing under the hedge with a whisk of his tail.

The traveler reached the wood and looked around for a place to make a temporary nest, but each paw prickled with restlessness, and none of the hollows or the spaces under the tree-roots seemed quite suitable. A mouse crept out from under a bush, nibbling at fallen grass seeds. Remembering long-forgotten lessons, the traveler dropped into the hunter's crouch and sprang, killing the mouse with a single swift blow. But the limp body looked unappetizing with the life chased out of it; the cat scraped a few pawfuls of earth over it and left it.

Dusk was falling as the traveler continued, heading up the hill more swiftly through the spindly trees.

It's been a long time. Will the cats that I remember best still be there?

As the day began to fade, the cat left the trees behind and reached the crest of a hill covered in tough moorland grass. Below, a scarlet sunset was reflected in the lake, transforming the water to the color of blood. Above the stranger's head, the first warriors of StarClan were glimmering in the sky.

The traveling cat took a deep breath. *I have returned. Let vengeance begin.*

CHAPTER 1

❧

Jayfeather's dream dissolved into darkness as he woke and stretched his jaws in a massive yawn. His whole body seemed heavy, and when he sat up in his nest he felt as though ivy tendrils were wrapped around him, dragging him back to the ground. The air was hotter than usual for late newleaf, filled with the scents of prey and lush green growth. Noise filtered through the brambles that screened the medicine cat's den from the rest of the stone hollow: paw steps and the excited murmuring of many cats as they gathered for the first patrols of the day.

But Jayfeather couldn't share his Clanmates' excitement. Although a moon had passed since he and his companions had returned from their visit to the Tribe, he felt cold and bleak inside. His head was full of images of mountains, endless snow-covered peaks stretching into the distance, outlined crisply against an ice-blue sky. His belly cramped with pain as he recalled one particular image: a white cat with green eyes who gave him a long, sorrowful look before she turned away and padded along a cliff top above a thundering waterfall.

Jayfeather shook his head. *What's the matter with me? That was all a long, long time ago. My life has always been here with the Clans. So why do I feel as if something has been lost?*

"Hi, Jayfeather." Briarlight's voice had a muffled, echoing sound, and Jayfeather realized she must have her head inside the cleft where he stored his herbs. "You're awake at last."

Jayfeather replied with a grunt. Briarlight was another of his problems. He couldn't forget what Lionblaze had told him when he returned from the mountains: how Briarlight was so frustrated by being confined to the hollow, trapped by her damaged hindlegs, that she'd persuaded her brother Bumble-stripe to carry her into the forest to look for herbs.

"There was a dog running loose," Lionblaze had told him. "A cat with four functioning legs would have been hard-pressed to outrun it. If it hadn't been for me and Toadstep luring it away, Briarlight would have been torn to pieces."

"Mouse-brain!" Jayfeather snapped. "Why would she put herself in danger like that?"

"Because she's convinced that she's useless," Lionblaze explained. "Can't you give her more to do? Cinderheart and I promised her we'd help her find a proper part to play in the life of the Clan."

"You had no right to promise her anything without speaking to me first," Jayfeather retorted. "Are you suggesting I take her as my apprentice? Because I don't want an apprentice!"

"That's not what I meant," Lionblaze meowed, his tail-tip twitching in annoyance. "But you could find more interesting duties for her, couldn't you?"

Still reluctant, Jayfeather had done as his brother asked. He had to admit that Briarlight was easy to teach. She had been stuck in the medicine cat's den for so long that she had already picked up a lot.

She's actually useful, he mused. *Her paws are neat and quick when she sorts the herbs, and she's good at soaking wilted leaves in the pool without letting them fall to pieces.*

"Jayfeather?" Briarlight's voice roused Jayfeather from his thoughts. He heard her wriggling around, and then her voice came more clearly as if she was poking her head out of the cleft. "Are you okay? You were tossing and turning all night."

"I'm fine," Jayfeather muttered, unwilling to dwell any longer on the dreams that had plagued him.

"We're running low on marigold," Briarlight went on. "We used up a lot on Dovewing's scratches when you got back from the mountains. Should I ask Brightheart to collect some more?"

"No, I'll go," Jayfeather muttered.

"Fine." Briarlight's voice was determinedly cheerful. "I'll get on with sorting the herbs. Oh, one more thing . . ."

Jayfeather heard the young she-cat dragging herself across the floor of the den until she reached his nest and pushed something toward him. "Could you throw this out on your way past the dirtplace?" she asked. "It was stuck at the back of the herb store."

Jayfeather stretched out his neck until his nose touched a tuft of fur with a few dried scraps of leaf dusted on it. He stiffened as he recognized the faint scent that clung to it.

"Who would have put an old bit of fur among the herbs?" Briarlight continued. "It must have been in there for ages. I don't recognize the scent or color."

For a moment Jayfeather didn't reply. He breathed in his lost sister's scent, overwhelmed by longing for the time when he and Hollyleaf and Lionblaze had played and trained together, before they knew anything about the prophecy, before they learned how Squirrelflight and Leafpool had lied to them.

I don't know how Hollyleaf's fur got into the store, he thought, *but I should have thrown it out when I first found it there, not left it for another cat to find.*

"I wonder where it came from," Briarlight meowed. "Maybe a cat from another Clan got in here to steal herbs." She stifled a *mrrow* of laughter. "Maybe the kits got in and hid it."

"How would I know?" Jayfeather snapped, irritated at being jerked out of his memories. "You should stop letting your imagination run away with you."

Turning so that Briarlight couldn't see what he was doing, he tucked the scrap of fur deep inside the moss of his nest, and rose to his paws. "I'm going to fetch that marigold," he mewed, and headed out of the den.

Before he had taken half a dozen paw steps into the clearing, Bumblestripe's scent washed over him as the young tom bounded up. "I was coming to see you," Bumblestripe blurted out. "I'm really worried about Dovewing."

"Why? What's the matter? Her scratches have healed, haven't they?"

"It's not that. She keeps having bad dreams—she had another one last night. She woke up screeching, and she was muttering about giant birds and snow."

Jayfeather struggled to suppress a stab of impatience. *I know how bad it must have been, watching Swoop carried off by the eagle. But Dovewing has to be stronger than this.*

"How do you know about it?" he asked Bumblestripe.

"There's a leak in the warriors' den right above my nest," the young tom replied. "And there's no more room in there, so I thought I'd spend a few nights in the apprentices' den with Dovewing and Ivypool. And every night Dovewing has these awful dreams. Are there any herbs that can help her?"

Jayfeather picked up waves of deep anxiety rolling off Bumblestripe. "There are no herbs that can take away memories," he meowed. "You just have to learn to live with them." *Don't we all?* he added silently.

"But—" Bumblestripe began.

Brambleclaw's voice rang out across the clearing, cutting across his protest. "Hey, Bumblestripe! You're supposed to be on hunting patrol. Sorreltail's waiting."

"Okay!" Bumblestripe called back. "Coming! Bye, Jayfeather!" He bounded away.

Jayfeather headed toward the apprentices' den, where Dovewing and Ivypool were sleeping since the warriors' den was so crowded, only to halt when he realized that Brambleclaw had gotten there ahead of him.

"Ivypool, Dovewing, wake up!" the ThunderClan deputy yowled, sticking his head into the den. "You've overslept again."

Jayfeather heard muffled mews of protest; a couple of heartbeats later the two she-cats staggered into the open.

"You look dreadful!" Brambleclaw meowed, annoyance in his tone. "I've never seen such messy fur! Have you been hunting at night?"

Though Jayfeather couldn't see them, his twitching nose picked up dusty, ruffled fur, and he could sense echoes of fear coming from both cats. He knew very well why their sleep had been disturbed. Bumblestripe had just told him about Dovewing's troubled dreams, while each night Ivypool was visiting the Dark Forest, training with the cats who had been spurned by StarClan.

I wish she'd tell me more about what happens there, Jayfeather thought. *But no—she just says that she'll let me know when there's anything important to report.*

"Why don't I check them out in my den?" he suggested to Brambleclaw, hoping for the chance to get some information out of the two she-cats in private. "Maybe they're coming down with something . . ."

Jayfeather's voice trailed off as he realized that no cat was listening to him. As he was speaking, the swift patter of paws announced the arrival of Whitewing.

"Brambleclaw, don't get angry with them!" she meowed. "They're working so hard, now that we don't have any apprentices." She paused, then added, "I'll help them with their duties today."

"I need you to go on border patrol," Brambleclaw told her.

"And I *need* to stay here with my daughters," Whitewing retorted. "Some other cat can go on border patrol instead of me."

Brambleclaw gave a disapproving sniff. "Fine," he muttered, and stalked away.

"Now, tidy yourselves up," Whitewing went on, rasping her tongue busily over Ivypool's ears.

"Get off me!" Ivypool protested. "I'm not a kit!"

"You'll always be *my* kit," Whitewing told her, turning to give the same brisk licks to Dovewing, who jumped back and exclaimed, "Stop! I'm a *warrior*! I can do my own fur!"

"Then prove it. We need to fetch moss for the elders' bedding," Whitewing went on as her daughters gave themselves a quick grooming. "And for StarClan's sake make sure there are no thorns in Purdy's, or we'll never hear the end of it. Come on!"

She bustled them toward the camp entrance, but before they reached the thorn tunnel Firestar appeared at the head of the dawn patrol. Jayfeather's nose was flooded with the scents of his Clanmates. Brambleclaw bounded across the clearing to meet them, with Dustpelt, Cloudtail, and Brightheart hard on his paws. Foxleap raised his head from the fresh-kill pile, a mouse dangling from his jaws, while Berrynose strode importantly up to the patrol, followed more slowly by Leafpool and Squirrelflight.

Molekit and Cherrykit burst out of the nursery, scampered out into the clearing, and hurled themselves at Berrynose's paws, tripping him.

"Careful!" he murmured, recovering his balance and sweeping his tail around the two excited kits.

Berrynose can be a real pain in the tail, Jayfeather pondered.

How come he's such a good father?

"Is ShadowClan attacking?" Molekit squeaked. "Can we go and fight?"

"I've learned a really good move!" Cherrykit exclaimed, pouncing on a leaf and shredding it with her tiny claws.

"Of course you can't fight!" Poppyfrost panted as she caught up to her kits. "You're not even apprentices yet!"

Brambleclaw skirted the kits and halted in front of his Clan leader. "Any news?" he asked.

"No, everything's quiet," Firestar responded as Jayfeather padded over to listen. "It looks as if all the Clans are at peace with one another."

"Right," Thornclaw agreed; the tabby tom had followed Firestar into the camp. "There was no evidence that either WindClan or ShadowClan had been anywhere near the borders, except to renew the scent markers."

"That's good news!" Brightheart exclaimed.

Jayfeather wasn't so sure. He knew that the Clans were keeping to themselves because of the deep divisions within StarClan along Clan boundaries. All the warrior ancestors were warning every cat to stay apart from the other Clans, to trust none but their Clanmates, and prepare for something dreadful that lay in the future like storm clouds on the horizon.

At least ThunderClan has the three cats mentioned in the prophecy, Jayfeather thought. *There will be three, kin of your kin, with the power of the stars in their paws. Me, Lionblaze, and Dovewing, all in the same Clan. That must make us safer, right?*

He flexed his paws. After his sleepless night they didn't feel particularly powerful, but at least they would carry him as far as the patch of marigold above the hollow. Then he remembered the other prophecy, from the Tribe of Endless Hunting barely a moon before. For a moment Jayfeather was plunged back to that dark, windswept mountaintop, surrounded by dead cats who fixed their luminous eyes on him. Once again he seemed to hear the whispers of a long, long line of Stonetellers.

The end of the stars draws near. Three must become four to challenge the darkness that lasts forever.

Rousing from the trance, Jayfeather was once more aware of the sounds and scents of the camp around him.

How are we going to recognize the fourth cat? We had enough problems finding the first three. And this new prophecy says nothing about Firestar's kin. Jayfeather bit back a hiss of frustration. *It could be any cat from the Clans!*

CHAPTER 2

Ivypool followed Whitewing until they stopped beside a tiny stream, not far from the camp. Leaves clustered thickly on the trees and the newleaf grass was long and lush, cool for Ivypool's tired paws. *Thank StarClan!* She puffed out a breath of relief. *Every hair on my pelt is aching.*

The night before, she had taken part in a tough training session with Sunstrike and Redwillow. Hawkfrost had been supervising, not letting up until all three cats bore the marks of their opponents' claws. Now Ivypool felt as if her body were nothing but a huge bruise, and one ear was still ringing from a well-aimed blow.

Glancing at her sister, Ivypool saw that she looked just as exhausted. *Jayfeather should never have taken Dovewing to the mountains,* she thought with a stab of anger. *It could have been her that the eagle carried off, and she's too important to the Clan to risk losing.*

"Let's rest for a bit," Whitewing suggested, more sympathetic now. "You can have a drink and finish grooming."

Ivypool could hear anxiety in her mother's voice. *I know she cares about us, even though she's concerned that we're falling behind with our duties.*

"No, we're fine," Dovewing meowed, straightening her shoulders and raising her head in an effort to look alert. "We should keep going. There's a good moss place a bit farther on."

"You're both a long way from fine," Whitewing pointed out. After a moment's hesitation, she added, "I know there's something troubling you. I'm not going to ask what it is, if you don't want to tell me. But remember that I'm your mother. Nothing you say could ever shock me or make me love you less."

Ivypool twitched her ears. *I bet I could prove you wrong.*

But she kept quiet, happy to sit in the long, cool grass and relax as Whitewing helped groom her pelt with long, rhythmic strokes of her tongue. It felt good to be taken care of for once after her visits to the Dark Forest, where she couldn't trust any cat, and always had to be on her guard.

"I had a bad dream last night," Dovewing confessed, twisting her neck to get at a clump of matted fur on her shoulder. "I thought I was back in the mountains. Swoop was being carried away by the eagle."

"You should try not to think about it," Whitewing mewed gently, turning to Dovewing and helping her to tease out the clump with swift rasping licks. "You know that eagles never come to the lake."

And if they did, Ivypool thought, *Dovewing would hear them before any other cat.*

Whitewing finished grooming Dovewing and rose to her paws, arching her back in a long stretch. Ivypool got up, too, ready to move on. Then she noticed that Dovewing was still sitting by the stream, shaking her head and pawing at her ear as if there was something lodged inside it.

Glancing at Whitewing, who was looking the other way, Ivypool leaned over to murmur quietly to her sister, "Are you okay? Are your senses still not working?"

"No . . . I still can't hear properly!" Dovewing's blue eyes were stricken. "I mean, I can hear you and Whitewing and what's around us, but I can't hear any farther than that. It's all just noise and shrieking and the sound of the wind."

Ivypool touched her nose to her sister's shoulder. "It must be because you heard so much when you were in the mountains," she meowed. "You said it was much louder when you crossed the ridge above WindClan. Maybe it will get better soon."

"I keep hoping that," Dovewing muttered. "But it's been a moon. I feel like I'm useless to the Clan."

"No way!" Ivypool shook her head. "Don't think like that!"

Dovewing sighed. "But it's like being deaf."

"No, it's like being *normal*," Ivypool told her. "You—"

She broke off as Whitewing turned around. "It's time we got moving," she called. "We have that moss to collect, and then I want to do some hunting for the elders."

She bounded off toward the lake. Ivypool exchanged a glance with Dovewing, and they both followed. They had just reached the gnarled oak whose roots were covered in thick green moss when Ivypool spotted a flicker of movement in the trees nearby. Her neck fur began to rise and she braced her muscles, ready to attack an intruder, then relaxed as she realized it was Jayfeather. She was still surprised by how confidently the blind medicine cat wove through the undergrowth.

Whitewing had paused, gazing through the trees at Jayfeather. "He shouldn't be out by himself," she murmured. "Ivypool, go see if he needs any help."

Ivypool hesitated. She didn't want to be alone with Jayfeather; she knew he had been waiting for the chance to interrogate her about the Dark Forest.

"Go on!" Whitewing flicked her tail toward Jayfeather. "He might be a bit moody, but you know he'll be glad to have your help."

And hedgehogs might fly! Ivypool thought as she padded after the medicine cat.

"Good luck!" Dovewing whispered after her.

Ivypool quickened her pace, following Jayfeather's thin tabby shape as he rounded a patch of nettles. "Hi," she meowed as she caught up to him. "Whitewing sent me to see if you need any help."

Jayfeather twitched one ear as if a fly had landed on it. "No," he replied curtly.

Great! I can get back to moss collecting! But then Ivypool realized that Whitewing would never let her get away with that. "At least let me tag along," she persisted. "Or I'll just be sent straight back to you."

Jayfeather shrugged. "Okay. But don't even *think* of trying to guide me. I was finding my way through this forest before you were kitted. I'm just going to collect some marigold leaves from the top of the hollow," he added as Ivypool fell in beside him. "There are some good clumps on the slope above the highest part of the cliff, where the trees have thinned out and sunlight reaches the ground."

Ivypool was surprised that the medicine cat could describe the spot so well when he had never seen it. She padded beside him over rough ground along the curve of the cliff, where stones poked out of the earth and roots snaked out as if trying to trip them. Soon they reached the edge, and Ivypool looked down into the hollow. She shuddered as she remembered her vision of blood and fighting cats, and wondered again if it had been an omen of the destruction of her Clan.

Then Jayfeather swung away from the cliff top and followed a steeper trail that led through dense brambles. Ivypool had to press herself close to the ground to avoid the tendrils that reached out over the path. She was so busy concentrating on crouching down that she almost bumped into Jayfeather's hindquarters when he halted with a hiss of disgust.

Ivypool realized that the medicine cat was caught on a bramble tendril, the thorns snagged in his pelt. She reached out a paw to pull the stem off, then stopped herself. *He'd claw me worse than the brambles if I tried to help him!*

Awkwardly Jayfeather lifted one paw and groped for the end of the bramble, muttering under his breath. After a moment he managed to free himself, though there was a tuft of tabby fur left on the thorns as he crept forward again. When another tendril raked its thorns along his side, he didn't even pause, just pulled himself away and went on.

Ivypool was glad when they emerged into a small clearing.

She flexed her muscles, letting the hot sun soak into her fur, and her jaws watered at the strong smell of rabbits.

"This is the place," Jayfeather meowed, "but I can't smell any marigold with this reek of rabbit."

Padding farther into the clearing, Ivypool looked around for the plants. But all she could see were clumps of nibbled stalks and a scattering of leaves, already shriveling in the sun.

"Oh, no!" she hissed.

"What's the matter?" Jayfeather demanded.

"There's no marigold here," Ivypool told him. "Something has eaten it all. It must have been the rabbits—I can see their droppings here, too."

Jayfeather was already stalking up to the ruined plants, thrusting his nose deep into the remains of the clumps and sniffing at the hard, dark droppings. "This is a disaster," he spat. "I've tried to grow marigold with my other plants beside the old Twoleg nest, but it only grows well up here in the sun."

Ivypool walked slowly around the clearing in case there were any plants the rabbits had missed. She couldn't see any, but suddenly the scent of marigold, strong and sweet, wafted over her. She halted, puzzled.

That smells like a lot of plants. So why can't I see them?

With her jaws parted to taste the air, Ivypool followed the scent. It led to a beech tree at the edge of the clearing; the scent was pouring down from the branches.

"Plants growing in a tree?" she murmured. "That's mouse-brained!"

But Ivypool couldn't deny what her nose was telling her.

Still confused, she scrambled up the tree until she reached the first branch. Crouching there, claws digging into the bark, she stared at the shallow hollow formed where the branch joined the trunk. It was filled with rainwater, and several marigold plants had been placed there, with their roots in the water so that they stayed fresh and alive.

"Jayfeather!" she called excitedly. "I've found marigold!"

Jayfeather looked around as if he couldn't figure out where her voice was coming from, then bounded over to the foot of her tree. "Plants up a tree?" His voice was sharp with annoyance. "If this is a joke, I'll—"

"It's not a joke," Ivypool assured him, describing the scoop of water with the plants carefully arranged there. "I'll drop them down to you."

"This is the weirdest thing I've ever come across," Jayfeather went on, as Ivypool picked up the plants one by one and dropped them to the ground. "How in the name of StarClan did they get up there?"

"Maybe the rabbits carried them up to keep them for later?" Ivypool guessed.

"When have you ever seen a rabbit climbing a tree?" Jayfeather asked in a scathing voice, making a bundle of the plants by his front paws. "Squirrels hoard nuts," he added thoughtfully. "Maybe this is one of their stores."

When have you ever seen a squirrel eating marigold? Ivypool didn't dare ask the question aloud. "It's a mystery," she meowed, dropping the last plant and scrambling back down the tree.

Jayfeather divided the marigold plants into two bunches so he and Ivypool could carry them back to camp. Then he padded across the clearing and took a final sniff of the ruined patch. "We ought to find a way to protect the plants so that they'll grow back," he mumbled around his mouthful.

Ivypool wondered how they could do that. Building a thorn barrier around the patch would be a huge task, and anyway it wouldn't be much good to keep rabbits out. They hardly stayed away from the wood just because there were bramble thickets in the way.

"Maybe we could bring the scent of fox up here," she suggested. "That would scare the rabbits away."

"How?" Jayfeather asked, his tone suggesting it was a mouse-brained idea.

Ivypool thought for a moment. "We could use fox dung . . . it would be yucky getting it here, but it might work."

"And how would you get it?" Jayfeather mewed. "Just stroll up to a fox and say, 'Please make some dirt for me?' I don't think so."

Ivypool rolled her eyes. *Jayfeather might be our medicine cat, but he's such a mouse-brain sometimes.* "Old dung," she responded. "You didn't think I'd march into a fox's den to get it fresh, did you?" She said the last part under her breath. It was pointless trying to argue with Jayfeather—somehow he always won.

But Jayfeather was nodding. "You could be right. Sort it out, will you, as soon as we've taken these plants back to the hollow?"

Ivypool sighed. *Great,* she thought as she followed Jayfeather back down the trail. *Why can't I keep my big mouth shut?*

Back in the stone hollow, Ivypool went with Jayfeather to the medicine cat's den to deposit her bundle of marigold.

"You found some!" Briarlight exclaimed, pulling herself across the den to plunge her nose into the aromatic stems. "I'll sort them out and store them right away."

"Thanks, Ivypool." Jayfeather gave her a curt nod. "You can get on with that fox dung now."

Wrinkling her nose in disgust, Ivypool padded back into the clearing and glanced around. She knew she would have to find another warrior to go with her. Looking for fox dung meant she might encounter a fox, and she knew she would get a talking-to if she took the risk alone. The first cat she spotted was Blossomfall, emerging from the thorn tunnel and bounding across the camp to drop a vole on the fresh-kill pile.

"Hi, Blossomfall," Ivypool meowed, heading up to her. "Will you come out with me to find some fox dung?"

Blossomfall stared at her as if she had sprouted a second head. *And I can't say I blame her,* Ivypool thought wryly. "To scare rabbits away from Jayfeather's marigold patch," she explained.

"I . . . I'm sorry, Ivypool, I can't," Blossomfall replied after a moment's hesitation. "I promised I'd help Purdy and Mousefur with their ticks." She hurried off toward the elders' den.

Huh! Ivypool thought. *So why aren't you collecting mouse bile from Jayfeather if you're going to do ticks?*

At first she thought that Blossomfall was just trying to get out of a messy and maybe dangerous task. *But she's not usually like that . . . no, she's still uneasy with me because we met in the Dark Forest. Maybe she's starting to realize how bad it is there, and that's why she doesn't want to talk to me.*

She jumped, startled, as she heard the paw steps of another cat approaching behind her. Glancing around, she saw her father, Birchfall, who padded up and dropped a squirrel onto the fresh-kill pile.

"You scared me out of my fur!" she gasped.

Birchfall twitched his ears. "I didn't think anything scared you, Ivypool."

Ivypool thought that was a weird thing to say, but she didn't have time to think about it. "I need to collect some fox dung to protect Jayfeather's plants against rabbits," she mewed. "Will you come with me?"

"Sure." Birchfall gave his chest fur a quick lick and bounded toward the thorn tunnel beside Ivypool.

Once in the forest, Ivypool took the lead and headed for the border between ThunderClan and the woods outside the Clan territories. "We're not likely to find foxes living anywhere else," she explained. "All the Clans are pretty good about driving them out."

Birchfall nodded. "I saw you three nights ago," he meowed after a moment. "Training with Hawkfrost in the Dark Forest."

Ivypool halted, staring in shock at her father. She hoped he couldn't hear how hard her heart was pounding. It was hard to think that any ThunderClan cats would join Tigerstar and the other dark warriors, and harder still when the cat was her own kin. *Can I trust any of my Clanmates?* she wondered. *Except for Lionblaze, Dovewing, and Jayfeather, they could all be visiting the Dark Forest!*

"It was my first visit," Birchfall continued. "I spotted you through the trees."

"I didn't see you," Ivypool replied, trying not to show him how disconcerted she was.

Birchfall's eyes glimmered with amusement. "No, you looked a bit busy."

"I've learned some useful stuff there," Ivypool meowed carefully.

Her father nodded, the amusement in his eyes replaced by confidence. "The training they give us is good. It gives us a chance to make the Clan even stronger," he meowed. "I thought I'd learned all I could, but now I see there are ways to be even more powerful in battle for my Clan."

Ivypool didn't want to go on talking about the Dark Forest. "It should help dealing with foxes," she conceded. "Can you scent anything yet?"

For a moment Birchfall watched her intently; Ivypool's pelt itched beneath his amber gaze. Then he raised his head and parted his jaws to taste the air. "No," he mewed. "We need to get closer to the border."

Ivypool felt even more uneasy as she and Birchfall crossed the ThunderClan scent marks and stepped into the unfamiliar forest. The ground here was uneven, the hollows filled with damp, decaying leaves; rocks poked up out of the tussocky grass. The trees grew close together, the branches arching overhead to cut out the light. Ivypool shivered, convinced that she was being watched, though when she spun around she couldn't see any gleam of eyes peering out from the undergrowth or the branches above.

"Fox!" Birchfall exclaimed with satisfaction. "And not far off, I'd guess. This way."

Ivypool followed him around a clump of bracken. She couldn't shake off the sensation that some creature was watching her, and kept glancing over her shoulder, vainly peering into the shadows.

"Ouch!" She let out a startled yowl. Bramble tendrils surrounded her, thorns clawing into her pelt. For a couple of heartbeats she struggled wildly, imagining foxes waiting for her to give up and turn into easy prey.

"Keep still." Birchfall's voice came from beside her. "Honestly, Ivypool, you were staring around like a kit on its first trip outside the camp. Didn't you see the bramble thicket in front of you?"

"Oh, sure," Ivypool muttered. "I just walked into it for fun." Raising her voice, she added, "Get me out, Birchfall. I don't want to be stuck here if a fox comes by."

Her father began pulling the prickly branches off her, and soon Ivypool was able to wriggle clear. Thorns were still stuck in her pelt, and several silver-white tufts were clinging to the tendrils.

"It looks as if it's been snowing," Birchfall meowed with a snort of amusement. "Are you sure you're okay?"

"I'm fine, thanks."

"Then let's keep going, and for StarClan's sake, watch where you're putting your paws this time."

Ivypool followed him, simmering with resentment. *He's talking to me like I don't know anything. He needs to remember I'm not just a kit anymore.*

On the other side of the thicket Ivypool spotted a dark hole between a couple of rocks, almost hidden behind trailing ferns. The smell of fox was very strong.

"There's the den," Birchfall pointed out with a flick of his tail.

"But the smell is stale," Ivypool added, eager to show off her scenting skills. "I don't think the fox is there now."

Birchfall nodded. "Right. So let's find some dung and get out of here before it comes back."

Gagging on the stench, Ivypool tracked down a pile of fox dung near the opening of the den. She picked up a stick and rolled one end in the dung until she had coated it thoroughly.

"Great StarClan, that stinks!" Birchfall exclaimed. "I can't believe we're doing this."

"You'll be glad to have the marigold if you're wounded," Ivypool told him through her teeth.

Birchfall rolled his eyes. "And there isn't an easier way?"

Ignoring his question, Ivypool hefted the stick in her jaws and headed back toward the ThunderClan border. To her relief, the feeling of being watched faded as soon as she was safely back in her own territory.

I wonder if it was the fox, watching us. But then, why didn't it attack?

The stick was awkward to carry, but taking it in turns Ivypool and Birchfall managed to transport it back to the clearing above the camp where the marigold plants grew. Ivypool traced a circle around the damaged clumps, daubing the dungy end in the grass.

"That should keep the rabbits away," Birchfall meowed with satisfaction.

Dropping the stick, Ivypool felt a brief claw-scratch of worry. "I hope we did the right thing. What if other foxes smell fox scent here? Will they think this is their territory?"

Birchfall shrugged. "They're mouse-brained if they do. But we'd better tell the patrols what we've done, or they'll be bringing back reports of fox invasion."

Ivypool nodded. "I'll find Brambleclaw and tell him." *I hope this* was *a good idea,* she thought, misgiving stabbing her like a thorn in her pad. *We've just brought the scent of our worst enemy into the heart of our territory.*

She headed for the trail back to the camp, with Birchfall just behind her. "Let's go back the long way, by the stream on the WindClan border," he suggested. "I want to wash the fox stink off my paws."

On their way to the border, they pushed through clumps of cool green ferns, the fresh green tang beginning to mask the fox scent on their fur. Ivypool felt herself relaxing in the familiar surroundings. But heading down the slope toward the stream she failed to see a branch lying in the grass. As she tripped over it, pain stabbed her leg where she had been wounded in the training exercise the night before.

"Mouse dung!" she muttered, wincing.

"You'll need to be quicker next time," Birchfall commented; clearly he knew exactly how she had gotten her injury. "You should watch where you're putting your paws. It would be a shame if you couldn't fight anymore because of a stupid accident. You must know how tough the training is."

Ivypool gave him a swift glance. "Yeah."

Her pads prickled with the strangeness of sharing her nocturnal life with a Clanmate, especially when that Clanmate was her father. *Birchfall must think I want to be part of Tigerstar's plans,* she thought uneasily. *He doesn't know that I'm spying for ThunderClan. And he can't find out,* she added to herself uncomfortably.

Ivypool knew that the Dark Forest cats meant to destroy the Clans. But she found it hard to believe that Birchfall and Blossomfall were enemies of ThunderClan. *They must have been tricked. I know Birchfall only wants to do the best he can for his Clan.* And yet she couldn't entirely stifle her doubts, like a small worm of unease eating into her.

Trying to push her disturbing thoughts away, Ivypool reached the bank of the stream and stood beside Birchfall, gazing down into the water. "Do we really have to get down into there?" she asked.

"We could go back to camp stinking of fox," Birchfall replied. "Not much of a choice, really."

Reluctantly he slid down the bank until his paws splashed into the water. Ivypool followed, wading a little farther into the stream and flinching as the cold current flowed around her legs. She rubbed one paw against another to get rid of the clinging scent. Behind her, Ivypool could hear Birchfall splashing around. Suddenly the sounds stopped.

"Uh-oh," Birchfall muttered. "We've been spotted."

Four cats were looking down at them from the WindClan side of the stream. Narrowing her eyes against the light, Ivypool recognized Breezepelt and his apprentice, Boulderpaw, and beside them Heathertail with her apprentice, Furzepaw. Neither Breezepelt nor Furzepaw showed any signs of exhaustion after their training session in the Dark Forest the night before, when Ivypool had faced them in a drawn-out mock battle.

"What are you doing in our stream?" Breezepelt demanded. "Get out!"

Birchfall stood his ground. "It's not *your* stream," he pointed out. "We have as much right to be here as you do."

"Your territory ends at the bank," Heathertail snapped. "That's where you've put your scent markers."

"And you've put *yours* on your own bank," Birchfall retorted. "As if any cat can put scent markers in running water!"

Ivypool felt completely stupid standing belly-deep in the stream and tilting her head up to see the cats on the bank. She waded back to Birchfall and touched his shoulder with her tail. "Let's get out of here," she murmured.

Birchfall didn't move. "The stream doesn't belong to either Clan," he insisted. "We can wash our paws here if we want."

Breezepelt rolled his eyes and leaned farther over the bank so that he could talk to them without Heathertail hearing him. "Look, I don't want to fight you over this," he muttered.

"But I'll have to if you keep arguing. Just clear out, okay?"

Birchfall looked as if he might have agreed, but just then Heathertail stepped forward. "Why are you wasting time talking?" she hissed. "We should fight them if they don't leave. Furzepaw, why are you hanging back there?"

"I'll fight them!" Boulderpaw announced.

"No, Boulderpaw," Breezepelt told his apprentice. "This isn't a battle worth fighting. These are just a couple of ThunderClan fleabags."

Ivypool realized with a pang of anxiety that the WindClan Dark Forest warriors were allying themselves with her and Birchfall, not with their own Clanmates. *That can't be right!*

"They're fleabags who are trespassing on our territory." Heathertail padded forward and gazed down into the stream. Her eyes glittered with fury. "Leave now, or fight."

"Come on," Ivypool urged Birchfall. "We don't want any more trouble."

"No, we don't," Birchfall agreed. "But we're not the cats who are causing it." His neck fur fluffed up with anger as he met Heathertail's gaze. "I'm not going to back down when we're not doing anything wrong."

To Ivypool's dismay, he waded across the stream and leaped up onto the bank on the WindClan side. Breezepelt let out a snarl and came to stand beside his Clanmate. "Mousebrain!" he hissed at Birchfall. "Now I'll have to fight you! Just wait until I see you in the Dark Forest. You need to be taught where your loyalties lie."

"Yeah, we'll get you then as well!" Furzepaw added, her

paws tearing up the grass as she crouched for a pounce.

To Ivypool's relief, Heathertail seemed so focused on Birchfall that she wasn't paying attention to her Clanmates, and their voices were so soft that she would have had to strain to overhear what they were saying.

Reluctantly Ivypool waded across the stream. *I have to support my Clanmate! Am I going to spend the rest of my life fighting, awake or asleep?*

But before Ivypool could leap up onto the opposite bank, she heard the sound of cats crunching over dry leaves in ThunderClan territory. Sorreltail appeared from behind a hazel thicket, with her patrol hard on her paws: Bumblestripe, Hazeltail, and Berrynose. All four cats were carrying prey.

"What's going on?" Sorreltail asked, dropping her vole.

Thank StarClan! Ivypool turned to face the tortoiseshell warrior. "Birchfall and I were washing our paws in the stream," she explained. "Then this WindClan patrol came along and told us to get out, so—"

"So you're going to fight," Sorreltail sighed. "Over cats washing their paws. I never heard anything so ridiculous! Ivypool, Birchfall, get over here right now."

Ivypool obeyed with relief, climbing out of the stream and shaking water from each leg in turn. Birchfall was more reluctant, giving Heathertail and Breezepelt a baleful look before he slid down into the stream again and waded back to his own territory.

Horror clawed at Ivypool's belly. *My father never used to be so battle-hungry,* she thought. *The Dark Forest is changing him!*

"We'll settle this later!" Birchfall meowed over his shoulder.

"You bet we will," Breezepelt retorted, twitching his tail-tip from side to side.

Anxiety surged up inside Ivypool like a flooding stream as she followed Sorreltail and the others back to camp. *More trouble tonight,* she thought wretchedly. *Training in the Dark Forest is bad enough, but now we have a score to settle with Breezepelt as well. Will there ever be an end to it?*

CHAPTER 3

Dovewing clawed at the moss, pulling great pawfuls away from the roots of the oak tree.

"It's nice and dry," Whitewing commented. "That should please Mousefur and Purdy." She paused, then added hesitantly, "Dovewing, I'm worried about these bad dreams you're having. I—"

"I'll be fine, honestly," Dovewing interrupted, wishing she hadn't said anything about the dreams in which she saw Swoop, over and over again, carried away by the eagle, the Tribe cat's heartrending cries shattering the air. Avoiding her mother's gaze, Dovewing bent her head over the growing pile of moss, checking it for thorns. "The dreams will go away eventually."

Whitewing shook her head. "It's been a whole moon since you got back, and you're still having them." She pulled off another clump of moss, raking her claws down the oak root. "I blame myself for letting you go to the mountains. You're too young, and you haven't got enough warrior experience to travel so far."

"You can't say that!" Dovewing protested, looking up from the moss. "You didn't *let* me go. Firestar *chose* me."

"Yes, and I would expect a Clan leader to have more sense," Whitewing meowed.

I wish I could tell you why he made that decision, but I can't, Dovewing thought. "Don't forget I led the expedition to find the beavers," she reminded her mother. "I got lots of experience there."

"I know." Whitewing still looked anxious. "StarClan shouldn't have sent the dream about the beavers to an apprentice. It was far too much responsibility."

Except they didn't send a dream. . . . Dovewing bent even more busily over the moss to hide her expression. *Whitewing would never sleep again if she knew how much responsibility I was born with, thanks to the prophecy.*

"I'll get over it, I really will," she reassured her mother. "And it's not all bad. I'm lucky to have traveled such a long way beyond the Clan. There's so much out there to see!"

Whitewing sniffed. "There's plenty to see here beside the lake, too."

"Yes, yes, I know there is . . . oh, there's a huge thorn!" Dovewing exclaimed, snagging it in one claw and tossing it aside. "It's a good thing that didn't end up in Mousefur's pelt."

For a few heartbeats Dovewing and Whitewing worked side by side, clawing more moss off the oak roots. Laying a particularly thick clump on the pile, Whitewing paused. "I was talking to Bumblestripe earlier," she remarked. "He's a nice young warrior—so polite! He likes you a lot, you know."

Dovewing began to feel hot and uncomfortable in her pelt. "I know," she muttered, squirming with embarrassment.

"You'll need to find a mate one day, to keep the Clan going," Whitewing pointed out.

"There's plenty of time," Dovewing meowed. *Will the prophecy allow me to have a mate? How can I have kits if I might be called on to save the Clan at any moment?* An image of Tigerheart flashed into her mind, his eyes sparkling as if he were going to spring at her and roll her over in a play fight. *Tigerheart would understand. . . .*

Dovewing thrust the thought away. "This is plenty of moss," she announced. "Let's get it back to camp."

Whitewing rolled the moss into two balls and the she-cats picked them up to carry back to the stone hollow. Now that Whitewing wasn't fussing anymore, Dovewing enjoyed being with her; it wasn't often that she and her mother could work together without any other cats. In spite of her disturbed night, she began to feel better. But her ears were full of weird buzzing noises, and she still couldn't reach out with her senses.

What if my powers have gone forever? she wondered, a cold trickle of fear passing through her from ears to tail-tip. *No,* she told herself. *I'm not going to think about that.*

As she passed a thick bank of ferns not far from the entrance to the camp, there was a sudden flash of gray-and-white fur, and Mousewhisker leaped out of the undergrowth in front of her. Dovewing let out a startled squeak and jumped back, dropping the ball of moss.

"Got you!" Mousewhisker exclaimed with a *mrrow* of laughter. "I've never seen you jump like that. Have you got moss in your ears, Dovewing? Usually no cat manages to sneak up on you."

Dovewing batted at him with one paw, trying not to feel annoyed. *If I'd had my proper senses, I'd have heard you stomping along like a fox in a fit!*

"Do you want to come hunting?" Mousewhisker went on. "The border patrol heard squirrels fighting in the grass clearing near the ShadowClan border. And tired, injured squirrels make easy prey!"

Icecloud and Toadstep emerged from the ferns behind Mousewhisker.

"Yes, come," Icecloud mewed. "It'll be fun!"

Dovewing glanced at her mother. "I'm supposed to take this moss back. . . ."

"I can do that," Whitewing meowed cheerfully. "You go and hunt."

"Thanks!"

While Whitewing gathered the moss balls together, Dovewing joined Mousewhisker and the others, heading into the forest. Mousewhisker picked up the pace until they were running full-pelt through the trees. Dovewing felt her night fears and exhaustion melt away as she bunched and stretched her muscles, her paws skimming the ground.

"Bet I can jump higher than any cat!" Toadstep announced.

"Bet you can't!" Icecloud retorted, leaping over a fallen tree trunk to show off her skills.

Toadstep sprang over the trunk after the white she-cat and landed hard on top of her.

"Oof! Get off!" Icecloud spluttered, shoving Toadstep away and jumping to her paws. "You're as heavy as a badger."

"Let's race," Mousewhisker suggested. "Last cat to reach the dead tree is a mouse!"

He streaked off before he had finished speaking, leaving the other three to scramble after him. Dovewing sprinted with her belly fur brushing the ground and her tail streaming out behind her. Toadstep overtook her and Mousewhisker, but Dovewing gradually drew ahead of Icecloud.

It's easier to run fast and dodge trees when I can't hear everything from far away, she realized in surprise. *There's nothing to distract me. This is what it must be like for other cats!*

She passed Mousewhisker as they skirted a bramble thicket so that only Toadstep was in front of her, his black-and-white shape pelting easily along. Dovewing gathered herself and put on a spurt, her paws barely touching the ground with each bound. The dead tree was within sight when she came up alongside her Clanmate, glimpsing his astonished look as she scampered past him and hurled herself at the tree, scoring her claws down the trunk.

"I win!" she yowled.

Toadstep ran up after her, followed by Mousewhisker and last of all a panting Icecloud.

"Okay, I'm a mouse." The white she-cat let herself flop to

the ground. "Dovewing, that was a great race!"

"Yes, you even beat Toadstep," Mousewhisker meowed. "And he's fast!"

Toadstep gave her an approving nod. "Well done."

When all the cats had caught their breath, Mousewhisker rose to his paws. "It's time to start looking for those squirrels. We'd better be quiet now; we're pretty close to the clearing."

He took the lead; Dovewing and the others followed him, brushing through the undergrowth on stealthy paws. At the edge of the clearing Dovewing peered out of a clump of long grass to see that Twolegs were already starting to build their green pelt-dens there.

"Mouse dung!" she muttered as three Twoleg kits ran across the open space, yowling and tossing something red from paw to paw. "They'll scare away all the prey from here to the lake."

Mousewhisker led his patrol around the edge of the clearing, slinking through the shadows so that the Twolegs wouldn't notice them. Dovewing shivered to the tips of her claws as she crossed the old ShadowClan boundary. There were still traces of ShadowClan scent, and she half-expected to hear the challenge of a ShadowClan patrol.

That's the bush where I first met Tigerheart, she thought as she passed it. *Everything was so different back then. . . .*

At the other side of the clearing the patrol scattered, tasting the air to pick up the scent of squirrel.

"Over here," Icecloud called in a low voice. She was standing at the foot of a tree, gazing up into the branches. "There's a squirrel up there. I think it's injured."

Mousewhisker bounded over. "You're right. You climb this side, and I'll take the other."

Dovewing and Toadstep watched as their Clanmates clawed their way up the tree. But as they reached the lowest branches there was a rustling among the leaves and the squirrel leaped out, skimming the top of Icecloud's head, and sprang to the ground, streaking straight past Dovewing and Toadstep. Dovewing whirled and gave chase with Toadstep beside her. The squirrel made a dash for the clearing.

It's not so badly injured that it can't run, Dovewing thought as she pelted after it.

She and Toadstep gained on the squirrel as it raced across the open space. They swerved past the pelt-dens, their paws splashing briefly in the stream. Dovewing drew ahead; the squirrel was so close that she was bunching her muscles for a leap when the reek of ShadowClan scent brought her skidding to a halt.

Great StarClan! I nearly crossed the border.

The squirrel bounded ahead and disappeared up a nearby ash tree with a flick of its tail. Dovewing glanced around as she stood panting at the edge of her territory, but she couldn't see Toadstep or the rest of the patrol.

"You stopped this time."

Dovewing's heart thumped in her chest at the sound of the voice. She spun around to see Tigerheart padding out from a thicket of brambles. He paced up to his own side of the border and dipped his head.

"I haven't set paw on your territory!" Dovewing meowed

defensively, her neck fur beginning to fluff up with anger. *I wish the others would get here,* she thought.

"Relax. I'm alone," Tigerheart responded. "You haven't done anything wrong. Actually, I was hoping to see you."

Dovewing narrowed her eyes. "I told you, we can't talk like this anymore. It's . . . it's over."

Tigerheart blinked. "No, there's something else." He hesitated and added reluctantly, "It's about Dawnpelt."

Dovewing's fur began to lie flat as curiosity overtook her nervousness.

"She's been acting weird ever since Flametail's death," the tabby tom went on. "She . . . she thinks it was Jayfeather's fault that he drowned."

"That's not true!" Dovewing hissed. "Jayfeather was trying to save him."

Tigerheart sighed. "He probably was. But I guess it's hard to know the truth, and Dawnpelt wants revenge."

Dovewing stared at him, carried back in her mind to the terrible day when the young ShadowClan medicine cat, Tigerheart's and Dawnpelt's littermate, had fallen through the ice on the frozen lake and drowned.

"You know the medicine cats have been acting strange," Tigerheart went on. "Not going to the Moonpool at the half-moon, that kind of thing. Dawnpelt thinks that Jayfeather had a quarrel with Flametail, and then murdered him when he fell through the ice."

"That's nonsense!" Dovewing's claws tore at the grass in front of her. "Dawnpelt needs to grow up. Jayfeather would never do anything like that—he was devastated that he couldn't save Flametail. I can't believe you'd listen to that kind of rumor!"

"I'm not telling you because I think it's true." Tigerheart's voice rose. "I'm trying to warn you. I think Dawnpelt might do something to hurt ThunderClan in revenge." His voice dropped and he shook his head. "She's acting really weird."

Dovewing couldn't feel sympathetic. "I think we can handle Dawnpelt losing her temper, thanks," she snapped. "Please don't talk to me again. We'll both be in trouble if we get caught." She turned, poised to run into the woods on the other side of the clearing.

"I was just trying to help." There was anger and sorrow in Tigerheart's voice. "I want to prove to you that we don't have to be enemies."

"It's too late for that," Dovewing mewed.

Without looking at Tigerheart again she headed for the trees. Before she reached them, the squirrel shot past her, and Dovewing let out a hiss of irritation. *I know Tigerheart chased it back onto our territory. Doesn't he think I can hunt on my own?*

But at the same time her paws carried her swiftly after her prey, and she killed it with a neat blow to the spine. Picking it up, she plunged into the shelter of the trees, spotting Mousewhisker and the rest of the patrol a few tail-lengths away.

"Great catch!" Toadstep exclaimed as she bounded up to them.

"Yeah, you're really fast on your paws," Mousewhisker added, while Icecloud gave the fresh-kill an admiring sniff.

As the patrol headed back toward the camp, Dovewing cast a final glance back across the clearing. Tigerheart had vanished. *Is what he told me true?* she wondered. *Is Dawnpelt planning revenge for a murder that never happened?*

CHAPTER 4

❧

Lionblaze padded through the thorn tunnel into the camp and stood flexing his aching muscles. "That was a great training session," he meowed to Blossomfall as she emerged behind him. "You certainly caught me with that backward leap and twist."

"Yeah, will you show me how to do it?" Foxleap asked as he followed Blossomfall.

The young she-cat's eyes glowed at her Clanmates' praise and she gave her chest fur a couple of embarrassed licks. "It's not that hard," she murmured. "I'm sorry if I hurt you, Lionblaze."

"I'll be fine." Lionblaze gave her a friendly flick over her ear with the tip of his tail. "I should have been a bit quicker."

Cinderheart padded up, her eyes glimmering with amusement as her gaze traveled over Lionblaze's ruffled pelt. "You look like you've been pulled through the thorn barrier backward," she mewed.

"I feel like it, too," Lionblaze replied. "Blossomfall and Foxleap didn't give me a chance to catch my breath. They're turning into great fighters."

He was heading toward the fresh-kill pile when a yowl broke out behind him. "Firestar! Firestar!"

Whirling around, Lionblaze saw Sorreltail burst into the clearing with Bumblestripe, Berrynose, and Hazeltail hard on her paws. Birchfall and Ivypool followed more slowly.

"Great StarClan!" Lionblaze exclaimed, his neck fur rising. "Are we under attack?"

While Sorreltail was struggling to get her breath back, Firestar appeared from his den on the Highledge, then ran lightly down the tumbled rocks to the floor of the hollow. Sandstorm leaped down behind him, while Dustpelt and Brackenfur bounded over from the fresh-kill pile.

"What's going on?" Firestar demanded as he halted in front of Sorreltail's patrol.

"Trouble on the WindClan border," Sorreltail explained. "Birchfall and Ivypool got into an argument with some WindClan cats. I think if we hadn't turned up, there would have been a fight."

"Is this true?" Firestar asked, fixing his green gaze on Birchfall and Ivypool.

For the first time Lionblaze noticed that Birchfall was looking sulky, while the tip of Ivypool's tail flicked irritably to and fro.

"They started it," Birchfall mewed defensively. "They didn't want to let us wash our paws in the stream."

"We weren't on their territory," Ivypool added. "We weren't doing anything wrong."

"For StarClan's sake!" Dustpelt snapped, before Firestar could respond. "Aren't the tensions high enough between the Clans, without going out to look for more trouble?"

"We *weren't* looking for it!" Ivypool flashed back at him.

As Firestar raised his tail for silence, Brackenfur padded to Sorreltail's side and touched her ear lightly with his nose. "I hope you haven't been getting into any skirmishes," he murmured.

His mate blinked at him affectionately. "No. But it's no thanks to these mouse-brains."

"Mouse-brain yourself!" Birchfall retorted.

"Let's all keep calm," Firestar meowed, padding into the middle of the hostile group. "No cat is saying you broke the warrior code," he went on to Birchfall and Ivypool, "but washing your paws on the WindClan border wasn't the most sensible thing you've ever done."

"Yes, what's wrong with the lake?" Sandstorm put in.

Ivypool opened her jaws to reply, but just then excited squealing came from the direction of the nursery. Lionblaze glanced over his shoulder to see Molekit and Cherrykit scampering up.

"What's happening?" Cherrykit demanded, her tail straight up in the air with excitement. "Can we help?"

"Tell us what to do!" Molekit puffed his chest out importantly. "Who are we going to fight?"

Lionblaze felt warmed by the kits' enthusiasm. They were almost six moons old, ready to be apprentices, and their mother, Poppyfrost, was ready to return to warrior duties. He bent his head and touched noses with each kit in turn. "Settle down," he purred. "WindClan isn't about to attack. You can put your claws away."

Straightening up again, he caught Cinderheart's blue gaze, and saw a flash of pain in her eyes. He understood exactly how she was feeling. *We could have kits of our own, as soon as you like, if you could only get past the prophecy.* He suppressed a growl of frustration that the gray she-cat found his destiny such a big obstacle. *I didn't ask to be picked out by StarClan before I was even born!*

"Having fun with the kits?" Brightheart asked, padding up with her mate, Cloudtail. "You'll be a great father one day, Lionblaze."

And that doesn't help, either, Lionblaze thought, his fur itching with embarrassment.

More cats emerged from the thorn tunnel. Mousewhisker was in the lead, ahead of Dovewing, Icecloud, and Toadstep. Dovewing held a squirrel clamped in her jaws, while Icecloud was carrying a blackbird. They padded into the center of the clearing, casting curious glances at the group of cats around Firestar, then headed for the fresh-kill pile to deposit their prey. Most of the other cats drifted after them, the argument about the encounter with WindClan breaking up.

As soon as Dovewing had dropped her squirrel, Purdy padded up to her from the elders' den. "Hey, young 'un," he began, "it was you collectin' moss this morning, wasn't it?"

Dovewing tipped her head on one side. "Yes, Whitewing and I fetched it. Is there a problem?"

"It's really dry an' prickly," Purdy meowed, blinking apologetically. "I don't want to fuss, but Mousefur can't get comfortable."

Lionblaze glanced across at the elders' den to see Mousefur crouched at the entrance, her head lowered. A pang of pity clawed at him; the outspoken old she-cat hadn't been the same since her denmate Longtail was killed by the falling tree. Lionblaze would have given anything to hear Mousefur complain about her own prickly moss.

"I'm sorry," Dovewing mewed. "I thought I got all the thorns out. I'll go through the bedding again, if you like."

"No, that's going to take forever," Graystripe put in; he and Millie were sharing a vole beside the fresh-kill pile. "Bumblestripe and Blossomfall can go out and find some feathers. That should be soft enough."

"That is so not fair!" Blossomfall exclaimed, looking up from choosing a piece of fresh-kill.

"Yes, we always get the boring jobs." Bumblestripe came to stand beside his sister. "Just because there aren't any apprentices in the Clan! When will some of the older warriors do the apprentice duties for a change?"

Graystripe narrowed his amber eyes. "Maybe when you learn not to answer back to a senior warrior," he rasped.

Bumblestripe and Blossomfall exchanged mutinous glances, but before either of them could reply, Sandstorm padded up to Graystripe and gave him a poke in the side. "Come on, Graystripe," she meowed. "You're always tougher on your own kits than the rest of the Clan. They have a point. They're warriors, but they *do* get stuck with the apprentice tasks. I'll go with you," she added to the two younger warriors.

"No, I've got a better idea." Firestar bounded over to the rockfall that led up to his den and sprang onto one of the boulders at the bottom. "Let all cats old enough to catch their own prey join here beneath the Highledge for a Clan meeting!" he called.

Most of the cats were already out in the clearing, and they gathered around Firestar with murmurs of surprise. Lionblaze headed to sit beside Cinderheart, noticing that Jayfeather had emerged from his den and was crouched beside Briarlight, who had dragged herself to the edge of the bramble screen. Daisy, Poppyfrost, and Ferncloud slipped out of the nursery and sat together at the edge of the crowd.

"Foxleap, Rosepetal, come and stand here with me," Firestar continued.

Exchanging mystified glances, the two warriors rose to their paws and joined their Clan leader at the foot of the cliff.

"Since the Clan is having problems because of the shortage of apprentices," Firestar went on, "I think the best solution is to create some more. Molekit and Cherrykit—"

"What?" Molekit exclaimed, springing to his paws with every hair on his pelt fluffed out until he looked twice his size.

"Us?" Cherrykit bounced up and down with excitement. "Oh, cool!"

"Firestar, you can't!" Poppyfrost leaped up, her paws pattering as she raced across the clearing to her kits. "We've had no warning! They're so untidy—Molekit, just *look* at your pelt!"

She flung herself on the little tom, licking frantically, while Berrynose got up and hurried over to groom Cherrykit. Lionblaze thought the warrior looked as proud as if it were his own apprentice ceremony.

Firestar looked on for a moment with a purr of amusement, then beckoned the two kits with a wave of his tail. "They're fine," he meowed. "Come over here and stand in front of me."

The two kits obeyed him, their fur still rumpled and sticking up here and there. Firestar reached out with his tail and touched Cherrykit on the shoulder. "From this time forward," he announced, "this kit will be known as Cherrypaw. Foxleap, you have shown courage and perseverance in serving your Clan, and I trust that you will pass on these qualities to your apprentice."

Foxleap's eyes were shining with pride as he stepped forward and touched noses with Cherrypaw. She stayed by his side as they returned to the crowd of cats.

But when Firestar turned to Molekit, the little tom took a leap backward, out of reach of the Clan leader's tail. "I don't want to be an apprentice," he squeaked. "You only want us so we can do all the nasty jobs!"

Gasps of astonishment came from the assembled cats. Lionblaze saw Cherrypaw gazing wide-eyed with horror at her brother. Berrynose lashed his tail, while Poppyfrost shut her eyes and dug her claws into the ground as if she wished she were somewhere else.

But Firestar, far from being angry, was stifling a purr of laughter. "Yes, there are duties to be done," he agreed. "But every single warrior here did them. And training is just as important. That's why I've chosen Rosepetal to be your mentor. She's a skilled and swift fighter, and I know she'll pass her training on to you." He beckoned Molekit again.

Molekit stayed where he was, his eyes narrowed suspiciously. "Can I do some training first?" he checked. "Before I have to search any cat for ticks?"

"That's up to Rosepetal," Firestar purred.

Rosepetal's eyes were sparkling with amusement. "Even better than training," she promised. "Today we'll explore the whole territory. Duties start tomorrow."

"They'd better!" Molekit growled.

At last he padded up to Firestar, who touched him on the shoulder with his tail-tip. "From this time forward, this kit will be known as Molepaw," he declared. "Now, go and touch noses with Rosepetal."

The young tom did as he was told, his eyes gleaming with satisfaction.

"The Clan meeting is over," Firestar meowed.

But before any cat could move, Brackenfur came bounding over. "Just a moment, Firestar. I have some news to share with the Clan."

Firestar waved his tail, giving the ginger warrior permission to speak.

"Sorreltail is having kits again," Brackenfur announced.

Yowls of congratulation rose up from the Clan. Lionblaze spotted Cinderheart and Poppyfrost, the kits of Sorreltail's first litter, exchanging a delighted glance.

Sorreltail raised her voice above the noise. "They'll be born in just under a moon."

Daisy padded over to her and gave her ear a lick, and Ferncloud pressed her muzzle into Sorreltail's shoulder. "It's great that you'll be moving into the nursery with us," she mewed.

Listening to them, Lionblaze couldn't help glancing at Cinderheart, but she had moved away from his side and was talking excitedly to Poppyfrost.

Foxleap and Rosepetal were padding toward the thorn tunnel, their apprentices bouncing alongside them. Molepaw seemed to have forgotten his misgivings, and looked as excited as his sister.

"They're so little," Poppyfrost murmured as they passed her. "I hope they won't be too tired, walking all the way around the border."

"They'll be fine," Cinderheart reassured her.

"Of course they will," Berrynose added, touching his nose to his mate's ear. "*Our* kits will be the best apprentices the Clan has ever seen."

Lionblaze turned away, trying to push down his envy. As the Clan meeting broke up, he spotted Ivypool heading for her den, and bounded across to intercept her. "What was all that about WindClan?" he asked. "Which warriors were involved?"

Ivypool paused as if she was reluctant to answer. "Heathertail and Breezepelt, and their apprentices," she mewed at last.

It would be, Lionblaze thought. "They just challenged you? There wasn't any actual fighting?"

Ivypool shook her head.

"It was fine," Birchfall meowed, overhearing. "We were never in any danger. Breezepelt wasn't going to cause trouble. Sorreltail overreacted, that's all."

Lionblaze studied Birchfall for a heartbeat, surprised at how confident he sounded. Normally any ThunderClan cat returned from an encounter with Breezepelt ruffled and hissing. Why had this time been so different? He narrowed his eyes. Was it because Birchfall and Breezepelt had a connection that went beyond a shared border?

"Tell me more about what happened," he prompted Ivypool as soon as Birchfall was out of earshot again. "Is there something between Birchfall and Breezepelt? Have you seen Birchfall in the Dark Forest?"

"N-no," Ivypool replied.

Her hesitation made Lionblaze suspicious. "But you know he goes there, right?" Frustrated, he added, "You're supposed to tell us everything about the Dark Forest! Even if it involves your father. I think you need to consider where your loyalties lie."

Fury flared in Ivypool's eyes. "How dare you question my loyalties?" she snarled. "I risk my life for my Clan every time I go to sleep!"

"What's going on?" Dovewing's voice sounded behind Lionblaze, and he turned to see her racing up to him. "What are you doing to Ivypool?"

"Nothing," Lionblaze defended himself.

"So accusing me of being disloyal is *nothing*, is it?" Ivypool challenged him, her eyes still blazing with rage.

"That's not fair!" Dovewing exclaimed. "Just back off, Lionblaze. If we can't trust our Clanmates, who can we trust?"

Lionblaze snorted. "I don't know. I'd trust Ivypool more if she'd give me a straight answer."

Ivypool didn't answer, just spun around and stalked off. Dovewing was about to follow when Lionblaze blocked her with his tail.

"Make sure you listen carefully for anything happening on the WindClan border," he meowed.

To his surprise, Dovewing hung her head and muttered something that Lionblaze couldn't catch.

"What?" he asked.

Dovewing looked up; Lionblaze felt his pelt prickle with apprehension as he saw real fear in her eyes.

"My extra senses haven't come back after my trip to the mountains," she confessed. "What if I've lost my power?"

Lionblaze stared at her. "But you're one of the Three."

Dovewing shook her head. "I don't know if it's because I heard and saw too much when I was beyond the ridge of hills, or if I've become too good at blocking out far-off sounds. I had to do that when we were traveling, or everything would have overwhelmed me."

"I'm sure you'll be all right," Lionblaze soothed her instinctively, remembering the time when she was his apprentice.

"You just need to give it time. Your senses will come back."

But though he tried to sound confident, inwardly he wasn't so sure. Anxiety bubbled up inside him. *If Dovewing loses her power, does that mean the prophecy is reduced to two?*

CHAPTER 5

"Hi, Jayfeather." Sandstorm's voice came from the entrance to the medicine cat's den. "We've got some cobwebs for you."

Jayfeather turned, picking up the scent of cobwebs, and faintly beneath it the scent of Cherrypaw and Molepaw. It had been a quarter moon since their apprentice ceremony, and he had to admit they were settling well into their duties.

As the two young cats bounced into the den there was a splutter of laughter from Briarlight.

"Oh, Jayfeather, I wish you could see these two. They're walking cobwebs—it's stuck all over them from nose to tail!"

"We found lots," Molepaw announced proudly. "Sandstorm lifted up a log for us."

"I'd better untangle them," Briarlight went on. "Come here, both of you, and watch out for that pile of burdock root."

Jayfeather heard the patter of paws as the two apprentices padded across the den, and the sound of Briarlight dragging herself over the ground to meet them.

"Do your legs hurt?" Cherrypaw mewed. "Is it tough, not being able to move them?"

"Yes, it's tough," Briarlight replied calmly. "But I'm used to it. And it doesn't hurt."

"Bumblestripe says you're the bravest cat in the Clan," Molepaw told her.

Jayfeather could feel Briarlight's embarrassment. "I don't know about that," she murmured. "Now keep still so I can get this cobweb off your fur."

Jayfeather squeezed past the kits and joined Sandstorm in the clearing. "Thanks for taking them out," he mewed. "Those cobwebs will come in handy."

"No problem," Sandstorm responded. After a moment she added, "It seems like you're overworked. Maybe you should think about taking an apprentice sometime soon."

I'm planning to be around for a while yet, Jayfeather thought. "Briarlight is being very useful," he meowed out loud.

To his relief, Sandstorm didn't push it. "I'll see you later," she murmured.

"Could you find Sorreltail for me?" Jayfeather called after her. "Tell her I'd like to see her."

"Sure." Sandstorm padded off.

Jayfeather was turning back toward the den when the scent of more approaching cats drifted over him. He halted as the sound of their paw steps grew louder.

Brightheart . . . Foxleap . . . Rosepetal . . . What do they want?

"Have you come to pick up your apprentices?" he asked. "They're inside, being untangled."

"Yes, we're going out for a training session," Rosepetal

replied. "Brightheart is going to teach them some of her battle moves."

"Firestar wants every apprentice to learn them." Brightheart's voice was full of quiet pride. "That way, if they injure their eye in a battle, or they have to fight at night when it's hard to see, they'll know what to do."

The scamper of paws told Jayfeather that Molepaw and Cherrypaw had appeared from the den.

"Are we training now?" Molepaw mewed eagerly. "We collected *masses* of cobwebs."

"Yes," Brightheart told him. "You're training with me today. I'm going to teach you some moves that none of the other Clans know about."

"Cool!" Cherrypaw exclaimed.

"You'll need to have your wits about you," Brightheart warned. "We're going to the slope above the hollow, and the brambles are very thick there."

"Great! Let's go!" Molepaw squeaked.

Jayfeather listened as they moved away, enjoying the sunshine soaking into his fur, and the cool breeze that kept the air fresh. Around him the camp was humming with activity. A hunting patrol had just left, passing Thornclaw at the entrance as he returned with a border patrol. Jayfeather padded over when Brambleclaw emerged from the warriors' den to hear Thornclaw's report.

"WindClan seems *very* jumpy at the moment," Thornclaw meowed.

"So what else is new?" Jayfeather could picture Bramble-claw rolling his eyes.

"More jumpy than usual, I mean," Thornclaw went on. "We met a WindClan patrol on the border, and they were convinced they'd seen one of our cats crossing into their territory."

"Oh?" Brambleclaw's voice grew sharper. "Did they say which cat?"

"No, they didn't get a good look. So I told them no way was it a ThunderClan warrior. It must have been a loner—if there was a cat there at all."

"Hmm . . ." Jayfeather could tell that Brambleclaw was thinking hard. "Did they believe you?"

"I have no idea," Thornclaw admitted. "Those cats jump at their own shadows! But Sedgewhisker was leading the patrol, and she's a decent cat, so maybe they did."

"We'd better tell Firestar," Brambleclaw decided. "If WindClan starts throwing accusations around, he'll need to know. Come with me, Thornclaw."

The two cats padded off toward the tumbled rocks, and Jayfeather headed back to his den. Sorreltail was waiting for him at the entrance.

"Hi, Jayfeather. Sandstorm said you wanted to see me."

"Right. Come in. I need to check you over."

"I'll be fine, honestly," Sorreltail went on as she followed Jayfeather into the den. "I've done this before, you know."

"I know. And that was many seasons ago. Older she-cats

need their medicine cat to keep an eye on them when they're having kits."

"Who are you calling older?" Sorreltail bristled, but Jayfeather could tell she wasn't really annoyed.

He made her lie down in the bracken and felt her belly gently with one forepaw. Then he leaned close to her to listen to her heartbeat. Briarlight dragged herself over to watch; Jayfeather could feel her breath on his neck fur.

"Will she be okay?" Briarlight whispered.

Jayfeather nodded. "Everything seems fine," he replied, adding to Sorreltail, "I've noticed a bit of stiffness in your hip joints. You might need some poppy seeds to take the edge off the pain when you give birth."

"I'll be fine," Sorreltail told him. "Leafpool has already given me some exercises to help keep the joints flexible."

Jayfeather stiffened. "Leafpool is not your medicine cat," he hissed through gritted teeth.

"She's still my friend," Sorreltail pointed out, "and I'll listen to her, no matter what happens."

Jayfeather suppressed a sigh. *I can't be bothered to argue.* With the flick of an ear to dismiss Sorreltail, he followed her out into the clearing. Sitting in a pool of sunlight, he listened to what was going on in the camp. Dovewing had just come back from a hunting patrol, and was settling down beside the fresh-kill pile to eat with Hazeltail and Graystripe. Dustpelt was leaving at the head of a hunting patrol. Leafpool, Ivypool, and Poppyfrost followed him; Jayfeather detected Poppyfrost's delight at going out on warrior duties again.

The patrol had scarcely left the clearing when a commotion broke out at the top of the hollow. Jayfeather sprang to his paws, every hair on his pelt bristling. Yaps and snarls and the shrieking of cats came from up above, and wails of dismay broke out in the camp.

"That's Molepaw and Cherrypaw!" Berrynose yowled, leaping out of the warriors' den and charging across the clearing. "And that sounds like a fox!"

He hurled himself toward the thorn tunnel, with Firestar, Cloudtail, Graystripe, and Brackenfur hard on his paws. Jayfeather ran back into his den. Briarlight was dragging herself toward the entrance; Jayfeather could sense her shock.

"What's happening?" she asked. "What's that awful noise?"

"Fox," Jayfeather replied tersely. "Get the supplies for wounds ready."

As Briarlight headed for the storage cleft, Jayfeather heard Dovewing behind him, standing by the bramble screen. "A fox?" she gasped. "But that's not possible! I didn't hear anything."

Jayfeather wanted to ask her what she meant, but he was distracted by the yowls and screeching that still came from the top of the cliff.

"It sounds really bad!" Briarlight's voice was shaking. "There'll be terrible injuries."

"We'll deal with it." Jayfeather made himself sound calm, but he was still worried by what Dovewing had just said. *Why didn't she hear the fox coming?*

Gradually the sound of battle died away; moments later Jayfeather heard the voices and paw steps of his Clanmates returning through the thorn tunnel. He padded out to meet them, bracing himself for the scent of wounds and spasms of pain.

But as soon as he emerged into the clearing Jayfeather realized that things weren't as bad as he had feared. He could hear that Brightheart and Rosepetal were limping, and picked up the scent of blood coming from Foxleap, but their injuries were nowhere near as serious as the wounds an angry fox could inflict.

"Go into my den," he instructed them. "I'll be with you in a couple of heartbeats. Where are the apprentices?"

"Here!" Cherrypaw bounced up beside him. "Molepaw and I are fine."

"Yeah, the fox nearly ate us up." Excitement was rolling off Molepaw in fizzing waves. "But the cat came and chased it off!"

Firestar pushed his way through the cats crowding around Jayfeather. "What cat?" he asked Molepaw. "Do you mean Brightheart, or your mentors?"

"No," Cherrypaw replied. "They chased after the fox, but it came back, and we thought we'd be eaten. But there was another cat! It hissed at the fox, and the fox ran away!"

Firestar shook his head, a puzzled look in his green eyes. "I didn't see any other cat up there."

"It sounds unlikely to me," Brackenfur murmured.

"Yes." Berrynose agreed. "Look, you two, it's not funny to

make up stories about something so dangerous."

"You had a big scare," Sandstorm added, sounding sympathetic. "But there's no need to invent mysterious cats coming to the rescue. Brightheart and your mentors did a great job scaring the fox away."

"But we're not making it up!" Cherrypaw protested.

"Right," Molepaw insisted, pressing up close to his sister. "There *was* another cat."

Jayfeather could sense that the young cats were telling the truth, or at least that they believed what they were saying. He realized that Firestar was taking their story seriously, too.

"What was this cat like?" the Clan leader asked.

"We never saw it clearly," Molepaw confessed. "We were hiding in a bramble thicket. And we couldn't smell it above the scent of fox."

"We're not even sure it was a ThunderClan warrior," Cherrypaw added.

Firestar was quiet for a moment. "I'll ask the other warriors if they saw anything," he mewed at last. "The only thing that matters is that every cat is safe."

The group of warriors began to split up.

"Not you," Jayfeather meowed, sweeping his tail around the two apprentices. "I want you in my den so I can check you out."

"But we're fine," Cherrypaw told him.

"I'm your medicine cat, and you're not fine until I say so. Inside."

He herded the two young cats into his den, to find that Briarlight was already treating the warriors' injuries.

"Brightheart's paws were full of bramble thorns," she explained to Jayfeather. "I pulled them out, and gave her dock leaf to rub on."

"I feel fine now," Brightheart mewed. "Briarlight did a great job. I'll get out of your way, Jayfeather, so you can treat the others."

Jayfeather gave her paws a sniff to make sure everything was okay, then waved her out of the den with a flick of his tail.

"Foxleap has a fox bite and some scratches on his shoulder," Briarlight went on. "I've given them a good lick, but I don't know what herbs are best for bites."

Jayfeather sniffed carefully at the wounds; the scratches had already stopped bleeding, but the bite was deep. "We'll put a poultice of burdock root on that," he decided. "Chew it up small, Briarlight, and fix it on with some cobweb. You'll need to rest it for a day or two," he added to Foxleap.

"But who'll be my mentor?" Cherrypaw asked anxiously. "I don't want to be stuck in camp while Molepaw is learning stuff."

"You can do the elders' ticks," her brother told her, then squeaked, "Ow! Keep your claws to yourself!"

"That's enough," Foxleap scolded them. "Of course you'll have a mentor, Cherrypaw. I've already asked Cloudtail. He says he'll take over your training for a couple of days."

"Cool." Cherrypaw sounded satisfied.

"I'm just scratched a bit," Rosepetal told Jayfeather. "And I've lost some fur from one side, but I don't think there's anything serious."

Jayfeather checked, and found that the scratches were quite shallow. Since Briarlight was still fixing Foxleap's poultice, he went to the store for some marigold, and trickled the juice onto Rosepetal's wounds.

"Come back tomorrow for some more of that," he instructed her. "You'll need to take it easy at first, but I think you can carry on with your duties. Let me know if the pain gets any worse."

"Okay, thanks," Rosepetal meowed.

When she and Foxleap had gone, Jayfeather sent Briarlight out of the den. "You've done really well," he told her. "Go do your exercises and get some fresh air."

He waited until the dragging sound of her movement had died away before turning back to the apprentices. He was pretty sure that they weren't hurt, but he wanted the excuse of checking them over.

"Tell me more about the other cat you saw," he mewed as he sniffed Cherrypaw's fur.

"Don't want to," Molepaw muttered sulkily. "You'll only say we're lying."

"Yeah, or that we got scared and imagined it," Cherrypaw added.

Jayfeather tipped his head on one side. "Try me."

"Well, we don't really remember anything," Molepaw went on after a moment's hesitation. "Brightheart sent us deep into the brambles. We couldn't see much, but we heard this other cat."

Jayfeather grunted. Pretending to check Molepaw for injuries, he pressed his paws down on the young tom's shoulders and let his mind drift into Molepaw's memories.

Sunlight dazzled Jayfeather's eyes as it shone on the slope above the hollow. On an open stretch of grass surrounded by ferns and brambles, Brightheart was showing a move to the two apprentices, while Foxleap and Rosepetal sat close by, looking on. The fur on Jayfeather's neck began to rise as he waited for what he knew would happen.

"That's great, Cherrypaw, but try—"

A loud snarling interrupted Brightheart as the fox leaped out from a clump of brambles. Foxleap and Rosepetal sprang to their paws as it lunged toward the apprentices.

"Hide!" Foxleap yowled as he hurled himself at the intruder.

Rosepetal let out a screech as she dashed past the fox and raked her claws down its side. Brightheart spun around and shoved both apprentices toward the nearest bramble thicket. "Get under there and don't move!" she hissed.

Molepaw and Cherrypaw burrowed into the brambles; Jayfeather could feel their fear surging over him like waves. Once they were in the thicket, he couldn't see much of the fighting, but he heard yelps and snarls from the fox, a shriek of pain from Foxleap, and furious caterwauling from Rosepetal and Brightheart. Through a gap in the tendrils he spotted the fox driven back from the clearing, with all three cats in pursuit.

The fox scent faded and everything went quiet.

"Do you think we can get out now?" Cherrypaw whispered. "I've got thorns digging into my pelt."

"Better not," Molepaw replied. "Brightheart told us to stay here."

They waited a little longer, their fear gradually dying away. Jayfeather tensed as the fox scent grew stronger again, and Molepaw muttered, "I think it's back."

He peered out through the gap in the brambles and spotted the fox sniffing along the ground a couple of tail-lengths away.

"It's looking for us!" Molepaw's voice was a terrified whisper.

"What if it finds us?" Cherrypaw asked. "Where are the others?"

The fox drew closer; Jayfeather guessed it had picked up the apprentices' scent. Then a loud hiss and a snarl came from the shadows underneath a nearby bush. The fox raised its head. The hiss was repeated, and after a heartbeat's hesitation the fox turned tail and slunk away out of sight.

"That was close!" Molepaw gasped.

Jayfeather realized there was definitely another cat under the bush. But the brambles blocked his view and in the shadows he could make out nothing more than a vague shape. He strained to catch a scent.

"Ow!" Molepaw squealed. "You're pressing too hard!"

Jayfeather's vision vanished, leaving him in darkness again. "Sorry," he muttered, frustrated to be thrown out of the young tom's memory just when he thought he might have learned something. "Okay, you can go."

When the two apprentices had scampered off, Jayfeather padded into the clearing to discover that the patrols had returned. Poppyfrost was in the middle of the hollow with Cherrypaw and Molepaw. Other cats had gathered around her, listening to the apprentices retell their adventure.

"What?" Poppyfrost screeched. "A fox nearly ate you? This is dreadful! Brambleclaw, what are we going to do about it?"

"Calm down, Poppyfrost," the deputy meowed. "There's no harm done—"

"Don't tell me to be calm!" Poppyfrost retorted. "My kits could have been eaten!"

"I know it's worrying." Brambleclaw's voice was reassuring. "I'm surprised there's a fox in the territory at all. It hasn't been long since we chased the last one out, and I wouldn't have expected it to come back so soon."

Jayfeather padded across, wanting to discuss the mysterious cat who had rescued the apprentices, but in the tumult around Poppyfrost no cat wanted to listen.

He shouldered his way into the group and became aware of Ivypool beside him, shrinking in a wave of guilt. "What's wrong with you?" he asked.

"I think this was my fault," Ivypool replied miserably. Raising her voice to make herself heard, she meowed, "I think I might have brought the fox into the territory."

"How?" Firestar demanded.

Jayfeather located the Clan leader bounding over from the Highledge; the other cats quieted down as he confronted Ivypool.

Ivypool began by describing how she and Jayfeather had found the marigold plants eaten by rabbits. "So I went to find some fox dung and put it on a stick," she went on, her voice shaking. "I put the dung around the plants to frighten the rabbits off. The fox must have smelled it and followed the trail over the border. I'm really sorry," she finished.

"Mouse-brain!" Cloudtail commented loudly.

"Yes, you nearly got my kits killed!" Poppyfrost hissed.

"Hey, that's not fair." Lionblaze thrust his way forward to stand beside Jayfeather and Ivypool. "How was Ivypool to know what would happen? We don't normally train up there."

"That's right," Sorreltail added. "And we'll all be glad of the marigold once it grows back."

More voices broke out, talking all at once so that Jayfeather couldn't make paws or tail of the argument. Finally, Firestar's yowl rang out.

"That's enough. What's done is done." As the noise began to die down, he added, "Now we need to focus on regular patrols to make sure the fox doesn't come back." He let out a snort. "And keep a lookout for strange cats hiding in bushes!"

Jayfeather could tell that his leader was only half joking. Strange things were happening, and the Clan needed to be extra vigilant. Molepaw's memory was still fresh in Jayfeather's mind, and he knew there had been a cat on the cliff top.

"Hey, Dovewing," he meowed, picking up her scent as the Clan cats separated. "What was that you were meowing about earlier? What did you hear happening on the cliff top?"

He sensed Dovewing's defensiveness as she halted and faced him. "Nothing," she replied.

"Not the first attack?" Jayfeather persisted.

"No."

"And what about afterward? Were there any signs of a cat you weren't expecting to find?"

"No!" Dovewing burst out. "I didn't hear anything, okay? Stop expecting me to look after the whole Clan!"

She turned her back on Jayfeather and stalked off. A moment later Lionblaze's scent wafted over Jayfeather, and his littermate came to stand beside him.

"What's going on?" Lionblaze asked.

"I think the apprentices were right," Jayfeather told him. "There is an intruder."

Alarm surged through Lionblaze; Jayfeather could imagine his neck fur fluffing out. "I've got to get a patrol together to track it down," he meowed.

"No, wait." Jayfeather reached out and curled his tail around his brother's foreleg. "If this cat saved the apprentices, then I don't think she's any threat. In fact, I don't think she was a threat to begin with."

For a moment Lionblaze said nothing; Jayfeather could almost hear thoughts buzzing in his head like bees in a hollow tree. He knew Lionblaze would reach the same conclusion as he had. "Really? You think so?" Lionblaze mewed at last. There was an undercurrent of hope in his voice, as well as nervousness.

"We didn't find her in the tunnel," Jayfeather pointed out. "Would she really come back?"

Jayfeather took a long breath. "We learned long ago that we didn't know her as well as we thought. Maybe she would."

CHAPTER 6

❧

"Climb higher! Higher than that!"

Twigs lashed across Ivypool's face and raked through her pelt as she clawed her way up the tree.

"Faster!" The insistent yowl came from the ground below. "Higher! Now *jump!*"

"Great StarClan!" Ivypool muttered, digging her claws into the bark of the trunk. "I'll break my neck if I jump from this high up."

She and the cats with her were so far up the tree that the trunk was starting to bend under their weight. There wasn't enough room for four cats to climb safely.

Ivypool risked a glance downward, peering through the gloom of the Dark Forest. She could hear the sounds of cats training all around her, until the noise of fighting almost drowned out the slimy rustling of the leaves. *I wonder if Birchfall is here? And how many other ThunderClan cats?*

Below she could just make out Shredtail, who was in charge of the training exercise, sitting on the trunk of a fallen tree. Antpelt stood beside him. He had been Shredtail's apprentice when he first came to the Dark Forest, but now he was a full warrior; it was he who was doing all the yowling.

"That mange-pelt loves throwing his weight around," Breezepelt hissed, clinging to the trunk beside Ivypool. "Just because he died doesn't make him more important!"

Hollowpaw of RiverClan was trying to balance on a thin branch just below Ivypool, his eyes shut tight as he let out a low moan of terror. His Clanmate Minnowtail scrambled past him and headed for the top of the tree, almost knocking Ivypool off her precarious perch.

"Hey, watch it!" Ivypool growled, envying the RiverClan cat's light, strong body and confident movements.

"Minnowtail, you won!" Shredtail yowled from below. "You don't have to jump. The rest of you, I want to see you jump *now*!"

Ivypool took a deep breath. *I don't have any choice . . . .* Spotting a pile of dead leaves underneath the tree, she launched herself into the air. All the air was driven out of her body as she hit the ground, and before she could struggle to her paws Antpelt was on top of her, holding her down. His amber eyes glared into hers.

"Too slow, mouse-brain!"

Ivypool heaved at him, bringing up her hindpaws to batter at his belly. "I can't believe you've forgotten how I helped you," she panted. "Thistleclaw wounded you so badly on the woodpile that you *died*, remember?"

"Who cares about the past? This is my Clan now!" Antpelt hissed, slashing his claws toward her throat. "I deserve to be here."

Ivypool tucked in her chin and bit down on Antpelt's outstretched paw. *Yes,* she thought bleakly. *You do.* Above her, Antpelt let out a furious yowl and snatched back his foot. Gathering all her strength, Ivypool shoved Antpelt off in time to see Minnowtail jump gracefully down from the tree and land in a clump of fern.

"Well done," Shredtail meowed as she emerged, looking smug. "It's a pity more cats aren't like you." Swinging around to rake Ivypool, Breezepelt, and Furzepaw with a glare, he continued, "Right. Time for battle training. I want to see the backflip we practiced last time."

Ivypool paired up with Furzepaw while Breezepelt and Minnowtail worked together. The WindClan cat wasn't the same nervous apprentice Ivypool had tried to help when she first came to the Dark Forest a moon ago. Furzepaw had learned a lot since then, and her movements were strong and sure. Ivypool was shocked at the power behind her blows as she leaped on top of her, and shocked, too, at her own skill as she slid out from under the apprentice and raked her claws over her ears.

She was aware of how she and the others echoed one another's moves with barely a pause, like a well-ordered patrol who had trained together since they were kitted. *You would never think we come from different Clans,* she thought, dodging a blow from Furzepaw and leaping in again to give her a swipe across the ear. *Our fighting techniques fit together perfectly. This is a force beyond anything the Clans have seen before. And I'm a part of it.*

Ivypool was relieved when finally she heard Shredtail

call out, "That's enough!"

"Did we do well?" Minnowtail mewed, springing up to let Breezepelt get to his paws.

"You're not here for praise," Shredtail growled. "Leave that to your precious Clanmates. You're here to fight. If you survive, count yourself lucky." He flicked his tail dismissively. "Now get out of here."

Ivypool stumbled away into the shadowy trees, the other cats keeping pace with her. Breezepelt was limping, and Furzepaw had oozing scratches from a blow to her flank. Even Minnowtail had fur missing from her hindquarters.

None of the cats spoke to one another. Ivypool spotted Blossomfall through the trees, heading in the same direction and looking equally battered. She knew that Blossomfall had seen her, but she looked too worn out to call a greeting. Ivypool was aware of more cats padding around her, their heads lowered with exhaustion and their flanks heaving.

But we'll all come back next time we close our eyes, Ivypool thought. *The Dark Forest has us trapped like flies in a web.*

A full moon floated above the lake, turning its water to silver, as Firestar led his Clan out of the forest. Ivypool padded beside her sister. Even though she was bone tired, she was glad to be going to the Gathering.

I won't have to go to the Dark Forest tonight, because I'll be awake for too long.

As the cats followed Firestar along the lakeshore, Ivypool

noticed that Dovewing kept shaking her head as if she had just emerged from water. She was letting out soft hisses of frustration.

"Is your hearing still not back?" Ivypool whispered.

Dovewing turned toward her, distress in her wide blue eyes. "No," she replied. "It's worse than being deaf! How am I supposed to look after the Clan?"

"Don't worry," Ivypool tried to reassure her. "There are warriors all around us." Anger stabbed at her like a claw as she saw her sister was unconvinced. "But they don't count, because they're not part of the *prophecy*, right?" she added sarcastically.

"You wouldn't understand," Dovewing snapped back at her.

"You think?" Ivypool hissed. "I don't see you going to the Dark Forest every night!"

In her stress, she didn't realize that her voice was rising, until she saw Brackenfur dropping back to walk beside them.

"Stop it, both of you," he meowed. "You can at least present a united front at a Gathering. Do you want the other Clans to see ThunderClan warriors squabbling? Not to mention that StarClan will be angry if you argue under the full moon."

Ivypool gave a reluctant nod and Dovewing muttered, "Sorry." Brackenfur gave them a hard look from narrowed green eyes, then quickened his pace again to rejoin Cloudtail.

StarClan! Ivypool thought. *Sometimes I wonder if they have any power at all.* Suppressing a shiver, she recalled everything she had seen in the Dark Forest. *I know what those cats can do. How will we ever fight back?*

* * *

As Firestar led his Clan along the shore toward the tree-bridge, the RiverClan cats emerged from the shrubbery around the stream, with Mistystar at their head. For a few moments every cat milled around in confusion. Ivypool spotted a few hostile looks from the rival Clan.

We can't fight over which Clan gets to cross the bridge first!

Then Mistystar stepped forward and dipped her head politely to Firestar. "Please, go ahead," the RiverClan leader meowed, waving her tail for her Clan to retreat a few paces.

"Thank you," Firestar replied.

He waited on the shore beside Mistystar while Bramble-claw led the ThunderClan cats across the tree-bridge. Ivypool was waiting her turn when she glanced across at the River-Clan cats and caught the gaze of Minnowtail. For a heartbeat she couldn't look away, as if the memory of training together in the Dark Forest were a claw pinning her to the RiverClan warrior. Then Minnowtail turned her head aside, and the moment was past. Ivypool realized she was shivering.

"Come on!" Dovewing gave her a prod in the side. "Are you crossing, or are you going to stand there all night?"

"Sorry." Ivypool leaped onto the tree-bridge and ran across.

There were no other cat scents in the air as she jumped down onto the pebbly shore of the island, meaning that Thunder-Clan was the first to arrive. The clearing seemed very quiet as Ivypool wriggled underneath the surrounding bushes and padded toward the Great Oak. Dovewing and Brackenfur, who had followed her, set their paws down carefully as if they didn't want to break the silence.

Then a scamper of paws sounded from beyond the bushes and Ivypool jumped, startled, as excited squeals rose into the air.

"This way! I'll race you to the Great Oak!"

"I'll get there first! You couldn't race a hedgehog!"

Brackenfur let out a *mrrow* of amusement. "Our apprentices have arrived for their first Gathering."

Cherrypaw and Molepaw came squirming through the bushes, with Rosepetal right behind them.

"That's enough," she meowed. "Don't even *think* of racing around the clearing. We have to wait for the leaders and listen quietly while they're speaking." She gestured with her tail. "Sit there."

The two apprentices obeyed her, but they were wriggling with excitement, exchanging bright-eyed glances as they gazed around.

"Wow! The Great Oak is *big*!" Cherrypaw exclaimed.

The rest of the ThunderClan cats emerged from the bushes, closely followed by RiverClan and WindClan. A few moments later ShadowClan joined them. As the clearing filled up and the different Clan scents mingled, Ivypool crouched in the middle of her own Clanmates, not wanting to see the cats who were familiar to her from the Dark Forest.

I feel as if I half belong with them, she thought uncomfortably. *But I'm betraying them already. I wish I could tell the other Clans exactly what's going on. Maybe then we could make a plan to fight the Dark Forest from within.*

Firestar was the first leader to jump into the branches of the Great Oak, followed by Onestar, Mistystar, and Blackstar. Brambleclaw and the other deputies took their places on the tree roots. The other cats grew quiet at once; Ivypool noticed that most of them had stayed with their own Clans, instead of mingling to exchange news as they usually did.

Mistystar stood on a low branch and let out a yowl, sweeping her blue gaze around the clearing. Moonlight shone on her gray-blue fur. "I will begin," she announced. "RiverClan is prospering. The dry weather hasn't affected the water levels in the lake or the stream, so fishing is good."

A murmur of approval came from RiverClan, but the other cats were silent.

"Also," Mistystar went on, "we have two new warriors. Mossypaw and Hollowpaw are now Mossyfoot and Hollowflight."

"Mossyfoot! Hollowflight!"

Ivypool peered out from behind Lionblaze to see the two new warriors sitting with their heads high while the other cats called out their names. She noticed that most of the cheers came from their own Clan; the others weren't nearly as enthusiastic. When the yowling had died down, Mistystar dipped her head to the other leaders and sat on her branch, letting her tail hang down.

Firestar rose to his paws and advanced a couple of paces to the end of the branch where he had been sitting. "Prey is running well in ThunderClan," he reported. "Two days ago a fox appeared in our territory, but our warriors chased it off."

Ivypool breathed a sigh of relief that the Clan leader didn't mention what she had done with the fox dung, which led to the fox entering ThunderClan in the first place. *He hasn't mentioned injuries, either. He won't want ThunderClan to seem weak.*

"And we have two new apprentices," Firestar went on, "Cherrypaw and Molepaw."

The two young cats sat up straight, their eyes shining, as their Clanmates called out their names. Ivypool thought they were in serious danger of bursting with pride. But still there were only a few cats from other Clans who acknowledged them.

Redwillow of ShadowClan was eyeing the two apprentices thoughtfully, though he remained silent. *Paws off!* Ivypool wanted to tell him. *You're not having them for the Dark Forest!*

Firestar waited until the clearing was quiet, then began to step back. But before he could sit down again, Onestar leaped to his paws, rustling the oak leaves as he balanced on his branch.

"I noticed you haven't mentioned the way your warriors hang around on the WindClan border," he rasped. "Are you plotting an invasion?"

Ivypool's heart beat faster and she swallowed nervously. *Is this because Birchfall and I were caught washing in the stream?*

Instantly Firestar took a pace forward so that he was facing the WindClan leader. His eyes blazed with green fire. "No!" he exclaimed. "You're being ridiculous!"

"Ridiculous, am I?" Onestar hissed. "Then why have my warriors seen a ThunderClan cat scouting our territory?"

"Yes!" Crowfeather yowled from the clearing. He sprang to his paws with his gray-black fur bristling. "I've seen it!"

"So have I!" Whitetail agreed.

Ivypool realized that Lionblaze was stiffening beside her, clearly indignant about the false accusation. She was just relieved that this didn't seem to have anything to do with her and Birchfall.

"Can you identify this trespasser?" Firestar inquired icily. He waved his tail toward the ThunderClan cats in the clearing. "Is that cat here tonight?"

"No," Onestar replied. "My warriors never got a good look at the intruder, and the scent wasn't clear."

"Oh, *really*?" Firestar's green eyes narrowed. "So you have no evidence that this was a ThunderClan cat? It could easily have been a passing loner—unless it was a bit of mist or a skinny dog."

"Well, you would say that, Firestar," Onestar blustered.

"Yes," Firestar agreed. "I would always defend my Clan against an unfounded accusation. Onestar, I think you'd better give us your Clan news and sit down, before you fall any further into the hole you've dug for yourself."

There were murmurs of agreement from the cats in the clearing—and not only from ThunderClan, Ivypool realized. The WindClan cats were mostly looking embarrassed, except for a few like Crowfeather and Breezepelt, who were still furious.

"WindClan has two new apprentices," Onestar announced

abruptly. "Crouchpaw and Larkpaw." He sat down.

This time only WindClan called out the names of the two new apprentices. Ivypool felt sorry for the young cats. *Their special moment has been spoiled because their leader is such a mouse-brain!*

Firestar also sat down, waving his tail for Blackstar to speak.

"ShadowClan warriors fought a battle with the two kitty-pets at the Twoleg nest." The big white cat lashed his tail with satisfaction. "We won't be having any more trouble from *them* for a while."

There was a yowl of agreement from ShadowClan; Ivypool spotted Tawnypelt and Toadfoot with satisfied expressions on their faces, although Toadfoot's eye was swollen from a nasty scratch, which suggested the kittypets had put up a decent fight.

"Also," the ShadowClan leader went on, "we have three new warriors: Pinenose, Ferretclaw, and Starlingwing. Shadow-Clan is strong."

Blackstar sat down as the cats in the clearing yowled approval of the new warriors. Ivypool couldn't bring herself to join in. *Strong? That sounded like a threat. Does that mean they'll be causing more trouble?*

As the Clan leaders came down from the Great Oak, the Clans at last began to mingle and share tongues before they left the island. Ivypool saw Tigerheart staring at her and Dovewing, and immediately looked away. Dovewing seemed to be ignoring the ShadowClan cat, too.

A heartbeat later, Ivypool noticed that Tigerheart had left his Clanmates and was heading toward Dovewing. Ivypool turned to warn her sister, but at that moment Hollowflight thrust himself between them.

"Hi, Ivypool," he meowed.

"Hi. Congratulations on becoming a warrior," Ivypool offered, trying to peer around the RiverClan cat to see what had happened to Dovewing.

"Thanks." Hollowflight puffed out his chest proudly. "Hey, wasn't that great climbing last night?"

Oh, sure—you were scared out of your fur! Ivypool thought. "We can't talk about it here," she whispered.

Hollowflight didn't take the hint. "It's really weird, being in the Dark Forest," he went on, though at least he had the sense to keep his voice to a low murmur. "I mean, half of those cats are dead!"

"Yeah, weird," Ivypool agreed, still trying to watch for Dovewing and Tigerheart.

To her relief, she heard the voice of Reedwhisker, the RiverClan deputy. "Hey, Hollowflight! It's time to go!"

"See you tomorrow night," Hollowflight purred as he turned and pushed his way through the crowds of cats toward his Clanmate.

As soon as he had gone, Ivypool whirled around, looking for her sister. But there was no sign of Dovewing or Tigerheart. *Have they gone off together somewhere?*

Then she spotted Dovewing heading out of the clearing

behind a group of ThunderClan cats. Ivypool hurried after her, creeping under the bushes and running down the shore to catch up to her as Dovewing waited to cross the tree-bridge.

"What did Tigerheart want?" she asked in a low voice.

Dovewing looked stressed, working her claws into the sandy ground. "It's nothing," she snapped. "He's just trying to stir up trouble over Flametail."

A chill ran through Ivypool from ears to tail-tip. *Has Tigerheart told Dovewing what he saw me doing in the Dark Forest?* Her belly heaved as she remembered the moment when Brokenstar had tried to make her kill Flametail when he wandered into the Dark Forest from StarClan.

"What sort of trouble?" she pressed Dovewing, unable to bear the uncertainty. "You know, you can't believe everything Tigerheart says."

"Too right!" Dovewing burst out loudly, then lowered her voice again with a swift glance around to see if any warrior was listening. "He's trying to make me believe that Dawn-pelt has a grudge against Jayfeather because he didn't save Flametail. She thinks Jayfeather murdered him. According to Tigerheart, Dawnpelt is planning something really bad for ThunderClan." She twitched her whiskers. "Does he think that's going to scare me?"

Ivypool relaxed, trying not to let her sister see how relieved she was. "Maybe you should tell Brambleclaw," she suggested. "He might want to put extra cats on ShadowClan border patrols."

"And get into trouble for talking to Tigerheart?" Dovewing responded. "I don't think so." She leaped up onto the end of the tree-bridge and looked down at Ivypool. "Honestly, what damage can Dawnpelt do? It's all a lie, and she knows it."

CHAPTER 7

❧

On the morning after the Gathering, Lionblaze returned from the dawn patrol and headed straight for Firestar's den. The sun was shining down into the hollow, and puffs of white cloud scudded across a blue sky. The camp was filled with the noise of peaceful activity, but Lionblaze couldn't help feeling that trouble was heading for them like a swelling storm cloud.

As he climbed up to the top of the tumbled rocks, Lionblaze heard Brambleclaw's voice coming from Firestar's den.

"Do you think Onestar was making all that up?" the Clan deputy meowed. "Is he looking for a fight?"

"I hope not," Firestar replied. "But WindClan is certainly getting hostile."

"Firestar?" Lionblaze reached the entrance to the den and poked his head inside. "Can I talk to you?"

Firestar was sitting on his pile of bedding at the back of the den, with Brambleclaw standing beside him. "Come in," he invited with a wave of his tail. "We were just discussing Onestar's outburst at the Gathering."

Lionblaze padded into the den, dipping his head to Brambleclaw. "I heard what you were saying," he began. "That's what I wanted to discuss, too. What if WindClan is right?"

"What?" Brambleclaw's tail-tip twitched. "You think ThunderClan cats—?"

"No," Lionblaze interrupted. "I know that's not true. But suppose they have seen a cat hanging around? Remember what Cherrypaw and Molepaw said they saw. We might well have a rogue wandering about in the territory."

Firestar nodded. "That's a very good point."

"I'll track it down if you like," Lionblaze offered, "and send it on its way." Waiting tensely for his leader's reply, he added to himself, *And then I can find out if what Jayfeather and I suspect is true.*

"There's no need for that," Brambleclaw meowed. "We can just send out extra patrols."

"No," Firestar decided after a moment's thought. "Lionblaze can go alone if he wants. There's no need to be aggressive about this. We just need to find out if there's any evidence of an intruder."

Brambleclaw looked slightly puzzled, but dipped his head toward Firestar. "Fine, if you think that's best."

Lionblaze bade the two cats a hasty farewell, and ran down the tumbled rocks into the clearing. On his way to the thorn tunnel, he spotted Jayfeather outside his den, sniffing at the fox bite on Foxleap's shoulder. Lionblaze veered toward him.

"That smells fine," Jayfeather meowed to Foxleap as Lionblaze approached. "See me again tomorrow. If there are no more problems I think you can go back to warrior duties in a few days."

"Great, thanks!" Foxleap replied, heading toward the warriors' den.

Jayfeather turned to Lionblaze. "Well? What are you so excited about?"

Lionblaze paused for a heartbeat, still finding it odd after all this time that Jayfeather could judge his feelings so accurately without being able to see him. "Firestar has given me permission to go and look for the intruder," he told his brother.

Jayfeather twitched his ears. "Really? You'd better be careful, then." A heartbeat later, he added, "What will you do if we're right?"

"I don't know," Lionblaze admitted, feeling a tingle in his paws. "But I don't want any other cat finding out first."

"True enough," Jayfeather commented.

Leaving his littermate to return to his den, Lionblaze brushed through the thorn tunnel and headed to the slope above the hollow. Wind blew into his face and flattened his fur to his sides as he gazed out over the lake. It looked so peaceful, the water glittering in the sunlight, surrounded by rustling green leaves. Yet Lionblaze felt it was overshadowed by the Dark Forest and his knowledge of what was coming.

The acrid scent of fox dung trickled into Lionblaze's nose. He followed it until he reached the clearing where Cherrypaw and Molepaw had been training.

Phew, what a stench! Ivypool certainly did a thorough job.

He searched along the edges of the bramble thickets until

he discovered paw prints and scraps of fur clinging to the thorns, which showed him where the apprentices had hidden from the fox. Squeezing under the brambles, Lionblaze tried to work out what the young cats might have seen from their hiding place. Bramble tendrils cut off his view in most directions, but there was a gap low down, level with a scared apprentice's sight line. Through it he could see a hazel bush a few tail-lengths away that looked like a place where the mysterious rescuer might have been crouching.

Lionblaze wriggled out from underneath the brambles, hissing with annoyance as thorns raked his fur. Underneath the hazel bush the debris was disturbed as if a cat had stood there, and a few snapped twigs lay on the ground, but there were no clear paw prints.

The cat must have been a bit smaller than me to get under there, Lionblaze thought. *Too bad there are no scraps of fur left behind. And I can't smell a thing over this awful reek of fox.*

There was nothing more to be learned in the clearing. After a moment's thought, Lionblaze headed for the border with the unclaimed forest, then turned toward WindClan, since the intruder had been seen there. Scanning the ground carefully as he padded along, he spotted a place where the leaf-mold had been churned up, as if a pounce and a brief struggle had taken place there.

Sniffing carefully all around, Lionblaze couldn't find any signs that the prey had been eaten where it was caught. Then he stiffened, spotting tiny drag marks leading toward the border. Following them paw step by paw step, sometimes almost losing the trail among grass and leaves, Lionblaze finally reached the border. The drag marks continued; passing the ThunderClan scent markers, he found scattered feathers a few fox-lengths outside the boundary, in unclaimed forest.

So this cat killed prey, but knew enough to take it across the border before eating it. Lionblaze's heart started to beat faster. *This is a cat who knows about the territories! It's confident hunting and moving around here, but it doesn't want to be found.*

Lionblaze sat beside the feathers, wrapped his tail around his paws, and tried to think. If the intruder was living in this area, she had food and water, but she would need shelter, too.

Not too far from here, if she wants to keep an eye on ThunderClan, but not so close that scent would stray across the border while she's resting . . .

Rising to his paws again, Lionblaze ventured a little farther into the unknown woods. He soon came to a bramble thicket, which looked like a possible shelter for a loner.

No, he thought, eyeing it carefully. *I wouldn't live there. It would be too hard to escape, and a cat could be on top of me before I heard them.*

Searching farther, his pelt prickling with the feeling that he was very close to his quarry, Lionblaze came to a clearing where the ground was uneven and moss-covered rocks jutted out of the ground. Beneath one of the biggest boulders was a hole, like the entrance to a tunnel. Lionblaze set his paws down as lightly as if he were stalking a mouse. Reaching the hole, he stretched out his neck and took a sniff. Dampness and earth flooded his scent glands, but there was the scent of cat as well, though he couldn't identify it among all the other scents.

He was crouching down to enter when another thought occurred to him. *Wait. I wouldn't shelter in there unless I knew there was another way out.*

Still treading carefully, he slunk around the boulders, his gaze flicking from side to side in search of another hole. Finally he found it: smaller than the first, and well-hidden in a clump of ferns.

Yes!

After a moment's thought, Lionblaze searched until he found a fallen branch, and dragged it back to the second hole, jamming it firmly across the opening.

I don't know if the intruder is in there, but I'm taking no chances.

He returned to the first entrance, crouching down and straining to see inside. But it was impossible to make out anything in the darkness.

There's no other choice. I'll have to go in.

For a couple of heartbeats he hesitated. He really didn't want to squeeze himself into the dark hole. It was too small for him, and he felt as if he would hardly be able to breathe in the cramped space. *There could be anything down there . . . snakes . . . foxes . . .*

Then he gave his pelt a shake. *Are you a warrior, or a mouse?* Flattening himself to the ground, he began to thrust his shoulders into the narrow gap and crawl forward.

A voice spoke behind him. "Hello, Lionblaze."

Lionblaze's heart jumped. He whipped around, banging his head on the boulder that sheltered the hole. Then his jaw dropped open and he stared in astonishment. In front of him stood a cat that he had never expected to see again.

"Sol!"

Sol inclined his head. His mottled brown-and-black pelt gleamed in the sunlight and his whiskers arched with amusement as he looked at Lionblaze. "How appropriate that you're the first cat that I see when I return," he mewed, giving his chest fur a couple of licks. "After all, you were the last cat I saw before I left."

Guilt surged over Lionblaze as he remembered how he had helped Sol escape from the ThunderClan camp, genuinely believing that he didn't deserve to be kept prisoner.

"What are you doing here?" he demanded, his mind racing.

Sol's ears twitched in surprise. "No warm welcome for a former Clanmate?"

"You were never my Clanmate," Lionblaze retorted, struggling to keep calm, furious with himself that Sol had caught him off-balance, with his pelt covered in soil and debris. "And you're wrong to expect a welcome from any of us," he went on. "We know what you did to Blackstar and ShadowClan."

Sol's eyes widened in a hurt expression. "I simply suggested a different way of living. The world doesn't begin and end with the warrior code, you know." An ominous note crept into his voice. "But I also know that the warrior code insists that you treat visitors with courtesy. There's nothing wrong with wanting to visit old friends, is there?"

Lionblaze gritted his teeth. *This cat leaves me wrong-footed whatever I say!* "We were never your friends," he muttered.

"Oh, I think you were," Sol meowed. "After all, you helped me to escape, didn't you?" Blinking at Lionblaze's hiss of annoyance, he added, "Ah, I see that this isn't common knowledge. I can't say I'm surprised. Hardly your finest moment, was it, releasing a prisoner? Though I have to say I was never entirely sure what I was captured for." He examined the claws on one forepaw. "So, are you going to take me to Firestar?"

Surprise rippled through Lionblaze's pelt. "Really?"

Sol nodded. "Why not? I have no quarrel with him, even if he did imprison me for no reason. We can share stories about the old days by the lake. The vanishing sun—remember that?"

Lionblaze shuddered and looked up at the sky, remembering the unnatural darkness, chill, and silence all too clearly.

"It's all right," Sol purred. "I'm not going to make it disappear again. As long as I'm not treated unfairly, that is."

Lionblaze emerged from the thorn tunnel with Sol just behind him. Most of the patrols had returned by this time, and the stone hollow was filled with cats sunning themselves, sharing tongues, or gossiping beside the fresh-kill pile. Dustpelt was crossing the clearing, heading for the dirtplace tunnel; he halted when he spotted Sol.

"I don't believe it!" he exclaimed. "What are you doing here?"

Cloudtail and Brightheart, curled up together in a sunny spot, raised their heads and stared. "Sol! It can't be!" Cloudtail's voice was a yowl of astonishment.

Alerted by the noise, two or three warriors poked their

heads out of their den, then slid into the open. Brackenfur, who was sharing tongues with Sorreltail just outside, took one look, sprang to his paws, and raced up the rockfall toward Firestar's den.

"Sol!" Squirrelflight gasped, looking up from the fresh-kill pile with a vole in her jaws. "Oh, no!"

Cherrypaw and Molepaw scampered across the clearing and skidded to a halt in front of Sol, gazing at him with eyes stretched wide in wonder.

"Are you really Sol?" Cherrypaw asked. "Mousefur was just telling us about you!"

"Yeah, are you the cat who stole the sun?" Molepaw added.

Sol dipped his head. "Yes, but I gave it back again."

"Wow!"

Lionblaze didn't move as more of his Clanmates bounded across the clearing and surrounded him and Sol. He glanced around for Jayfeather and Dovewing, but couldn't see either of them.

"What do you want?" Graystripe growled, pushing himself to the front of the crowd. "Every time you set paw in our territory, it means trouble."

"Right." Dustpelt came to stand beside Graystripe, his neck fur bristling. "If I were you, Sol, I would turn around again and go back where you came from."

"So good to meet old friends," Sol purred, raising one paw and giving it a lick. "There's always such a warm welcome in ThunderClan."

Before any cat could respond, Firestar shouldered his way

forward and halted in front of Sol, looking him up and down with suspicion in his green eyes.

"Why are you here, Sol?" he asked, his flame-colored pelt fluffing up.

Sol blinked. "I was just passing through. I couldn't go on without stopping to greet my friends in ThunderClan."

Passing through . . . huh! Lionblaze thought. *He's been around for several sunrises, at least.*

Firestar seemed to consider Sol's answer for a moment, the tip of his tail flicking slightly. "ThunderClan has no quarrel with you now," he mewed at last. "But I can't say the same about Blackstar. And you've already caused enough trouble by hanging around on the WindClan border. All in all, it would be better if you just left."

Sol's only response was to twitch an ear.

"We can make him go, Firestar," Cloudtail growled, taking a pace forward. "Just say the word."

But at the same moment, a loud cry of "Sol! Sol!" came from the direction of the warriors' den. Poppyfrost came pelting across the camp and wriggled through the crowd of cats surrounding Sol.

"Sol, you saved my kits, didn't you?" she meowed, gazing wide-eyed at him. "Above the hollow, when the fox cornered them? It was you, wasn't it?" she went on insistently when Sol didn't reply. "They didn't get a good look at you, but they'd have known if it was a ThunderClan warrior."

Lionblaze's heart sank. Realizing that Sol must have been the cat under the hazel bush who scared away the fox didn't change his opinion at all. He wanted Sol gone.

"And what was Sol doing, wandering around ThunderClan territory?" Dustpelt muttered.

"Yeah." Cloudtail glared at the newcomer. "Why didn't he come straight here if he wanted to visit, or make himself known to a patrol?"

Poppyfrost's head swiveled and she returned Cloudtail's glare. "He probably wasn't sure about what sort of a welcome he'd get," she retorted, then turned back to Sol with a deep-throated purr. "Oh, Sol, thank you so much! You'll always be welcome here."

"Thank you, Poppyfrost," Sol replied. "But really, it was nothing."

"Fighting off a fox isn't nothing," Berrynose meowed, coming up behind Poppyfrost and dipping his head respectfully to the visitor. "Firestar, he can stay the night, can't he?"

Firestar looked disconcerted. Lionblaze could see that he didn't want to let Sol back into the camp, but he could hardly turn him away now. "Very well," he agreed, with a curt nod.

"Come over here and take your pick of the fresh-kill pile," Berrynose invited.

The cream-colored warrior escorted Sol across the camp, and most of the other cats followed. Cherrypaw and Molepaw were already asking excited questions about Sol's travels.

"Later," Poppyfrost told them. "Let Sol eat and rest first."

Lionblaze stayed where he was, near the camp entrance. *I can't believe this! Sol's back in ThunderClan as an honored guest.* He spotted Jayfeather, who had been listening at the edge of the crowd, and padded over to join him. "We were wrong," he mewed.

Jayfeather nodded, his head turned toward the fresh-kill pile as if he could see his Clanmates gathering around Sol. "I was so sure . . ." he murmured.

"I don't care how many apprentices Sol saved," Lionblaze went on after a moment. "I don't trust him, and I don't think Firestar trusts him, either."

"Neither do I." Jayfeather gave a disdainful sniff. "There's no way he was just passing by. He's here for a reason, and that reason is bound to be trouble."

CHAPTER 8

Dovewing followed Brambleclaw through the thorns with a squirrel clamped in her jaws. Hazeltail and Thornclaw followed, also carrying prey. It had been a good hunt.

At the end of the narrow tunnel, Dovewing almost bumped into Brambleclaw, who had halted abruptly just inside the camp. "Sorry," he muttered, moving out of the way.

When Dovewing emerged, she saw that the Clan deputy was gazing across the clearing at a strange cat who was sitting beside the fresh-kill pile, eating a piece of prey and chatting to the ThunderClan warriors who surrounded him. He looked sleek and well-fed, his pelt mottled brown and black, patched with white.

"Who is that?" she asked Brambleclaw, who was still staring at the newcomer, his neck fur beginning to bristle.

"Sol," the deputy replied, dropping the rabbit he was carrying. "He was here before you were born, and—"

"Mousefur told me about him, moons ago!" Dovewing interrupted, excitement beginning to prickle her paws. "Didn't he make the sun go away? I thought that was just a story."

Brambleclaw nodded. "It's no story."

"Do you think he'll do it again?"

"He'd better not," Thornclaw growled, coming to stand beside Brambleclaw. "That cat is trouble. I can't imagine what Firestar's thinking, letting him in here."

Brambleclaw picked up his rabbit and led the way across to the fresh-kill pile. The rest of the patrol followed to deposit their prey, weaving their way between the cats who were talking to Sol.

"Come and meet Sol," Mousewhisker meowed enthusiastically as Dovewing added her squirrel to the pile. "He's the cat who chased the fox away and saved the apprentices."

"Yes, isn't it great that he came back?" Whitewing added. "Just think what would have happened to those poor young cats!"

But Dovewing could tell that not all the cats around Sol were pleased to see him. Firestar was sitting with Sandstorm, Graystripe, and Millie, looking distinctly awkward about the newcomer's presence, while Dustpelt, Ferncloud, and Squirrelflight had their heads together, speaking in undertones and casting suspicious glances at Sol.

Purdy and Mousefur padded slowly across from the elders' den, looking curious; Purdy blinked in surprise when he spotted Sol.

"Well, what next!" the old tabby exclaimed. "Sol! I never reckoned I'd see you again."

Sol inclined his head. "Purdy. You're looking well. Mousefur, I—"

The brown she-cat lashed her tail as Sol turned to her, taking a pace back and letting out a hiss. "Don't come near me," she snarled.

For a moment Dovewing thought she detected a flash of anger in Sol's amber eyes. Then the mottled tom dipped his head again. "The same old Mousefur, I see," he mewed smoothly. "I'm so glad to see you again."

Mousefur spun around and stalked back to her den. Purdy cast a helpless glance at Sol before following her. Watching the cranky elder, Dovewing didn't notice that Ivypool had appeared at her side until her sister poked her with one paw.

"How weird is this?" Ivypool meowed. When Dovewing didn't answer, she went on in a whisper, "Did you see anything on the ShadowClan border?"

Dovewing guessed that her sister was referring to the threat from Dawnpelt. "You're taking that stupid she-cat seriously?" she asked, rolling her eyes. "No, I didn't see a thing. No cat's going to listen to her lies when there are bigger things to think about."

Firestar sent more patrols out to bring back extra prey, and as the sun went down the Clan feasted around the fresh-kill pile. Dovewing sat nibbling at a mouse, trying to work out what Sol's arrival would mean for ThunderClan. The younger cats were gathered around the newcomer, crouching with wide-open eyes and ears pricked to take in every word he said.

"Then there was the time I fought off a badger single-pawed," Sol was relating. "A huge, ugly brute it was, too. I came across it unexpectedly when I was hunting in a forest a long way from here." He gave his paw a long lick and drew it slowly over his ear. "But badgers aren't dangerous if you know how to handle them. It soon got out of there when I gave it a scratched nose."

I hope Cherrypaw and Molepaw don't think that's the right way to deal with a badger, Dovewing thought. The two apprentices were right at the front of the crowd, forgetting to eat as they gazed up at Sol with gaping jaws.

"Tell us more!" Cherrypaw begged. "Have you ever fought with dogs, Sol?"

"I've fought off more dogs than you've eaten mice," Sol replied. "There was a time—"

"No, that's enough," Poppyfrost mewed, flicking Cherrypaw's shoulder with her tail. "I'm sorry, Sol, but it's time they were both in their nests."

"No way!" Molepaw protested. "We're not kits anymore."

"You still need your sleep," Poppyfrost told him.

Berrynose leaned over to his mate and touched her ear with his nose. "Let them stay up for once," he murmured. "It's not every day they have the chance to learn about what's beyond these hills."

"Yes!" Molepaw gave an excited little bounce. "Go on about the dog, please, Sol."

"Well, it was with a couple of Twolegs and their kits," Sol began. "They were walking in the woods where I was staying at the time, and the stupid creatures let their dog off that tendril-thing they use to tie themselves to animals. It picked up my scent and came yapping through the ferns toward my den. So do you know what I did then?"

"No!" Cherrypaw breathed out. "Tell us!"

"I climbed a tree," Sol went on. "I waited until the dog came running underneath, and I dropped down right on top of it!"

Dovewing heard several cats catch their breath in excitement. *They actually* believe *this nonsense?*

"That mangy flea-pelt yowled to the moon and back, I can tell you," Sol went on. "It went yelping back to its Twolegs with its tail between its legs and me still clinging onto its neck."

"Did the Twolegs catch you?" Blossomfall asked breathlessly.

Sol shook his head. "Just before the dog ran up to them, I jumped off and hid in some ferns. They shouted at the dog for running off, and put its tendril-thing back on. And that was the last I saw of it."

Trying to ignore the admiring comments from her Clanmates, Dovewing stared at Sol. She cast back through her recent memories in case she could pick up any faint sounds that might have been him trespassing on ThunderClan territory. But there was nothing. She shook her head in frustration.

If only I had my proper senses. . . . What if I never get them back?

Dovewing jumped as a tail rested on her shoulder, and turned to see Cinderheart.

"Cheer up," the gray she-cat meowed. "Whatever's worrying you, I'm sure it'll be okay."

"I don't know," Dovewing murmured. "It's Sol . . . I don't like him, and I don't like the fact that he's here."

Cinderheart nodded, her blue eyes sympathetic. "I'm not too sure about Sol myself," she confessed. "But if he did save the apprentices, then the Clan owes him a decent meal and shelter, at least."

While Dovewing was thinking that over, she noticed Bumblestripe getting up from his place beside Blossomfall. The thick-furred warrior, his pelt just like his father's, stretched before padding over to her.

"Hi, Dovewing," he meowed. "I feel like going for a walk in the forest. Do you want to come with me?"

"Not right now," Dovewing replied. "I'll probably go to my den soon."

Bumblestripe blinked, a hurt expression in his eyes. "Oh, okay." He turned away and vanished down the thorn tunnel.

"That wasn't very kind," Cinderheart murmured. "Don't go trampling on Bumblestripe's heart. He really likes you."

Dovewing wriggled, feeling her pelt grow hot with embarrassment. "No, he doesn't. . . ." she began.

"Of course he does." Cinderheart sounded convinced. "You know," she added more seriously, "if there are no obstacles to getting to know a cat better, then you should take the opportunity."

"Does that mean that you and Lionblaze—"

Dovewing broke off as Cinderheart shook her head, her blue eyes clouding with sadness. "No," she mewed. "There *is* an obstacle to that, but you'd never understand."

Dovewing stared at her. *Does Cinderheart know about Lionblaze's special power? Is that the obstacle?*

She opened her jaws to question Cinderheart, but the gray she-cat never gave her the chance. "Off you go after Bumblestripe," she urged. "It's not too late. He'll be so happy to see you."

Though she still had misgivings, Dovewing didn't argue. Ducking through the barrier, she emerged into the cool, dusky wood. Moonlight shone through the leaves, turning the forest floor into a pattern of silver and shadow. A faint breeze stirred the grass and rustled the leaves above Dovewing's head.

"Bumblestripe!" she called.

There was no reply. Dovewing tried to send out her senses, straining to listen. After a moment she picked up the sound of paw steps, and the image of a cat sitting by the lake. Excitement tingled through Dovewing from ears to tail-tip. *Maybe my special powers are starting to come back!*

She raced through the forest in the direction of the cat she had seen. It was harder to stay focused, and the image was fainter than before, but when she burst out of the undergrowth onto the lakeshore she was delighted to see Bumblestripe sitting at the water's edge, his face turned upward to the stars. The stripes on his pale pelt stood out sharply in the silver moonlight.

"Bumblestripe!" she called, her voice high-pitched with joy that she hadn't lost her power for good.

Bumblestripe sprang to his paws and whirled around. "Dovewing!" he exclaimed, running to meet her. "You came," he added, purring so hard he could hardly get the words out. "Come and sit beside me. It's beautiful here."

Dovewing suddenly felt awkward. "Is it okay if we go for a walk instead?" she asked.

"Sure."

Together the two cats turned to pad along the shore, Bumblestripe walking close enough that their pelts brushed. Dovewing fished for something to talk about.

"Do you remember Sol from when he was here before?" she asked as the silence began to drag out.

"Sort of," Bumblestripe replied. "I recognized him when he turned up today. But I was only a kit then."

"What do you think of him?"

Bumblestripe shrugged. "He thinks a lot of himself, doesn't he?"

A sudden spurt of amusement bubbled up inside Dovewing. "Yes! All those stories! Jumping down onto a dog's back . . . please! I know we leaped out of trees when we were fighting ShadowClan, but you'd have to be totally mouse-brained to try it with a dog."

"Oh, I've had enough of Sol," Bumblestripe meowed. "Let's not talk about him here as well. Toadstep told me how you won that race the other day. Do you want to race with me?"

"Great!" Dovewing responded. "Where to?"

"That tree stump over there?" Bumblestripe asked, angling his ears toward a stump at the edge of the forest farther along the shore.

Dovewing nodded and bounded off, her paws flicking up little stones behind her. For a few moments Bumblestripe kept pace with her, but soon she began to draw ahead. *Wow, I really can run fast!* But then Dovewing became aware of sounds from the other Clans across the lake: A RiverClan cat was fishing in the stream beside their camp, while in ShadowClan a gray-muzzled warrior was teaching his apprentice about night hunting.

She felt as though her senses were surging in and out, like a wave on the lake. Sometimes she picked up everything clearly, sometimes the images were blurred, but excitement and relief pulsed through her as she realized that she was recovering.

It just needed time, she thought. *Lionblaze was right! My senses were overwhelmed by the journey to the mountains, that's all.*

Dovewing was so pleased to have her senses back, and was concentrating so hard, that she didn't notice where she was putting her racing paws. Something coiled around one forepaw; Dovewing was flung down onto the pebbles, letting out a startled yowl that ended in a gasp as the breath was driven out of her body.

Bumblestripe flashed past her. Dovewing tried to scramble up and realized that an ivy tendril, snaking out from the edge of the trees, had tripped her. As she wrenched her paw free, Bumblestripe was by her side again.

"Are you okay?" he panted.

"Fine," Dovewing replied, struggling to get her breath. Even though she felt battered from her fall, happiness was surging through her like a stream in flood. *I haven't lost my senses. Everything's okay!* "I'm absolutely fine," she repeated.

Bumblestripe let her lean on his shoulder as she staggered to her paws, and stroked her pelt gently with his tail to get rid of the sand and grit. His eyes shone. "You would have won the race if you hadn't tripped," he mewed.

"Maybe." Dovewing had almost forgotten the race; getting her senses back was so much more important. "You're pretty fast, too."

She began to pad back along the lakeshore, and Bumblestripe stayed close to her side. "Dovewing . . ." he began, sounding a little shy, "can I show you something?"

"Okay," Dovewing agreed, only half-listening as she focused on a WindClan she-cat scolding her kits for putting a beetle in her nest.

"It's this way." Bumblestripe veered into the trees, and Dovewing followed, ferns brushing against her pelt on both sides.

Without following any path that Dovewing could see, they came to a tiny clearing where wild jasmine scrambled over a gnarled oak tree, forming an archway with a tiny space underneath it. A few white flowers had already appeared on the branches. Bumblestripe squeezed into the space, and beckoned Dovewing with his tail. She crept in after him, feeling his warmth against her side, and enjoying the sweet scent of the jasmine flowers.

"I've always loved this place," Bumblestripe confided in her. "It's even better in greenleaf, when all the flowers are out." He blinked at her anxiously, and Dovewing realized he was afraid that she might make fun of him.

"It's lovely," she assured him.

Bumblestripe relaxed and lifted his muzzle to gaze upward;

Dovewing spotted a gap between the branches through which they could see the stars.

"I like to look up at our ancestors," he meowed. "Sometimes I wonder which ones are mine." He hesitated, then added, "I think your ancestors would shine really brightly, Dovewing."

"I don't know about that," Dovewing replied. "I think my ancestors would be hiding behind a cloud, because they were always getting into trouble!"

Bumblestripe let out a little *mrrow* of laughter. "I think that's an ancestor of mine up there," he murmured, pointing with his tail. "The one that looks as if it's stuck in the branches!"

"I wonder if they're watching us," Dovewing mused. "Can they see everything we're doing from up there?"

"I think they can," Bumblestripe meowed seriously. "They glare down at us and see all the things we're doing wrong. I bet that one over there knows all about the time I put fire ants in Blossomfall's nest!"

"You didn't!" Dovewing exclaimed, half-amused and half-shocked.

"I did." Bumblestripe ducked his head, embarrassed. "When we were apprentices. She got back at me, though; she pushed me into the stream when I wasn't looking."

Dovewing snorted. "There must be a star glaring down at her, then. Maybe it's that one." She pointed at it with one paw. "And the one beside it is annoyed with me because I forgot to change the elders' bedding one time."

"Oh, no!" Bumblestripe leaned over and touched her ear

with his nose. "I bet Mousefur told you off."

Dovewing winced. "I think they must have heard her in RiverClan!"

Bumblestripe lapsed into silence. *This is good,* Dovewing thought, reveling in the cool grass and the scent that wreathed around her. *Just sitting here, talking to a Clanmate, looking at the stars. . . .*

It wasn't exactly the same as the nights she had spent with Tigerheart—she couldn't feel her heart thumping hard enough to burst out of her chest, and her paws weren't tingling as she ran through forbidden territory—but right at that moment, she was very happy to be sitting beneath the jasmine with Bumblestripe, and nowhere else.

"Okay," Cinderheart meowed. "Let's see your hunter's crouch."

Dovewing watched as Ivypool took up her position at the edge of the training clearing, while Cinderheart padded around her, checking that she had it right.

"Tuck your tail in a bit more," she instructed. "Yes, that's great. Now spring, and see if you can hit that primrose under the tree over there."

Ivypool bunched her muscles and exploded in an enormous pounce, leaping through the air and bringing her forepaws down on the primrose, flattening it to the ground.

"Well done," Lionblaze commented. "Now let's see you do it, Dovewing."

As she crouched down, trying to make sure her paws and

tail were in the right place, Dovewing thought that once she might have resented going back to this kind of basic training with her former mentor. But today she felt too happy to resent anything. She had slept well the night before, after her walk with Bumblestripe, and this morning her senses were even clearer.

She felt a claw-scratch of fear, knowing how fragile her special senses were. But then she shrugged off the feeling. *I have to protect them, that's all, just like I protect my paws on stony ground, or the soft parts of my belly in a fight.*

While Lionblaze checked her position, she took a moment to reach out. WindClan had a new litter of kits. *Noisy little things!* Dovewing thought as they burrowed into their mother's belly to feed. In RiverClan the newly-made warriors were overwhelmed by excitement at being out on patrol, while in ShadowClan Tigerheart was teaching a couple of apprentices how to stalk a squirrel. Dovewing let out a *mrrow* of laughter as something alerted their prey. The squirrel dashed one way, then doubled back and ran right across Tigerheart's back before leaping to safety up a tree.

"You're in a good mood today," Lionblaze commented.

"Mmm," Cinderheart agreed with a twitch of her whiskers. "That must have been a really good walk last night!"

"What walk?" Lionblaze asked.

Cinderheart glanced at him, her blue eyes glimmering. "I couldn't possibly tell you."

Lionblaze flicked his ears. "Okay. Meanwhile, Dovewing, bring your hind paws a bit farther forward and see if you can pounce on that primrose."

"If Ivypool hasn't demolished it," Dovewing muttered.

Drawing her paws in to give more power to her spring, she launched herself across the clearing and landed beside her sister, shredding what was left of the pale yellow primrose with her claws.

"Good!" Lionblaze commented. "You're both on form today."

"What did Cinderheart mean about a walk last night?" Ivypool whispered. "You were really late coming back to the den."

Dovewing didn't want to talk about her evening with Bumblestripe, but she knew that her sister would be upset if she refused. "Nothing," she replied. "I went down to the lake with Bumblestripe, that's all."

Ivypool's eyes widened with surprise. "Oh, that's terrific!" she exclaimed. "He's really nice. Are you two going to be mates?"

"That's the last thing on my mind!" Dovewing twitched her tail irritably. "It was just a walk. It was fun, but no big deal."

Her sister gave her a poke in the side. "The two of you would have the cutest kits together!"

Dovewing rolled her eyes. To distract herself from Ivypool's teasing, she extended her senses into the forest again. Almost at once she picked up the image of a cat heading through the trees toward the WindClan border. It took her a moment to identify his scent and appearance; she stiffened when she realized it was Sol.

Is he leaving already? she wondered. *Or just going for a walk? He's a strange cat, that's for sure.*

"Why don't we do some hunting before we go back to camp?" she suggested, dismissing Sol from her mind. She wanted to show Lionblaze that her senses had returned.

"I'm surprised you have the energy after that training session," Lionblaze remarked.

Dovewing bounced on her paws. "I feel like I could run right around the lake!" she purred. Then she spotted Cinderheart blinking with pleasure. *Oh, no, she thinks it's because of Bumblestripe!*

"Okay, let's hunt," Lionblaze meowed. "And to make it a bit more interesting, we'll have a contest. We'll all start from here, and the first to make a catch wins."

Ivypool pricked up her ears. "Wins what?"

"Oh . . . how about first pick of the fresh-kill pile?" Cinderheart suggested.

Dovewing crouched down and waited, sending out her senses as delicately as the seeds from a dandelion, drifting on the wind. Soon she picked up a bird—a moorhen—beside the lake, pecking its way along the shoreline. Concentrating intensely, she held her focus as Cinderheart and Ivypool set off in different directions, holding their heads high to scent the air.

Lionblaze was still watching her. Dovewing fixed on the exact location of the moorhen, still pecking among the little stones at the water's edge, then sprang to her paws. She took off toward the lake, winding her way through the trees, leaping over dead branches and tiny streams.

I didn't realize how far we were from the lake!

Pausing beside a hazel bush, Dovewing checked that the moorhen was still there, then carried on. As she burst out of the trees the bird fluttered up, but she batted it out of the air with a massive pounce, and gave it a sharp bite to the neck. Picking up her prey, she headed back to the clearing. She wasn't surprised, given how far she had run to make her kill, to see that the three others had all gotten there before her.

"Bad luck," Ivypool mewed sympathetically, a plump mouse lying at her paws.

Cinderheart had caught a squirrel, and Lionblaze a blackbird.

"Ivypool was first back, so she wins," Cinderheart announced.

Dovewing dipped her head to her sister. "Well done."

Picking up her prey, Cinderheart led the way back to the clearing with Ivypool at her side. Shrugging, Dovewing followed. Secretly, she wasn't disappointed to be the last back. She had done what she set out to do. Lionblaze was watching her intently, and as she met his gaze, he gave her a nod. He wasn't disappointed, either. He knew her power had come back.

CHAPTER 9

Jayfeather shivered as a cold wind probed his fur with icy claws. He stood at the crest of a hill; around him a copse of pine trees bent their tops into the gale, their branches rattling together. Above the trees, the sky heaved with gray clouds.

"I've had enough of this," Jayfeather muttered, gazing out across the bleak landscape. "I'm leaving."

But before he could wake from his dream he heard the puffing breath of a cat climbing the hill, and spotted a skinny gray shape struggling through the thorny undergrowth.

"Yellowfang," he sighed as the cat emerged into the open. "Did we really have to meet here? This wind is blowing my fur off."

Yellowfang halted in front of him and stared at him from narrowed amber eyes. Jayfeather thought that she looked even scruffier than usual. Her pelt was ruffled by the wind, her breath stank, and her eyes were gummy, as if she hadn't groomed herself for moons.

"I chose this place because I can't risk any cat overhearing us," Yellowfang informed him, wheezing.

"There's still a bad feeling in StarClan, then?" Jayfeather asked.

"Yes!" the old she-cat hissed. "And you must trust no cat!"

Jayfeather dug his claws into the cold ground. He felt chilled to the bone, and wanted nothing more than to wake into his warm den. "What do you want?" he mewed impatiently.

"To tell you what you must do," Yellowfang replied. "You need to recruit another medicine cat. I don't mean an apprentice. I mean the other fully trained cat who lives in ThunderClan."

Jayfeather's pelt prickled with surprise. "But Leafpool isn't a medicine cat anymore," he pointed out. "That's beyond my control—or yours."

Regret clouded the old gray cat's eyes. "I know," she mewed sadly. "I don't mean Leafpool. What she did was so wrong when judged against the medicine cat code, it's as if her training had never existed. Don't underestimate the depth of her punishment, Jayfeather. She hasn't only given up her place as medicine cat. She's forbidden to use her knowledge, even though she worked so hard to achieve it."

Jayfeather felt a flash of frustration. *Like you didn't have a kit of your own, even if your Clan never knew the truth.* "That's like punishing the whole Clan for one cat's mistake!" he hissed.

"It was a grave mistake." Yellowfang's voice was somber.

"Then what do you mean about another medicine cat?" Jayfeather prompted. "Not Briarlight or Brightheart, surely? They know more than the others, but they haven't had any real training. Brightheart hasn't even been to the Moonpool."

Yellowfang lashed her scraggy tail. "You should know who I mean, mouse-brain," she rasped. "ThunderClan has a third medicine cat—Cinderheart. Perhaps it's time to tell her who she really is."

Jayfeather flinched. "You think so? Will she believe me?"

"She will if you walk in her dreams," Yellowfang meowed. "Take her back to the life she had before. All the knowledge is there; she just needs to reach out for it."

Disconcerted by the burning intensity in Yellowfang's amber eyes, Jayfeather took a step back. "Wait. Cinderpelt was your apprentice; she doesn't have to be mine. How can I train a new medicine cat with everything else that's going on?"

Yellowfang rolled her eyes. "You won't need to train her!" she spat. "She already knows more than you do. She just needs to remember who she is."

Jayfeather bristled. "I'll think about it," he snapped.

"Make sure you do," Yellowfang mewed. "Or I might walk in her dreams myself."

That would scare Cinderheart out of her fur, Jayfeather thought, unable to imagine anything more unsettling for the young warrior.

"All right, I'll do it," he growled.

Yellowfang turned to leave, then glanced back over her shoulder. "You have to be ready for the worst battle the Clans have ever known," she reminded him. "One medicine cat will not be enough!"

* * *

Jayfeather woke to darkness. He was curled comfortably in the moss and fern of his nest in the medicine cat's den; the air around him was warm, and full of the fresh scents of early greenleaf. But although his body was at ease, his mind was troubled, and he felt as if he had scarcely rested at all.

Outside in the clearing, cats were moving around; Jayfeather could hear Brambleclaw's voice as the deputy organized the patrols. Paws scampered closer to his den, and Cherrypaw's voice rose above the background murmur.

"Sol—come and watch us training, please!"

"Yeah," Molepaw added. "I've learned this really cool battle move I want to show you."

Jayfeather raised his head out of his nest and tasted the air. He could pick up the apprentice's scent, along with Sol's, just outside the bramble screen. Rosepetal and Cloudtail, who was still mentoring Cherrypaw, stood a couple of tail-lengths farther away.

"That's really not a good idea," Rosepetal meowed. "Sol has better things to do than watch a couple of apprentices."

"And we want you to concentrate on your training session," Cloudtail added, his voice cool with dislike of Sol. "Not showing off for a visitor."

"It's kind of you to ask me," Sol mewed to the two young cats. "But I have other duties right now. I'll want to hear a full report of what you've learned when I get back."

Jayfeather heard a suppressed hiss from Cloudtail, and sensed a wave of annoyance rolling off him. He could understand what the white warrior felt. *Sol is talking as if he's our Clan leader!*

"Jayfeather?"

Focused on what was happening outside the den, Jayfeather hadn't noticed Briarlight dragging herself up to him.

"Jayfeather, can I go and speak to Sol?" she asked.

The eagerness in her tone irritated Jayfeather. "He's not going to mend your back, if that's what you're thinking," he snapped.

"I wasn't hoping for that," Briarlight huffed. "I'm curious about him, that's all."

"Well, don't be," Jayfeather retorted. "He's nothing special."

"He saved the apprentices from the fox," Briarlight reminded him.

Jayfeather snorted. "Maybe."

I can't believe Lionblaze and I got it so wrong, he thought. *Sol was the last cat we were expecting to turn up.*

The apprentices and their mentors moved away. Sol loitered for a few more moments outside the den, then he, too, retreated in the direction of the entrance. Jayfeather hauled himself out of his nest and began to groom the scraps of moss and bracken from his fur.

"Jayfeather!" Daisy's voice came from the other side of the bramble screen. "Can you come and have a look at Sorreltail?"

Leaving his grooming unfinished, Jayfeather brushed past the screen and out into the camp. Daisy was waiting for him a tail-length away.

"Is something wrong?" he asked.

"I'm not sure," Daisy admitted, falling in beside him as he

padded toward the warriors' den. "You're the medicine cat. But I've seen a lot of cats near to giving birth, and I'm not sure I like the look of Sorreltail."

Jayfeather replied with a grunt. As he slid between the outer branches of the warriors' den, his nose twitched at the musty scent of dried moss and fern. Most of the cats were already out on patrol; he located Sorreltail lying in a nest near the edge of the den, and picked his way through the bedding to her side.

"Hi, Jayfeather," the tortoiseshell warrior meowed. "You didn't need to come. I'm fine."

"I'm not so sure about that," Jayfeather muttered.

Sorreltail's voice sounded tired, and as Jayfeather sniffed at her he picked up her feelings of anxiety and exhaustion. "You're trying to do too much," he told her. "You're less than half a moon from giving birth, and keeping up with your warrior duties is wearing you out."

"But last time—" Sorreltail began.

"Like it or not, you're older than the last time you had kits," Jayfeather pointed out. "You need to slow down to give yourself a chance to stay in good health. Birth is a very difficult time."

Sorreltail sighed. "I know."

As both cats fell silent, Jayfeather felt her flank shudder beneath his forepaw, and he was plunged into a terrible whirlpool of memory. He felt Sorreltail's agony as she gave birth; he shared her horror as the badger forced its way into the nursery.

He saw Cinderpelt leap bravely to protect Sorreltail and heard her shriek cut off abruptly as the huge creature clamped its jaws on her neck and shook her. In the same heartbeat he heard the thin wail of a tiny gray kit, born as the medicine cat gave up her life.

Jayfeather shivered. *That was when Cinderpelt became Cinderheart. And now Yellowfang says that I need to bring her back, for the sake of the Clan.*

He started, jerked out of the memory, as he realized that Sorreltail was speaking again, her voice low and weary.

"I know you're right," she mewed. "These kits need to have the best possible start. And if that means sitting around for this last half-moon . . . well, so be it!"

"Thank you, Sorreltail," Jayfeather replied. "You've made the right decision." *And made my job a lot easier,* he added to himself.

"Come on, then, Sorreltail," Daisy mewed, bustling forward and nudging the tortoiseshell warrior to her paws. "Ferncloud and I have made you a really comfortable nest in the nursery."

Jayfeather's anxieties faded as he edged his way out of the warriors' den. *It's obvious Sorreltail is going to be thoroughly mothered before these kits arrive!*

Back in the clearing, Jayfeather listened for Cinderheart's paw steps, wondering whether this was the right time to speak to her. *What in the name of StarClan am I going to say?*

His ears twitched as he heard paw steps padding toward

him, but the scent that he picked up was Birchfall's. "Are you busy right now?" he asked.

"No," the tabby tom replied. "Do you want something?"

"Yes—Cinderheart," Jayfeather replied. "If you see her, would you tell her I want a word with her?"

"Sure." Birchfall padded off.

Jayfeather headed for the warriors' den, but when he paused to taste the air there was no trace of Cinderheart among the mingled scents. He stood lashing his tail with frustration. *She must be out on patrol.*

Then a voice spoke close to his ear. "Are you looking for Cinderheart?"

Jayfeather stiffened as Leafpool's scent washed over him. *How does she know that?*

"Yes," he replied warily. "Have you seen her?"

"Yes, but I need to speak to you first."

Jayfeather hesitated, unwilling to discuss Cinderheart—or anything else—with his mother. But he could sense Leafpool's determination, and knew he wouldn't be able to put her off. "Okay," he sighed. "Go ahead."

"Not here," Leafpool meowed. "Let's go into the forest. I don't think that what I have to say should be overheard."

Suppressing a sigh, Jayfeather followed her out of the forest and into the camp. As he padded beside her, he felt the usual sense of disbelief that Leafpool was his mother. Sometimes she felt more like a stranger to him than a cat from another Clan.

Leafpool halted beneath a broad tree with noisy, rustling leaves; Jayfeather could hear the trickle of water close by. "So?" he demanded.

"I had a dream last night," Leafpool murmured; Jayfeather had to lean close to hear her. "Spottedleaf came to me, and told me that Yellowfang wants to tell Cinderheart about . . . about who she was before. Is that right?"

"Yes," Jayfeather replied.

"Well, she can't!" Leafpool burst out; Jayfeather winced at the lightning bolt of her emotions. "Cinderheart has been given the chance to live a different life, as a warrior and as a mother. If you tell her about her previous life, you will rob her of that chance."

Jayfeather could hear Leafpool tearing at the grass with her claws. He tried to interrupt her, but she ignored him.

"I was Cinderpelt's apprentice," Leafpool went on. "I knew her well. I knew she had longed to be a warrior, a mate, and a mother, but all that was taken away from her when she had the accident on the Thunderpath. In spite of that, she was a good medicine cat, one of the best that ThunderClan will ever have. I won't let her life be taken away from her again!"

"But the Clan has to come first," Jayfeather argued. "More medicine cats are needed."

Leafpool was silent for a moment. Both of them knew that she was a fully trained medicine cat quite capable of caring for her Clan, if only she hadn't broken the medicine cat code, as well as the warrior code, by taking a cat from another Clan as her mate. But neither she nor Jayfeather mentioned that. The silence stretched out until it tingled between them as if a storm were about to break.

"Individual cats are important, too," Leafpool went on at last. "You could take an apprentice. Briarlight is already doing a great job."

"Oh, sure!" Jayfeather lashed his tail. "Wouldn't that just be great? One medicine cat who can't see, and another who can't walk. ThunderClan would be invincible!"

"I know you see much more than the rest of us," Leafpool stated calmly. "You can't use that as an excuse. But I'm telling you, Cinderheart deserves a different life this time. That's why StarClan gave her a second chance. Spottedleaf said so, in my dream. I won't let you spoil everything for her again."

Without giving Jayfeather a chance to respond, she rose and walked away.

Jayfeather stayed beneath the tree, thoughts swirling in his head. He had to admit that Leafpool had a point: If StarClan had interfered enough to let Cinderheart have another life, he knew there must be a very good reason for it. *And Yellowfang isn't thinking straight at the moment,* he reminded himself. *She's too closely caught up in the rivalries inside StarClan, and her fear of the Dark Forest.*

Jayfeather returned slowly to the camp, still unsure about what he should do. Before he had even reached his den, he picked up Cinderheart's scent and heard her paw steps approaching.

"Birchfall said you were looking for me," she meowed. Her

voice was cheerful. "Do you need me to do something?"

As clearly as if he could see, Jayfeather was aware of Leafpool's gaze fixed on him. He took a deep breath. "Nothing important," he told Cinderheart. "It can wait until another day."

CHAPTER 10

Ivypool slid cautiously through the Dark Forest. It seemed positively crowded now, as busy as a disturbed anthill, with clusters of cats training in every clearing, racing along every path, and splashing through the sludgy river. Anxious not to be called into a training session, Ivypool clung to the shadows, her senses alert for traces of one particular cat. Hearing voices, she dived into the middle of a clump of ferns, then poked her head out warily to spot Tigerheart and Mapleshade a few tail-lengths ahead.

Ivypool felt her heart begin to pound faster. She had been terrified of Mapleshade ever since the old she-cat had almost drowned her in the river in a so-called training exercise. Now Mapleshade looked paler than ever; Ivypool's eyes widened as she realized that she could see the tree trunks behind the she-cat's misty shape.

But Mapleshade's eyes still burned as she leaned close to Tigerheart. "The Dark Forest will rise up and stamp out the Clans," she told him, her voice a spitty, rasping hiss. "StarClan will bow down to us, and the warriors who chose not to join us will be punished beyond the end of their lives."

Horrified, Ivypool shrank back among the ferns. Tiger-heart was listening intently, nodding as the old she-cat went on.

"Every cat who ever lived will know—" Suddenly Maple-shade broke off, sniffing the air. "I smell fear," she growled. Ivypool's heart almost stopped as the pale she-cat's bale-ful gaze swept past the ferns where she crouched, shivering. "Who has come here with insufficient courage to face their Clanmates?"

Mapleshade swung her massive, scarred head around, still sniffing. Then she hauled herself to her paws and stalked in the opposite direction from Ivypool, pushing through dead, slimy brambles. Ivypool stayed very still, trying not to let her breath stir the fern fronds around her.

"Snowtuft!" Mapleshade snarled. "I might have known! You mangy pile of dung, get back into the fight and show some mettle." Ivypool winced at the sound of a heavy blow and a high-pitched shriek of pain.

Several heartbeats passed, and at last Ivypool realized that Mapleshade wasn't coming back. Swallowing her fear, she emerged from the ferns and padded up to Tigerheart. The ShadowClan warrior sat grooming himself, passing one paw over his ears; he glanced up casually as she approached. "Sneaking around, Ivypool?" he mewed.

"Just looking for you," Ivypool replied carefully. Tigerheart had seemed to lap up what Mapleshade was telling him; if he really agreed with her about destroying all the Clans, he was a dangerous enemy. "What's this about Dawnpelt?" she asked.

"Dovewing said you tried to warn her at the Gathering."

Tigerheart's gaze raked over her contemptuously. "Are you worried I said something about what happened with Flametail? You shouldn't be. I haven't told Dovewing anything—not for your sake, but because I don't want her to know what you did."

"I didn't do anything!" Ivypool hissed, her neck fur beginning to rise.

"Only because I stopped you," Tigerheart growled.

Ivypool's claws worked in the cold, dark grass. "It was a test! What could I do?"

"*Nothing* could justify you destroying my brother's spirit," Tigerheart retorted.

Ivypool knew that he was right. *But there's no way I can tell him. I have to hide the fact that I'm spying for ThunderClan.* "So what's all this about Dawnpelt?" she prompted.

Tigerheart hesitated. "Dawnpelt blames Jayfeather for Flametail's death in the lake," he meowed at last.

"That's ridiculous!" Ivypool exclaimed.

Tigerheart shook his head, his hostility swallowed up in sadness. "You don't know what it's like to lose a littermate," he told Ivypool. "You want to blame anyone, anything. Not just a crack in the ice."

Ivypool felt a claw-scratch of sympathy. *I couldn't bear it if I lost Dovewing.* Then she reminded herself that Tigerheart had been listening to Mapleshade's tirade. She couldn't trust him. *He doesn't deserve pity!*

"I don't know what Dawnpelt thinks she can do against

ThunderClan," she went on aloud. "Or maybe you're thinking of bringing her here?"

"That's not up to me," Tigerheart replied.

"I'm sure you could put in a good word for her," Ivypool suggested mockingly.

Tigerheart didn't react. Before Ivypool could say anything else, the ferns parted again and Hawkfrost emerged into the open.

"There you are, Ivypool!" he hissed. "Come with me. You're keeping the other apprentices waiting." He turned and padded off without waiting for a reply. Ivypool winced at being called an apprentice. *But why should I care?* she asked herself, shocked. *Do I wish I were a Dark Forest warrior?*

Padding after the dark tabby tom, Ivypool wondered if the Dark Forest had anything to do with Sol turning up. *There's something about Sol that I don't trust. Especially with all the stories the elders tell about the time the sun vanished! Maybe the Dark Forest is plotting to hide the sun again.*

Gathering her courage, Ivypool sped up until she was walking beside Hawkfrost. "Do you know Sol?" she asked, trying to sound casual.

Hawkfrost twitched an ear. "Who?"

"Sol," Ivypool repeated. "The cat who arrived in ThunderClan five sunrises ago. He was here before, when the sun vanished."

"Ah," Hawkfrost mewed. "That was after my time in RiverClan, but I know what happened. What about him?"

"I just wondered if he had . . . er . . . ever been here."

Hawkfrost paused, narrowing his ice-blue eyes as he gazed at her. "So, you want to know if Sol is a true Clanmate?"

"Yes," Ivypool mewed, trying not to flinch under that freezing gaze. "Something like that."

The dark tabby tom hesitated before he replied, as if he were wondering how much to give away. "Sol is a welcome presence in ThunderClan," he meowed.

That means Sol is very bad news, Ivypool realized. Too scared to ask any more questions, she followed Hawkfrost until he halted at the edge of a stretch of marsh. Four other cats were waiting there, belly-deep in mud and bristly grass. All of them turned as one, watching as Ivypool and Hawkfrost approached.

"Right," Hawkfrost announced. "Fighting in difficult terrain . . ."

The sky was flushed with rose-pink the next morning as the dawn patrol set out. Drops of dew glittered on every stem of grass and sparkling cobwebs spread across the bramble thickets. Ivypool's paws dragged as she forced herself through the forest. She was exhausted from the night's training, and she was convinced that her fur still smelled of the stinking mud of the marsh.

"Stop sniffing," Toadstep muttered. "It's so annoying! Do you think you have greencough?"

"No, I just need to wash my fur," Ivypool responded.

"Your fur is fine." Millie, who was leading the patrol,

glanced over her shoulder. "Concentrate on what we're doing, please."

Hazeltail, who had been scouting a few tail-lengths ahead, suddenly froze. A moment later she came creeping back through the long grass. "I heard a cat walking close to the border," she murmured.

Millie gave her a brisk nod. "Ivypool, head that way," she directed, flicking her tail at a narrow path around a clump of elder bushes. "I'll go this way."

Ivypool obeyed, setting down her paws with all the stealth she had learned in the Dark Forest as she skirted the elder clump, then ducking low to avoid brambles that trailed across the path. Soon she picked up the cat's scent and the sound of its paw steps. It was heading confidently toward the border, seeming not to care whether any cat spotted it or not. Ivypool recognized the scent at once.

Sol!

She crept forward until she could see him brushing through the undergrowth. He halted as Millie appeared from his other side.

"Is everything okay?" the gray tabby she-cat called.

For a heartbeat Sol seemed startled, then he recovered his poise. "Am I being followed?" he meowed. "Look, I'm not stealing any prey. You fed me too well last night for that."

"Then where are you going?" Millie prompted.

Sol arched his back and relaxed. "I thought I'd visit ShadowClan," he explained. "Catch up for old times' sake."

"You won't be welcome there," Millie warned him.

"I had friends there." Sol's eyes flashed at her. "And it was a long time ago. I come in peace!"

Ivypool bristled with distrust, but there was no way she or Millie could stop him from going. Looking after him as he strode away, she muttered, "Maybe you can eat *their* fresh-kill, then."

Toadstep and Hazeltail arrived in time to hear what she said.

"That's a bit unfair," Toadstep protested.

"Yes," Hazeltail agreed. "Don't forget that Sol saved the apprentices from the fox. He must have changed."

Millie gave a disdainful sniff. "Tabbies don't change their stripes," she growled.

Ivypool stared at Sol's vanishing hindquarters and wondered just how much he knew about the Dark Forest. *Has he been sent here to stir up trouble?*

When the patrol returned to camp, Ivypool spotted Firestar and Brambleclaw beside the fresh-kill pile. Millie padded straight across the clearing to join them, the rest of the patrol following her.

"We met Sol while we were out," she reported. "He said that he was going to pay a visit to ShadowClan."

"What?" Brambleclaw sprang to his paws, his neck fur bristling and an angry look in his amber eyes. "The treacherous mange-pelt! What is he going to tell them about Thunder-Clan?"

Firestar calmly finished his mouthful of vole and twitched his ears at his deputy. "Take it easy, Brambleclaw. We've got no proof that he's going to betray us. Anyway, what can he tell them that we would want to keep secret?"

"I still don't like it," Brambleclaw muttered. "Every time I set eyes on Sol my paws itch and I want to claw his pelt off."

Firestar blinked in surprise. "I don't want to encourage Sol to stay here in ThunderClan," he meowed, "but if we persecute him without reason, he could go to the other Clans and cause trouble."

"I'm not afraid of Sol or the other Clans," Brambleclaw growled.

"Neither am I," Firestar told him. "But if we have a chance to keep our enemies close, let's not turn that down."

Some of the other cats had drifted up to listen. Dovewing came up to Ivypool and gave her a prod with one paw. "What was all that about?" she asked.

Ivypool told her sister what Sol had said when they met him near the border.

"That cat is bad news," Dovewing hissed. "Ivypool, do you know if he's connected to the Dark Forest?"

Ivypool twitched her tail. "I'm not sure. I've never seen him there, but when I asked Hawkfrost about him, he said he was pleased that Sol was here in ThunderClan."

Dovewing's neck fur began to fluff up, and her eyes reflected Ivypool's own uneasiness. "That proves it's bad to have him here," she mewed.

Ivypool nodded. "But we can't do anything about it as long

as Firestar lets him stay. We'll just have to keep an eye on him. I'll tell you one thing, though," she added. "Even if we find out he's chased every fox in the woods out of our territory, I wouldn't trust Sol a single mouse-length."

CHAPTER 11

The sun was beginning to descend as Lionblaze led Graystripe, Spider-leg, and Blossomfall into the forest.

"I want to check the WindClan border," Lionblaze meowed. "And we'll keep a lookout for any more signs of fox, too."

Golden sunlight was pouring through the branches, and the trees rustled gently in a fresh breeze. The fresh scents of grass and leaves surrounded the patrol. But all Lionblaze could see were the shadows under the trees, and his mind was filled with imagining the day when they might spread and engulf everything.

He took his patrol to the border stream where it flowed into the lake, then turned to follow it away from the shore, renewing the scent markers on the way. Everything was quiet; although the WindClan scent markers on the opposite bank were fresh, there was no sign of any WindClan patrols. They had covered about half the length of the border when the WindClan scent suddenly grew stronger, carried on the breeze that blew down from the moorland. Lionblaze raised his tail for the patrol to halt.

"Now what?" Spiderleg muttered.

As the black warrior spoke, a WindClan patrol appeared from behind a rocky outcrop and bounded up to the edge of the stream. Onestar was at the front; Crowfeather and Sedge-whisker were with him.

Lionblaze dipped his head. "Greetings, Onestar."

The WindClan leader didn't return the greeting. Instead, he stared across the stream at the ThunderClan cats with hostility in his eyes. "I was hoping to meet some of your Clan," he rasped.

"Oh?" Lionblaze could feel anger stirring inside him at the challenge in Onestar's voice, but he forced his fur to stay flat. "What can we do for you?"

"One of my warriors overheard a patrol of yours talking," Onestar replied. "It seems you have that StarClan-cursed excuse for a cat, Sol, staying with you. Is that right?"

Lionblaze nodded. "Yes."

"Then you have to drive him out at once!"

Lionblaze heard an annoyed hiss from Spiderleg, standing at his shoulder, but he still refused to let his anger show. "Why?" he meowed. "Has Sol done you any harm?"

"That's not the point!" Onestar spat. "Every cat knows Sol is bad news. Firestar has to get rid of him now!"

The tip of Lionblaze's tail began to twitch. "Firestar won't be ordered around by the leader of another Clan," he warned.

"Then maybe WindClan will have to force him." Onestar drew his lips back in the beginning of a snarl. "Every cat knows that Sol is an enemy to all the Clans."

Lionblaze's indignation spilled over and he bounded to the very edge of the stream, his tail lashing and his fur fluffed up. "If you want a fight, you can have one now!"

"Right!" Spiderleg leaped up to stand beside his Clanmate and slid out his claws.

Instantly Onestar and Crowfeather stepped up to the bank on the WindClan side of the stream. A growl began deep in Onestar's throat, but before any cat could make another move, Graystripe shouldered Lionblaze back. Lionblaze glared at him. Surely he was as furious as Lionblaze at the way Onestar was trying to give orders to ThunderClan?

"That's enough, Lionblaze." Graystripe's voice was firm and calm, and Lionblaze recalled that once he had been Clan deputy. "There's no need to fight over this. Onestar, you need to remember that it's not up to you to decide who receives ThunderClan's hospitality. You're insulting Firestar if you think he would offer shelter to a cat who didn't deserve it."

Though Lionblaze didn't try to interrupt, he could tell that Graystripe's words were sticking in his throat. He knew that Graystripe didn't like Sol any more than Lionblaze did. *We'd both like to see him gone. But that's not the point. It's not up to another Clan to tell us what to do.*

Onestar was unimpressed by what Graystripe had said. "Send Sol away," he growled. "Or I'll make you."

Graystripe shook his head, and there was sadness in his eyes now. "Onestar," he began, "do you remember when you were Firestar's friend, back in the old forest? How can we have come so far from that time? We don't need to be enemies."

Onestar lashed his tail. "Your Clan makes it impossible to be anything else."

Lionblaze watched the younger warriors welcome Sol when he strolled back into the camp as the sun went down.

"The hunting patrols are just back," Blossomfall meowed. "Come and choose some fresh-kill."

"Will you tell us more stories?" Cherrypaw added, bouncing along at Sol's side as he strolled across to the fresh-kill pile.

"Yes, did you ever see that dog again?" Molepaw asked eagerly.

Toadstep and Rosepetal gathered to listen, and Briarlight dragged herself over from the medicine cat's den. Foxleap and Icecloud, who were sharing a blackbird, looked up as Sol approached; Whitewing, Birchfall, and Hazeltail appeared from the warriors' den and sat nearby.

Lionblaze noticed that Dovewing remained within earshot, but a few tail-lengths off, with Ivypool and Bumblestripe. None of them looked enthusiastic about Sol's return, and they made no move to join him and the others.

Good. Not all the young warriors want to be friends with him.

While Sol gulped down a plump vole, Blossomfall told him about the clash with WindClan earlier that day. "Lionblaze and Graystripe told Onestar that he can't tell ThunderClan what to do," she meowed. "But Onestar said that if we don't send you away, then he'll make us!"

Sol swallowed the last bite of vole and swiped his tongue appreciatively around his jaws. "You can't possibly be afraid of WindClan," he taunted. "Those scrawny rabbit-chasers? They're no match for our warriors!"

"We're not *your* warriors! You're not a ThunderClan cat!" Ivypool blurted out.

Several cats gasped, and Whitewing turned and glared at her.

"Ivypool! That's no way to talk to a visitor."

"Well, he's not," Ivypool muttered.

Dovewing pressed her muzzle sympathetically against her sister's side and Bumblestripe let his tail-tip rest for a heartbeat on her shoulder. The young warrior exchanged a glance with Dovewing over Ivypool's head, and she gave a tiny nod in reply.

Dovewing and Bumblestripe seem to be getting very close, Lionblaze thought, and added to himself grimly, *I wonder what will happen when Bumblestripe finds out about the prophecy?*

Meanwhile, the young cats around Sol raced to reassure him that they weren't afraid of WindClan at all.

"We'll show them," Foxleap yowled. "They can't order us around like that!"

"Yes, we'll rip their pelts off if they try," Blossomfall growled.

Lionblaze listened to them with a growing sense of unease. The last thing any cat should want was a battle with another Clan. But Firestar couldn't ignore Onestar's challenge. Now he would be forced to offer hospitality to Sol purely in order to preserve the honor of ThunderClan. Anything else would look like Firestar was obeying orders from WindClan.

We can't back down now, Lionblaze realized. *Onestar has forced us to ally ourselves with Sol, even though he isn't welcome here.*

CHAPTER 12

Dovewing found herself walking through shadowy trees, and for a heartbeat she was terrified that somehow she had found her way into the Dark Forest. But moonlight was filtering down through the branches, and when she looked up she could see the stars.

All was quiet except that in the distance Dovewing could hear the wails of a cat in distress. She began to search among the ferns and brambles, but she couldn't figure out where the wails were coming from. They grew louder and more urgent, but the cat still remained hidden.

Panicking, Dovewing started to run. Her flying paws tripped over a dead branch; letting out a startled screech, she rolled over on the ground and woke in her own nest, her legs flailing in the struggle to get up. Ivypool was sleeping beside her, while Cherrypaw and Molepaw were curled up together at the opposite side of the den.

"Whew!" Dovewing muttered. "That was some dream!"

Then she realized that she could still hear the wails of distress. They were fainter than in her dream, but loud enough to reach her through the walls of the camp.

"That's Sorreltail!" she exclaimed. "And she's somewhere outside the camp."

Struggling to her paws, Dovewing scrambled out of the den and raced across the camp to find Jayfeather.

"Wake up!" she panted, brushing past the bramble screen at the entrance to the medicine cat's den. "Jayfeather, it's Sorreltail!"

"Wha'?" Jayfeather raised his head, his blue eyes blurred with sleep. "What's the matter?"

"It's Sorreltail," Dovewing repeated. "I can hear her wailing. She must be having her kits, and she's way outside the camp!"

Jayfeather was instantly alert, springing to his paws and shaking bits of moss and bracken from his pelt. "Her kits are coming early!" he exclaimed. "Show me where."

Briarlight was waking, too, dragging herself out of her nest. "Can I help?" she meowed.

"No, it'll be too far for you," Jayfeather replied. "But be ready to give herbs to Dovewing. I'll send her back to fetch them when I know what I need."

As he finished speaking he whisked out of the den with Dovewing hard on his paws. Cloudtail was on watch at the entrance to the tunnel through the barrier.

"What's going on?" he asked, rising to his paws.

"Sorreltail's out in the forest, and her kits are coming," Jayfeather panted, hardly breaking stride as he plunged into the thorns.

As Dovewing followed, she thought Cloudtail looked

confused, and realized that no other cats could hear Sorrel-tail's heartrending cries. Cloudtail must be wondering how they knew. "Fetch Brackenfur," she called over her shoulder. "Tell him to follow our scent trail."

Cloudtail waved his tail in acknowledgment as Dovewing headed out of the camp. Jayfeather was waiting for her at the other end of the tunnel, his claws digging impatiently into the ground.

"Lead the way," he ordered.

Sorreltail's pitiful wails were even louder now, flooding Dovewing's senses. She could hardly believe that Jayfeather couldn't hear them.

"She's near the lake," Dovewing meowed, pointing with her tail before remembering that Jayfeather couldn't see her. "Follow me."

She bounded through the undergrowth, skirting bramble thickets and clumps of nettles. At first she kept looking back, uncertain whether the medicine cat would be able to keep up with her, but every time she turned her head he was hard on her paws.

"Sorreltail, we're coming!" he yowled as they drew closer to the lake; Dovewing guessed that by now he must be able to hear the tortoiseshell she-cat for himself.

At last they broke out of the undergrowth into a clearing not far from where Dovewing had walked with Bumblestripe. Sorreltail lay stretched out on her side underneath an arching clump of ferns. She raised her head as Dovewing and Jay-feather raced across to her. "Oh, thank StarClan!" she gasped.

"I was afraid no cat would hear me."

Jayfeather crouched down beside her, studying her intently. "Lie still," he murmured. "These kits will be born soon."

"It hurts so much!" Sorreltail moaned. "It was never this bad with my first litter."

Still concentrating, Jayfeather ran one paw down Sorreltail's belly and felt her hips. "There's the problem," he told her. "It's the stiffness I warned you about."

"But I did my exercises—oh!" Sorreltail's words ended in a gasp of pain as a powerful ripple passed down her belly.

"Should she have poppy seed?" Dovewing suggested.

"No!" Jayfeather snapped. "She's already tired, and she needs all her energy to give birth. Go and fetch me some chervil root," he added after a moment's thought. "That should help things along."

Dovewing turned and dashed back through the forest. *I have no idea what chervil root looks like,* she thought. *I hope Briarlight knows.* She hadn't traveled many fox-lengths before she met Brackenfur and Ferncloud hurrying to meet her.

"Is Sorreltail okay?" Brackenfur demanded.

"She will be," Dovewing responded, pausing briefly. "Jayfeather's with her."

Brackenfur nodded and raced on with Ferncloud at his side. Feeling reassured that Sorreltail's mate and the most experienced queen in the Clan were heading to help, Dovewing bounded on toward the stone hollow. As she panted up to the thorn barrier, Brambleclaw emerged, closely followed by Dustpelt and Thornclaw. Dovewing halted until they had all cleared the thorn tunnel.

"This way?" Brambleclaw checked, angling his ears in the direction from which Dovewing had come.

Dovewing nodded.

"We're going to guard Sorreltail," the Clan deputy explained. "A cat crying out, and the scent of blood, could attract foxes."

He led his patrol away, the three cats slipping easily through the trees, their jaws parted as they followed the scent trail.

Dovewing brushed through the thorns to find Cloudtail still on watch; with a nod to the white warrior she bounded across the camp and into the medicine cat's den.

Briarlight was at the back of the den, her head inside the storage cleft. She pushed herself back and looked over her shoulder as Dovewing came in. "How's—" she began.

"Jayfeather sent me for chervil root," Dovewing interrupted. "Do you know what it looks like?"

"There." Briarlight pointed with one forepaw, and Dovewing realized that she had set out several different herbs in a neat line across the floor of the den. "Right at the end. You'd better take some fennel, too," she added, pointing to an herb with thin, spiky leaves. "It should help the pain in Sorreltail's hips."

"Thanks." Dovewing grabbed up the knobby brown root and the herb in her jaws and raced out again.

When she returned to the clearing, she found Sorreltail still lying underneath the ferns. Brackenfur was close beside her, bending over her and licking her ears. Brambleclaw,

Thornclaw, and Dustpelt had spread out around the clearing, facing into the forest, their jaws parted and their ears pricked for the first sign of danger.

As Dovewing crossed the clearing, Ferncloud appeared from the direction of the lake with a bundle of dripping moss in her jaws. She set it down beside Sorreltail so that the tortoiseshell queen could drink.

"Thanks, Ferncloud," Sorreltail murmured as she lapped at it; Dovewing could tell how exhausted she was. "That's so good."

Jayfeather was sitting beside her, listening closely, unmoving except for the tip of his tail, which twitched back and forth. He glanced up as Dovewing dropped the chervil root and fennel beside him. "I thought you'd gone to the mountains for that," he commented.

"Briarlight sent the fennel," Dovewing explained, her chest heaving as she gasped in air.

Jayfeather gave a satisfied nod. "Good thinking." He fixed Dovewing with a blank stare. "Well, chew up the chervil root for her. You don't think she's going to do it herself, do you?"

How do I know? Dovewing thought resentfully, setting her teeth into the hard root. *I'm not a medicine cat.*

"Break the fennel stalks," Jayfeather added brusquely to Ferncloud. "Squeeze the juice into her mouth."

Ferncloud looked slightly surprised at the medicine cat's tone, but she did as he told her and let the fennel juice trickle between Sorreltail's jaws.

When Dovewing had chewed up the chervil root, Brackenfur urged Sorreltail to eat the pulp, but the tortoiseshell she-cat was in so much pain that she could hardly get it down between her gasps of distress.

"Oh, it hurts so much!" she wailed. "Leafpool! Leafpool!"

Dovewing felt her pelt tingle. Did Sorreltail know she was calling for the wrong medicine cat? Then she noticed that Leafpool had appeared at the edge of the little group. She was blinking uncertainly, looking as if she didn't know if she was allowed to do anything more than watch.

"I'm here," Leafpool murmured. She settled down beside Sorreltail, but keeping out of Jayfeather's way. "Don't be afraid, Sorreltail. Jayfeather knows what to do."

"Is there something wrong?" Brackenfur hissed to Jayfeather. "Shouldn't the kits be here by now?"

"Kits take their own time," Jayfeather responded, though Dovewing thought that there was worry in his eyes. It was clear that Sorreltail was growing weaker with every spasm.

"Stupid furball," Brackenfur purred to his mate. "What were you thinking of, leaving the camp like that?"

"I needed air," Sorreltail replied, her words coming in short puffs. "I wasn't expecting the kits to come yet, and I thought it would be cooler by the lake . . ."

"Never frighten me like that again," Brackenfur meowed. "Stay where you're told next time!"

Sorreltail flinched as another spasm racked her body. "There won't be a next time!" she spat through gritted teeth.

Spotting a stick in the middle of the clump of ferns, Dovewing pulled it out and took it to Sorreltail. "Bite down on this," she suggested. "It should help when the pain comes."

"Thanks, Dovewing," Sorreltail meowed, gripping the stick in her jaws.

Dovewing saw Jayfeather giving her a nod of approval. *At last I've done something right!*

Then Sorreltail gave a massive heave. Her jaws clamped down on the stick until it began to splinter. In a rush, a small wet bundle slipped out from under her tail and lay motionless on the grass.

"Well done!" Ferncloud cried. "There's your first kit, Sorreltail. It's a little she-cat."

"She's wonderful!" Brackenfur purred, nudging the tiny kit toward her mother.

Sorreltail turned her head to look and licked feebly at the small body, only to break off a moment later as her belly convulsed again and the second kit—another tiny she-cat—was born.

Dovewing couldn't share Brackenfur and Ferncloud's delight. Both the kits were very small, and looked weak; they were hardly moving, and Sorreltail was too exhausted to give them the vigorous licking they needed.

Jayfeather was examining Sorreltail, carefully patting her belly with one forepaw. "You're done," he announced. "Let's get you and the kits back to camp."

Brackenfur nudged Sorreltail to her paws and let her lean

on his shoulder. Brambleclaw came to support her on her other side.

"What about my kits?" she whimpered, her eyes wide with distress.

"They'll be fine," Ferncloud promised. "Dovewing and I will bring them."

She picked up one kit, and Dovewing took the other. As she lifted the tiny cat from the ground, the kit let out a feeble squeak, then hung as limp as a piece of fresh-kill. The weight was less than a sparrow in Dovewing's mouth.

Thornclaw took the lead, still keeping watch for foxes, while Sorreltail staggered along between the two toms. Leafpool hovered at her side, and Jayfeather brought up the rear with Dustpelt.

The sky was growing pale with dawn by the time they reached the camp. The Clan was beginning to stir: Brightheart was near the entrance to the tunnel, talking to Cloudtail, and she followed Sorreltail and the others across to the nursery.

"Everything's ready for you," she told Sorreltail.

As Brackenfur and Brambleclaw supported the queen into the nursery, Daisy got up from a nest of thick moss and bracken. "Here," she mewed to Sorreltail, touching noses with her. "I've made the nest warm for you. Lie down and rest."

"Thanks, Daisy." Sorreltail's voice was an exhausted murmur.

Once Sorreltail was settled, Dovewing and Ferncloud set the two kits down in the curve of her belly. Ferncloud and

Daisy began to lick them with strong, rhythmic tongue-strokes, until they started to wriggle and let out tiny squeals of hunger. They huddled close to their mother and began to suck.

Dovewing let out a faint sigh of relief. *Maybe they'll be okay.* "I'm worn out after all that!" she told Jayfeather. "You should get some rest, too."

Jayfeather shook his head. "I need to stay here and keep an eye on Sorreltail and the kits."

"No, you don't." Brightheart padded up to his side. "I'll stay. I know enough to tell if I should wake you."

Jayfeather hesitated for a moment, then dipped his head. "Okay. Thanks, Brightheart."

Dovewing followed Jayfeather out of the nursery and headed back to her own den. Ivypool was still curled up asleep beside Molepaw and Cherrypaw. Suddenly feeling as if her legs wouldn't support her anymore, Dovewing flopped into her nest and closed her eyes.

At first she thought that she was stumbling through a tangled forest, where ivy and bramble tendrils reached out to trip her paws. All around her she could hear the shrieks of cats and kits in agony, but she couldn't find them or do anything to help them. Then she broke out of the trees and found herself on a bare hillside. Two tiny kits were squirming on a flat rock in front of her. But as Dovewing started to head toward them a shadow fell across the rock. An eagle swooped out of the sky and caught up the kits, one in each talon. They squirmed helplessly as they were carried into the sky.

"No!" Dovewing screeched. She leaped into the air, her claws stretching for the murderous bird. But it was far out of reach; she crashed to the ground again in a tumble of feathers. Her eyes flew open and she saw that she was in her own nest, with Ivypool bending anxiously over her.

"Are you okay?" her sister mewed. "You were thrashing around. You must have had a really bad dream."

Raising her head, Dovewing saw that the moss and bracken from her nest was shredded and scattered all over the floor. She was still shaking from the horror of her dream, and her heart was beating fast.

"I'm okay," she whispered. "Thanks, Ivypool." She needed to get outside and clear her head.

Clambering out of her den, she ran lightly across the camp. By now the sun was above the trees at the top of the hollow and Brambleclaw stood in the middle of the clearing, organizing the patrols. Dovewing dodged around them and stuck her head inside the nursery. In the dim light she could see that Sorreltail was asleep, her kits enclosed in the warm curve of her belly. Their fur was dry and fluffy now, and they were feeding eagerly.

Brightheart was still on watch, while Ferncloud and Daisy were drowsily sharing tongues. Daisy looked up as Dovewing looked in through the entrance.

"They're all fine," she purred. "And it's thanks to you, for realizing that Sorreltail was in trouble. You must have really sharp hearing!"

"Er . . . yeah." Dovewing backed away, not wanting to discuss how she had managed to hear Sorreltail from so far away.

"You're a hero!" Bumblestripe spoke behind Dovewing, making her jump. "You saved Sorreltail's life, and the kits!" he added as she whipped around to face him.

"Any cat would have done the same," Dovewing replied, embarrassed.

"I wouldn't." Bumblestripe's eyes glimmered with amusement. "I'd sleep through falling off a cliff!" The amusement faded from his eyes, to be replaced by a glow of admiration. "I'm really proud of you," he murmured. "I'm glad you're my Clanmate."

Feeling warm beneath her pelt, Dovewing took a step forward and touched her nose to his. "I'm glad you're my Clanmate, too."

"I'm convinced Sol is up to something," Dovewing muttered into Ivypool's ear.

The littermates were heading toward the abandoned Twoleg nest, bringing up the rear of a hunting patrol led by Millie. Spiderleg and Birchfall were just ahead of them; Ivypool slackened her pace until the rest of the patrol was out of earshot.

"What makes you think that?" she prompted.

Dovewing stopped walking for a moment and concentrated hard. "I can hear him talking, somewhere on the far side of the hollow," she replied.

"You're sure?"

"Positive."

"Hey, are you on this hunting patrol or not?" Millie's voice floated back to them. The rest of the patrol had disappeared into the undergrowth.

"Coming!" Ivypool called back. "You go and check out what he's up to," she added to Dovewing in a whisper. "I'll cover for you."

"Thanks." With a swift nod to her sister, Dovewing turned and slid noiselessly into the ferns. She headed for the opposite side of the camp, close to the place on the cliff where a determined cat could climb out. As she drew closer to the sound of Sol's voice, she flattened herself to the ground, setting her paws down as carefully as if she were stalking a mouse.

The noise grew clearer as she approached, and Dovewing realized that several cats were there, talking to Sol. A strong ThunderClan scent was coming from the other side of a bramble thicket. Cautiously Dovewing raised her head so that she could peer through the stalks of long grass.

Sol was still out of sight, screened by the brambles, but Dovewing's eyes stretched wide with dismay as she recognized Blossomfall, Hazeltail, Mousewhisker, and Rosepetal. Were she and Ivypool the only cats in the Clan who didn't want to hang on Sol's words?

"You're right, Sol," Rosepetal was meowing as Dovewing crept up. "We can't just sit here and wait for WindClan to attack us."

Dovewing bit back a shocked yowl. Her claws slid out and dug into the ground. *Why are they discussing an attack from Wind-Clan?*

"Quite true." Sol's voice was a deep-throated purr. "They might get the idea that ThunderClan cats are scared."

"ThunderClan cats aren't scared of anything!" Mouse-whisker leaped to his paws, his neck fur fluffing out. "We have to strike first!"

"That's an excellent idea, Mousewhisker."

But it wasn't Mousewhisker's idea at all. Dovewing's forepaws kneaded the ground in her fury. *It was yours! You're putting words into his mouth.*

"We'll prove we're not afraid of a battle," Hazeltail agreed, her tail lashing. "We'll rip their treacherous fur off!"

"Don't you think we should discuss this with Firestar first?" Rosepetal suggested.

"Would he agree?" Sol asked.

"No, of course he wouldn't," Mousewhisker retorted. "He's the Clan leader. He can't show that he's hostile to another Clan without good reason."

"We *have* good reason," Blossomfall meowed. "We know that WindClan is plotting an attack. Firestar might not be able to order his Clan into battle, but that doesn't mean he'll be angry with us when we've sorted out those rabbit-chasers once and for all!"

"Yes!" Mousewhisker's eyes shone. "Let's do it!"

All Dovewing's instincts were pushing her to leap into the open and tell them all how mouse-brained they were being. But she knew that it wasn't her Clanmates who were making this disastrous decision. *It's Sol's fault.*

As quietly as she could, she slid backward until she was well away from the bramble thicket. Then she spun around and sped off, sending out her senses to locate Ivypool. She found her sister beside the old Thunderpath with a vole in her jaws. There was no sign of Millie or the rest of the patrol.

"Come quick!" Dovewing hissed when she reached Ivypool. "Sol is planning an attack on WindClan!"

CHAPTER 13

♣

Ivypool stared at her littermate in astonishment. She dropped her vole and hastily scraped earth over it. "He can't do that!" she exclaimed.

"He can," Dovewing replied grimly. "Enough of our cats will follow him. Come with me—and hurry!"

Together the warriors raced back to the top of the stone hollow. But while they were still scrambling up the path, they met Hazeltail, closely followed by Mousewhisker, Rosepetal, and Blossomfall.

"What are you doing?" Dovewing gasped.

"What does it look like?" Hazeltail's voice was curt. "We're a hunting patrol, mouse-brain."

"Yeah, thanks for scaring all the prey away," Mousewhisker added. "Trampling through the bushes like a herd of badgers!"

Ivypool exchanged a frustrated glance with her sister. "Have you seen Sol?" she asked.

"No." It was Blossomfall who replied. "Did you want him?"

Dovewing twitched her whiskers at Ivypool, a tiny gesture warning her to hide the fact they'd been eavesdropping. She could see her own anger glittering in her sister's eyes. *They're supposed to be our Clanmates—and they're lying to us!* "No, we just hadn't seen him for a while," she responded. "We wondered if he was still around."

Mousewhisker shrugged. "I haven't heard that he's left."

Dovewing and Ivypool had to step back and let their Clanmates go on their way. Ivypool was tempted to tell them that if they wanted to pretend to be a hunting patrol, they should at least catch something before they returned to camp. Once they were out of sight, Dovewing waved her tail at Ivypool for silence, then stood alert; Ivypool guessed she must be sending out her senses.

After a few heartbeats, Dovewing shook her head. "I can't pick up any signs of Sol," she mewed. "That's really weird. He *was* there with the others."

"Should we go and search?" Ivypool suggested.

"No, we can't do any more now," Dovewing replied. "We have to get back to the hunt."

Ivypool nodded, though every hair on her pelt was prickling with anxiety. "What if they're going to attack right now?"

"They won't do that," Dovewing reassured her. "Four cats aren't enough to launch an attack on WindClan. They'll have to convince a few more of our Clanmates to join them."

"I can't believe ThunderClan cats would do this," Ivypool meowed. "Dovewing, are you sure about what you heard? I mean, your hearing hasn't been great since—"

"My hearing is fine now," Dovewing snapped. "And I know what I heard. Except . . ." Her voice trailed off.

"Well?"

"I didn't hear Sol say very much," Dovewing confessed. "I thought he was putting ideas into our Clanmates' heads, but maybe . . . maybe it was just the usual sort of warrior boasting."

"Maybe." Ivypool ducked under a low hazel branch. "But we can't be sure of that."

"There's no scent of Sol around here," Dovewing went on, "so he didn't come this way. I wish I knew where he was now." She shook her head. "Let's get back to our patrol."

"Are we going to tell Firestar?" Ivypool asked, her paws tingling with apprehension.

Dovewing thought for a heartbeat, then shook her head. "I don't want to get our Clanmates into trouble when I can't be sure exactly what was going on. And it's all Sol's fault, anyway. You can bet that I'll keep a close watch on him from now on," she added more forcefully as she bounded away.

Ivypool followed, her belly still churning. Even if Dovewing doubted what she had overheard, Ivypool was convinced that her sister's first instincts had been right.

Something's going on, and Sol is at the bottom of it.

Ivypool woke with a start. Dovewing was curled up close beside her, while at the opposite side of the den Molepaw was snoring softly and Cherrypaw's tail was twitching as if she were deep inside a dream.

I wish the warriors' den weren't so crowded, Ivypool thought. *We're warriors; we shouldn't be stuck in here with the apprentices!*

But there was no time to worry about that now. Somehow in her sleep an idea had come to her, and she knew she had to check it out right away. She gave Dovewing a gentle prod.

"Wake up," she breathed into her sister's ear. "And keep quiet. We don't want to wake the apprentices."

Dovewing sat straight up, instantly alert. "Is something happening in the Dark Forest?"

Ivypool shook her head, relieved that her dreams hadn't taken her there that night. "No, this is about Sol," she replied in a whisper. "I think I know where he vanished to today."

The visiting cat hadn't returned to the camp before dark, and no cat had seemed to know where he was. Ivypool had heard Dustpelt muttering, "Good riddance. I never trusted him anyway."

Cloudtail had agreed with a lash of his tail. "That cat is trouble wherever he goes."

Now Ivypool leaned even closer to murmur into Dovewing's ear. "Come with me. We have to go right away, or it might be too late."

Side by side, the two she-cats slipped out of their den. Clouds drifted across the moon; its light was faint and uneven. Here and there a warrior of StarClan glittered frostily. Graystripe was on watch; they waited until his head was turned the other way, then raced across the camp and plunged into the dirtplace tunnel. Heartbeats later they were once more climbing the path that led to the top of the hollow.

"Take me to the place where you heard Sol," Ivypool meowed.

She followed Dovewing until they reached a bramble thicket near the edge of the cliff. Jaws parted to pick up Sol's scent, Ivypool began to search, poking among the bramble tendrils, crouching low so that she could see underneath them.

"I don't think Sol would hide under there," Dovewing objected. "He likes to be comfortable."

"I'm not looking for a cozy hiding place," Ivypool replied. She knew exactly what she *was* looking for. *It has to be here somewhere.*

At last she spotted what she was searching for; her paws tingled with a mixture of fear and excitement as she clawed aside a pawful of bramble tendrils to reveal a dark hole leading deep into the ground.

"Sol went down there?" Dovewing asked, sounding incredulous.

"It's a tunnel," Ivypool explained. "The hillside is full of them. Remember when Icecloud fell into one, when we were doing our assessment? Well . . ." She went on more hesitantly as Dovewing flicked her ears. "Blossomfall and I . . . er . . . went down there, too. We walked underground for ages."

"You never told me!" Dovewing exclaimed indignantly.

Ivypool shrugged, unwilling to get into an argument. "If Sol knows about these tunnels," she pointed out, "then he could have gone down one and be anywhere by now."

Dovewing crept closer and took a deep sniff. "Sol's scent is here," she meowed. "It's faint, but it's definitely his." She paused for a heartbeat, then added, "What do we do now?"

"Follow him," Ivypool declared. She was half-scared by her own suggestion, but she didn't see any other option. They couldn't accuse a cat who was considered a hero by half her Clanmates of plotting with WindClan—not unless they had real evidence.

Dovewing's eyes stretched wide, but she didn't argue, just gave her sister a brief nod. "Lead on," she mewed.

Ivypool squeezed into the tunnel. It was so narrow that her fur brushed the walls on either side, and their bodies blocked the dim light from outside. Her heart began to pound as she walked into the dark, but she made herself keep going.

"This shouldn't be as bad as last time I was underground," she whispered after a few moments, trying to reassure herself as much as Dovewing. "With your special senses, you should be able to work out where we're going, just as easily as if we could see."

"I'm not sure." Dovewing's voice quivered. "It's all so strange down here . . . so confusing . . . Give me a moment to get used to it."

To Ivypool's relief, she felt her sister's fear begin to ebb as they padded forward. She lost count of how much time had passed before she sensed that the passage was growing wider. She couldn't feel the walls any longer, and the steep downward slope leveled out. There was hard stone beneath her paws, not close-packed earth, and the small sounds of their movement echoed eerily around them.

"Let's stop a moment," Dovewing mewed. "I think I can reach out now."

Ivypool halted. All she could hear was the sound of their breathing, and the occasional drip of water, but she knew that the whole of this strange underground world would be open to Dovewing.

"Voices!" Dovewing whispered after a long, tense silence. "I can hear voices."

"Where?" Ivypool asked.

"Let me go in front."

There was enough space in the tunnel now for Dovewing to slip past her sister, and lead the way farther into the depths. Ivypool couldn't see or hear anything; all she could do was follow her sister's scent and the sound of her paw steps. The tunnel twisted in front of them, sometimes plunging deeper, sometimes leading upward again. Sometimes it felt as though they were turning back to follow their own trail. But Dovewing walked without hesitating, taking side tunnels that were hidden to Ivypool, skirting pools and patches of broken rock.

Ivypool was acutely aware of the weight of earth and rock above their heads, and the cats who were sleeping above, not knowing that two Clan warriors were so far beneath them. With a shudder, she pushed these thoughts away.

Focus. Concentrate on what we have to do.

"You're doing really well," she told Dovewing encouragingly. "We'll soon find out what's going on."

At last Ivypool thought she could hear the murmur of voices some way ahead of them. At first she thought she was imagining things. But as she followed in Dovewing's paw steps, the sounds grew clearer. She felt every hair on her pelt rise as she began to make out some of the words.

"WindClan!" she whispered. "And Sol!"

"Shhh." Dovewing's voice was no more than a breath. "If you can hear them, they can hear us." She led the way forward more cautiously, until the voices grew clearer still.

"I will lead you through the tunnels," Sol was meowing. "I can bring you out above the ThunderClan camp. Those mouse-brains won't know what's happening."

"Traitor!" Ivypool hissed, taking a pace forward.

Dovewing blocked her, and slapped her tail over her sister's mouth. "Shut up and listen!"

"How do we know we can trust you?" Ivypool recognized Owlwhisker's voice. "How do we know that you haven't told ThunderClan to attack *us*?"

WindClan cats aren't completely mouse-brained, Ivypool reflected.

"Of course I have." Sol's tone was scornful. "How else would I get them to trust me? But it's WindClan that I'll be leading into ThunderClan territory."

Another WindClan cat spoke, the words too soft for Ivypool to make out. She leaned forward, and felt a pebble slip underneath her paw. The clinking sound it made seemed as loud as a crack of thunder.

Ivypool froze, but the damage was done.

"What was that?" Owlwhisker growled. "Who's there? Is some cat eavesdropping on us?"

"Get us out of here!" Ivypool whispered into Dovewing's ear.

But Dovewing didn't move. "I followed the voices to get here," she confessed. "I'm not sure of the way out."

Ivypool heard movement from Sol and the WindClan cats.

"They're coming to look for us! We have to go." But even as she spoke she was terrified at the thought of wandering blindly through the dark tunnels. *Will we ever find our way out?*

Before either of the she-cats could move, they heard paws padding toward them from the tunnel behind. Cat scent washed over Ivypool; she thought she ought to recognize it, but she was too scared to think clearly. She slid out her claws, her heart thumping in panic at the thought of being trapped between two enemies.

Then the newcomer spoke. "Come with me. Quick!"

"No way!" Ivypool hissed, bunching her muscles to spring. "You could be with them."

"I'm not," the strange cat mewed.

"Prove it," Dovewing challenged her.

"I shouldn't have to," the newcomer replied irritably. "For StarClan's sake, let's go."

Ivypool's eyes widened in shock and she exchanged a glance with her sister, picking up the gleam of Dovewing's eyes. "StarClan? Then you . . ."

"Do you want to get out of here or not?" the newcomer interrupted.

"Yes, we do," Ivypool snapped back. "But how do we know you won't lead us farther in?"

The strange cat let out a hiss of annoyance. "Because I'm a ThunderClan cat like you," she replied, a darker shadow in the darkness of the tunnel. "My name is Hollyleaf."

Ivypool felt her mouth drop open. "Hollyleaf? But you . . . you're dead!"

"Obviously not," the newcomer replied, with an edge to her voice. "And we don't have time to stand here discussing ancient history. We have to leave now."

The paw steps of the WindClan cats were drawing closer, speeding up as they sensed their quarry was near. Ivypool could picture them bounding along the tunnel toward them, jaws parted to take in their ThunderClan scent.

"Okay," Dovewing mewed. "Show us the way."

Hollyleaf spun around and whisked down a narrow side tunnel. Ivypool and Dovewing followed her, just as the first of the WindClan cats raced past. Ivypool heard their flying paw steps halt suddenly, followed by a murmur of confused voices.

"Where did they go?"

"They were here, I know they were."

"Fox dung! We've lost them!"

Hollyleaf ignored the WindClan cats, heading deeper into the tunnels. Ivypool pressed close up behind her, terrified of losing her. She knew that she and Dovewing would never find their way out alone. After a while Hollyleaf paused; in the pitch-blackness of the tunnels Ivypool almost barged into her.

"You can trust me, you know," Hollyleaf meowed. "I led you out once before, remember?"

"Oh!" Ivypool gulped, realizing why Hollyleaf's scent had seemed familiar. "That was you?"

Hollyleaf padded on without saying more. Soon Ivypool realized that a pale light was filtering into the tunnel; Hollyleaf's head and ears were outlined against it. A moment later they emerged into a shallow dip of tumbled rocks and fern on the hillside; Ivypool drew in the fresh night air, loaded with the scents of ThunderClan. She turned to their rescuer, a slender, long-legged black she-cat with piercing green eyes. "Thank you!"

"We'd never have made it without you," Dovewing added, following them out of the tunnel and giving her pelt a shake.

Hollyleaf gave her a curt nod. "Listen," she meowed. "I've heard Sol plotting with the WindClan cats for the last half-moon, and—"

"What?" Ivypool interrupted. "That's even before he came to ThunderClan."

"They're going to attack through the tunnels," Hollyleaf continued, as if Ivypool hadn't spoken.

"Then we have to warn the others," Dovewing mewed, her eyes wide with dismay. "Come on, Ivypool!"

"Wait." Hollyleaf raised her tail as Dovewing spun around to head for the camp. "It's not going to happen yet. Sol wants to win more support from your Clanmates first. The WindClan cats know that he's winning ThunderClan's friendship so he can betray you." A soft growl rumbled in her throat. "You should never have let him come back!"

"It wasn't up to us," Ivypool pointed out. "And he did save the apprentices from a fox."

"Sol didn't save them," Hollyleaf hissed scornfully. "That was me."

Shock kept Ivypool silent for a moment. Before she could recover, she saw Dovewing's ears flick up, and a heartbeat later she heard voices coming from the direction of the camp.

"Dovewing! Ivypool!"

"Mouse dung!" she muttered. "They're looking for us."

Panic flared in Hollyleaf's green eyes. "Don't tell any cat you saw me," she begged.

"Why not?" Dovewing asked. "Why can't you come home? You belong here!"

"You don't understand," Hollyleaf whispered, beginning to back away toward the tunnel opening. "I have to go!"

But before she could plunge back into the darkness, a shaft of moonlight broke through the clouds, fixing all three cats in a pool of silver light. At the same moment Lionblaze appeared on a rock at the edge of the dip, and stood looking down at them.

"No!" His voice rang out in the night air. "Hollyleaf, I won't let you run away again."

CHAPTER 14

❧

Movement outside his den woke Jayfeather, and he padded into the clearing to discover several of his Clanmates milling around outside their dens.

"What's going on?" he asked, hurrying up to Graystripe, who was standing beside Firestar near the thorn tunnel.

"Cherrypaw woke up," the gray warrior replied. "She realized that Ivypool and Dovewing weren't in their nests. She told Firestar, and we've been searching the camp."

"There's no sign of either of them," Sandstorm reported worriedly, bounding over to join them.

"Then we have to send out search parties," the Thunder-Clan leader decided. "I don't trust WindClan since Onestar threatened us. Dovewing and Ivypool could have been captured."

"If WindClan has laid a claw on our warriors, we'll rip their pelts off," Graystripe growled.

Since Jayfeather couldn't help with the search, he returned to his den, but he couldn't sleep. He wasn't as worried about Dovewing and Ivypool as the rest of the Clan, knowing what he did about them.

But it's odd that they'd vanish in the night without giving me any idea of what they're doing, he thought. He shivered as a new thought struck him. *They wouldn't put WindClan's threats to the test on their own, would they? They've already gotten in trouble for visiting their camp in the past.*

He could hear Briarlight moving around in her nest, and picked up a stifled gasp of pain. "Are you okay?" he asked sharply.

"Yes, I'm fine," Briarlight replied. "I'm just a little stiff."

Jayfeather heaved himself out of his nest and padded over to her. *Since I'm awake, I might as well do something useful,* he decided, settling down beside Briarlight and starting to massage her wasted muscles.

"Thanks, Jayfeather." Briarlight let out a long sigh. "That feels better." A moment later, she added, "Do you think Ivypool and Dovewing will be okay?"

"I'm sure they will," Jayfeather meowed, crushing down his own misgivings. "They've probably just gone out for a night hunt."

Soon Briarlight drifted back into sleep, soothed by Jayfeather's reassurance and the rhythmic rubbing from his paws. But Jayfeather was fully awake. He rose, arched his back in a long stretch, then made his way out into the clearing again.

Firestar was sitting in the center of the camp, while Daisy paced beside the thorn barrier. Jayfeather could sense her anxiety, as sharp as if two of her own kits were missing. Locating Mousefur outside her den, Jayfeather crossed the camp to her side. "You should be in your nest," he meowed. "I'm sure there's no need to worry about Ivypool and Dovewing."

"I'm fine where I am," Mousefur snapped back at him. "I can sit and look at the stars if I want."

"Of course you can," Jayfeather responded, making his voice more gentle. *I wonder if she's looking for Longtail.*

Padding off again, he drew closer to the nursery, and picked up a murmur from Sorreltail. "That's right, kits. Have a good feed. Grow big and strong."

The tortoiseshell she-cat still sounded tired, but not with the dragging exhaustion she had felt just after she gave birth. She was recovering well, Jayfeather thought with satisfaction, and her kits were growing stronger. She and Brackenfur had named them: Lilykit and Seedkit.

They'll all be fine. Jayfeather was warmed by the thought of more kits in the Clan. They meant hope and new life, a faith that the Clan would go on in spite of everything that the Dark Forest was planning. His ears pricked at the sound of a rustle from the thorns. He recognized the scents of Whitewing and Birchfall; their sense of defeat washed over him like a muddy wave.

"There's no sign of Dovewing and Ivypool by the lake," Whitewing reported to Firestar. Her voice was taut with worry for her kits.

Foxleap and Icecloud followed their Clanmates in a moment later. "There's no trace of them between here and WindClan," Foxleap announced.

"We thought we picked up a scent trail early on," Icecloud added. "But it faded out, and we couldn't find it again."

Jayfeather's anxiety was rising now, and he padded closer to Firestar. Other cats were emerging into the clearing from their dens: Cloudtail and Brightheart talking quietly to each other; Dustpelt sliding his claws in and out as he stalked around the clearing; Ferncloud popping her head outside the nursery to listen to the news, then disappearing back inside. Leafpool and Squirrelflight slid quietly out of the warriors' den and sat close together; Cinderheart joined them after a few heartbeats.

More movement from the barrier alerted Jayfeather. This time Brambleclaw and Sandstorm were reporting back, and he could sense their failure before either of them spoke.

"They're not between here and ShadowClan," Brambleclaw told Firestar.

"That just leaves Lionblaze and the abandoned Twoleg nest," Firestar meowed. His voice was heavy with concern. "If they don't find them—"

He broke off as more cats emerged from the tunnel. Lionblaze was in the lead.

"I found them," he announced.

Jayfeather tensed at the sound of his brother's voice. Lionblaze wasn't pleased or relieved; instead he sounded strained. *Something's wrong.*

"Are Dovewing and Ivypool okay?" he called out.

"We're fine," Dovewing replied, pushing through the thorns after Lionblaze.

Ivypool followed her, and Whitewing bounded across the clearing to meet them.

"Where have you been?" she demanded, her furious words broken up with purrs of joy as she pressed herself against her daughters. "We've been frantic!"

Jayfeather could sense the young she-cats' embarrassment.

"What's the big deal?" Ivypool muttered. "We only went for a walk."

Firestar rose to his paws and padded over to them. "You're safe, and that's the most important thing," he meowed. His voice grew stern as he went on. "Tomorrow we'll have a talk about letting your Clanmates know where you are at all times, especially when we're being threatened by our neighbors."

"Okay," Dovewing responded in a small voice.

"We're sorry," Ivypool mewed.

The she-cats were heading for their den when Lionblaze spoke again. "Wait." His voice was still strained. "That's not all I found."

Jayfeather heard another rustle from the entrance, followed by a gasp from his Clanmates. He strained to detect a scent. The newcomer was a cat that smelled more of earth and stones and ferns than the other warriors, but underneath there was a faint layer of ThunderClan scent.

Can it be . . . ?

"Hollyleaf!" Cinderheart gasped. There was a patter of paw steps as she rushed past Jayfeather. "You're alive!"

Jayfeather felt as if the ground were unsteady beneath his paws, and he staggered. *She's come back!* Even though he had suspected that his sister hadn't died in the tunnels ever since he and Lionblaze had found no trace of her body, it was still a shock to have her walk into the camp. He stood back as the other cats crowded around her, the quiet air buzzing with their comments and questions.

"It's really Hollyleaf!"

"Where have you been all this time?"

"How did you survive?"

It was a few moments before Hollyleaf could get a word in. When she spoke at last, her voice was muted and a little hoarse, as if she weren't used to speaking.

"I lived underground," she mewed, "and I hunted in the woods on the other side of the hills, outside the territory."

"But the tunnel collapsed!" Poppyfrost protested.

"Not on top of me," Hollyleaf meowed. "I found a way out."

Jayfeather thought that she sounded tired and troubled, as if the very last thing she wanted to be doing was standing in the center of the hollow answering questions from her old Clanmates.

"Well?" Lionblaze spoke close to Jayfeather's ear. "It looks like we were right."

"Was it Hollyleaf who chased off the fox?" Jayfeather asked.

"It seems so," his brother replied. "And she found Dovewing and Ivypool in the tunnels tonight, and brought them out."

So they didn't just go for a walk, Jayfeather thought. *Why am I not surprised?*

There would be time later to question the sisters about that. "Hollyleaf could have gone much farther if she didn't want to stay in the Clan. She must have known that we would find out she was there eventually," he commented.

Lionblaze let out a sigh. "Perhaps that was what she wanted. Perhaps she was tired of living alone."

"She took a risk." Jayfeather twitched his whiskers. "What if the truth had been discovered about Ashfur's death?"

"It must have been a risk worth taking." Lionblaze's voice was full of sympathy.

Jayfeather realized he wasn't as ready as his brother to welcome Hollyleaf back. The Clan seemed to be treating her as a returning hero, and he couldn't share that. All along he had suspected—hoped with every hair on his pelt—that his sister was alive. He had wanted her to come back because he missed her so much, but now that Hollyleaf was actually here, all he could think about was how complicated the future was going to be.

"She told all the Clans about Leafpool and Crowfeather," he reminded Lionblaze. "It's because of her that every cat knows we are half-Clan, and that Squirrelflight lied about being our mother."

"That wasn't Hollyleaf's fault," Lionblaze pointed out.

"But she didn't stay here to deal with it afterward, did she?" Jayfeather hissed. "And how will the other Clans react to her? She caused a lot of trouble, there's no getting around that. Cats have long memories." He paused and then added, "What do you think will happen now? Will she stay?"

"I don't know," Lionblaze mewed. "I guess we'll have to let her decide."

There was a stir among the knot of cats in the center of the clearing as Leafpool pushed her way through to Hollyleaf's side. "Oh, my precious daughter, you came home!" Her voice was quivering. "I'm so, so sorry for what happened. None of it was your fault, none of it."

Jayfeather could tell from the tension in the air that Hollyleaf was shrinking away from Leafpool. He wasn't surprised that she didn't want the joyous reunion that most of the Clan seemed to be expecting.

He felt another cat brush past him, heading for the warriors' den. *Brambleclaw. No wonder that he wants out of this happy gathering.* Squirrelflight had lied to him, too, letting him believe that the three cats were his. Was there any part of Brambleclaw that wanted to welcome Hollyleaf home as a daughter?

Squirrelflight wriggled through the cats until she reached Hollyleaf. "I'm glad that you're alive," she mewed, her voice steady. "And that you're looking so well."

"Thanks. I . . ." Hollyleaf didn't seem to know how to respond.

"That's enough for now," Firestar broke in. "It's time we all went back to our dens. Hollyleaf, Molepaw and Cherrypaw will make a nest for you."

"Thanks," Hollyleaf repeated. She sounded confused as she continued, "The hollow . . . something looks different."

"A tree fell into it!" Molepaw meowed excitedly. "Come with us, and we'll tell you all about it . . ."

As the cats dispersed, their paw steps and their astonished comments dying into silence, Firestar padded up to Jayfeather and Lionblaze. "You too," he ordered. "Rest now. You can spend as much time as you want with your sister tomorrow."

I'm not sure I can face that, Jayfeather thought. *I don't know what to say to her.*

Before he could leave for his den, Ivypool and Dovewing padded up, their uneasiness as plain as if they had yowled it from the Highledge.

"Firestar, we've got some urgent news," Dovewing began. "When we found Hollyleaf—or when she found us—we were listening to Sol plotting with some WindClan cats to attack ThunderClan!"

"I knew we couldn't trust Sol," Jayfeather hissed. "Where is he now?"

"Not here." Firestar sounded grave.

Jayfeather snorted. "What a surprise!"

"Firestar, should we attack WindClan?" Ivypool asked.

"That's not a good idea," Firestar responded; Jayfeather could feel his anxiety rising. "Onestar is already looking for any sign of hostility, so we'll have to wait for him to make the first move. But we'll be ready," he added. "I'll order extra patrols, and every cat must be ready for battle at a moment's notice."

Jayfeather heard Lionblaze working his claws into the earth of the camp floor. "It's not that simple," he meowed. "Wind-Clan will attack through the tunnels, like they did before. ThunderClan cats have no experience in fighting underground, and that means we'll have to wait until the attackers are right in the heart of our territory."

"We have the advantage in forests," Firestar reminded him. "Whatever the risk, we will have to bring the battle to us."

For the rest of the night Jayfeather slept uneasily, shifting about in his nest, the darkness broken by flashing images of places he didn't recognize: a rocky slope; a pool by the gnarled roots of an oak; a wide river glittering in starshine. The sound of a cat brushing past the bramble screen brought him back to full wakefulness. He recognized Hollyleaf's scent, carried on a damp dawn breeze.

"Hi." Briarlight greeted her confidently. "I'm Briarlight; I'm Jayfeather's assistant. I'll wake him for you."

Jayfeather heard the sound of Briarlight dragging herself out of her nest, followed by a surprised meow from Hollyleaf. "Oh, you can't . . ."

"Walk?" Briarlight finished for her. "Not really. But that doesn't mean I can't be useful."

"N-no, I guess not," Hollyleaf mewed.

Jayfeather rose to his paws and padded into the middle of the den. But when he stood facing his sister, his mouth went dry. He had no idea what to say to her.

"I'm back," Hollyleaf mewed after a long silence.

"Yes." Jayfeather had to force out the word.

"Can we go for a walk?" Hollyleaf suggested. "Lionblaze, too? There's . . . there's a lot I need to tell you."

Clouds covered the sky as Jayfeather, Lionblaze, and Holly-leaf headed out into the forest. The air carried the scent of rain and a chilly breeze blew into their faces. But Jayfeather felt ruffled by more than just the wind. None of the three spoke until they emerged from the trees onto the grassy slope that led down to the lake and sat in the shelter of an elder bush. Then Hollyleaf took a deep breath.

"Thank you," she mewed. "I guess you didn't tell Firestar what . . . what I did."

"There was no point," Lionblaze replied. "It was much easier for every cat to think it was a rogue who killed Ashfur."

Jayfeather couldn't entirely agree, but he said nothing, keeping his face turned toward the lapping of waves on the shore.

"Didn't any cat think it was odd?" Hollyleaf asked. "The timing, I mean?"

"I don't think any cat stopped to wonder about it," Jayfeather grunted. "There was a lot of other stuff going on, if you remember."

"Yes, of course." Hollyleaf's voice was meek. "What about now? Will you tell Firestar the truth?"

"Why would we?" Lionblaze burst out. Jayfeather could imagine his brother's golden neck fur bristling.

"Because I got away," Hollyleaf pointed out.

"But you didn't really," Lionblaze meowed. "You exiled yourself from the Clan; that's quite a punishment."

Something about his brother's words made Jayfeather's pain well up and spill over like rain overflowing the edges of a leaf. "No!" he hissed. "You let us think that you were dead! How could you do that?"

For a few heartbeats Hollyleaf was silent. "I had no choice," she murmured at last. "You were better off without me."

"That wasn't your decision to make," Jayfeather told her. "And you were wrong. You're our littermate. Nothing you could do will ever change that."

Hollyleaf sighed. "But I'm not one of the prophecy, am I? Does that mean I've ruined everything? That the prophecy won't come true?"

Jayfeather felt Lionblaze look sharply at him. He took a deep breath. "There is a third cat. You met her last night. She's Dovewing, Whitewing's daughter."

Hollyleaf let out a puff of breath. "Well . . . maybe it wasn't a coincidence that I met her in the tunnels last night. What . . . what can she do?"

"Her senses are very sharp," Lionblaze explained. "I mean, *really*. She knows what's going on in the other territories . . . and even farther away. A few seasons ago, when the lake dried up, she knew it was some animals called beavers who had built a dam way upstream."

Hollyleaf made a small noise that sounded as if she was impressed. But Jayfeather picked up feelings of grief and envy, too . . . not a bitter jealousy that would make her Dovewing's enemy, but a deep regret that she was excluded from something that her littermates shared.

If only Hollyleaf had been part of the prophecy, he thought. *She would have taken her place in it so seriously . . . maybe it would have stopped her from doing what she did.*

The words of the latest prophecy came back to Jayfeather's

mind. *Three will become four* . . . He wondered if Hollyleaf could be the fourth cat, even if she hadn't been part of the original prophecy. But sensing the trouble in his sister's mind, he decided not to say anything yet. *I'll discuss it with Lionblaze first.*

"Are you going to stay?" Lionblaze asked Hollyleaf.

"I think so," she replied. "For a while, at least. After all, you've got a problem with Sol. If . . . if I can help you, then I will."

"Isn't it great that Hollyleaf came back?" Briarlight purred as soon as Jayfeather pushed past the bramble screen into his den. "Why did she stay away for so long?"

"Maybe you should ask her," Jayfeather grunted. "Meanwhile, you can sort out those borage leaves and take some to Sorreltail to help her milk come."

"Okay." Briarlight didn't sound offended, just a bit mystified that Jayfeather didn't want to answer.

"And after that, do your exercises," Jayfeather went on. "I'll be away until tomorrow. I'm going to the Moonpool."

Until he spoke, Jayfeather hadn't been aware that he had made the decision. But when he left the camp, after a quick word with Brambleclaw to tell him where he was going, he felt a burden lifting from his shoulders. It was good to be alone with his thoughts. His fears about the Dark Forest had receded into the background. Sol was their biggest threat.

And Hollyleaf has come back. That could change everything.

The air was growing cooler as Jayfeather slid through the bushes that ringed the Moonpool and padded down the spiral

path. Though he couldn't see, he knew that darkness was falling. His paws slipped easily into the prints left by the ancient
cats, and grief welled in his heart.

Half Moon . . .

Jayfeather pushed away the thought of the cat he had
loved, the cat who had been dead for seasons upon seasons.
He crouched at the water's edge and touched his nose to the
surface of the pool.

After a little while the splashing of the waterfall faded and
Jayfeather slept. He opened his eyes on sunlight, and rose to
his paws to find himself in a clearing in StarClan territory.
The grass was long and lush, and the trees that surrounded
him were weighed down with damp green leaves. He let out a
sigh of relief when he realized that Yellowfang wasn't waiting
for him.

But there was no sign of the cat he wanted to see, either.
Choosing a direction at random, Jayfeather set out. His ears
were pricked and he glanced rapidly from side to side as he
headed into the trees, passing through glades and leaping
over small streams. The air was fresh and clear, loaded with
prey-scent, and a warm breeze ruffled Jayfeather's fur. But his
errand was too urgent for him to stop and hunt, or bask in the
sun.

From time to time as he searched, Jayfeather passed
other cats; some of them were old and faded, the trees visible
through their misty outlines, while others were young and
bright against the green ferns. They didn't notice Jayfeather,
or if they did, they didn't recognize him.

Then Jayfeather spotted the cat he was looking for. He stood a little way off through the trees: a muscular gray warrior, his tail twitching as he scented the air for prey.

Ashfur.

Jayfeather crept closer, using the shadows of the trees for cover, then jumped in surprise as Bluestar leaped down from a branch above his head and stood in front of him.

"I don't think that's a good idea," the former ThunderClan leader meowed.

"I just want to talk to him," Jayfeather retorted defensively.

"Why?" Bluestar asked.

"Hollyleaf is back," Jayfeather replied, craning his neck to see if Ashfur was still there. "I . . . I want to know if Ashfur thinks that's okay." When Bluestar didn't respond, he continued, "I mean, he's here, so StarClan must believe he was a good cat, and that means he shouldn't have died the way he did."

Bluestar still stood in front of him, blocking his path, her intense blue gaze fixed on him. "But you've kept Hollyleaf's secret, haven't you?" she prompted. "You could have told Firestar or any cat the truth before now."

"No, I couldn't have! She's my *sister*!" Jayfeather protested.

Bluestar rested her tail on his shoulders, drawing him away from the gray warrior. "You won't learn anything by talking to Ashfur," she mewed. "He knows who killed him, and why. Perhaps he did a lot to bring it on himself, perhaps not. It is not StarClan's place to judge him." As Jayfeather opened his jaws to argue, she added more sternly, "If he found his way here, then he must deserve to be here. That is what we all have to believe."

Jayfeather sighed and shook his head. "I don't understand . . ."

"There are some things that are beyond understanding," Bluestar told him, sounding more sympathetic. "How can we say that Hollyleaf deserved to be in StarClan and Ashfur didn't, or the other way around? Things are different here. Some cats even forget parts of their life that they don't want to remember."

"But . . . I don't know if Hollyleaf deserves to be back in ThunderClan," Jayfeather meowed.

"That's not your decision, either." Bluestar twitched the tip of her tail. "Hollyleaf has her own conscience to answer to. Ashfur paid a high price for what he did wrong—and so did she. Perhaps justice has been served."

CHAPTER 15

Lionblaze opened his eyes in his nest in the warriors' den. Gray dawn light was filtering through the branches; a breeze found its way through the gaps and probed his mossy bedding with cold claws. Lionblaze yawned and tried to blink away sleep, then sat up sharply as Cloudtail crashed into him.

"Hey!" he yelped.

"Watch where you're putting your tail," the white warrior snapped, pushing his way out into the open.

Lionblaze rose to his paws. *It's too crowded in here,* he thought. *We're all tripping over one another.*

Skirting carefully past Squirrelflight, who was just beginning to stir, Lionblaze headed into the clearing. Brambleclaw stood in the middle of the camp with warriors gathering around him as he sorted out the morning's patrols. Firestar stood a little to one side, looking on.

"Sandstorm, will you lead a patrol along the WindClan border?" Brambleclaw was meowing as Lionblaze padded up. "Take Thornclaw and Ivypool. Cloudtail, you and Brightheart can do the WindClan border as well, but start from the other end. Take Blossomfall with you. Make sure the scent markers are fresh and strong."

"And make sure there's no WindClan scent on our side of the stream," Firestar added. "Report back right away if you find any."

"Hunting patrols," Brambleclaw continued, glancing around at his Clanmates, "stay away from the WindClan border. We don't want to give WindClan any reason to complain about us."

"What?" Spiderleg's neck fur bristled. "Are you telling me we can't hunt on our own territory because of those flea-ridden rabbit-eaters?"

"Yeah," Thornclaw added, the tip of his tail twitching. "Why should we have to creep around like mice when we've done nothing wrong?"

Brambleclaw avoided the question, just continued dividing up the hunting patrols. Lionblaze guessed that Firestar had warned his deputy about Sol's plot with WindClan, though he had said nothing to the rest of the Clan.

"What's Firestar thinking?" Dovewing whispered, padding up to Lionblaze's side. Her blue eyes were puzzled. "Shouldn't he tell the Clan that there's a threat?"

Lionblaze shrugged. "I don't know," he admitted. "I guess there's no point starting a panic when we don't know what will happen, or when."

"I notice Sol hasn't come back to camp," Dovewing observed with a twitch of her whiskers.

Lionblaze snorted, feeling his neck fur begin to fluff up. "Are you surprised? He must know that he was seen last night, so he's staying away." Guilt weighed down his belly like a stone as he remembered how he had helped Sol escape from the camp all those moons ago. *After I helped him, Sol has betrayed us! And I can never tell any cat what I did.*

As the cats milled around, splitting up into their patrols, Lionblaze noticed that Millie was looking around with a confused air. "I don't see Sol," she mewed to Dustpelt. "Where do you think he can be?"

"I don't know and I don't care," Dustpelt growled. "Good riddance is what I say."

"And so do I," Thornclaw agreed. "But I'd like to know where the mange-pelt is, all the same."

"Sol hasn't done any harm," Berrynose argued.

A chorus of arguments broke out, and Brambleclaw had to raise his voice to a yowl to be heard above it. "That's enough! Can I have a bit of quiet around here?"

Lionblaze felt the tension in the deputy's voice, and watched his slowly lashing tail. *I don't blame him for getting frustrated,* he thought with a stab of sympathy.

"Millie," Brambleclaw went on more quietly as the querulous voices died down. "You're leading a hunting patrol with Toadstep, Mousewhisker, and Hollyleaf."

Lionblaze heard several gasps of shock as Brambleclaw announced the names, a protest rippling like a cold wind through the Clan. Toadstep muttered something to Foxleap.

"What was that, Toadstep?" Brambleclaw's voice was icy.

Toadstep hesitated for a moment, then raised his head defiantly. "I don't want to be on a patrol with Hollyleaf," he meowed. "I don't know her! Patrols are supposed to trust one another with their lives, but we have no idea what Hollyleaf has been doing since she vanished."

Lionblaze stared at the young warrior in dismay. *Did he really say that?* As more murmurings broke out around him he realized that Toadstep wasn't the only cat who was suspicious about Hollyleaf.

"She could have been *anywhere*," Icecloud whispered.

"Yeah, how do we know she wasn't with one of the other Clans?" Hazeltail responded.

"No offense, Hollyleaf." Mousewhisker stepped forward and confronted the black she-cat. "I know we were friends before, but you've hardly said anything about where you've been. And now you've come back just when Sol reappears—is there a connection?"

Hollyleaf looked startled.

"There's no need for this," Brambleclaw meowed, before any other cat could say anything. "The past is the past. You're making a fuss about nothing."

"Really, Brambleclaw? Nothing?" Birchfall padded up to the deputy, his amber eyes serious. "Why won't Hollyleaf tell us where she's been? And why did she leave in the first place?"

Lionblaze took a breath for an indignant protest, but left it unspoken. Perhaps these questions would have to be answered before Hollyleaf could stay in the Clan.

"Yes, why did you leave?" Thornclaw sounded much more belligerent than his Clanmates.

Brightheart let her tail rest lightly on the tabby warrior's shoulder. "No need to ruffle your fur, Thornclaw," she mewed. To Hollyleaf she added gently, "If you tell us, we'll understand, whatever it is. Did some cat do something to hurt you? We need to know."

Hollyleaf was still silent.

Thornclaw shook off Brightheart's tail. "You left not long after Ashfur was killed." He spoke slowly, as if he was thinking about every word. "Hollyleaf, did it have something to do with that?"

Lionblaze thought that his heart had stopped beating. A thick silence hung in the clearing, as though every cat had been turned to ice.

Then Poppyfrost called out, "No, of course it doesn't! If Hollyleaf had seen who had killed Ashfur, she would have told us back then."

Thornclaw blinked. "I'm not asking if she witnessed another cat killing him."

This time Lionblaze thought that the silence would last forever. Berrynose turned to Thornclaw. His whisper sounded throughout the clearing like the shriek of trapped prey. "You think *Hollyleaf* was the killer?"

Poppyfrost's eyes stretched wide. "She can't be!"

"I won't believe it," Cinderheart declared.

"Nor will I," Leafpool agreed. "Oh, Hollyleaf . . ." Her voice faded into silence.

Birchfall's gaze was fixed on Hollyleaf. "I don't want to believe it," he rasped. "But it makes sense."

More voices rose around Hollyleaf where she stood,

hunched and small, in the middle of the clearing. Lionblaze stared desperately at his Clanmates, wondering what in the name of StarClan he could say; he felt as if a piece of fresh-kill was lodged in his throat, choking him. He glanced at Firestar for help, but the Clan leader was standing in silence, his eyes slightly narrowed and his gaze fixed on Hollyleaf. There was nothing to tell Lionblaze what he was thinking.

"Hollyleaf, you have to speak for yourself," Graystripe called out.

"Yes, let's hear what happened," Thornclaw demanded, sliding out his claws with a menacing look at Hollyleaf.

Lionblaze stepped forward, putting himself between his sister and the tabby warrior. "Stop!" he snarled. "This is ridiculous. There's no way that Hollyleaf knows anything about Ashfur's death."

Hollyleaf took a pace toward Lionblaze until they were so close that their pelts brushed. Her green eyes were full of misery, and she was gaunt from the hardship of her life as a loner, but Lionblaze could read determination in every hair on her pelt.

"No, Lionblaze," she whispered. "I know you're only trying to help, but you must let me speak. I think it's time for the truth to come out."

Lionblaze heard a whimper from somewhere at the back of the crowd. Without turning to look, he knew that it had come from Squirrelflight. The rest of the Clan was silent, pressing around Hollyleaf in a circle, a barrier of eyes.

Hollyleaf raised her head and spoke clearly to her Clan.

"Thornclaw is right. I was there when Ashfur died. And his death was my fault."

Her confession was greeted with a horrified gasp from the cats. As if at a word of command, they shrank back, widening the circle. Lionblaze spotted Foxleap swiftly thrusting Cherrypaw behind him. Sorreltail, who had brought Lilykit and Seedkit into the clearing for the first time, gathered them close to her with a sweep of her tail.

Hollyleaf looked terrified, her glance darting around the clearing as if she expected some cat to leap on her and rip her throat out. Lionblaze suddenly wished that she had never come back, that she had gone away to the mountains if that would have kept her safe. *Dovewing and Ivypool would have found their own way out of the tunnels,* he thought, his belly shaking from the force of his fear and anger. *She didn't have to help them!*

"I was there . . ." Hollyleaf's faltering voice began again. "I saw Ashfur, beside the stream. He had threatened to kill me and my littermates. Most of you know how much Ashfur wanted Squirrelflight to be his mate. He hated us all because he thought we were Squirrelflight's kits with Brambleclaw. Even when he knew he was wrong, he still hated us. So . . ."

Lionblaze stared at his sister in horror, wanting to hold back the words he knew she was about to speak. *She can't confess to killing Ashfur! She mustn't!*

But while Hollyleaf was gathering herself to go on, Brambleclaw pushed his way to the front of the crowd and stood beside her.

"I was there, too, that day, beside the stream," he announced.

He glanced at Hollyleaf as she opened her jaws to protest, and added, "You didn't see me there, but I saw you, and Ashfur." He paused for a moment, letting his glance rake across the Clan. "When Ashfur saw Hollyleaf alone by the stream," he continued, "he sprang at her. He was determined to hurt one of the three cats Squirrelflight loved most, to punish her for not loving him. Hollyleaf fought bravely, but before I could help her, Ashfur slipped on the edge of the stream and fell in. He was still alive when he hit the water. There was nothing Hollyleaf could do to save him. She was only defending herself."

The clearing exploded as the tabby warrior finished speaking.

"Why didn't you tell us that at the time?" Thornclaw demanded.

"Yes, we spent moons suspecting one another," Berrynose growled. "Firestar, they should both be punished for not telling the truth back then."

"No!" Leafpool protested, her amber eyes full of pain.

Lionblaze stepped forward and glared at Berrynose. "You might want to know that it was Hollyleaf who saved your kits, not Sol," he snarled. "Think about that before you start meowing about punishment."

Berrynose stared at him in disbelief. "It was Hollyleaf?"

"Then we *have* to let her back into the Clan!" Poppyfrost mewed. "She risked her life for my kits!"

"Besides, Ashfur only got what he deserved," Dustpelt declared. "He tried to kill four cats—his own Clanmates! If you ask me, Hollyleaf did us a favor."

Firestar padded into the middle of the crowd, raising his tail for silence. His fur was bristling and his tail twitched. "What happened was a tragic accident," the Clan leader began as soon as he could make himself heard. "I agree that Hollyleaf should have spoken up at the time." His green gaze rested sternly on Hollyleaf. "She should have trusted us to believe her, and deal with her fairly. But she has been punished enough by living away from her Clan for so many moons." Firestar transferred his gaze to his Clan. "She will not be punished again, and nor will Brambleclaw for not speaking out before. Their silence has been a burden for both of them, and that has eased now." With a drawn-out sigh he added, "What's done is done. Let Ashfur be judged by our ancestors."

Lionblaze puffed out a breath of relief, but he could see that not all the cats were satisfied. And Hollyleaf still looked as if she wished the ground would open up and swallow her.

Firestar beckoned her with his tail. "You should have told the truth back then," he meowed quietly; Lionblaze strained to overhear. "It's going to be hard for you now, do you understand that?"

Hollyleaf nodded, her eyes bleak. "I shouldn't have tried to come back—"

"Never say that," Firestar interrupted. "You are back, and I wouldn't have it any other way. The Clan will settle down now that the truth is out." He paused, but Hollyleaf had nothing to add. "I won't include you on any patrols today," Firestar went on more briskly. "Go to the elders' den and see what you can do for them."

"They'll know, won't they?" Hollyleaf asked, glancing around at the rapidly dispersing Clan.

Firestar nodded. "News travels fast around here, you know it does. But you are strong enough to deal with this. Put it behind you, Hollyleaf. Your Clan still needs you."

Hollyleaf bowed her head. "Thank you," she whispered.

As Lionblaze watched his sister padding away toward the elders' den, he was aware of Cinderheart coming up beside him. "Poor Hollyleaf!" she murmured, her eyes wide with shock and excitement. "Who would have expected that?"

She doesn't know I knew, Lionblaze thought.

"I feel so sorry for her," Cinderheart went on. "She must have felt so terrible, all the time she was away. And I never realized Ashfur felt that way about Squirrelflight."

"It happened before we were born," Lionblaze replied shortly. He didn't want to talk about any of it, and to his relief Cinderheart seemed to understand that.

"Brambleclaw wants you to lead a hunting patrol," she meowed. "Foxleap and Rosepetal are coming, with their apprentices."

"Good," Lionblaze grunted. It would feel good to work off some of his tension with his claws in prey. Turning toward the thorn tunnel, he saw that the rest of the patrol was already waiting. Cherrypaw and Molepaw were bouncing up and down in front of their mentors.

"How did it happen?" Molepaw was asking, his eyes wide with excitement. "What did you do when you found out that Ashfur was dead?"

"Hollyleaf's a killer!" Cherrypaw breathed out.

Rosepetal stood over her with her lips drawn back in a snarl. "If I ever hear either of you say that again, you'll see nothing but Mousefur's hindquarters and ticks for a moon! Firestar said that the past is to be left behind. I don't want any gossiping from you, I don't want any more bouncing about, and I definitely don't want to hear any more accusations. Have I made myself clear?"

Subdued, the two apprentices nodded. "Sorry, Rosepetal," Cherrypaw muttered.

Lionblaze was grateful for Rosepetal's loyalty, but he could see how shocked the she-cat had been by Hollyleaf's confession.

"They'll calm down soon, you'll see," Cinderheart whispered into his ear.

Lionblaze nodded, though he wasn't sure that Cinderheart was right. *Will my Clanmates ever get used to Hollyleaf being back in the hollow?*

CHAPTER 16

❧

Dovewing stood motionless in the clearing while around her the cats split up into their patrols. Her mind was whirling.

No wonder Hollyleaf wasn't part of the prophecy, she thought. *She killed a cat!*

Ivypool came over, her fur fluffed up with excitement and her blue eyes showing the same confusion that Dovewing felt. "I can't believe this!" she murmured.

"Ivypool," Dovewing mewed hesitantly, "have you ever seen Ashfur in the Dark Forest?" Her belly clenched as she waited for her sister's reply; she knew how defensive Ivypool could be if any cat questioned her about her visits to the Place of No Stars.

But Ivypool merely looked thoughtful. "I wouldn't know him if I saw him," she admitted. "But I don't think I have. At least, no cat has ever pointed him out to me."

"He was horrible to Squirrelflight before he died," Dovewing reflected. "But maybe he got to go to StarClan because he died so terribly."

Before she got the last words out she was aware of

Brambleclaw looming over her, his amber eyes gleaming with annoyance.

"Stop gossiping," he ordered. "Ivypool, I thought I told you to join Sandstorm's border patrol. Dovewing, you're in a training session with me, but Firestar wants to see you first. You'll find him in his den."

Ivypool scuttled off, and Dovewing turned toward the Highledge. Climbing the tumbled rocks, she wondered briefly why Firestar wanted her. The answer wasn't difficult to guess. *WindClan!*

Dovewing reached the Highledge and approached the entrance to the den. "Firestar?" she called, looking in.

Firestar was sitting in the shadows at the back of his den, on his nest of moss and bracken. His green eyes gleamed in the dim light. He beckoned Dovewing with his tail. "Come in."

When Dovewing was sitting beside him, Firestar went on. "I asked you to come because of your special senses," he began. "I expect you can guess why."

Dovewing dipped her head. "You want me to tell you what's going on in WindClan."

"That's right," Firestar meowed with a nod. "If you can."

Pride surged through Dovewing as she sent out her senses and settled down to listen, tucking her forepaws under her chest. *This isn't sneaking around,* she thought. *I'm truly using my powers to protect my Clan.* She let her senses range across the border stream and over the moor until they were focused on the WindClan camp. Onestar was standing in the middle of the shallow scoop in the ground, with some of his senior warriors clustered around him.

"I can see their camp. Onestar is there with Crowfeather and Sedgewhisker," she reported to Firestar. "Ashfoot just joined them. And there are a couple of cats I don't know."

"Is Onestar speaking?" Firestar asked. "Can you hear anything?"

Dovewing nodded, concentrating hard as the WindClan leader's words faded in, as if he were approaching from a long distance.

". . . trouble with ThunderClan," Onestar meowed. "Border patrols need to keep a special lookout. If you pick up their scent on our side of the stream, I want to know about it."

"You will, don't worry," Crowfeather growled, digging his claws into the earth.

Dovewing repeated what she could hear to Firestar, who twitched one ear in surprise.

"That's almost word for word what I said to Thunder-Clan," he murmured. "Has Onestar mentioned Sol at all?"

Dovewing kept listening, but the WindClan leader had gone on to give Ashfoot instructions about hunting patrols.

"Not a word," she replied to Firestar.

"Then either he doesn't know what Sol is planning," Firestar mewed, "or he's being very careful about what he says. At any rate, it doesn't sound as if the attack will happen anytime soon. Can you see Sol?" he added.

Dovewing cast her senses out again, carefully searching the WindClan camp, then widening her focus to take in the whole of the WindClan territory as far as the horseplace. Sweeping back toward the ThunderClan border, she encountered one of the tunnel entrances and tried to penetrate the tunnels, but after a few fox-lengths the weight of stones and earth blocked her from continuing.

Returning to reality in Firestar's den felt like coming back to the surface after sinking for a long time into dark water.

"Not a trace," she replied to Firestar's question. "He doesn't seem to be in WindClan, unless he's down one of the tunnels. My senses don't work too well underground."

Firestar nodded thoughtfully, not speaking.

"I suppose it's too much to hope that Sol has gone away?" Dovewing suggested after a moment.

"No, he's still here," Firestar assured her. "He has a score to settle with the Clans—I just don't know why."

When Firestar dismissed her, Dovewing ran lightly down the tumbled rocks to find Bumblestripe waiting for her.

"Brambleclaw went ahead with the others," the young warrior explained. "He asked me to wait for you and show you where we're going to train."

"Okay, thanks," Dovewing mewed. It felt comfortable to head across the clearing beside Bumblestripe.

"What did Firestar want?" the gray tom asked. "Are you in trouble?"

"No, it was just . . . stuff." However much she liked Bumblestripe, she couldn't tell him what Firestar had asked her to do. *That would take a whole moon to explain!*

"Firestar has never invited me into his den," Bumblestripe continued, sounding slightly envious.

Dovewing shrugged. "It was no big deal."

Leading the way through the thorn tunnel, she realized that she wanted to push her special powers to the back of her mind when she was with Bumblestripe. She just wanted to be an ordinary cat. *It's a nice change from when I was with Tigerheart! Then I always had to be listening to make sure no other cats found us.*

Brambleclaw had taken the rest of the group to a small clearing on the ShadowClan side of the territory, not far from the dead tree. Holly and elder bushes lined the rim of a shallow dip, which was filled with long grass and ferns.

When Dovewing and Bumblestripe arrived, Brambleclaw was sitting at one side of the hollow, watching Toadstep and Blossomfall as they stalked around each other. Without warning, Blossomfall darted in, skillfully hooked Toadstep's legs from under him, and delivered a blow to his hindquarters before leaping back out of range.

"Well done," Brambleclaw meowed. "You've got that move perfectly, Blossomfall."

Toadstep scrambled to his paws and shook scraps of fern out of his pelt. "She sure has!"

Brambleclaw looked up as Dovewing and Bumblestripe padded down the slope to join the others. "Good, you made it. Now I'm going to show you a new move."

"Great!" Blossomfall exclaimed, bounding over to Bumblestripe. "Come on," she urged him, "let's work on it together."

Bumblestripe looked briefly embarrassed. "Er . . . sorry, but

I'm going to partner with Dovewing."

Blossomfall's ears shot straight up in surprise. "Excuse me, but who's your littermate?" she muttered. "You could show a little loyalty, you know."

Dovewing was slightly shocked at Blossomfall's hostility. *Why is it such a big deal?* "I don't mind if you partner with Blossomfall," she told Bumblestripe.

"No, Blossomfall's being ridiculous," Bumblestripe retorted. "Of course I'm not being disloyal if I partner with you."

"Do you mind?" Brambleclaw rose to his paws and padded over to them, his strong shoulders thrusting the ferns aside. "Stop twittering like a lot of starlings and let's get on with it."

Blossomfall spun around, stuck her tail in the air, and stalked across the clearing to Toadstep.

"I'll demonstrate the move first, and then you can try it yourselves," Brambleclaw meowed. "Dovewing, you're a WindClan cat. Come and attack me."

Instantly Dovewing let out a yowl and hurled herself at the Clan deputy. Brambleclaw reared up on his hindpaws, his forepaws stretched out with claws sheathed. As Dovewing tried to duck under his guard and claw his exposed belly, he flipped backward, away from her. She lost her balance, and as she tried to recover Brambleclaw leaped on her and braced his forepaws on her belly.

"Like that," he purred, stepping back to let her get up.

Dovewing rolled over and sprang up to see the Clan deputy watching her with a faint trace of pride in his amber eyes.

"That's brilliant!" she panted. "Let's try it."

First Brambleclaw made them practice the backflip until they could do it and land squarely on their paws. When he was satisfied and let them work with their partners, Dovewing was surprised at how strong and agile Bumblestripe was.

It's been a long time since I trained with him, one on one like this. He's so bulky, I'd expect him to be slow. . . .

As Bumblestripe flipped neatly away from her attack, Dovewing's paws skidded out from under her. She flopped onto her side; while she was struggling to get up Bumblestripe sprang toward her and reached out with one forepaw to touch her gently.

"I win, I think," he mewed, his eyes narrowed with amusement. "Paws belong on the ground, not in the air."

Huh! Dovewing thought, stung. When Bumblestripe attacked her, she backflipped on the opposite side, catching him unawares. The gray tom missed his footing and landed hard among the ferns, his paws flailing.

"What was that about paws going on the ground?" Dovewing teased as she pounced on him.

"Why don't we watch each other?" Blossomfall suggested when all four cats had practiced the move several times. "We might pick up some helpful tips that way."

Brambleclaw nodded. "Okay. You and Toadstep go first."

Watching the other pair, Dovewing noticed how good Blossomfall was already, both in attacking and performing the new move. She had worked out how to stay balanced, and knocked her weight into Toadstep before he could recover from the backflip.

"Blossomfall, that's really great!" she told her Clanmate. "You'll have to be a bit faster, Toadstep."

Toadstep nodded. "I'm working on it."

When it was her turn to demonstrate with Bumblestripe, Dovewing felt that they had both done pretty well. She was surprised to see Blossomfall looking at her with a disdainful expression.

"Bumblestripe was fine, but Dovewing, you need to do a *lot* more work," she meowed. "Your paws were all over the place. And you seem to have forgotten that you even have a tail. It's there for balance, you know."

Dovewing muttered something noncommittal, embarrassment flooding over her until every hair on her pelt burned. "Blossomfall wouldn't have said that if you hadn't chosen me as your partner," she whispered to Bumblestripe. Trying to set her own hurt aside, she added, "I'm sorry if I've made things difficult between you."

Bumblestripe rested his tail comfortingly on Dovewing's shoulder. "Don't worry, it's not you causing the problem," he mewed, glaring across the clearing at his sister.

"I think that's enough for one session," Brambleclaw announced. "Back to camp, all of you, and take your pick of the fresh-kill pile. You've all worked hard."

"You should walk with Blossomfall now," Dovewing murmured as the group moved off. "Littermates are more important than friendship."

Bumblestripe paused and gave her a long look. "I was kind

of hoping that what we have is more than friendship," he mewed at last.

Dovewing stared at him, not knowing what to say. To her relief, Bumblestripe didn't press her. He just ducked his head and trotted off, catching up with Blossomfall and touching his nose to her ear.

Dovewing padded on; a moment later Toadstep bounded up to join her.

"What's going on between you and Bumblestripe?" he asked with a little *mrrow* of amusement.

Dovewing felt her neck fur beginning to fluff up, and forced it to lie flat. "Bumblestripe is a great cat," she replied calmly.

As she spoke, an image of Tigerheart popped into her head: the gleam of green eyes as he thrust his dark tabby head out of a clump of ferns. Resolutely she pushed it away. *That was different. I can't think about him anymore,* she decided. *Tigerheart can't be part of my life . . . but Bumblestripe could be.*

CHAPTER 17

❧

Jayfeather pushed through the thorns into the camp just after sun-high. The chill dawn wind had dropped as he journeyed back from the Moonpool, and warm light bathed the clearing. The stone hollow was deserted, and Jayfeather realized that all the warriors and apprentices would be out on patrol. He was heading for his den when he heard Mousefur's voice.

"Jayfeather! Come here a moment."

Jayfeather padded across and found the elder crouching alone outside her den. "Where's Purdy?" he asked.

"Hollyleaf took him for a walk in the forest," Mousefur replied. "I didn't want to go. My legs are aching too much."

"We can sort that out," Jayfeather assured her. "I'll go and fetch you some daisy leaves."

"I didn't call you over for that," Mousefur snapped at him. "It's about Hollyleaf."

Jayfeather stood frozen with shock as Mousefur described the scene that had taken place in camp that morning. "Then Brambleclaw told every cat that he'd seen what happened," she meowed. "That Ashfur attacked Hollyleaf and then fell into the stream by accident. I was sitting right here and I heard everything."

She paused and Jayfeather could feel her gaze burning into his pelt. His mind was whirling. *What does it all mean? What's going to happen, now that every cat thinks they know the truth? What happens if the real truth comes out?*

"You knew this all along, didn't you?" the old cat asked shrewdly.

Jayfeather nodded.

"But you said nothing?"

"What was the point? Hollyleaf had gone, and the situation was more complicated than it looked because of Ashfur's threats. He threatened me, too, you know."

Mousefur sniffed. "So it suited you to have him dead."

"It suited the whole Clan," Jayfeather retorted, refusing to be disconcerted by the elder's plain speaking. "Ashfur was determined to cause trouble for every cat."

"I won't say that no harm was done," Mousefur grunted, "because harm has been done. To Ashfur, to Hollyleaf, to Brambleclaw, to you. And now the Clan has to carry on as normal, is that what you want?"

Jayfeather licked one paw and drew it over his ear, giving himself time to figure out a reply. "I think there are bigger things to worry about right now than the death of one cat many moons ago."

Mousefur snorted, then lapsed into silence. Jayfeather was

getting ready to leave when she spoke again. "Darkness is coming, isn't it?"

Jayfeather felt every hair on his pelt begin to rise. "What do you know?" he asked hoarsely. *Could Mousefur be the fourth cat in the prophecy? An elder?*

"I don't know anything that could help us," Mousefur admitted. Her voice was bleak. "But my dreams have been troubled for a long time." She let out a weary sigh. "I never thought that I would live to see the end of the Clans."

Jayfeather leaned close to her. "This will not be the end of the Clans," he meowed. "As long as I have breath in my body, the Clans will be safe."

He waited beside Mousefur until the old cat drifted into sleep, muttering and twitching. *She's so old,* he thought. *Does she really know what she is saying?* As he rose and headed for his own den, Jayfeather's fur prickled at the truth of what Mousefur had said about keeping quiet about Hollyleaf and Ashfur.

But the Clan must move forward, he told himself. *There's no time to waste looking back at what can't be changed.*

Before he reached his den, Jayfeather heard the sounds of cats brushing through the thorn barrier, and he heard Purdy's voice.

"There was this fox, see, took to wanderin' through my Upwalker's garden. Well, I wasn't havin' any of that, so what do you think I did?"

"I have no idea, Purdy," Hollyleaf replied, sounding distracted. "Hey, watch out for that bramble!"

"I can see it," Purdy muttered. "I'm not a young 'un like

you, but I've got eyes. Anyway," he went on, "I hid under this holly bush, see, right next to my Upwalker's fence, an'—"

He broke off as Jayfeather approached. "Hollyleaf, I need to talk to you."

"We were talkin'," Purdy retorted with dignity, before Hollyleaf could reply. "Don't they raise young cats with manners anymore?" He gave a disgusted sniff. "I'll be in my den when you've finished, Hollyleaf, an' I'll tell you the rest of the story."

Jayfeather heard him stalking away. "Come over here," he meowed to Hollyleaf. With his sister following him, he padded over to the bottom of the cliff and sat in a sheltered spot underneath an elder bush.

"You know, don't you?" Hollyleaf guessed as she settled down beside him. "What happened this morning?"

"Mousefur told me," Jayfeather replied. He hesitated for a moment and then went on, "Hollyleaf, do you understand what Brambleclaw has done for you?"

Jayfeather knew what it must have cost the Clan deputy to speak out as he had. It was hard for him to appreciate what it meant, how much Brambleclaw—and Squirrelflight, too, he admitted to himself—had loved him and his littermates. *And maybe they love us still.* He felt as uncomfortable as if ants were making their nest in his pelt.

"They all know now," Hollyleaf murmured, her voice stricken. "They know I killed a cat."

Jayfeather reached out and rested his paw on her shoulder. "It was an *accident*, remember."

He could feel Hollyleaf's gaze on him, scorching him like a

flame. "But it wasn't," she whispered.

Jayfeather heard Mousefur's words echoing in his ears, telling him how much harm had been done as a result of that single moment. He shook his head as if he could get rid of her voice like a buzzing insect.

"Enough," he insisted. "We have to live with what has happened. I'm glad you came back. I missed you."

"I missed you, too," Hollyleaf murmured. Jayfeather felt the light touch of her nose on his ear, only for a moment. "I just hope I've done the right thing by coming back. Perhaps it would have been better if you'd all forgotten about me."

"We would never have done that," Jayfeather told her, leaning closer to her and drinking in her scent. "Never."

In the silence that followed, Jayfeather could hear the breeze rustling in the trees overhead, and farther away the sound of cats approaching the camp. As they drew closer, he heard the excited voices of the apprentices.

"I caught *two* mice!"

"And I caught a squirrel! It's *huge!*"

The hunting patrol emerged from the thorns, Cherrypaw and Molepaw scampering ahead. Lionblaze and Cinderheart followed, with Rosepetal and Foxleap bringing up the rear.

"Hey, take it easy," Cinderheart warned the apprentices. "You'll make every cat think that badgers are invading." Her tone was gently teasing. "But you've hunted very well today," she went on. "Molepaw, why don't you take your mice to Mousefur and Purdy? They're so nice and plump I'm sure they'll tempt their appetites."

Jayfeather heard Molepaw scurrying off, while Cherrypaw dragged her squirrel to the fresh-kill pile.

Cinderheart is a natural mentor, he thought, *even though these aren't her apprentices. And she couldn't be a more loyal warrior to ThunderClan. StarClan made the right decision when they let her live a second life.*

Grief sharp as thorns suddenly pierced Jayfeather, as if he had stumbled into a bramble thicket. Tensing, he realized that it came from Lionblaze.

"What's the matter?" he asked.

"You wouldn't understand," Lionblaze snapped. "All you ever think about is this dumb prophecy."

Jayfeather bit back a sharp reply as he realized that his brother's grief was tangled with longing for Cinderheart. "Try me," he suggested.

For a few heartbeats Lionblaze was silent. "I know Cinderheart wants to be with me," he meowed grudgingly at last. "But she thinks she can't, because I have a destiny. She thinks I'm too *important!*" He spat out the last word and stalked away before Jayfeather could reply.

Anger surged up inside Jayfeather, and for a moment he wanted to yowl his pain to the sky. *Half Moon* . . . No cat in ThunderClan knew of his love for the long-ago cat, lost to him now through the passing of so many seasons. He would have given anything to have her beside him again. Remembering her now helped him to understand his brother's hurt and frustration.

"She thinks *he's* the only cat who's important?" he muttered to himself. "Maybe it's time some cat showed her just how wrong she is."

That night Jayfeather curled up in his nest and took a deep breath before letting himself sink into sleep. He knew exactly where he wanted to go.

Somehow we have to settle this, once and for all. Not for Lionblaze, or even the Clan, but for Cinderheart. I have to show her what a great cat she is.

His eyes opened in a sun-filled forest, where thick foliage rustled above his head and the undergrowth was filled with the murmurings of prey. Jayfeather padded through the ferns, enjoying the cool grass beneath his pads and the warmth of sunbeams that struck down through the canopy. All his senses were alert as he searched for one particular cat.

Soon he heard a rush of paws, a pounce, and a hiss of disappointment. "Mouse dung! I missed it!"

Heading in the direction of the voice, Jayfeather bounded around a tree stump and burst into a sun-dappled clearing. Cinderheart was standing at the foot of a tree, looking up with a disgusted expression on her face. On a branch above her head a squirrel was chattering crossly.

"Bad luck," Jayfeather meowed.

Cinderheart started. "Wow! Jayfeather—I didn't expect to see you here." A fearful look flickered in her eyes. "I am still dreaming, right? I'm not in StarClan?"

"Don't worry," Jayfeather reassured her. "This isn't

StarClan. Everything's fine, and yes, you are dreaming. There's something I need to tell you."

Cinderheart faced him warily. "What is it?"

For a moment Jayfeather stood in silence, not sure where to begin. *Get on with it!* he told himself. *You started this, so you'd better finish it.* "It will be easier if I show you," he mewed aloud. "Come with me."

He set off with Cinderheart padding at his shoulder. Jayfeather pictured in his head the old ThunderClan camp, with the former cats leading their busy everyday lives. Gradually as they passed through the trees the old forest took shape around them. A stream appeared, splashing beneath arching fronds of bracken, and a jay swooped out of the branches of an oak tree. Jayfeather heard a gasp from Cinderheart as she realized that she had somehow left the territory of her dream and was on unfamiliar ground.

A patrol flashed through the undergrowth a couple of fox-lengths away; Jayfeather recognized younger versions of Firestar, Graystripe, and Sandstorm. Turning to follow, he saw them halt at the foot of a tree where a young gray she-cat was gathering celandine.

"Picking flowers again?" Sandstorm teased.

The young she-cat flicked her tail. "Flowers and leaves," she replied, unruffled, though her blue eyes were sparkling with amusement. "Do you have a problem with that, Sandstorm? Because if you do, you'd better take it up with Yellowfang."

Sandstorm took a pace back, shaking her head. "Anything but that!" she yelped in mock alarm.

"Yeah, she doesn't want to get her ears clawed," Graystripe meowed.

"Why don't we keep on hunting?" Firestar suggested. "Maybe we'll catch something good and fat for Yellowfang to put her in a good mood for once. You're doing a great job," he added to the gray she-cat as he led the patrol away.

"Make it a squirrel!" the she-cat called after them. "That's Yellowfang's favorite at the moment!"

Jayfeather was aware of Cinderheart standing beside him, her pelt bristling as she stared in astonishment. "That . . . that's me," she stammered. "I mean, it's not, but it looks just like me."

"No, it's not you," Jayfeather responded. "At least, not then."

Cinderheart shot him a baffled look, but said no more.

When she had collected enough celandine, Cinderpelt picked up the bundle in her jaws and headed off, limping heavily. Jayfeather and Cinderheart followed. The medicine cat apprentice wove her way confidently through the undergrowth until she came to the head of the ravine that led down to the camp.

"Does she know we're following her?" Cinderheart whispered.

Jayfeather shook his head. "She can't see us. We aren't really here."

Cinderpelt padded down the ravine and vanished into the gorse tunnel. Jayfeather and Cinderheart followed and soon they emerged into the old ThunderClan camp. Jayfeather's gaze swept the clearing, taking in the dens, the fresh-kill pile, and the Highrock where the Clan leader's den was. *Not Firestar,* Jayfeather reminded himself. *He's not Clan leader yet.*

"This is so weird . . ." Cinderheart murmured.

They padded behind Cinderpelt as she carried her bundle of herbs through the ferns and into the medicine cat's den. Yellowfang sat in the smaller clearing, looking just as scrawny and ungroomed as she did whenever Jayfeather met her in StarClan.

"That's a good bundle," Yellowfang praised her apprentice gruffly, trudging over to sniff the celandine. "Some of the leaves are a bit wilted, though."

"They'll be fine if we use those first," Cinderpelt pointed out.

Yellowfang snorted. "All right. Put them away and then come over here."

While Cinderpelt stowed the celandine in a cleft in the rock at the back of the den, Yellowfang padded over to a clump of ferns a couple of tail-lengths away. For the first time Jayfeather saw that a large white tom was sitting among the ferns, his fur rumpled and a look of pain in his eyes.

"Whitestorm had an argument with a bramble thicket," Yellowfang rasped as Cinderpelt returned. "He has a thorn in his paw. What do you think we should do for him?"

"Advise him to stay away from brambles," Cinderpelt meowed, provoking a snort of amusement from the white tom. "But for now, we need to get the thorn out, tell him to give the paw a good lick, and rub it with marigold to make sure it doesn't get infected."

"Quite right." Yellowfang gave a nod of satisfaction.

"I have a good mentor!" Cinderpelt responded, warmth in her blue eyes.

Yellowfang gave her an affectionate nudge, but all she said was, "Better get on with it, then."

"Whoever she is, she's a great medicine cat," Cinderheart commented, as Cinderpelt bent her head over Whitestorm's paw and swiftly extracted the thorn with her teeth.

"Yes, she was," Jayfeather agreed.

"Did you know her?" Cinderheart asked curiously, her gaze still fixed on the gray cat.

"Not then. This was before ThunderClan came to the lake."

Cinderheart turned to gaze at him, her eyes as big as moons. "So this is ThunderClan in the past? Is that why Firestar and the others look so much younger? But how . . . why . . . ?"

"You don't need to worry about that," Jayfeather reassured her. "Just keep watching. That medicine cat apprentice is called Cinderpelt." He felt a pulse of shock run through Cinderheart as she heard the name that was so like her own, but she didn't interrupt him. "She wanted to be a warrior just like you," he continued, "but she was injured before she finished her training. Did you notice that she limps? Her leg will never heal properly. She knew she would never be able to keep up with patrols, so she became a medicine cat instead.

She taught Leafpool, you know."

"Wow . . ." Cinderheart breathed. "I've heard about her. Didn't she die saving my mother?"

"Her death meant more than that," Jayfeather replied, though he didn't explain any further. *She'll find out soon enough.*

While they were speaking, white mist drifted out of the ferns, wreathing around them until it blotted out the medicine cats' den.

"What's happening?" Cinderheart whimpered.

"It's okay," Jayfeather repeated. "Just wait."

After a few heartbeats the mist cleared. The two cats were standing on a hillside, where rough moorland grass swept upward to huge peaks of gray stone. A long line of cats was trekking across it, their fur buffeted by the wind. Cats from all four Clans—long-legged WindClan, broad-shouldered ThunderClan, sleek-furred RiverClan, and lean Shadow-Clan—walked side by side, talking quietly.

"It's the Great Journey!" Cinderheart exclaimed. "They're heading for the mountains. Jayfeather, why are you showing me this?"

"You'll find out," Jayfeather promised. "Look, there's Cinderpelt again. She's the only medicine cat in ThunderClan now."

Padding closer, Jayfeather saw that Mousefur—a younger, stronger Mousefur, before she retired to the elders' den—was talking to Cinderpelt.

"My paws hurt," she was complaining. "It's walking over all these sharp stones that does it. It's not natural for cats."

"I'm sure we'll rest soon," Cinderpelt replied sympathetically. "When we do, I'll bring you some dock leaves to rub on your pads. You'll find that helps a lot."

Mousefur gave her a brusque nod and limped on. Heartbeats later, a mottled brown kit bounced up to Cinderpelt and announced, "I've got burrs in my fur!"

That must be Applefur, Jayfeather thought, recognizing a tiny version of the ShadowClan warrior.

"Oh, it's Applekit!" Cinderpelt yelped with mock astonishment. "I thought for a heartbeat there was a giant burr chasing me. Never mind. When we stop, I'll help you untangle them. Until then, watch where you're putting your paws."

"Thank you!" Applekit charged off toward her littermates.

Not watching out at all, Jayfeather thought, unsurprised.

Cinderpelt watched the kit go, her head tilted and amusement glimmering in her blue eyes, then returned to the weary toil up the slope. As the cats drew closer to the cliff face, a few snowflakes began to drift down. A wind rose, and soon they were struggling through a blizzard. Jayfeather lost sight of the other cats, and could barely make out Cinderheart fighting her way forward against the wind.

"Over here!" Jayfeather recognized Firestar's voice. "Every cat shelter under the cliff!"

Together Jayfeather and Cinderheart huddled together in the lee of the gray rocks, at the edge of their Clanmates. The whole world seemed to be full of whirling white flakes. Even the sound of the other cats was lost in the whining of the wind.

Suddenly everything was quiet. The falling snow died

away and seemed to melt into the earth. Abruptly the air grew warmer. Jayfeather looked around and realized that he and Cinderheart were back in the stone hollow, crouched against the thorn barrier.

"Oh!" Cinderheart sighed, disappointment in her voice. "Are we back home already?"

"Not quite," Jayfeather warned.

His words were hardly out when darkness fell over the clearing. Jayfeather heard a grumbling roar growing closer through the trees. Along with it came the sound of trampling, as if twigs were breaking under heavy paws.

"What is it?" Cinderheart gasped.

Before Jayfeather could reply the thorns beside them gave way and badgers erupted into the camp. Warriors surged out of their den to meet them: Jayfeather spotted Squirrelflight hurling herself at one of the leading badgers, with Brambleclaw and Cloudtail just behind her. Firestar let out a yowl of defiance as he plunged into the fight with Dustpelt, Sandstorm, and Thornclaw. Spiderleg and Ashfur were attacking one of the huge creatures together, darting in from both sides to confuse it.

Cinderheart let out a screech of terror. "Jayfeather! What's happening?"

"It's okay," Jayfeather reassured her, thrusting her to one side. "They can't hurt us." *At least, I hope they can't.*

A horror-struck shriek sounded from the nursery, rising above the clamor from the fighting cats.

"I'm so sorry," Jayfeather murmured to Cinderheart. "There's one more thing you have to see. Follow me."

He led the way across the clearing to the nursery, slipping between the battling shapes that appeared without warning out of the darkness. Squirrelflight lay panting across the entrance, wounded but still guarding the nursery from attack. Jayfeather and Cinderheart passed straight through, somehow without disturbing her.

The nursery was crowded. At the far side, Sorreltail was lying in a mossy nest, her belly heaving as she struggled to give birth. Cinderpelt crouched beside her, gently stroking her belly with one paw. But a badger loomed over both of them, its jaws parted in a threatening snarl. As it raised a paw to swipe at Sorreltail, Cinderpelt turned and sprang between them. The badger's claws slashed down her side; blood welled out as she collapsed.

"Oh, no—no!" Cinderheart whispered.

Jayfeather was vaguely aware of Leafpool and Crowfeather bursting into the den and attacking the badger, driving it out into the clearing. All his attention was fixed on Cinderpelt. Blood still gushed from her side; she was struggling to breathe, and as Leafpool returned she managed to gasp out a few words before her eyes closed and she went limp.

Behind her in the nest, a tiny kit gave its first thin cry.

Cinderheart's eyes were wide with horror. "She can't be dead," she breathed. "Jayfeather, tell me she'll be okay."

"Look at the kit," was all that Jayfeather said.

Sorreltail was licking the newborn kit with strong, rasping strokes of her tongue. Its gray fur stuck up in tiny spikes. Its delicate nose, the shape of its head, the set of its stubby tail were all echoed in the cat that stood beside Jayfeather.

"That's me," Cinderheart murmured in amazement. "That's how I was born."

"Yes," Jayfeather mewed.

Cinderheart turned stricken eyes on him. "Then Cinderpelt gave her life to save mine."

"Not exactly." Jayfeather tensed.

Cinderheart blinked in confusion. "But you said she died!"

"Only for a heartbeat," Jayfeather replied. "And then she was given a whole new life."

Cinderheart stared at him and he saw the moment when understanding flashed into her eyes. Her voice was scarcely audible, no more than a breath. "And that life was . . . *me*."

Jayfeather nodded. A spiraling flock of emotions was chasing through Cinderheart's eyes: horror, shock, pride, and then memories upon memories, thicker than falling leaves.

"I'm an apprentice . . . and Fireheart's my mentor . . . he's such a great teacher!" Cinderheart's words were coming so fast that Jayfeather could hardly make them out. The she-cat's flanks twitched as Cinderpelt's long-buried memories surged through her like a river in full flood. "Hunting's such fun . . . and fighting . . . I want to be the best warrior in the Clan!"

Then she let out a screech of fear and pain. "The monster . . . no . . . oh, my leg hurts . . . I'll never be a warrior. But I'll learn all the herbs . . . marigold for infection, borage leaves for fever, juniper for bellyache, catmint for whitecough and greencough . . . what are the traveling herbs? Sorrel, daisy, chamomile . . . oh, and burnet! Must get it right . . ." Her voice took on a note of deep sadness. "Yellowfang is gone! And now I'm the only medicine cat . . . It's so cold here, by the Moonstone. Fireheart is so still . . . maybe he's dead. Will StarClan really give him his nine lives?"

Cinderheart began to pant hard, as if she were struggling up a steep slope; then she let out a little cry of wonder and joy. "The lake . . . it's so beautiful! Oh, StarClan, thank you for leading us here." Then the sadness came back, threaded through with a note of fear. "Is that truly my destiny? And Leafpool wants to leave us . . . what will become of my Clan?"

At last Cinderheart was silent, her breath coming in ragged gasps. In the ruins of the nursery she stared at Jayfeather. "Who am I?" she wailed. "What am I supposed to be?"

Jayfeather stepped forward until he could look down into her distraught blue eyes. "You are *Cinderheart*," he insisted. "That is your destiny. StarClan chose to let you live again so that you could follow your first path, to be a great warrior, to have a mate and kits of your own, to fight and hunt for your Clan after caring for them so long from the medicine cat's den." He took a deep breath. "Honor StarClan for their decision," he went on, "and be proud of everything you have achieved in both of your lives. This is all your destiny, Cinderheart."

"Are you sure?" Cinderheart whispered.

Jayfeather nodded. "StarClan chose that you should be a warrior this time."

"Who else knows?" Cinderheart asked.

"Only Leafpool," Jayfeather told her. "No other cats need

to know. You are not an echo of Cinderpelt, you are your own cat now. Your Clanmates know you and love you as Cinder-heart, which is all the truth they need."

Cinderheart sighed and gazed around at the nursery; it was still and silent now, as if it were drawing away to a great distance. Slowly she padded over to Cinderpelt's body, and licked the dead medicine cat's ears. "I will never forget who I was before," she murmured. "Thank you for living my first life."

Jayfeather moved to her side and touched his tail-tip to her shoulder. "Come," he meowed. "It's time to go home."

CHAPTER 18

❧

Ivypool opened her eyes in the Dark Forest to the sound of flying paw steps. She flinched backward to avoid a collision and found herself staring into Breezepelt's amber eyes.

"Get out of my way, mange-pelt," he snarled, and ran on.

Recovering her footing, Ivypool realized that she was surrounded by cats, all streaming past her, brushing through the undergrowth in the pale, sickly light. She recognized cats from all four Clans, seasoned warriors and young apprentices, as far as she could see through the dingy trees.

A call rang out in Brokenstar's rasping voice. "Let all cats old enough to kill their own enemies gather here!"

Ivypool gulped. That was a far more dreadful summons than she was used to hearing from a Clan leader. At the same moment Hollowflight rushed up to her.

"Come on!" the young warrior gasped. "Something's happening!"

He dashed on through the trees with Ivypool hard on his paws, joining the mass of cats. They were all intent on reaching the same place, all running in silence with somber expressions.

Great StarClan! Ivypool thought. *There are so many of us!*

At last she burst out into the clearing with the heap of fallen trees where she had once fought Antpelt. The crowd of cats massed around the tree trunks; Brokenstar stood on the topmost trunk, with Mapleshade and Tigerstar and two or three other cats unknown to Ivypool, even fainter shadows than Mapleshade. She shivered at the hungry glitter in their eyes.

Hawkfrost was pacing at the foot of the heap, in the place a Clan deputy would take. Ivypool spotted Darkstripe, too, crawling up on his belly and gazing up at the leaders with adoration in his eyes.

Striding across to him, Hawkfrost thrust his muzzle into Darkstripe's face. "Stay back with the others!" he hissed.

Darkstripe crept away, dragging his tail.

Ivypool looked around the clearing. She recognized Redwillow and Tigerheart from ShadowClan, and dropped her eyes quickly before Tigerheart noticed her watching him. Breezepelt had joined his Clanmate Sunstrike, and Hollowflight was pushing his way through the cats toward Icewing and Beetlewhisker.

Ivypool's belly lurched when she saw Birchfall and Blossomfall standing at the edge of the crowd; they hadn't spotted her. It still made her sick to think of her own father visiting the Dark Forest.

How can he stand here? And Blossomfall? she wondered. *They aren't evil! They must know what's going to happen!*

Brokenstar stepped forward and the murmur of voices in

the clearing faded to silence. "You have trained well," he told the gathered cats. "And now it is nearly time!"

Ivypool's pelt tingled. *He's going to tell us exactly what he intends to do to the lake Clans! Once every cat finds out the truth, I bet they'll rebel! Or at least not come back to the Dark Forest.* She knew that most of the living cats there didn't hate their Clans. They wouldn't want to hurt their Clanmates. *Will Brokenstar really tell the truth? Then the power of the Dark Forest will be destroyed. . . .*

"Soon you will have a chance to prove your skill, strength, and loyalty," Brokenstar went on, his gaze raking the cats like claws. "Your Clanmates here will honor you, and so will your Clanmates beside the lake. You will prove yourselves to be the greatest warriors ever."

Ivypool saw that the listening cats were nodding, their expressions proud and eager. She wanted to yowl, "No! Can't you see? He'll make you attack your own kin!"

But she knew that would be a big mistake. *Brokenstar wouldn't let me survive another two heartbeats. And then all these visits, all the information I have learned, would be for nothing.*

She spotted Breezepelt, whose eyes were gleaming; she guessed that he knew exactly what was going on. He was digging his claws into the marshy ground, as if he were imagining ThunderClan cats beneath his paws. Ivypool's tail-tip twitched in frustration as she realized that none of the cats around her were going to question Brokenstar. He hadn't given them any real instructions, just vague promises of glory. Even the Dark Forest cats seemed willing just to wait for further orders.

"He's not even telling us *when* this will be," she muttered to herself.

Too late she realized that some of the cats nearby had heard her murmur, and were turning shocked gazes on her.

"You shouldn't doubt Brokenstar's decisions," a white she-cat mewed. "Don't you trust him?"

Ivypool dipped her head, her fur hot with annoyance that she had made such a mouse-brained error. "Yeah, sorry."

"Go back to your training," Brokenstar continued from the pile of tree trunks, "and be ready for the final signal. It will come soon."

He and the other leaders jumped down from the fallen trees and the ranks of cats began to file into the shadows. Ivypool wriggled through the crowd, craning her neck to look for Hawkfrost. Finally she spotted him; he had seen her, too, and was beckoning to her with his tail. Shouldering her way through the crush of bodies, Ivypool reached his side.

"I want to speak to Brokenstar," she announced.

"He's busy," Hawkfrost replied, angling his ears to where Brokenstar and the other leaders were talking quietly together at the foot of the pile of tree trunks.

"But this is important," Ivypool insisted.

Hawkfrost twitched his whiskers. "Do you have information we should know about?"

"No," Ivypool answered, thinking fast. "I-I just want to know what I have to do to be treated like a warrior. I don't want to fight at the back, where cowards hide. I want to be at the head of the attack, doing the most that I can to help my

Dark Forest Clanmates."

Hawkfrost blinked, looking impressed. "I knew you were special," he meowed. "I'm glad I chose you. Come with me." He turned and led the way toward the senior warriors. "Excuse me, Brokenstar," he murmured. "My apprentice wants a word with you."

Mapleshade let out a furious hiss at the interruption, her amber eyes glaring at Ivypool. But to Ivypool's surprise Tigerstar beckoned her forward with a jerk of his massive head. "You can say what you have to say in front of all of us," he mewed.

As she took a deep breath, Ivypool felt Brokenstar's piercing stare burn her pelt. She tried not to flinch. *He challenged my loyalty when Flametail wandered into the Dark Forest,* she remembered. *Oh, StarClan, let him believe me now!*

She was aware, too, of other cats around her, hanging back from those who were filing into the trees. They were gazing at her in awe that a mere apprentice should dare to address the most senior cats in the Dark Forest.

This is the most important thing I will ever do for ThunderClan.

"Make me a warrior," she meowed to Brokenstar. "I will do whatever it takes to earn your trust. I want to help you defeat the Clans as much as any cat here, if not more. Use me however you wish."

The oldest of the leaders, little more than a faint shadow against the slimy trunk behind him, loomed threateningly over her. "Big words for one so small," he growled.

Ivypool forced herself not to shy away from his stinky

breath and his baleful eyes as he inspected her all over.

Brokenstar shoved him away. "Leave her alone, Maggot-tail." Glancing around, he flicked his tail to summon another cat. "Come here, Antpelt." When the brown tom was standing beside them, he addressed Ivypool. "You fought once before, and Antpelt lost. Can you beat him again?"

Ivypool swallowed hard. She knew exactly what Broken-star meant. *There can only be one survivor this time.* She glanced at Antpelt, whose neck fur was bristling in anticipation of a fight. *He's dead already. He's dead already,* she reminded herself desperately. *If I kill him here, it's not like killing him for real.* And maybe Antpelt would be better off out of this terrible place before the final battle. *He was a good cat when I first knew him. How will he feel if he has to attack his former Clanmates?*

For the sake of ThunderClan, for the sake of all the Clans by the lake, Ivypool knew she had to win this fight. She took a deep breath. *StarClan help me!*

Summoning all her strength, all the battle moves she had ever learned, and the last reserves of her courage, Ivypool sprang at Antpelt. He reared up to meet her; as she slammed into his belly he grasped her shoulders with his forepaws, raking his claws through her fur. The hot scent of her own blood hit Ivypool in the throat. Letting herself fall backward, she battered at Antpelt's belly with her hind claws, and felt savage satisfaction when she gouged out tufts of brown fur.

Antpelt screeched and rolled away from her but as Ivypool scrambled to her paws he crashed into her side, carrying her to the ground again and slashing his claws down her flank.

He's much stronger than before! Ivypool thought, fighting down panic. *He must have done nothing but train since he died. What if I can't beat him?*

In the midst of Antpelt's whirling claws, Ivypool grabbed his waving tail and bit down hard on it. Antpelt let out a yowl of pain and his attack wavered as he tried to tug himself free. Ivypool jumped free and crouched, panting, a fox-length away. Antpelt lay on the ground in front of her, his paws twitching as he tried to get up. He looked beaten. Bracing herself, Ivypool leaped in to deal the final blow, and in an instant he slid from underneath her and landed on her back, half squashing her. His teeth and eyes gleamed as he pushed his face close to hers.

"I can't believe you fell for that old trick, mange-breath," he hissed.

For a moment Ivypool lay still, unable to muster any more strength. Her wounds were screaming with pain and blood was trickling into her eyes. But then she felt the senior warriors watching her, curious but not concerned, as if they didn't really care which cat won, and Ivypool remembered how much depended on her victory. She made a wild, bee-brained promise to herself: *If I win this fight now, then the Clans will win the final battle.*

Ivypool pictured Dovewing, Firestar, and all her Clanmates, and the images gave her a surge of strength, right to the end of her claws. She heaved herself up, throwing Antpelt off. Before he could find his feet, she landed hard on top of him, slamming him to the ground. Then she lifted one paw, ready to rip his belly open from throat to tail.

Fear flashed into Antpelt's eyes, but Ivypool looked away. It was too late for her to back down—and too late to save Antpelt from the final battle any other way. Ivypool's paw sliced down, and she felt warm blood welling between her pads. Antpelt spasmed once, then lay very still. His outline wavered, as if Ivypool were seeing him underwater. Then she realized that she could see the withered grass beneath him, and a pool of dark scarlet spreading wider and wider. Antpelt grew paler and paler, his fur turning transparent until he was hardly a shadow on the floor of the clearing. Ivypool blinked, and he was gone. Only his blood remained, staining the cold damp earth, but even that was fading now.

Did I do the right thing? she wondered, numb with horror.

Brokenstar padded over to her. "Oh, you're a Dark Forest warrior, no doubt about that," he rasped in her ear.

Ivypool had to stiffen every muscle to stop herself shrinking away from him. *That's the worst thing that any cat could say to me!*

"So you'll tell me when the final battle will be?" Ivypool mewed, trying to sound eager. "And let me fight alongside you?"

Brokenstar blinked slowly. "Maybe."

"But I just proved my loyalty to you!" Ivypool protested.

Brokenstar turned away. As he padded off, he glanced over his shoulder and growled, "You should have been loyal already."

As Ivypool stared after him, Hawkfrost appeared at her side. "Well fought," he meowed. He sounded impressed, and

Ivypool thought she saw a flicker of fear in his ice-blue eyes. "You've earned your place among the warriors," Hawkfrost continued. "If you want to know anything, just ask me. I can see how much this means to you." Flicking his tail toward the edge of the clearing, he added, "Now go train some of the apprentices."

Ivypool watched him go, then began wiping her paw on the grass to clean off Antpelt's blood. The stain on the ground had already vanished. Ivypool wondered if she would ever get the reek of his death out of her fur.

A heartbeat later she was aware of another cat approaching, and looked up to see Breezepelt. The WindClan warrior was staring at her in horror. "What happened to Antpelt?" he whispered. "Did . . . did you kill him again?"

Ivypool wanted to tell him that she had been forced to kill Antpelt, that she only did it for the sake of the Clans. *And I've saved him from something worse.* But she knew that she was still being watched by the leaders of the Dark Forest; she could feel the prickle of their intent gaze in her fur.

"It was necessary," she replied with a shrug. "In the end, my loyalty was greater than his."

Breezepelt took a pace forward and loomed over her. "We may be in the same Clan here, but I am not your Clanmate," he snarled. "You will be punished for this. Wait and see."

A cold stone of dread weighed in Ivypool's belly. She knew that Breezepelt meant every word of what he said. But it was too late to bring Antpelt back. And too late for Ivypool to hide from what she had done. She had broken the warrior code by killing another cat—and she had to believe that it was the right thing to do.

Every sacrifice I make is for the good of my Clan—and for the other Clans around the lake. Even if that means sacrificing myself.

CHAPTER 19

Lionblaze brushed through the barrier of thorns and headed into the forest, his ears pricked for the sound of intruders. Hazeltail and Rosepetal followed him, and Cinderheart brought up the rear. As he led the way down toward the shore where the WindClan border stream flowed into the lake, Lionblaze heard muttered conversation behind him.

"Who'd have thought that *Hollyleaf* killed Ashfur?" Hazeltail whispered. "Isn't it awful? How did she ever keep it a secret?"

"Well, she left soon after," Foxleap pointed out. "Do you think she was brave or a coward to run away like that?"

There was a heartbeat's pause before Hazeltail replied. "She must have been brave, because she came back . . ."

Her voice trailed off as Lionblaze swung around and fixed his two Clanmates with a glare. Hazeltail exchanged a quick glance with Foxleap before giving her chest fur a couple of embarrassed licks.

So you've just remembered that Hollyleaf is my sister, Lionblaze thought, but he said nothing.

By the time they reached the WindClan border and headed upstream, both Hazeltail and Foxleap were fully alert, their ears swiveling, their gaze flicking back and forth along the undergrowth, and their jaws parted to pick up the tiniest trace of WindClan scent on ThunderClan territory. Watching them with approval, Lionblaze couldn't help noticing how distracted Cinderheart was, drifting along as if she weren't seeing or scenting anything in the forest. When he warned the others about a bramble stretching across their path, and heard Foxleap passing the message back, Cinderheart still managed to get tangled in it.

"Are you okay?" Lionblaze asked her.

"Fine!" she snapped, pulling herself free and leaving tufts of fur behind.

Lionblaze blinked at her uncharacteristically sharp tone. For a heartbeat he wished he had been put on a different patrol, or even ordered to fetch bedding for the elders. But then his concern for Cinderheart overwhelmed his brief annoyance. If she was behaving like this, there must be something wrong.

A few fox-lengths farther upstream, Lionblaze noticed that Cinderheart had wandered away from the border and was standing belly-deep in long grass, her eyes wide and unfocused. He let the others go ahead and padded through the grass toward her.

"WindClan patrol ahead!" he hissed.

Instantly Cinderheart was alert, her neck fur fluffing up as she gazed around. "Where?"

"Nowhere," Lionblaze meowed. "I was just testing to see if you were awake."

Cinderheart's fur bristled even more. "You're not my mentor," she growled. "You don't have to keep checking on me."

Lionblaze opened his jaws to ask her what was wrong, but the anger in her eyes told him to keep quiet. Instead he walked on, noticing that at least Cinderheart seemed to be concentrating now.

By the time they reached the stretch of territory where the hidden tunnels emerged, there had been no sign of WindClan or Sol. Without warning the others, Lionblaze slipped away briefly to check the tunnel entrances. *No need to tell every cat where they are. Some of them might be mouse-brained enough to mount an attack on WindClan from our side.*

As he sniffed at the tunnel openings, he thought of Heathertail, and wondered if she knew about Sol's plotting. Would she use her knowledge of the tunnels to help in her Clan's attack? Did Heathertail have any trace of loyalty to Lionblaze, or would she take delight in hurting his Clan because the friendship they once shared had turned to dust?

Returning to his patrol, Lionblaze looked at Cinderheart and sighed. *Why do relationships have to be so complicated?*

Sunhigh was approaching as the patrol returned to camp, with nothing to report. As they came in sight of the hollow, Lionblaze heard shrieks and wailing coming from the clearing.

"Something's wrong!" he yowled.

With his patrol hard on his paws he raced for the entrance. *Are WindClan warriors attacking? Now, when the patrols are out and the camp is almost empty?*

But when he burst out of the thorns, there were no Wind-Clan cats to be seen. The few ThunderClan cats who were not on duty were gathered in a ragged circle in the center of the clearing; Lionblaze thrust his way between Daisy and Ferncloud to see what was going on. In the middle of the circle, Mousewhisker and Cherrypaw were lying on the ground, writhing in pain, their legs flailing and their tails curled up in agony. There was foam on the lips of both cats, and their eyes were glazed with pain.

"What happened?" he demanded.

"I don't know," Poppyfrost replied, her eyes wide and scared. "They came back a few moments ago and collapsed like this."

"My kit!" Daisy whispered, blinking anxiously at Mouse-whisker. Ferncloud comforted her with the touch of her tail on Daisy's shoulder.

"Had . . . bellyache," Mousewhisker gasped. "Think the mouse we shared last night was . . . going off a bit."

"It hurts!" Cherrypaw wailed. Helplessly she stretched out a paw toward Poppyfrost, as if she were begging her mother for help.

"Where's Jayfeather?" Lionblaze snapped.

"Out in the forest somewhere," Molepaw meowed, gazing

at his littermate with horrified eyes. "He and Brightheart went to check on the herbs he's growing."

"Go and find him," Lionblaze ordered. "Try the old Twoleg nest first."

Molepaw nodded and raced off, looking relieved to have something to do. Lionblaze hesitated, uncertain what more he could do, then staggered as Leafpool shoved past him.

"What have you eaten?" she demanded, bending over Cherrypaw.

"Mousewhisker said they shared a rotting mouse last night," Lionblaze explained.

Leafpool flashed him a glance from her amber eyes. "A mouse shouldn't cause this." She was tense, but in control, her medicine cat skills surging back to meet the emergency.

"Didn't want to bother Jayfeather. We ate some parsley . . . cure the bellyache." Mousewhisker forced the words out between his teeth.

"Parsley?" Leafpool bent to sniff the foam around Cherrypaw's lips. "That wasn't parsley, it was water hemlock."

"Is that bad?" Lionblaze asked, already knowing the answer.

"There's nothing more poisonous in the whole forest, except for deathberries," Leafpool replied. "I need herbs to make them vomit."

But she didn't head for Jayfeather's den. Instead, she braced her paws on Cherrypaw's legs, trying to stop her from thrashing around.

"What are you doing?" Poppyfrost hissed.

"They have to keep still," Leafpool told her. "If they flail around like this they could choke on their tongues."

Instantly understanding the danger, Lionblaze rushed across to Mousewhisker and tried to hold the young warrior down; Mousewhisker's legs were jerking in agony and he raked his claws across Lionblaze's shoulder. Leafpool wasn't finding it any easier to control Cherrypaw; though her movements were strong and confident, her eyes were terrified.

"Foxleap, give us some help over here!" As Lionblaze called to his Clanmate he noticed that Cinderheart had appeared at the entrance to the camp. She was staring at the sick cats in horror, as if she couldn't bear to watch but couldn't tear her gaze away.

Suddenly she leaped forward, whisking past Lionblaze. "I'll get the herbs," she mewed, racing for Jayfeather's den.

Leafpool looked up. "We need—"

"I know," Cinderheart interrupted, casting a glance back as she vanished behind the bramble screen.

Foxleap went to help Leafpool with Cherrypaw, while Hazeltail bounded across to Lionblaze and joined him in holding Mousewhisker down. Her littermate's thrashing legs knocked her off her paws, but she scrambled up and grabbed at him again.

Within a few heartbeats Cinderheart was back with a bundle of yarrow in her jaws. Dropping the bunch beside Leafpool, she turned back to Lionblaze. "Hold his head," she mewed crisply. "No, not like that—your paw's in the way of his mouth. I need you to hold him so that I can get some yarrow between his jaws."

Lionblaze stared at her. "Where did you learn all this stuff?"

"We don't have time for this!" Cinderheart snapped as she slapped his paws into position. "Just do as I say." She chewed up a mouthful of the herbs and forced the pulp between Mousewhisker's jaws. Then she began to massage his belly, kneading it strongly as if she were a kit trying to get milk from her mother. Beside her, Leafpool was doing exactly the same for Cherrypaw.

Cinderheart glanced across to check on her. "More pressure a bit higher up," she instructed.

To Lionblaze's surprise, Leafpool nodded. Her eyes were a little wider than usual, but she didn't pause to ask why Cinderheart was suddenly telling her what to do.

What in the name of StarClan is going on? Lionblaze wondered. *Has Cinderheart been secretly training to be a medicine cat? Why would she do that?*

Heartbeats later, both sick cats vomited up mouthfuls of evil-smelling slime.

"That's very good," Cinderheart soothed Mousewhisker, stroking his shoulder as he choked wretchedly. "You'll feel better soon."

A tail-length away Leafpool was comforting Cherrypaw; the young apprentice looked worn out and utterly miserable.

"Are you sure she'll be okay?" Poppyfrost fretted, bending over her kit.

"She'll be fine," Leafpool assured her.

"Thank StarClan!" Daisy exclaimed.

As every cat relaxed, realizing that the crisis was over, Lionblaze studied Cinderheart more closely. She seemed to have changed her expression into something he didn't recognize at all. Her color and shape and size were still the same, but her eyes were not the eyes of the cat he knew and loved.

Leaving Cherrypaw with her mother, Leafpool padded over to check on Mousewhisker.

"Have you been training Cinderheart?" Lionblaze whispered to her.

"No, not at all," Leafpool whispered back, her eyes clouded with something unreadable.

"Then how does she know all this stuff?" Lionblaze demanded, raising his voice. "I don't understand!"

"I don't care," Hazeltail meowed. "Just as long as she saves Mousewhisker's life."

Cinderheart looked up at Leafpool, a world of sadness in her gaze.

"You know, then?" Leafpool murmured.

Cinderheart nodded. "Yes, I know."

Lionblaze heard paw steps behind him and turned to see Jayfeather striding across the clearing with Brightheart at his side. Both cats carried bunches of herbs in their jaws.

"What's going on?" Jayfeather called, his voice muffled by his mouthful of leaves.

As briefly as he could, Lionblaze told Jayfeather how Mousewhisker and Cherrypaw had poisoned themselves with water hemlock. "Leafpool—"

"This is what comes from Firestar's idea of teaching the Clan about herbs," Jayfeather interrupted, rapidly checking Cherrypaw and then Mousewhisker. "If they hadn't thought that they knew what to do, this would never have happened. They'll be okay," he added grudgingly. "Foxleap, Hazeltail, help them both into my den."

"Cinderheart knew exactly what to do," Leafpool mewed as the sick cats moved off shakily, leaning on Foxleap and Hazeltail.

Jayfeather's head whipped around, his eyes wide with shock. "What?"

Cinderheart faced him steadily. "How could I stand by and do nothing, knowing what I know now?"

"What have you done?" Leafpool hissed at Jayfeather. "I thought we agreed she should be allowed to live in peace?"

"She deserved to know the truth," Jayfeather snapped back at her. "And to know that StarClan chose a new destiny for her."

Lionblaze felt the ground tilt under his paws. *Cinderheart's destiny? What are they talking about?*

"I'm still here, you know," Cinderheart pointed out, narrowing her eyes at Leafpool and Jayfeather.

"Then I'm sorry you had to find out," Leafpool told her, glaring at Jayfeather. "I thought we had agreed to keep it from you."

A flame of anger flared in Cinderheart's blue eyes. "And let me live in ignorance of who I truly am? You had no right to decide that!"

"But this changes everything," Leafpool mewed, her tail drooping. "And nothing was wrong before."

"Everything was a *lie* before!" Cinderheart lifted her voice in a wail. "If I was truly given a second chance, StarClan should have kept those memories away. But I can't forget now, I can't stop memories pouring into my head."

"Cinderheart, I—" Leafpool began.

Cinderheart's fur bristled. "I know every path in the old forest!" she flashed back. "I know Snakerocks and Sunning-rocks. I remember Gatherings at Fourtrees. I remember delivering kits when I was Yellowfang's apprentice, but not being able to save their mother. Do you have any idea how that feels? I remember deceiving my Clan, when I was trying to save sick ShadowClan cats. I remember—" Her voice broke. "I remember everything."

Leafpool rested her tail-tip on Cinderheart's shoulder, and for a moment the gray she-cat didn't move away.

"I never meant for you to feel like this," Jayfeather whispered. "I just wanted you to know what StarClan did for you."

"But I can't help feeling like this," Cinderheart retorted. "I can't just forget about my former life, when I was Cinderpelt."

As he listened Lionblaze had felt like a kit struggling in a flooding stream, with nothing solid to hold on to. Now it was as if his paws had slammed against the bottom, leaving him stunned.

Cinderheart used to be Cinderpelt? How is that possible?

"I don't know who I am anymore," Cinderheart went on, her voice throbbing with sorrow. "All this time, have I been just the echo of a dead cat?"

"No." Leafpool spoke gently, but her voice was full of conviction. "No, you are so much more than that."

Cinderheart sprang away from her, whirling to face her, crouching as if she were about to pounce on prey. "I don't believe you!" she hissed. Without giving Leafpool the chance to reply, she sprang forward and bounded across the clearing, disappearing into the gap in the barrier.

"I'll go after her," Lionblaze meowed.

Jayfeather nodded. "I'll come with you."

"No." Lionblaze glared at his brother, rage welling up inside him. *You knew all along, and you never told me!* "I'm going alone."

"Okay, keep your fur on," Jayfeather muttered. "Tell me what happens."

"Be kind to her!" Leafpool called after Lionblaze as he bounded away.

Out in the forest, Lionblaze followed Cinderheart's scent trail. She seemed to have dashed blindly away from the hollow, breaking through the undergrowth, leaving tufts of gray fur on brambles that trailed across her path. He found her at last crouched under a leaf-laden hazel bush, shredding a twig to pieces with her claws.

"You'll need medicine cat skills to put that back together," Lionblaze joked as he slid underneath the hazel boughs and crouched beside her.

"Really?" Cinderheart looked up at him, her blue gaze savage with misery. "Aren't I lucky, then, that I have so many?"

Lionblaze realized that he had said the wrong thing. "I'm sorry," he mewed. "I hate this, too, for both our sakes."

The rage faded from Cinderheart's eyes. "I don't know who I am anymore."

"You're Cinderheart," Lionblaze assured her, touching her ear with his nose. "You always have been."

"No, not always," Cinderheart replied, blinking unhappily. "Once I was Cinderpelt. And I've walked this path before, every step of it."

"What do you mean?" Lionblaze asked, confused. "You're a warrior now, not a medicine cat."

"I don't know what I am." Cinderheart gave a last scratch at the remains of the twig. "But what I meant was . . . I've been in love before with a cat that I couldn't have." Her eyes clouded. "Poor Cinderpelt," she whispered. "There was so much that was taken away from her . . ."

Lionblaze flinched. *I can't take any more of this.* "We'll talk later," he murmured to Cinderheart, then scrambled out from underneath the hazel bush and headed for the lake.

When he reached the water's edge he sat down and stared out over the tossing gray water. *They're so lucky,* he thought moodily, picturing the life of the Clans going on all around the lake. *They're not tangled up in some dumb prophecy, or another cat coming back to life!*

"I don't know what to do," he whispered.

Lionblaze wasn't sure how long he had been sitting beside

the lake when he heard paw steps approaching behind him. Hoping that Cinderheart had come to find him, he turned, and spotted Squirrelflight padding down the shore toward him.

"Hi," she mewed, sitting beside him. "Do you want to talk?"

Squirrelflight was the last cat Lionblaze would have chosen to confide in, but his churning emotions wouldn't let him stay silent.

"It's so unfair!" he burst out. "Not just for me, but for Cinderheart, too. She wanted to be a warrior, but now she's convinced she has to be a medicine cat because some other cat was before."

Squirrelflight nodded. "All cats deserve to find happiness as a mate, and as a mother. I wouldn't have changed anything about my life."

Lionblaze tensed, digging his claws into the ground. He knew what he wanted to say, but the words seemed stuck in his throat like a hard piece of fresh-kill, and were just as difficult to dislodge.

"You were a good mother," he admitted at last, thinking longingly of the time when he had been young, when he and his littermates had believed that Squirrelflight and Brambleclaw were really their parents. The tension in his shoulders relaxed as he let go of the long-held grudge. "You should have kits with Brambleclaw."

"That's not going to happen." Squirrelflight sighed. More briskly she added, "And perhaps it's for the best that it never did. But I loved you and Jayfeather and Hollyleaf just as much as if I'd given birth to you myself, and it breaks my heart to see you unhappy."

Lionblaze turned his head to meet her brilliant green gaze. "I think Cinderheart is unhappier than any of us," he meowed.

CHAPTER 20

❦

"Let all cats old enough to catch their own prey join here beneath the Highledge for a Clan meeting!"

At the sound of Firestar's voice Dovewing sprang up from the fresh-kill pile and gazed up at the Highledge. Firestar was sitting there with Brambleclaw beside him.

Although it was the height of greenleaf, the sky was covered with clouds. A chill, restless breeze rustled the trees above the stone hollow and ruffled Firestar's flame-colored pelt. To Dovewing the murmuring of the leaves seemed to echo the murmuring within ThunderClan. She hardly needed her special senses to pick up the gossip.

"Did you hear that Cinderheart used to be Cinderpelt?"

"Yeah, and Leafpool and Jayfeather knew all along!"

"I can't believe that Sorreltail didn't realize. She and Cinderpelt were good friends, right?"

"They do look a bit alike. But how weird that Cinderheart knows all about that medicine cat stuff!"

Dovewing closed down her senses and blocked out the whispering. "This meeting must be about WindClan," she meowed to Ivypool, her heart beginning to pound with anticipation.

Her sister swallowed her last mouthful of blackbird, then led the way closer to the Highledge. She was moving awkwardly; Dovewing guessed that she had been injured in the Dark Forest, but as usual Ivypool was refusing to talk about it. Foxleap, Molepaw, Rosepetal, and Hazeltail came to sit beside them, while Dustpelt, Graystripe, and Millie settled a couple of tail-lengths away. Mousewhisker and Cherrypaw emerged from the medicine cat's den and joined the crowd on shaky legs, flopping down to listen beside Poppyfrost and Berrynose. Jayfeather and Briarlight remained beside the bramble screen.

"Everything is so strange right now," Dovewing muttered as yet more cats appeared from the warriors' den. "Hollyleaf coming back, Cinderheart being a cat that everyone thought was dead—"

"And a medicine cat, at that," Ivypool added. "With all Cinderpelt's memories and skills."

Hazeltail leaned closer. "So does that mean we have two medicine cats now?" she whispered.

"I guess we do," Mousewhisker agreed.

Ivypool shook her head. "Like you said, it's strange. She was my mentor!"

"Surely we need warriors more than another medicine cat?" Foxleap mewed.

"That's enough," came a gruff voice behind them. Dovewing

had been so intent on what her Clanmates were saying that she hadn't noticed Brackenfur had joined them. He flicked Foxleap's ear with his tail. "Firestar is waiting to speak."

While the last scraps of conversation died away, Dovewing spotted Hollyleaf by herself at the edge of the crowd. She looked awkward and self-conscious.

There's been a lot of gossip about her, too, Dovewing thought. *It's only dying down now because there's something else to talk about.*

When Hollyleaf had first returned, Dovewing had tried to avoid her, nervous of getting too close to a cat who had killed a Clanmate, even if it had been an accident. But now she felt a stab of sympathy for the black she-cat.

Maybe Firestar's right, and she's been punished more than enough for not speaking up at the time. After all, no cat is blaming Brambleclaw, and he saw it happen!

Dovewing was about to go and sit beside Hollyleaf to give her support, when she saw another cat slip out of the warriors' den: Cinderheart. The gray she-cat padded across to Hollyleaf; without speaking she inclined her head toward Hollyleaf's until their ears touched.

"I see the odd ones are sticking together," Foxleap commented.

"That's enough!" Millie hissed. "Don't speak like that about your Clanmates."

Foxleap ducked his head, embarrassed.

"Cinderheart was Hollyleaf's best friend before she . . . went away," Millie continued. "And now they have something in common, a big secret revealed. They should be treated with kindness, nothing else."

"Well, Millie, you should know what it's like to be the odd one out. Having been a kittypet and all."

Dovewing's head whipped around as she tried to find the source of the whisper, but she couldn't spot which cat had spoken. *So many rumors and secrets,* she thought with a shiver, wondering what else might be revealed. Her gaze fell once more on Ivypool, who was flexing one foreleg as if she were testing its strength. *Definitely a Dark Forest injury,* Dovewing decided. *That's one secret that must be kept whatever happens.*

Firestar rose to his paws. "I have grave news," he began, "and I've decided to share it with the Clan after discussing it with Brambleclaw and the senior warriors. I know you're all curious about the extra patrols, and the fact that I've forbidden you to hunt along the WindClan border. It seems that Sol has betrayed us; he's planning an attack with cats from WindClan."

"What?" Mousefur screeched, shakily struggling to her paws from where she was sitting at the entrance to the elders' den, with Purdy beside her. "Didn't I tell you that cat was trouble?"

Several cats had jumped to their feet along with Mousefur, letting out caterwauls of shock and defiance. Dovewing glanced around at the cats she had overheard plotting with Sol, and noticed that Hazeltail and Rosepetal were exchanging horrified glances, while Blossomfall's jaws were gaping in utter shock. Mousewhisker was on his paws with the rest. "Traitor! Mange-pelt!" he yowled.

Dovewing narrowed her eyes. *Maybe you're just as furious as you seem,* she thought. *And maybe you're not. But you'd better not put a paw wrong now, because I'll be watching.*

"Mouse-brains!" Ivypool muttered with an icy glare. "They're lucky we never told Firestar what you heard."

"Thank StarClan Sol left, and they never got pulled deeper in," Dovewing responded in a whisper.

Firestar waited until the worst of the noise had died down.

"I can't say I'm surprised to hear what Sol is up to," he went on. "It explains why he hasn't shown himself here in the hollow for the last few sunrises."

"He'd better stay away if he knows what's good for him," Thornclaw growled.

"We have to attack WindClan now!" Cloudtail's neck fur fluffed up as he spoke, and several other warriors caterwauled in agreement.

Dovewing half expected her Clan to stream out through the thorn barrier and race for the WindClan border without any more discussion. Even though she knew what a bad idea that would be, her paws itched to be on the move.

But Firestar raised his tail for silence. Gradually the tumult died away and the cats sat down again, but their neck fur was still fluffed up; their eyes glared with hostility and their claws scratched at the bare earth.

"We are not at war with WindClan yet," the Clan leader meowed. "We have no way of knowing whether Onestar is aware of this, or whether Sol is making plans with a few cats he has befriended. And we're not going to approach Onestar about it, because we don't want to give him the idea of attacking."

"Then what are we going to do?" Dustpelt challenged. "We can't just sit here and wait."

"Of course not," Firestar replied. "We'll plan for a battle with the whole of WindClan, but it might not come to that. We'll wait for WindClan to come to us, because we're strongest in our own territory. We all know that WindClan doesn't like fighting among trees."

"That's right!" Birchfall called out. "We can climb trees and drop on their heads, like we did when we fought Shadow-Clan."

"And ambush them from the undergrowth," Sandstorm added. "WindClan cats are used to being able to see a long way in all directions."

"Good suggestions," Firestar responded, dipping his head.

"I can't *believe* this!" Dovewing heard Poppyfrost murmur to Berrynose a couple of tail-lengths away. "That flea-pelt even lied about saving our kits!"

Berrynose nodded, flexing his claws. "How dare he betray us! I'll claw his fur off the next time I see him."

"I knew we shouldn't have trusted him again," Graystripe meowed, overhearing them. He had an expression of grim satisfaction on his face. "He's treacherous through and through."

While they were speaking, Brambleclaw had risen to his paws and stepped forward to the edge of the Highledge. "We need extra border patrols," he announced. "Sandstorm, will you lead one with Cloudtail and Hazeltail? Graystripe, you lead the other; Spiderleg and Bumblestripe, go with him. And all the hunting patrols still need to stay away from the WindClan border. We don't want to look for trouble, so no more washing your paws in the stream!"

"As if we would!" Dovewing exclaimed indignantly, while Ivypool hunched her shoulders and gave her chest fur a couple of embarrassed licks.

"Dustpelt and Brackenfur," Brambleclaw went on, "I want you to work out a way to block off the entrances to the tunnels nearest the camp. We have to stop WindClan from attacking us in the heart of our territory."

Hollyleaf sprang up. "Don't block all of them!"

There were a few gasps of shock, as if some cats couldn't believe that the newly returned warrior would dare to interrupt the Clan deputy. Brambleclaw looked startled, his neck fur fluffing up as he turned his gaze on the black she-cat.

"Why not?" he queried.

"It's better that we keep the WindClan cats contained in a small area when they do attack," Hollyleaf explained. Her voice was quiet, and she dipped her head respectfully to the deputy. "There are tunnels at the edge of our territory that we should block off first, to stop the WindClan cats from surrounding us."

Brambleclaw blinked thoughtfully, recovering from his surprise, his neck fur flattening again. "So, which tunnels should we block?"

"Come down here, and I'll show you."

While Firestar and Brambleclaw ran down the tumbled

rocks, Hollyleaf used her tail to clear fallen leaves from a patch of earth. She began to sketch a plan with her claws; Dovewing wriggled in frustration that she was too far away to see.

"These are the farthest tunnels," Hollyleaf mewed, slicing her claws at the ground. "They should be blocked first."

Dustpelt and Brackenfur shouldered their way through their Clanmates so they could watch.

"There's sense in that," Dustpelt admitted.

"What's the best way to block the openings?" Brackenfur asked.

"Use stones to shut out the light." Dovewing was surprised at how confident Hollyleaf sounded. *She's thought all this out!* "Sticks will let light through, and so cats will try to get out that way. If you use stones, they'll just think it's a dead end."

Remembering her own time in the tunnels, Dovewing winced at the thought of meeting darkness at every turn. She had to remind herself that WindClan was the enemy. *No cat asked them to attack. I shouldn't feel a mousetail of sympathy for them!*

"Hollyleaf," Brambleclaw meowed, "will you train us in fighting skills that are suitable for the tunnels, in case we have to take the battle underground?"

"Of course I will," Hollyleaf replied. "I—"

"What?" Spiderleg interrupted, thrusting himself forward. "Is she coming straight back as a warrior, then?"

Brambleclaw gave him a steady glance. "Why not?"

"Well . . ." Spiderleg scuffled his forepaws in the dust. "She's been away for so long. What if she's forgotten everything?"

Hollyleaf looked up from her plan, her neck fur bristling

and her green eyes sparking with annoyance. "You think I didn't have to catch my own food while I was away?" she hissed. "Or fight off rogues and foxes without help? I promise you, Spiderleg, my skills are as sharp as they ever were."

"Just like your tongue," Berrynose muttered.

There were no more interruptions while Brambleclaw organized the hunting patrols, and named warriors for battle training sessions with Hollyleaf and to help Dustpelt and Brackenfur block up the farthest tunnels. He paused when he came to Dovewing and Ivypool, looking them up and down as he flicked the tip of his tail.

"Since you've already been underground," he mewed, "you'd better learn to look after yourselves properly. You can go into Hollyleaf's training group."

Dovewing and Ivypool crossed the clearing to where Hollyleaf was waiting. Brackenfur, Brightheart, Thornclaw, and Toadstep were clustered around her.

"Okay, let's go," she meowed. "Listen to everything I tell you, because it could save your life."

CHAPTER 21

Hollyleaf led the way out of the camp and up the steep path that brought the group to the top of the hollow. Pushing through the undergrowth, she halted beside an outcrop of stones.

"This is near the place where I found those marigold plants in water up a tree," Ivypool told Dovewing. With a gasp she swung around and faced Hollyleaf. "Wait—was that you?"

Hollyleaf nodded.

"And the yarrow?" Brightheart asked.

Dovewing could tell that Hollyleaf was uncomfortable with the attention of all the cats fixed on her. "I trained as a medicine cat first, remember," she muttered. "I knew that I could help, so I did."

"So you were watching us all the time?" Brightheart murmured.

Hollyleaf stiffened. "It wasn't like that! I wasn't spying!"

"I wasn't accusing you of spying." Brightheart reached out with her tail to rest it on Hollyleaf's shoulder. "It's just good to know that you didn't forget about us."

"I would never do that," Hollyleaf mewed. Giving her pelt a shake, she ducked behind the stones. Following her,

Dovewing saw the gaping hole in the ground where she and Ivypool had ventured before, following Sol into the tunnels.

"You mean we're going down there?" Thornclaw asked, his whiskers twitching nervously. "It's not natural. We're not moles or foxes! Cats shouldn't be trapped down a hole!"

Toadstep shoved him to one side. "We won't be trapped, mouse-brain! Let's go!"

Before he could plunge into the darkness, Brackenfur stopped him with his tail across the entrance. "Hold on a moment. You can't just go rushing into danger." He sniffed warily at the stones that surrounded the hole. "These might fall and block us in."

"You're right, Brackenfur," Hollyleaf agreed, "but if they did, it wouldn't be a disaster. There are plenty of other ways out. Don't forget that I know these tunnels." Stepping back, she gestured with her tail. "All of you, have a good sniff. We're not going anywhere until every cat is ready."

While the other cats crowded around the hole, Toadstep glanced at Dovewing and Ivypool. "You two aren't saying much," he remarked.

He doesn't know we've already been down there, Dovewing thought. *And he'd better not find out. If Firestar knew we entered the tunnels on our own, we would be back on apprentice duties before you could say* mouse.

Aloud she mewed, "We're just looking forward to learning how to move through the tunnels."

Ivypool nodded. "Right."

"Right," Hollyleaf went on when every cat had taken a good look at the entrance. "We'll go in now. Follow me, and don't even *think* about trying to explore on your own." She gave Toadstep a hard look.

"Okay," he muttered.

Hollyleaf led the way into the tunnels followed by Brackenfur and then Brightheart. Dovewing hung back to take the last place, guessing that she might be able to use her senses to guard their rear, in case any WindClan warriors were lurking in the tunnels. Thornclaw was hanging back, too; Dovewing could see how reluctant he was to go down into the darkness.

"It'll be fine," she mewed as he hesitated at the entrance.

Thornclaw shot her a glare and plunged into the tunnel; Dovewing could guess how much he must hate being reassured by a much younger Clanmate, especially when he didn't know that she had experience of being underground.

The light from the tunnel entrance soon died away behind them. Dovewing padded along in darkness, adjusting her senses to the unfamiliar surroundings and remembering how freaked out she had been when she first followed this path with Ivypool. Now the damp earth beneath her paws and the sensation of her fur brushing the walls of the tunnel didn't bother her nearly so much. It was better because they had a confident leader in Hollyleaf. Now and again her voice would echo back along the tunnel.

"Watch your paws here; the ground is uneven."

"It's a tight squeeze just here, but it doesn't last long."

As the floor began to slant more steeply downward, Dovewing became aware of Thornclaw in front of her; he was breathing hard and once or twice his tail lashed across her face.

He's getting scared. I know how he feels.

In the next heartbeat she collided with Thornclaw's hind-quarters and realized he was trying to back away. "I've got to get out of here," he muttered.

"No—you can't!"

The tunnel was so narrow that Dovewing was blocking Thornclaw's retreat. Panting, he started to claw at her. "Let me out!" he gasped.

"Hollyleaf!" Dovewing called. "Thornclaw needs help."

"Okay, I'm coming!"

In the blackness Dovewing couldn't see a thing, but she could hear grunts and hisses from the other cats as Hollyleaf squeezed her way past them until she reached Thornclaw.

"There's nothing to be scared of," she told Thornclaw calmly. "The dark can't hurt you, just because you can't see. And you have other senses, remember?"

Her words seemed to soothe Thornclaw; at least, he stopped struggling, though Dovewing was close enough to feel him trembling. "I'll walk with you," Hollyleaf went on. "I've lived for moons down here, and nothing bad has happened to me."

Thornclaw took a deep breath. "Okay," he whispered. "Sorry."

"Brackenfur!" Hollyleaf raised her voice. "Will you take the lead? Just keep on going straight, and ignore any side turns."

"Right." Brackenfur's voice echoed back.

Thornclaw's brief panic had unsettled Dovewing, and she

began to feel uncomfortable, acutely aware of the contrast between bright, warm daylight and this cold blackness. She managed to slide forward past the others until she could pad between Brackenfur and Ivypool, feeling reassured by their closeness. Brackenfur especially was a solid and calm presence, apparently too curious about the tunnels to feel any fear.

"What keeps the roof up?" he asked, sounding impressed. "And what made the tunnels in the first place?"

"Water," Hollyleaf replied from farther back. "There's a river, and when it floods the tunnels fill."

"Will they fill now?" Thornclaw fretted.

"Not a chance," Hollyleaf told him. "There has to be really heavy rain for a long time before that happens. Run your paw along the stone," she added, "and you can feel ridges like ripples in a windblown lake. That's from when the tunnels were first worn away by water."

Reaching out to feel the tiny furrows, Dovewing felt strangely comforted. *Hollyleaf is really at home down here,* she thought. *She knows every mouse-length of these tunnels!*

"I thought we were down here to learn about fighting?" Toadstep remarked as they padded on.

"You are," Hollyleaf countered. "But you wouldn't be able to fight a beetle in these narrow tunnels. When it comes to a battle, we'll have to confront our enemies in larger spaces. The tunnels are useful to flee or pursue, but not for combat. If you try, you're more likely to hit the walls than your opponent."

"Sorry I asked," Toadstep muttered.

As the tunnel grew slightly wider Hollyleaf took the lead again and headed along a twisting side passage. At last Dovewing realized that she could see, very dimly, the shapes of the cats in front of her. The sound of running water came from up ahead; her pelt prickled at the thought of a flood rising to engulf them.

Moments later the cats emerged into an underground cave. A crack in the roof, high above their heads, gave them enough light to see one another. A river ran across the center of the cavern; Hollyleaf flicked her tail at it.

"See? It's greenleaf now, so the water level is very low. Nothing at all to worry about." She seemed hesitant as the cats gathered around her. "I wonder what's best . . ." she murmured, half to herself. "Attack or defense?"

"Don't you even know that?" Thornclaw snapped. "What did you get us down here for?"

Toadstep shot Thornclaw a sharp look, though he said nothing.

"I didn't spend my time down here fighting," Hollyleaf retorted. "I had no enemies because I saw no other cats."

That must have been so lonely, Dovewing thought, with a sympathetic glance at the black she-cat.

"But you know more than any of us about moving around in darkness and confined spaces," Brackenfur meowed. "That's what will be helpful. What should we do if a patrol of Wind-Clan cats ambushes us here?"

Hollyleaf gave him a brief nod. "Right," she began. "You need to remember that the space is small, so you have to change your fighting moves. Keep your blows short and tight, otherwise you risk knocking your paws against the walls."

Toadstep reared up on his hindpaws, keeping his forelegs tucked into his body while extending his claws against an imaginary enemy. "Like this?"

"Very good," Hollyleaf mewed. "But don't rear up unless you know there's enough space above your head. Braining yourself on the tunnel roof would be a *bad* idea."

Dovewing stifled a *mrrow* of amusement. "Is it better to fight in the light or the dark?" she asked.

Hollyleaf paused for a moment. "It depends," she replied. "If you think you can beat your opponent, lead them away from the light so you can take advantage of the darkness. But if not, keep them close to the light so you can aim your blows accurately."

Dovewing glanced around the cavern, suppressing a shiver as she imagined it full of clawing, screeching cats. The advice Hollyleaf was giving suddenly made the coming battle seem closer.

"Right," Hollyleaf mewed briskly. "Let's practice. Toadstep, you seem keen, so you can be a ThunderClan warrior. Dovewing, you be the WindClan warrior that's attacking him."

"Great!" Toadstep crouched down, lashing his tail. "Come and get me, WindClan scum!"

"Scum yourself!" Dovewing retorted.

She leaped at Toadstep, but forgot what Hollyleaf had said about keeping moves small and tight. As Toadstep dodged aside, her leap took her too far, and she narrowly missed charging into the cave wall. Her paws skidded, while Toadstep took the chance to deliver a couple of hard blows to her hindquarters.

"Well done!" Hollyleaf called.

Dovewing gritted her teeth. Turning tightly, she reared up as Toadstep came in for the attack, and used the backflip she had learned in the training session with Bumblestripe. Toadstep saw the move coming, but too late, and lost his balance. Dovewing leaped on top of him, battering at him with her forepaws.

But as Toadstep rolled over, wriggling to free himself, one of Dovewing's flailing paws hit the wall. She let out a yowl of pain. Taking advantage of her brief distraction, Toadstep threw her off and wrapped his forepaws around her neck. However hard she struggled, Dovewing couldn't dislodge him. Their fight had taken them right up against the cave wall. Heaving Toadstep around, Dovewing managed to trap him in a corner. Though he was still clinging to her neck, he had no way of escaping when she raked at his belly with her hindpaws.

"That'll do." Hollyleaf came to separate them. "Very good, both of you. Dovewing, that was a good move, to keep him pressed up against the wall like that. Do you know what you could have done?" she asked Toadstep.

"Not much. I'll have bruises for a moon," Toadstep muttered.

"I'll show you. Brackenfur, come over here and shove me into the corner."

As the golden brown warrior charged at her, Hollyleaf sprang up against the wall and pushed off in an enormous leap that carried her right over Brackenfur's head. She landed lightly and spun around, ready to attack.

"Brilliant!" Dovewing exclaimed.

There was a murmur of appreciation from the other cats.

"You need space, of course," Hollyleaf meowed, dipping her head. "And you have to be careful not to scrape your pads. The walls aren't always smooth. Why don't you all pair up and practice that?" she suggested.

Within a few heartbeats the cave was full of leaping cats. Dovewing took Ivypool as her partner. It took a few tries before either of them could do the move effectively.

"This is hard!" Ivypool panted. "But it might come in handy you-know-where," she added in a lower voice.

"Think of it as stalking and pouncing on prey," Dovewing mewed. "I've found that helps."

"Okay," Hollyleaf called. "Now I want to try something else. Brightheart, you've developed new fighting moves to take advantage of your blind side. Is there anything you can tell us that would help us here?"

Brightheart dipped her head, clearly pleased at being invited to contribute. "I'm used to darkness on one side," she began, "so the darkness down here doesn't bother me all that much. You need to make sure you're using your whiskers and your tail-tip. They'll help you judge how far away you are from the tunnel walls."

Hollyleaf nodded. "Let's try a practice round to show us

how that works. Ivypool, come and fight with her."

Ivypool leaped forward and tried to trap Brightheart against the cave wall. But Brightheart seemed to know exactly where she was without needing to look behind her. She slid to one side and raked her paw down Ivypool's flank.

"Great!" Ivypool wheezed, struggling to get her breath back. "If your claws were out, I'd be crow-food."

Brightheart repeated the sequence, but this time slowed down her moves so that every cat could see how she used her tail and whiskers. "Don't forget you can't always see your enemy down here," she added. "You'll need to use hearing and scent much more than you do when you're fighting out in the open."

"Good point," Hollyleaf meowed. "We'll do an exercise now to practice that. I'm going to take you into the tunnels one by one, and leave you there. You have to find your way back to us by listening and smelling."

"What if we can't?" Thornclaw asked with a twitch of his tail-tip.

"Then I'll come and get you, mouse-brain," Hollyleaf retorted. "Come on, you can be first. Meanwhile, the rest of you can practice Brightheart's moves."

She disappeared into a nearby tunnel, with Thornclaw trailing reluctantly after her. Dovewing was surprised when the tabby warrior returned soon after Hollyleaf, giving himself a couple of complacent licks as he emerged into the cave again.

"Good," Hollyleaf mewed. "Now you, Dovewing."

Hollyleaf led the way down a series of tunnels that twisted and branched so that Dovewing knew she would never have found the way out again without something to guide her.

"All right, this'll do," Hollyleaf told her as they reached a dead end. "Wait for as long as it takes to eat a mouse, and then follow me back."

Dovewing waited much longer than that. Thanks to her special senses she could pick up the sounds of the cats in the cavern and knew exactly where she had to go. She didn't want to give her powers away, so she tried to judge how long she should have taken before she rejoined them. From the moderate praise Hollyleaf gave her, Dovewing guessed her calculations had been right.

Toadstep was the last cat to go. Growing tired, the rest of the cats had stopped practicing and waited in the cave as the moments dragged out and he didn't reappear.

"Hollyleaf, do you think—" Brightheart began.

A panic-stricken yowl interrupted her, seeming to come from right inside the walls of the cave. "I'm lost! I can't get out!"

"It's okay!" Hollyleaf called back. "We can hear you. You can't be far away."

"But I can't find the right tunnel!"

"Just keep calm," Hollyleaf instructed him. "Let your senses go still before you try again. Now taste the air for scent. Is it stronger in one direction?"

There was a pause before Toadstep answered, "I . . . I think so."

"Okay, try that."

A few heartbeats' silence passed before Toadstep popped out of the tunnel entrance again. "Thank StarClan!" he exclaimed.

"If you get lost down here," Hollyleaf addressed the whole group of cats, "it's vital not to panic. There's always something that will tell you the right way. Pay attention to the direction of the airflow. And if the air feels damp and heavy, that means the tunnel will go deeper."

"And head for the light, right?" Ivypool added.

Hollyleaf hesitated. "Mostly . . . but don't forget that some cracks reach far, far down into the rock. They don't necessarily offer a way out. Like that one," she added, gesturing with her tail toward the gap in the cave roof.

"What next?" Toadstep asked.

"Next we go back to camp," Hollyleaf replied. "It's been a really good session, but we're all tired now."

"We've learned a lot," Dovewing meowed. "Thanks, Hollyleaf."

Murmurs of agreement came from the other cats as Hollyleaf led them back through the tunnels. The sun was setting by the time they emerged, and shadows lay thick under the trees as they padded back through the twilit forest.

"Hollyleaf's training will be really useful for night fighting, too," Brackenfur remarked.

"Yeah, we could practice that," Toadstep agreed eagerly. "I've got another idea, too. Down in the tunnels, we could think of ways of getting our enemies lost."

Ivypool nodded. "Maybe work out a system of signs so that we know where we are but the WindClan cats don't?"

"Or we could work on ways of luring them into an ambush," Dovewing added, her pads tingling with excitement. "Wind-Clan won't know what hit them!"

As the entrance to the hollow came into sight, Toadstep halted and gazed through the shadowy trees toward the WindClan border. "Let them come!" he yowled, his neck fur bristling and his tail lashing. "We are ready!"

CHAPTER 22

❧

"Hi, Dovewing, Ivypool!" Foxleap called as they emerged from the thorns at the rear of Hollyleaf's training patrol.

The last streaks of scarlet were fading from the sky and half the stone hollow lay in deep shadow. Most of the other patrols seemed to have returned, too, and almost the whole Clan was settling down to eat. Ivypool looked across the camp to see Foxleap sitting beside Bumblestripe near the fresh-kill pile.

"Come and share our squirrel!" Foxleap added.

Ivypool raced across the clearing with Dovewing at her shoulder. She noticed the welcoming purr that Bumblestripe gave her sister, and how he made room for her to sit next to him and eat.

"How was the training?" Foxleap prompted.

Every muscle in Ivypool's body was aching as she flopped down and bit into the prey. "We learned loads," she mumbled around the mouthful of fresh-kill.

"Yes, all about how to fight underground," Dovewing put in. "You have to keep your moves small, and not bang your paws against the walls."

"And Hollyleaf taught us to push off the tunnel wall and

leap over our enemies," Ivypool mewed, swallowing the squirrel. "That's so you don't get trapped."

"Wow, it sounds tough!" Foxleap commented.

"It is," Dovewing admitted, "but it's kind of logical, too. You'll see, when it's your turn."

"This is a great squirrel," Ivypool meowed, taking another huge bite. "Who caught it?"

"Actually, it was me," Bumblestripe confessed, giving his shoulder an embarrassed lick. "I was lucky to get it."

"No, it was a brilliant catch," Foxleap insisted. "Especially since you were on your own. Cinderheart was supposed to be in our hunting patrol," he explained, "but she said she wanted to stay here in the hollow and help Jayfeather."

Dovewing's whiskers twitched in surprise. "What did Brambleclaw say?"

Bumblestripe shrugged. "Not much. What could he say? He would never challenge a medicine cat, would he?"

"But *is* Cinderheart a medicine cat?" Foxleap asked.

Ivypool felt a pang of sympathy for Cinderheart; she knew very well what it was like to have a paw in two worlds. But when the gray she-cat emerged a moment later from Jayfeather's den and padded over to eat with Hollyleaf, she seemed contented enough.

Maybe she's found her destiny after all, Ivypool thought.

A few moments later, Jayfeather emerged from the den and bounded across to the fresh-kill pile, where he chose a mouse for himself.

Cinderheart looked up from the vole she was sharing with

Hollyleaf. "Jayfeather, should I sleep in your den from now on?"

Ivypool realized that the gray she-cat wasn't contented at all. She was trying to put a brave face on her situation, but underneath it she seemed confused and unhappy.

"We wanted to talk to you about that," Brackenfur mewed, padding up to Jayfeather with Sorreltail beside him. "About everything, really."

"Yes," Sorreltail joined in. "What does it all mean, that Cinderheart used to be Cinderpelt? Why has StarClan done this to her?"

Jayfeather shook his head. "I don't know. It was their decision."

Sorreltail padded up to her daughter and pressed her muzzle comfortingly against Cinderheart's shoulder. "I love you for who you are," she murmured. "And that is Cinderheart."

Cinderheart looked up at her with pain in her blue eyes. "But I don't know if I am Cinderheart anymore. Jayfeather, should I sleep in your den or not?"

Jayfeather hesitated. "You don't have to, but—"

Millie interrupted by springing to her paws and stalking forward, her tail-tip twitching. "What about Briarlight?" she demanded. "I don't want her moved out of the den just to make room for Cinderheart. What if she stops breathing in the night?"

"I don't think that's likely," Jayfeather responded. He raised his tail to stop Millie as she drew breath for another protest. "But I don't want Briarlight moved either," he added.

"She's really useful where she is."

Briarlight, who was sharing a sparrow with Graystripe, blinked. "I'm fine," she mewed. "I don't mind where I am."

"But there isn't room for three cats in there," Brightheart pointed out, joining the discussion. "You'd all be really squashed."

"And what if you need space for sick cats?" Leafpool added.

Ivypool felt her head start to spin as more cats joined in to add their opinions, and she couldn't follow the argument anymore. A flash of flame caught her eye and she spotted Firestar bounding down from the Highledge.

"Brackenfur, Dustpelt," the Clan leader meowed as he approached the fresh-kill pile, flicking his tail to summon the two toms. "Do you think that we could make more space in the medicine cat's den, along with the warriors' den?"

Dustpelt and Brackenfur turned to eye the fallen tree.

"It might work," Dustpelt murmured, tilting his head to one side. "What do you think, Brackenfur? If we could move that branch there, and pack the space with brambles . . ."

Ivypool was distracted from the warriors' plans when Hollyleaf padded across to her and Dovewing. "Are you still okay with me sharing your den?" she meowed.

"Of course," Ivypool replied at once. Now that she was over the shock of Hollyleaf's reappearance, she thought that the black warrior was one of the most intriguing cats she had ever met. She wanted to know her better. "You can stay as long as you want."

"What was it like, living in the tunnels for such a long

time?" Dovewing asked curiously; Ivypool thought that she looked more confident around Hollyleaf since their training session underground.

Hollyleaf shrugged. "Dark. Cold."

"Did you really not see any other cats?" Dovewing persisted.

"And what did you do all day?" Bumblestripe added; he was still sitting close beside Dovewing and the remains of the squirrel.

"No, I didn't see any others," Hollyleaf meowed. "As for what I did . . . stalked prey, explored the woods just outside the territory . . ."

Ivypool could tell that she really didn't want to talk about her exile from the Clan. *She must have been so lonely . . . and felt so guilty about Ashfur, without any other cat to talk to. . . .*

Suddenly Hollyleaf let out a small *mrrow* of amusement. "Did Lionblaze ever tell you about the time he and I went hunting mice on the way to the mountains? We were only apprentices."

"No—tell us!" Ivypool urged her.

"We were passing a farm," Hollyleaf went on, tucking her paws under her chest. "The scent of mouse was so strong, and we were so hungry! So we sneaked away while the others were having a rest. Breezepelt was with us, too."

"Breezepelt!" Ivypool exclaimed, feeling her neck fur begin to fluff up.

"Yes, he was there on the journey," Hollyleaf told her. "Even though he is a pain in the tail, we had to let him come."

"What happened?" Dovewing prompted.

"We got trapped in a barn by some dogs. I was scared out of my fur! Breezepelt nearly lost his tail, they got so close."

Ivypool leaned in. "How did you escape?"

"Purdy rescued us," Hollyleaf meowed.

"Purdy!" Dovewing's eyes stretched wide. "Purdy was there?"

"Yes, we met him on the way."

"ThunderClan has good reason to be grateful to Purdy," Squirrelflight purred, padding over to listen. "That wasn't the first time he helped us. And it was more than you mouse-brains deserved."

"True," Hollyleaf agreed. "We would have been crow-food without him."

"You almost were crow-food, once we found out what you'd done," Squirrelflight added. "Walking straight into danger like that!"

"And we never even got a taste of mouse!" Hollyleaf finished.

"Maybe you should tell them about some of the mischief you got into when you were kits," Sandstorm put in; she had been grooming herself on the edge of the group while Hollyleaf told her story. "I never thought the three of you would survive to be apprentices!"

Hollyleaf glanced at the ginger she-cat, then gave her chest fur a couple of licks. "That was a long time ago," she murmured. Memories flickered in Hollyleaf's eyes like minnows in a stream, but she said nothing more, to Ivypool's disappointment.

The discussion about Cinderheart was still going on around the fresh-kill pile. Ivypool glanced across as Firestar rose to his paws.

"That's settled then," the Clan leader meowed. "Cinderheart will sleep in the warriors' den for now, but she will be relieved of all warrior duties. That is what you want, Cinderheart?"

The gray she-cat nodded. "Yes, that's what I want, Firestar."

Ivypool thought that Firestar looked surprised and disappointed to hear the certainty in Cinderheart's voice, but he didn't argue with her.

The Clan is losing a valuable warrior, Ivypool thought sadly. *I know it's useful to have another medicine cat, but . . .* She shook her head. *This is too weird.*

Murmurs of agreement had greeted Firestar's announcement, although Ivypool noticed that Lionblaze was gazing forlornly at Cinderheart.

Why would he be upset that she's not a warrior anymore? Ivypool wondered. *Oh . . . maybe he wanted to be her mate. Wow, that's really bad luck.* Cinderheart's decision was causing ripples right across the Clan, like a stone thrown into the lake. Did StarClan realize what would happen when they decided to give her a second life?

Ivypool slid softly through the undergrowth on the way to the ShadowClan border. The sky was clear and sunlight slanted down through the branches, but a brisk wind was fluttering the leaves and rustling the cats' fur.

Ivypool was pleased to have been chosen for Hollyleaf's patrol, padding close behind her with Brackenfur and Berrynose bringing up the rear. As sunrise followed sunrise since Hollyleaf's return, she had gained more and more respect for the black she-cat's courage and her occasional sharp tongue. *She knows how tough life can be, and she still keeps going.*

"Hollyleaf is doing everything she can to fit into the Clan again." Ivypool's ears swiveled back to pick up Brackenfur's low-voiced remark.

"Yeah, she even takes on the worst chores to help the apprentices," Berrynose murmured.

Ivypool thought how unusual it was to hear Berrynose praising another cat, then remembered that it was Hollyleaf who had saved his kits from the fox.

Brackenfur let out a faint *mrrow* of amusement. "Yes, to go on this patrol Brambleclaw had to drag her away from searching for the elders' ticks!"

Hollyleaf glanced back. "Less noise," she ordered. "We're getting close to the border."

Tasting the air, Ivypool picked up the reek of the Shadow-Clan scent markers, mingled with the scent of Twolegs. Emerging from the trees at the edge of the clearing, she saw that it was full of Twoleg pelt-dens, with Twolegs sitting or lying on the grass, or jumping up and down tossing brightly colored objects at one another.

"What in StarClan's name are they doing?" she muttered.

Hollyleaf shrugged. "Maybe it's a training exercise."

From farther downstream, Ivypool could hear the happy yowling of Twoleg kits as they splashed around at the edge of the lake. *I wonder if they're fishing, or just cooling their paws. They'll scare all the fish away with that racket!*

Silently, swiftly, the four cats slipped across the clearing, avoiding the Twolegs. Ivypool wondered if Hollyleaf was tempted to set the markers at the ThunderClan side of the clearing, and leave the open grass to ShadowClan.

"I can't believe ShadowClan fought so hard to keep this useless bit of territory," Brackenfur muttered.

I can't believe we fought so hard to win it, Ivypool thought. A sharp pang of guilt pierced her as she remembered how it had been her fault that ThunderClan had gone into battle. *But now that it's ours, we're stuck with it. We have to set these wretched markers every day.*

All her fur stood up as she dodged around the pelt-dens; she hated being in the open like this, so close to Twolegs. And she couldn't relax when they reached the opposite side, because now the scent of ShadowClan was all around them.

"Okay," Hollyleaf meowed as they reached the border. "Let's split up. Brackenfur, you and Berrynose go upstream and renew our markers there. Ivypool, you and I will go downstream."

Brackenfur gave her a brisk nod and headed off with Berrynose beside him. "Go straight back to camp when you've finished," Hollyleaf called after them.

Hollyleaf set the first marker; by the time she had finished the two toms were out of sight. Ivypool padded at her shoulder as she turned toward the lake. Pausing to set another marker, Ivypool picked up more ShadowClan scent, strong and fresh.

"A patrol!" she whispered.

As she spoke the ferns on the other side of the border were thrust aside and three cats emerged into the open. Dawnpelt was in the lead; with her were Redwillow and Scorchfur.

Dawnpelt drew her lips back in a snarl as she spotted the ThunderClan cats. Ivypool felt her neck fur beginning to rise at the naked hostility in the cream-furred she-cat's gaze.

"Set one paw across—" Dawnpelt began, then broke off as she noticed Hollyleaf. "You!" she exclaimed. "I thought you'd left the Clans."

Hollyleaf shrugged. "I came back."

For a few heartbeats Dawnpelt's hostility faded, to be replaced by a look of interest. But Ivypool hoped that she wouldn't want to stand around and chat. *I've got nothing to say to that flea-pelt. I don't trust her one bit. Before we know it, she'll be accusing Hollyleaf of murdering Flametail, too.*

"We're not doing any harm," Ivypool meowed. "Just setting markers."

Dawnpelt snorted disbelievingly. "I'd better check where you're putting them," she hissed, padding forward and craning her neck to sniff the marker Ivypool had just placed. "I'll tell Blackstar if any of them are a leaf's depth out of place."

"Feel free," Hollyleaf retorted. "If you can find anything wrong, I'll tell Blackstar myself."

Dawnpelt's only reply was a snarl. Ivypool knew that she was spoiling for a fight and didn't much care how she provoked one. *Does she think she can make two Clans go into battle just because she wants to?* Ivypool remembered Tigerheart's warning to Dovewing at the Gathering, but she found it hard to take Dawnpelt's threats seriously. *Tigerheart probably just wanted an excuse to talk to Dovewing.*

"Dawnpelt, stop fussing," Redwillow meowed, stepping forward. "The ThunderClan scent marks are fine."

Ivypool was reassured by the brown-and-ginger tom's brisk tone, but her belly churned a moment later when she caught Redwillow's eye and he gave her a nod.

He's on my side because we're Dark Forest Clanmates, Ivypool thought, wincing. *No! I'm loyal to my own Clan. And he should be loyal to his!*

"Come on, Hollyleaf," she urged. "Let's keep moving."

Hollyleaf nodded, leading the way along the border, past the ShadowClan patrol. Dawnpelt let out a loud yowl behind them, as if she'd won some kind of victory.

"Great StarClan!" Hollyleaf meowed when they were out of earshot. "Who made dirt in Dawnpelt's fresh-kill? Or has she got a furball stuck somewhere?"

"She's a pain in the tail," Ivypool agreed.

"And what's the deal with Redwillow?" Hollyleaf went on, glancing at Ivypool with narrowed eyes. "He seemed to know you better than I'd expect from a ShadowClan cat."

She has eyes like a hawk! Ivypool thought, startled. "It's nothing," she mumbled aloud. "We've talked once or twice at Gatherings, that's all."

Hollyleaf paused, fixing Ivypool with an intense look.

"Becoming too close to a cat from another Clan is the worst act of disloyalty," she mewed. "No cat is—"

"But I'm not!" Ivypool interrupted, horrified at where Hollyleaf's suspicions were heading.

Hollyleaf ignored her protest. "No cat is worth breaking the warrior code for in that way," she insisted. "It only leads to unhappiness." Without waiting for Ivypool's reply she strode on down the border, disapproval quivering in every hair on her pelt.

"I don't know what got into her," Ivypool meowed to Dovewing when the sisters met beside the fresh-kill pile later that day. "You don't think she suspects I'm in the Dark Forest with Redwillow, do you?"

Dovewing rolled her eyes. "Oh, please! It's hard when my only sister is such a mouse-brain. The Dark Forest is the last thing Hollyleaf would be worried about. Just think of who her parents are! She's half-Clan, remember?"

"Oh." Embarrassment flooded over Ivypool. "I hadn't thought of that. Well, she needn't be afraid that I'll take up with Redwillow, or any cat from another Clan."

And it looks as if Dovewing's sights are set on Bumblestripe now, she told herself with satisfaction. *That's much better than mangy Tigerheart!*

CHAPTER 23

Lionblaze pushed his way between the branches of the warriors' den and bounded across the clearing to join the cats clustered around Firestar. The full moon floated high in a clear sky, the warriors of StarClan glittering around it. Lionblaze's paws tingled with anticipation of the Gathering.

"I'm not going to mention Onestar's threats," Firestar was meowing as Lionblaze reached his side. "There's no point in drawing the other Clans' attention to what could just be a minor dispute." He twitched his whiskers at the murmurs of uncertainty that came from his Clanmates. "Besides," he went on, "we haven't seen Sol in ThunderClan territory for a half-moon. Onestar has no reason to attack us now."

Lionblaze agreed, though part of him wished that Onestar could be called to account for his outburst of hostility toward ThunderClan. *It's none of his business that we let Sol stay in our camp!*

Jayfeather and Cinderheart emerged from the medicine cat's den and padded over to the group of warriors.

"I want you to stay here," Jayfeather told the gray she-cat. "Lilykit has a fever, and I'd be happier if you kept an eye on her."

Cinderheart looked briefly disappointed, then dipped her head and padded off toward the nursery.

I bet Sorreltail's kit would be fine without a medicine cat hovering over her, Lionblaze thought as he joined his brother on the edge of the group. "You don't want to make awkward explanations about why Cinderheart has suddenly changed to being a medicine cat," he murmured in Jayfeather's ear.

Jayfeather's tail lashed irritably. "She's not the first cat to switch roles!" he growled.

"No, but she's the first cat to be another cat first. Kind of . . ." Lionblaze responded.

Jayfeather opened his jaws to reply, but in the same heartbeat Firestar raised his tail and beckoned. He headed out through the thorn tunnel with the rest of the cats streaming behind him.

As they made their way down to the lakeshore, Lionblaze found himself walking beside Graystripe and Millie. "What did you think of the session this morning?" he asked. All three of them had gone with Birchfall and Hazeltail for underground battle training with Hollyleaf. "I have to admit that I don't like fighting in the dark. I'd rather see my enemy and know where I can strike without risking my paws on hard stone."

Millie twitched her shoulders. "I wasn't comfortable in the tunnels at all," she confessed. "I couldn't stop thinking about the amount of rock above my head!"

"But you were brilliant," Graystripe meowed, resting his tail on his mate's shoulder. "I think we all felt the same. Fighting underground isn't natural, but neither is Sol. What kind of cat would keep trying to befriend a Clan, only to betray them?" The gray warrior ducked under a hawthorn bough, and went on, "Sol did it with Blackstar and ShadowClan, and now he's turning WindClan against ThunderClan. If he has a reason, I'd like to know what it is."

Whitewing caught up in time to hear the gray warrior's last few words. "Sol knew that the sun was going to vanish," she pointed out, suppressing a shiver. "That suggests he has more power than any of us."

Lionblaze snorted. *No cat has the power to challenge me when it comes to a battle!* His paws itched to take on Sol in single combat. *He made me help him to escape from ThunderClan all those moons ago.* The memory surged up inside Lionblaze, making him feel as if flames were scorching his pelt. *I'd like to punish him for that. And for bringing more trouble to the Clans now, when we should be thinking about the Dark Forest.*

A sudden thought struck Lionblaze, briefly freezing his paws to the ground. *Was Sol sent by the Dark Forest cats to stir up trouble? Is this the beginning of the end?*

Forcing himself to move on, he spotted Jayfeather a couple of tail-lengths away, slipping unerringly through the undergrowth. "I just had a horrible idea," Lionblaze hissed. "Do you think Sol is helping the Dark Forest?"

Jayfeather paused, then shrugged. "I don't know. But I wouldn't be surprised."

* * *

In the clearing around the Great Oak, the air was filled with tension, as if a greenleaf storm was about to break. Lionblaze noticed that the medicine cats especially seemed hostile, sitting loosely in a group underneath a pine tree, but not acknowledging one another. *Every Clan is going it alone,* he thought, twitching his whiskers apprehensively. *It's really bad when even the medicine cats are enemies.*

Only Mothwing was speaking to her fellow medicine cats, but they barely replied. Lionblaze saw her flex her claws in exasperation and finally give up, sitting down beside her apprentice, Willowshine.

The rest of the cats settled down within their own Clans, without any of the mingling and gossiping that used to be part of a Gathering. Lionblaze watched carefully for any signs that cats knew one another in the Dark Forest. Once alerted, he spotted plenty of indications: Redwillow exchanging a glance with Breezepelt; Icewing of RiverClan nodding to Ivypool; the twitch of a tail as Tigerheart's gaze met Hollowflight's.

They know each other, Lionblaze thought, chilled. *Better than any warrior should know a cat from another Clan.* Then he gave his pelt a shake. *Don't get carried away,* he told himself. *Not every cat is being trained by unseen enemies.*

He was distracted from thoughts of the Dark Forest when he noticed Crowfeather among the WindClan cats. The gray-black warrior had just spotted Hollyleaf, and he was staring as if his eyes were about to leap out of his head. Beside him, his mate, Nightcloud, followed his gaze and drew back her lips in a snarl.

Lionblaze realized that Hollyleaf had seen them, but she turned her back on them, staying close to her own Clanmates. Surprised murmurs spread around the clearing as more cats realized that she was there. One or two younger cats sprang to their paws to get a better view of her.

"This feels kind of weird," Hollyleaf muttered, picking her way over to sit beside Lionblaze.

Lionblaze touched her ear with his nose. "You must have known it wouldn't be easy."

"It's what kept me away for so long," Hollyleaf admitted. "I can't bear the whispers, the gossip . . ."

The compassion Lionblaze felt faded into a flash of annoyance. *Jayfeather and I have had to put up with whispers and gossip for a very long time.* But he realized that Hollyleaf felt genuinely uncomfortable, and pushed aside his resentment. Wrapping his tail around her shoulders, he stared straight ahead, ignoring the whispers.

The atmosphere seemed to be growing more and more hostile. Lionblaze was relieved when Mistystar rose to her paws on her branch of the Great Oak and announced that the Gathering would begin.

"We have had a few problems with Twolegs," she reported. "As always in greenleaf, they come to fish in the lake and the streams around our camp. But we have managed to stay out of their way, and they didn't catch enough fish to threaten our stocks of fresh-kill."

"Huh!" Mistystar's deputy, Reedwhisker, exclaimed. "Two-legs couldn't catch a fish if it leaped out of the water and begged them."

Mistystar gave her deputy an amused glance from glimmering blue eyes, and sat down again.

Firestar rose in his turn and advanced along his branch, carefully avoiding a cluster of oak leaves. "I have good news to report from ThunderClan," he began, gazing down into the clearing. "Our warrior Hollyleaf has returned, after we believed she was dead for so many moons."

Murmurs and gasps rose from the other Clans. "Where has she been?" some cat called out loudly. Beside him, Lionblaze felt Hollyleaf grow tense.

Firestar ignored the question. "We welcome her back," he continued, turning his warm green gaze onto Hollyleaf. "We are glad to have her in ThunderClan once again, and I look forward to patrolling alongside her for many future moons."

Lionblaze was relieved that Firestar had kept to his earlier intention of saying nothing about Sol or WindClan. But now he braced himself for cats from the other Clans to mention Ashfur and the time that Hollyleaf had disappeared, just after she revealed the terrible truth about Leafpool and Crowfeather at a Gathering.

But no cat asked the crucial questions, only murmured comments as they reacted to Firestar's announcement.

"I'm surprised she showed her face after what she told us!"

"I bet Crowfeather isn't pleased to see her."

Nightcloud rose and lashed her tail, raking Hollyleaf with

an icy gaze. "Does she think she's welcome?" she snarled.

Firestar still refused to react to any of the comments; he dipped his head to Hollyleaf and retreated to sit down again farther back on his branch. Immediately Onestar took his place.

"This is surprising news, Firestar," he mewed smoothly. "But I'm sure that any Clan leader would welcome back a trained and loyal warrior."

Is he suggesting that Hollyleaf isn't loyal? Lionblaze wondered, beginning to bristle.

"My patrols are as vigilant as ever," Onestar continued. "We will do anything to defend our territory from rogues and strays."

Lionblaze's belly churned. *Now he's insulting all of us! He's suggesting that ThunderClan is a bunch of rogues and strays!* Glancing up at Firestar, half-hidden by the leaves of the Great Oak, Lionblaze could see that his Clan leader was struggling to keep his fur flat and his mouth closed.

With a triumphant glance at Firestar, Onestar sat down again. When Blackstar stood up, Lionblaze could see that he looked puzzled by the hostility between ThunderClan and WindClan, but after a moment's hesitation he gave a tiny shrug and began to speak.

"Like RiverClan, we have had problems with Twolegs by the lake," he began. "The warm weather brings them out like earthworms after rain. But they haven't come into the forest far enough to bother us close to our camp."

When he had finished he was about to sit down again, only

to check as a voice rose up from among the cats in the clearing. "Blackstar, may I speak?"

Lionblaze glanced across to where the ShadowClan cats were sitting, and saw that Dawnpelt had risen to her paws, her cream-colored fur luminous in the moonlight. Blackstar blinked in surprise, then dipped his head. Instantly Dawnpelt leaped up onto a tree stump. Her neck fur was bristling and her tail fluffed up to twice its size.

"There is a murderer among us!" she yowled.

Silence crashed down on the clearing. Lionblaze tensed, and wrapped his tail more firmly around his sister's shoulders. *Oh, Great StarClan! How could she have found out about Hollyleaf?*

But Dawnpelt raised a paw and pointed toward the pine tree where the medicine cats were sitting. "Jayfeather killed Flametail!"

The cats in the clearing exploded into yowls and screeches of horror. At first Lionblaze couldn't make sense of what any of them were saying. Then Brambleclaw rose to his paws on the root of the Great Oak and made his voice heard above the clamor.

"We all know about Flametail's death, and we grieve for him, too. But how was Jayfeather involved?"

"And why speak up now?" Graystripe added.

Dawnpelt turned her gaze onto the ThunderClan cats; her eyes were filled with hatred. "Jayfeather was there when Flametail drowned," she hissed. "We all saw him struggling in the water beside him. Why do we believe his story that he was trying to save Flametail?"

"Why not believe him?" Brambleclaw challenged her.

"Since when has Jayfeather shown compassion for cats in other Clans?" Dawnpelt snarled. "I believe that he deliberately drowned Flametail in front of all of us!"

Firestar sprang to his paws, thrusting his way out of the leaves. "That's ridiculous! It goes against the warrior code and the medicine cat code. Jayfeather would never murder Flametail!"

Lionblaze, too, had risen to his paws, his fur bristling. He wanted nothing more than to rake his claws across Dawnpelt's accusing face. Feeling a nudge from Hollyleaf, he glanced down at her.

"Sit down," she murmured. "Don't give Dawnpelt the satisfaction of provoking a fight."

Lionblaze flexed his claws, then realized the sense of what his littermate was saying, and forced himself to sit down. *This is a Gathering,* he reminded himself. *ShadowClan would be delighted if ThunderClan broke the truce.*

"I met Dawnpelt on border patrol," Hollyleaf continued quietly. "She was doing her best to pick a fight then, too."

"What's her quarrel with ThunderClan?" Lionblaze asked, bewildered.

Hollyleaf gave him a long look. "Her brother drowned and Jayfeather was there," she mewed. "That's enough."

The clearing had descended into turmoil again, with no cat able to make themselves heard. Lionblaze spotted Dovewing and Ivypool weaving their way among their Clanmates until they reached his side.

"I knew Dawnpelt was planning something," Ivypool whispered. "But I didn't know this was it."

Lionblaze wondered if Ivypool had heard something in the Dark Forest, perhaps from Dawnpelt herself. But he didn't want to ask where other cats might overhear.

"It's ridiculous!" Dovewing exclaimed. "I . . . I heard Flame-tail drown. I know Jayfeather was trying to save him."

But there's no way we can tell that to Dawnpelt and get her to believe it, Lionblaze thought. Gazing across the clearing at the medicine cats, he saw that his brother had risen to his paws. He looked icy calm, though Lionblaze could guess at the emotions that must be surging through him. Jayfeather waited, not even try-ing to speak, until the noise in the clearing died down.

"Dawnpelt, I was there when your brother died," he began. There was an edge to his voice, telling Lionblaze of his resent-ment that he had to defend himself in public over such an absurd accusation. "But I was trying to save him. That I failed is a tragedy for all of us." His voice shook on the last few words and he paused until he could go on steadily. "I had no reason to want him dead. And the water would have killed him on its own; he didn't need me as well."

Muttering rose from the ShadowClan cats around Dawn-pelt. "Are you sure you weren't just helping the water kill him?" Ratscar called out.

"The medicine cats have been very separate recently," Rowanclaw, the ShadowClan deputy, added more thought-fully. "Is their code changing? Are they even still allied across Clan borders?" He stared straight at Jayfeather. "Perhaps

Flametail knew too much about you?"

Lionblaze stiffened. *Do any other cats know about the prophecy? I never thought of that!*

"Enough!" Firestar ordered from his place in the Great Oak. "This accusation is groundless! Jayfeather could have drowned in that water just as easily as Flametail. He risked his own life by going to help him. Surely no cat takes this accusation seriously?" Firestar gazed around at Mistystar, Blackstar, and Onestar. All three Clan leaders were looking uncomfortable.

"I find it hard to believe that any cat would do something like this," Mistystar mewed.

Onestar nodded. "I'm sure Jayfeather could have found an easier way to eliminate an enemy."

Blackstar said nothing at all.

That's hardly the best defense they could come up with! Lionblaze thought angrily. But when he looked back at Dawnpelt, he saw that she had begun to look small and uncomfortable, as if the force of her accusation was ebbing like floodwaters after the rain is over.

While Firestar still waited, as if he were hoping that Blackstar would speak, Tigerheart rose to his paws from the clearing below.

"I believe what my sister says," he announced. "Jayfeather murdered our littermate, and he must be punished."

Beside Lionblaze, Dovewing drew in her breath in a gasp of horror.

"I will punish no cat for a crime that cannot be proved,"

Firestar answered coldly.

"It's not a case of not being proved," Dovewing hissed. "Jayfeather didn't do it!"

"But it's hard to ignore the accusation," Onestar meowed in response to Firestar. To do the WindClan leader justice, Lionblaze thought, he sounded reluctant, as if his respect for Jayfeather as a medicine cat outweighed his hostility toward ThunderClan. "Firestar, perhaps you should suspend Jayfeather from medicine cat duties until he has proven his innocence."

Mistystar dipped her head in agreement. "That would be sensible. With StarClan's help, it might not take long."

Lionblaze noticed that the other medicine cats had suddenly started to talk among themselves, their heads close together as quick meows passed from one to another. Then Littlecloud, the ShadowClan medicine cat, rose to his paws.

"We agree to this, too," he announced, his voice regretful as he looked at Jayfeather. "Without determining the truth, this accusation could poison the Clans for seasons, like an infected wound."

"Then how do you propose finding out what happened?" Brambleclaw challenged him. "It's impossible, unless Flametail returns to tell us himself. Have any of you seen him in dreams?"

The medicine cats conferred together quickly, then Littlecloud shook his head.

"I've seen Flametail," Ivypool confessed, leaning closer to Dovewing to murmur into her ear. Lionblaze could just pick up her quiet words. "But he's in StarClan, not the Dark Forest."

"Did you ask him if Jayfeather killed him?" Dovewing whispered back.

"No!" Ivypool's eyes stretched wide in astonishment. "Why would I ask him a thing like that?"

All the other medicine cats turned toward Jayfeather; Lionblaze could see that his brother was trying not to flinch. Though Jayfeather couldn't see them, he would be able to feel the force of their attention, all focused on him.

"Surrendering your duties is the only honorable thing to do," Littlecloud meowed. He sounded helpless; Dovewing guessed that he was torn between his dismay at the accusation and the horror he felt that it might be true.

Jayfeather's head jerked up. "But we walk alone now, don't we?" His voice was clear and steady. "I know you've all had visits from your ancestors, telling you that each Clan must look to its own future. You have no right to tell me what to do! I shall remain as ThunderClan's medicine cat!"

There were gasps from the clearing as Jayfeather defied his fellow medicine cats. Dawnpelt looked furious. Her jaws were open to protest when lightning crackled down from the sky, splitting the night. Its pale light outlined the pine trees and the bushes that surrounded the clearing, and rimmed the leaves of the great oak with a line of silver.

Lionblaze shuddered as the lightning was followed by a massive crash of thunder, so loud that it sounded as if the ground beneath his pads were cracking apart. A sharp wind rose, thrashing through the leaves and flattening the cats' fur to their sides. Clouds blotted out the moon.

In the darkness one of the cats wailed, "StarClan is angry!"

Then rain poured out of the sky, an icy curtain sweeping across the clearing. Lionblaze's fur was soaked within the first heartbeats. The cats let out wails of shock and terror as they began to flee for cover.

From the Great Oak Lionblaze heard Firestar's voice ring out. "Home, quickly!"

The Gathering broke up in chaos as cats fled through the bushes, heading for the tree-bridge. Lionblaze sprang across the clearing, making for the spot where he had last seen his brother.

"Jayfeather!" he yowled. "Over here!"

To his relief lightning flashed out again; by its light he spotted Jayfeather struggling toward him around a knot of terrified WindClan cats. He looked skinnier than ever, his tabby fur plastered to his body.

"Let's get out of here," Lionblaze muttered, thrusting through the crowd of cats to his brother's side.

As they turned toward the bushes Dawnpelt bounded past them, halting for a heartbeat to hiss at Jayfeather. "This is not over!"

Trying to force a way out of the clearing, Lionblaze realized that the cats had divided along battle lines as suddenly as the lightning had struck. Clan snarled at Clan, their claws extended and their lips drawn back to reveal sharp teeth. Their leaders yowled for control, but between fear and anger their warriors ignored them.

Lionblaze halted for a heartbeat to look up at the veiled moon. *Great StarClan! The Clans are turning on one another, just when we need to stand side by side against a greater enemy than anything we have ever faced before!*

CHAPTER 24

Thunder crashed overhead as Jayfeather raced back along the shore. His mind was whirling so much that he kept stumbling, blinder than usual. Somewhere in the chaos he had lost Lionblaze, and the pelting rain smothered his senses. He wasn't even sure where he was.

Through his confusion he realized that another cat was bounding at his side, matching him stride for stride. Squirrelflight's voice spoke in his ear. "Here, lean on me. Let me guide you."

Jayfeather's instinct was to hiss at her to leave him alone. But her pressure on his side was too comforting, supporting him through the tumult of his thoughts.

How could Dawnpelt think I killed Flametail? I nearly drowned myself—I would have died if it hadn't been for Rock, forcing me to let Flametail sink into the depths. He shuddered, and almost tripped over a boulder.

"Steady," Squirrelflight warned. "Come farther this way." After a moment she murmured into his ear, "Don't worry, no cat believes Dawnpelt. She's been driven mad by grief, that's all."

Jayfeather wasn't convinced. *Then why did they want me to give up being a medicine cat? The Clans are too eager to believe the worst of one another just now.*

Back in the stone hollow, Jayfeather headed for his den. Though the torrential rain had eased off, his pelt was drenched and he was utterly miserable, each paw step a massive effort. But before he reached the screen of brambles, he heard Firestar splashing up to him through the puddles that had formed on the floor of the hollow.

"Get some rest," his Clan leader ordered. "We'll discuss this in the morning. But don't doubt the loyalty of any of your Clanmates. We'll defend you whatever happens."

Firestar's voice was bone-weary, and Jayfeather wondered if he was tired of his cats being accused of murder. He gave Firestar a brief nod and brushed past the brambles into his den.

"Hi," Briarlight greeted him, raising herself in her nest. "How was the Gathering? Did any cat mention Sol? What did the other Clans think about Hollyleaf coming back?"

"Disastrous, no, and not impressed," Jayfeather listed, making for his nest and collapsing into it.

"Okay." Briarlight sounded puzzled rather than offended. Jayfeather heard her dragging herself across to him, and tensed at the feeling of her tongue licking his sodden fur. "It's obvious that something's wrong. Let me look after you for once," she mewed.

Jayfeather was too exhausted to protest; he was already

sliding into sleep. He opened his eyes to find himself in a sunny clearing, the air warm and filled with delicious prey-scent. A ruffled gray she-cat was sitting on a fallen tree trunk, waiting for him.

"Oh, no!" Jayfeather groaned. "Not you again!"

"Show a bit of respect," Yellowfang snapped, jumping down from the tree trunk and padding across to him. "It's all happening now," she continued. "But don't worry. No cat in StarClan thinks you murdered Flametail."

Oh, great! Jayfeather thought. *I'm so glad. It's a pity that doesn't help me much, isn't it?* He wondered if any of the StarClan warriors had seen Rock with him in the lake when Flametail died, but before he could ask, Yellowfang turned on him with a lash of her tail.

"What were you thinking, letting Cinderheart give up her warrior duties to become a second medicine cat? That's not what StarClan wanted!"

"Hey, hang on!" Jayfeather leaped out of range of her claws. "It was *you* who told me to walk in Cinderheart's dreams and show her that she used to be Cinderpelt. You said Thunder-Clan needed a second medicine cat. Don't start blaming me now because I did what you wanted."

"Yes . . . well . . ." Jayfeather's eyes stretched wide in amazement as he realized that Yellowfang was embarrassed. "I . . . er . . . might have got that wrong," she admitted, not meeting his gaze. "I was thinking too much about ThunderClan's needs. Cinderheart's destiny is to be a warrior."

Some StarClan cats must have told her off about this, Jayfeather realized, suppressing a purr of laughter. *Wow, I wish I'd been a bird on a branch when that conversation was going on!*

"Cinderheart is confused," he meowed. "She doesn't know who she is."

"Then you must show her that she is a warrior, nothing else," Yellowfang told him.

"It might be useful to have a second medicine cat when the final battle comes," Jayfeather mused. "But I guess Cinderheart can still use her knowledge of herbs and medicine, even if she is a warrior. Like Leafpool does."

Yellowfang let out a hiss, her embarrassment completely gone. "What did I tell you about Leafpool? She is not allowed to use her medicine cat skills anymore, and neither can Cinderheart, if she chooses to be a warrior."

Jayfeather's irritation spilled over. "If you don't mind my saying so," he snapped, "that's just a load of badger droppings. Leafpool helped Cherrypaw and Mousewhisker when they accidentally ate hemlock, and nothing bad happened because of it. Okay, no cat expects StarClan to send her messages for the Clan in her dreams anymore, but why should she forget what she knows? There's nothing *secret* about using marigold to fight infection or juniper berries for bellyache! Most of the cats in the Clan know that."

Yellowfang's tangled gray fur had begun to bristle. "Who are you to tell StarClan what a medicine cat may or may not do?"

"I am a cat who cares for his Clan!" Jayfeather hissed back. "I'm not going to tell Cinderheart or Leafpool to ignore what they know when they might be able to save lives."

Yellowfang's shoulders sagged suddenly; she looked weary and discouraged. "Perhaps StarClan underestimated the strength of Cinderpelt's spirit to survive," she admitted, "and carry on her loyalty to her medicine cat duties. Cinderheart will have to make her own choice, medicine cat or warrior. She has the right to choose her destiny."

"What, and I don't?" Jayfeather muttered.

"Because of the prophecy?" Yellowfang retorted, her momentary weakness vanishing. "That's different. It has nothing to do with StarClan. It was decided long ago, by cats who have been forgotten more moons back than you can possibly imagine. We have waited a long time for this moment, Jayfeather. And now the moment has nearly come."

Jayfeather still felt exhausted when he woke, depressed by his memories of the Gathering: the accusation, the turmoil, and the storm. He let out a long sigh, trying to summon up the energy to climb out of his nest.

"Here." Briarlight dropped a mouse in front of his nose. "Eat!" she prompted when Jayfeather did no more than sniff it.

He thought of protesting that he wasn't hungry, but he knew that Briarlight would nag him until he had finished every scrap of the fresh-kill. "Thanks," he mumbled, taking a bite. His jaws watered at the taste of the juices, and he realized how hungry he was.

"I heard what happened at the Gathering," Briarlight went on. "I'm really sorry. Surely no cat will believe what Dawnpelt said?"

"I don't know," Jayfeather replied between mouthfuls. "Strange things are happening in all the Clans, so why shouldn't one medicine cat murder another?"

"Because that would never happen," Briarlight insisted. "Especially not you."

Jayfeather was touched by her loyalty. "Go and visit the nursery," he told her, running his tongue over his whiskers to capture the last scraps of mouse. "See how Sorreltail's kits are doing."

"Okay." Jayfeather could tell Briarlight was pleased to be given the task. "But what about Cinderheart?" She sounded baffled and uncertain.

"I need to talk to her today," Jayfeather meowed. "You go to the nursery."

As soon as Jayfeather headed out of his den, he located Cinderheart padding toward him. Her paw steps were weary, dragging on the ground. Behind her, the first patrols were leaving the clearing. Hollyleaf was leading another underground training group.

"We've had to wait so long to go into the tunnels!" Molepaw meowed, bubbling over with excitement. "I don't care how dark and scary the others say it is. I'm not scared."

"Neither am I." Cherrypaw was bouncing on her paws. "I'm

going to be the best underground fighter in ThunderClan."

"You are not! I am!" her brother insisted, and the two apprentices rolled over in a scuffle.

"That's enough," Foxleap growled. "Or Hollyleaf won't take you down there at all."

Molepaw and Cherrypaw instantly sprang to their paws; Jayfeather could picture them with head and tail erect as they followed Hollyleaf and their mentors out of the camp.

"Don't tell me I should be going out with the patrols," Cinderheart sighed as Jayfeather padded up to her.

How many cats have been telling you that you shouldn't be a medicine cat? Jayfeather wondered, picking up her defensiveness, but he didn't ask the question aloud. Instead, he mewed, "I'm not going to tell you what to do. Come for a walk with me."

Branches rustled gently over their heads as Jayfeather and Cinderheart headed for the lake. As the end of greenleaf approached, the leaves smelled tired, sap-heavy, and dusty. Some of Jayfeather's weariness faded as he sat beside the lake, enjoying the fresh breeze that blew off the water.

"Try to think of it this way," he began. "You should feel very lucky. StarClan has given you the chance to choose your own destiny: to be a warrior, a mate, a mother—all the things that you were denied as Cinderpelt."

"But is it a real choice?" Cinderheart asked miserably. "What about my duty to my Clan?"

"There are many ways to fulfill your duty," Jayfeather murmured.

Cinderheart turned to him; he could feel the force of her

gaze. "It's true, I'm lucky to be here at all!" she burst out. "I know what a debt I owe to my ancestors. But I'm so confused. . . . I don't know what I'm supposed to do."

"What do you want?" Jayfeather asked quietly.

He felt a small start of surprise from Cinderheart, as if no cat had ever asked her that before.

"I wanted Lionblaze," she whispered. "But I can't have him."

"Oh? Really?" *Great StarClan, mouse-brain, he's been padding after you for moons!* "Why not?"

"Because of his destiny," Cinderheart replied.

Jayfeather gave an awkward wriggle; he wasn't comfortable discussing another cat's relationship problems. But he remembered Half Moon, and felt again the piercing pain he had suffered when he realized that he couldn't stay with her in her long-ago Tribe.

"You have a destiny, too," he mewed gently. "But that isn't the whole of who you are. You can still shape your own life."

Cinderheart was silent for a long time; Jayfeather could sense a tiny seed of hope stirring inside her.

"You have a chance to be happy," he prompted, "and to make Lionblaze happy, too. Don't throw that away because you spent too long trying to figure out the right thing to do."

"Thank you, Jayfeather," Cinderheart responded with a long sigh.

Together they sat on the bank overlooking the lake; Jayfeather could hear the soft lapping of the water on the pebbly shore. For a few moments he and Cinderheart seemed to be wrapped in a cocoon of peace.

It can't last, Jayfeather thought. *Not in these turbulent times. But I'm glad of it now, that's for sure.*

CHAPTER 25

❧

Gray light was seeping into the apprentices' den when Dovewing opened her eyes. Her fur felt ruffled; cold claws probed into her nest, as if she were lying in a draft. In the days since the Gathering the weather had turned colder, and she knew leaf-fall was not far away.

Dovewing wriggled deeper into the moss, trying to escape from the stream of chilly air. Then she realized that something else had woken her. Her senses were always turned toward WindClan, and as she concentrated she picked up a familiar voice.

"Follow me," Sol was meowing. "Those lazy ThunderClan mange-pelts will still be snoring in their dens."

The murmuring voices of many cats surrounded him, growling as they braced themselves for battle.

Scrambling out of her den, Dovewing raced across the clearing and up the tumbled rocks. "Firestar!" she gasped, bursting into her leader's den. "WindClan is heading for the tunnels. The attack is happening now!"

Firestar was curled up on his bedding at the back of the den. As Dovewing spoke, he raised his head, instantly alert, and slipped out past her onto the Highledge.

"Wake up!" he yowled. "Every cat, into the clearing! Wind-Clan is attacking!"

Once he had raised the alarm, he ran down the rockfall into the clearing. Dovewing paused for a moment on the Highledge before she followed him. The moon had set, but a few faint warriors of StarClan still lingered overhead. The trees above the hollow were outlined against a pale sky. Dovewing took in a deep breath of cold dawn air and bounded after her leader.

Warriors were beginning to emerge from their den, vague and clumsy from sleep. Daisy appeared at the entrance to the nursery, then vanished straight back inside. Jayfeather poked his head out from behind the bramble screen of the medicine cat's den, his ears pricked to hear what was going on.

Dashing back to her own den, Dovewing met Ivypool as she staggered out into the open. Her fur was ragged and there was a pained look in her eyes.

"Are you okay?" Dovewing asked. "Did something happen in the Dark Forest?"

"It's nothing to worry about," Ivypool replied, shaking her head to clear it. "I'm a warrior there now. I have to train the others." Her eyes were haunted and her gaze kept flicking from side to side as if she thought some cat was on her tail. "I'll be fine," she insisted. "I can still fight."

Hollyleaf followed her out of the den, looking brisk and ready for action. She ran into the middle of the clearing to join Firestar and Brambleclaw.

"We will meet the WindClan cats in the tunnels," Firestar

announced as his Clan gathered around him. "We won't let them set a single paw in ThunderClan territory. As far as I know," he added, with a glance at Dovewing, "WindClan hasn't trained to fight in the tunnels." Dovewing gave him a quick nod. "ThunderClan will have the advantage!"

A yowl of enthusiasm greeted the Clan leader's words. Every cat was awake now, ready to defend their Clan. Dovewing spotted Brightheart and Foxleap running through the new battle moves, while the two apprentices bounced up and down with excitement.

Dovewing was still listening to the approaching WindClan warriors as they crossed the moorland and approached the border with ThunderClan. Suddenly the noise of their voices and paw steps was cut off and their images faded to nothing. Dovewing's belly churned; she knew what that meant.

"We must hurry!" she meowed to Firestar.

Several other cats looked at her in surprise, not understanding the reason for her eagerness. *Of course they don't know that I can sense WindClan as far away as their own territory.*

Hollyleaf came striding over to her. "Lionblaze tells me that you can hear things," she mewed quietly. "Far away, I mean."

Dovewing nodded.

"Because of the prophecy about the Three?" Hollyleaf's voice was strained.

Feeling awkward, Dovewing replied, "Yes." She could guess how difficult it must be for Hollyleaf not to have a part in the prophecy with her littermates. *It can't be easy for her to talk to me about it.*

Hollyleaf was silent for several heartbeats, then gave her ears a decisive twitch. "Well, let's make the most of it. What are the WindClan cats doing now?"

"They've entered the tunnels," Dovewing told her. "It's really hard to hear them underground."

"All the same tunnel?" Hollyleaf prompted.

Dovewing stretched her senses to their limits and found that she could still pick up faint traces of the advancing enemy. "Yes, I think they're all together," she muttered, concentrating with every hair on her pelt. "Now they're entering the cavern with the river running across it . . . now they're entering another tunnel . . ."

"I think I can work out where they are," Hollyleaf hissed. "And where they're likely to head . . ." She turned to Firestar, Brambleclaw, and Lionblaze, who had come over to listen. "We'll split into three," she went on. "One patrol will enter the tunnel above the camp, a second will take the tunnel near the old Twoleg nest, and a third the one by the lake. Our aim is to push the WindClan cats back into the cavern with the river, where there'll be more room to fight."

Brambleclaw gave her an approving nod. He leaped up onto a boulder and began dividing the warriors up into patrols. "I'll lead one," he announced, gesturing with his tail, "Hollyleaf another, and Brackenfur, you take the third. Hollyleaf tells me you're the best at underground fighting."

Looking pleased and a bit embarrassed, Brackenfur moved to stand with his patrol.

"But we're not in a patrol!" Cherrypaw objected.

"We want to fight WindClan," Molepaw agreed.

"Wrong, Cherrypaw—you're in *my* patrol," Firestar told her. "We'll stay here in the hollow to defend the elders and the nursery if WindClan manages to break through."

The two apprentices exchanged a glance; Dovewing could see they weren't sure whether to be disappointed not to be fighting underground, or pleased to be chosen for a patrol by their Clan leader.

"We can fight, too, if we have to," Daisy meowed, padding up with Ferncloud. "We'll guard Sorreltail and the kits."

"And me," Purdy added, lumbering across from the elders' den. "Just because I'm old, don't mean I can't fight. I've clawed more cats than you young 'uns have eaten mice. There was a time—"

"Thanks, all of you," Firestar meowed, cutting off Purdy before he could embark on one of his interminable stories.

As the three tunnel patrols set off for the camp entrance, Cinderheart appeared from the medicine cat's den. "I will fight, too," she announced, padding over to join Hollyleaf.

Oh, really? Dovewing thought, pricking her ears with interest.

A few cats muttered something in response to Cinderheart's announcement, but there was no time for questions. Hollyleaf broke into a run, taking the lead as she raced through the thorn tunnel and out into the forest.

Dovewing and Ivypool were in Hollyleaf's patrol, along with Cinderheart, Sandstorm, Mousewhisker, and Berrynose. Hollyleaf led them in a swift scramble up the path to the top of the hollow and up to the tunnel entrance.

"Follow me in," she murmured to Dovewing. "I need you to tell me what WindClan is doing. Sandstorm," she added, raising her voice, "bring up the rear. Let me know if there's any trouble behind."

"Got it," Sandstorm responded, her pale green eyes gleaming in the strengthening dawn light.

Dovewing took a deep breath and followed Hollyleaf into the tunnel. Instantly the sound of WindClan burst into her ears. "They're running so fast!" she gasped.

"Where?" Hollyleaf's voice was terse.

"Not here, not yet," Dovewing whispered as she and Hollyleaf raced down the tunnel at the head of the patrol. "They've come up against one of the entrances Dustpelt and Brackenfur blocked off . . . now they're turning around . . . they're coming this way!"

As well as the WindClan cats, Dovewing could hear the other ThunderClan patrols as they headed down their tunnels. The whole hill was alive with scurrying creatures, like an ants' nest. The noises were growing so loud that Dovewing could hardly distinguish one patrol from another, or work out exactly where they were.

Then as they rounded a corner, the scent of WindClan suddenly grew stronger. Dovewing barely had time to gasp, "They're here!" before they collided head-on with the WindClan warriors.

WindClan had no warning at all. As they charged into the ThunderClan cats, they let out yowls of shock. For a few moments they were helpless, shoving at one another in the dark, not knowing whether to advance or retreat.

Hollyleaf and Dovewing lashed out, raking at their unseen attackers with claws extended. At first it was easy to push the WindClan cats farther down the tunnel, but after a moment they recovered and started to push back. Dovewing screeched as unseen claws slashed at her shoulder. Forcing her way forward, she felt chest fur against her muzzle, and stretched up to sink her teeth into the cat's throat. Her opponent reared back; there was a dull thump and a shriek, and Dovewing realized her attacker had banged their head on the tunnel roof.

"You should have trained!" she hissed.

"Get back!" Hollyleaf ordered. "Let fresh cats come through."

Remembering the battle plan Hollyleaf had worked out earlier, Dovewing flattened herself against the tunnel wall to let Cinderheart and Berrynose slip forward. She had a few moments' respite, gasping for breath at the back of the patrol, while her Clanmates took on the WindClan warriors. Mouse-whisker, Ivypool, and Sandstorm moved smoothly up to take their places, until the attackers were forced backward, toward the cavern with the river.

At last light began to filter into the tunnel from up ahead and Dovewing managed to make out the cats in the Wind-Clan patrol. Breezepelt was leading them, with Whiskernose, Weaselfur, and Harespring. Heathertail and Furzepelt brought up the rear.

The WindClan cats stumbled backward into the cavern

and the ThunderClan warriors sprang out of the tunnel after them. Glancing around swiftly, Dovewing saw that they were the first to arrive; extending her senses she picked up the sounds of fighting in the other tunnels.

The WindClan cats bunched together, panting and glaring at their rivals. Their fur was ragged and several of them showed the marks of ThunderClan claws. Dovewing guessed they had expected to emerge into ThunderClan territory and launch their attack on an unsuspecting camp.

Then they had a nasty surprise, she thought with satisfaction.

Hollyleaf pushed her way to the front of her patrol and faced the WindClan warriors. "End this now," she meowed. "You cannot win."

"Mange-pelts!" Breezepelt snarled. "You tormented Sol!"

"We did no such thing!" Dovewing hissed. "*We* invited Sol into our camp. It was *your* leader who wanted him chased off."

"And Jayfeather murdered Flametail!" Heathertail added, stepping forward to stand beside Breezepelt. Her eyes were blazing with hatred. "And you've been crossing our boundaries and stealing our prey!"

"That's right!" Whiskernose put in. "You always think you're better than us, just because we once needed your help before the Clans came to the lake."

"What do you know about that?" Sandstorm challenged the young warrior. "You weren't even kitted then!"

Dovewing was shocked at the strength of hostility directed at them from even the youngest cats. *It's so unfair!* she seethed. *We can't even defend ourselves, because they won't listen!*

Suddenly Breezepelt let out a bloodcurdling yowl and hurled himself straight at her. Taken by surprise, Dovewing was swept off her paws and hit the ground with a thump. But before Breezepelt could pin her down, she rolled to one side and sprang to her paws again in time to catch him a sharp blow on his shoulder.

"You'll have to be faster than that!" she taunted him.

With a snarl of defiance, Breezepelt launched himself at her, trying to force her back against the cavern wall. Remembering her training, Dovewing backed away, letting him think he was winning, then pushed herself off the wall and leaped over his head. The look of surprise on the WindClan cat's face made her fur feel hot with satisfaction.

The other cats were battling it out alongside her now, and as Dovewing landed, Cinderheart and Heathertail knocked into her as they rolled past in a screeching bundle of fur. Dovewing lost her balance and as her paws scrabbled on the cavern floor, Breezepelt was on top of her.

"Think you're clever?" he growled, his teeth gleaming close to her throat. "But you're not clever enough."

Dovewing battered at him with her hindpaws, but she couldn't dislodge him. She could feel his claws digging into her shoulders and blood starting to flow.

I can't die like this! she thought despairingly. *Not under Breezepelt's claws!*

Suddenly Breezepelt's weight vanished. Dovewing scrambled up to see that Ivypool had sunk her teeth in his scruff and was shaking his head from side to side. After a moment she released him, and while he was still groggy, she hooked his paws out from under him and dealt him a couple of hard blows on the soft part of his belly. Breezepelt rolled away from her, struggled to his paws, and fled.

"Thanks!" Dovewing gasped. "Ivypool, you fight really well!"

"You're welcome," Ivypool mewed, before spinning around and flinging herself back into the battle.

Dovewing realized that the sounds of fighting she had heard in the tunnel were all around her now. She didn't need her special senses, as the other patrols were pouring into the cavern, filling it with fierce caterwauls and shrieks of pain. Everywhere Dovewing looked, she saw a mass of wailing, thrashing cats.

"No sign of Onestar," Ivypool panted, reappearing beside Dovewing for a brief moment as she glared around to find her next enemy.

Dovewing nodded. "I can't see Ashfoot either. This isn't the whole of WindClan, just the cats Sol managed to trick." *And we outnumber them, thank StarClan!* she added to herself.

She leaped forward and let the battle sweep her away, lashing out at any cat that dared to face her. As she grew tired, she kept forgetting to keep her moves small and tight, and her paws ached from being banged against the cavern walls.

How long can we keep this up? she wondered.

In a tight knot of battling cats she leaped onto a brown tabby's back. A heartbeat later she was shocked to see Dustpelt glaring up at her.

"For StarClan's sake, get down," he snapped, shrugging her off. "Haven't we got enough trouble with WindClan?"

"Sorry," Dovewing muttered, jumping back into the fray.

Hollyleaf's voice rang out above the sounds of battle. "Force them into the tunnels!"

Dovewing did the best she could, charging into the side of Owlwhisker and shoving him toward the nearest tunnel opening. Owlwhisker pushed back, but his paws were unsteady, and after a few heartbeats he turned and limped away. Glancing around, Dovewing realized that the other WindClan cats were on the run, fleeing into the tunnels. ThunderClan warriors screeched in triumph as they gave chase.

But then another voice was raised in a yowl. "WindClan! Stand and fight! You have no greater enemy than ThunderClan!"

Dovewing whipped around to see Sol standing in the entrance to the biggest tunnel. Defeated cats were stumbling past him; his eyes brimmed with fury, glowing in the half-light, as he tried to stop them.

"Traitor!" The shriek of rage came from Hollyleaf, who raced past Dovewing and flung herself at Sol. "Liar!"

Sol turned tail and fled into the tunnel; without a heartbeat's pause Hollyleaf hurled herself after him.

"Hollyleaf, no!" Dovewing cried out. The black she-cat was so much smaller and lighter than Sol. "Wait!" she added. "Wait for me!"

Forcing her tired paws to move, she pelted across the cavern and into the tunnel. Almost at once she caught up to the two cats; Hollyleaf had trapped Sol in a side tunnel, a dead end still faintly lit by the light from the cavern.

Dovewing could hear Sol hissing in the darkness. Both he and Hollyleaf were moving confidently, striking out at each other as they prepared to come together in a close tussle. Dovewing noticed that Sol was unwounded, his sleek fur barely ruffled, while Hollyleaf had scratches over her shoulders and down one side, and tufts of fur missing from her hindquarters.

I don't think Sol has been fighting at all, Dovewing thought. *He's been hiding, and letting WindClan do his dirty work!*

"Leave the Clans alone," Hollyleaf growled. "You have hurt us enough."

"Never!" Sol retorted. "Not until I've destroyed everything the Clans stand for." His lips peeled back in a snarl. "Many seasons ago, I knew another of your Clans, far away in a gorge. They scorned me, too; they told me I wasn't good enough to be one of their precious warriors! So I vowed to prove to all of you that the warrior code means nothing. In the end, you will kill one another for reasons that aren't worth so much as a mousetail."

"No, you're wrong," Hollyleaf hissed softly, crouching ready to spring. "The way of the Clans is always worth fighting for—and dying for, if necessary."

With a screech of fury she leaped on Sol, battering at him with all four paws. The loner fought back, trying to overwhelm her with his greater weight.

He's no fighter, Dovewing realized, shocked. *He doesn't have warrior skills.*

She was poised to come to Hollyleaf's aid with teeth and claws, but quickly she realized that she wouldn't be needed. Hollyleaf fought with swift, neat blows, remembering her own tunnel training, while Sol was soon flailing around at random shadows as Hollyleaf slid nimbly away from his blows.

At last Hollyleaf darted in with her belly brushing the floor, and knocked Sol's legs out from under him. As Sol fell on one side she pinned him down with one forepaw on his belly and the other across his throat. Sol looked up at her with fear and hatred in his eyes.

"I would gladly kill you," Hollyleaf told him. "But the warrior code tells us to show mercy to a defeated enemy. I will let you escape once and for all, if you promise never to come back and trouble the Clans again."

Sol was silent as Hollyleaf stood back and allowed him to stand up. He stood over her, his eyes gleaming in the darkness. "I cannot make that promise," he hissed.

Hollyleaf didn't flinch. "Then I will kill you, if you return and threaten my Clanmates."

"I'll be ready." Sol's voice was soft and menacing. Then he slipped past Hollyleaf and was lost in the darkness.

"Why did you let him go?" Dovewing demanded, every hair on her pelt quivering. "He was at your mercy!"

"We have to let the warrior code rule our hearts," Hollyleaf answered. Her voice was blurred with exhaustion. "The death of a warrior does not mean victory."

Dovewing took a pace forward and pressed her muzzle into Hollyleaf's shoulder. Sending out her special senses, she could hear WindClan retreating to their camp, and her own Clanmates heading back through the tunnels, bleeding and battered, but triumphant. Later, there would be time to think about Sol's strange threat, about this mysterious Clan that had wronged him so long ago. For now, the battle had been won. A much greater battle lay ahead, one that would be lost unless the four Clans by the lake could unite and fight side by side. Every moment that the Clans were at war with one another, they were at the mercy of the Dark Forest. They had to find a way to settle their quarrels, to join together against their greatest enemy. Was that what the prophecy meant, that Dovewing, Jayfeather, and Lionblaze would be able to unite the cats around the lake?

Dovewing felt bone-weary from her ears to the tip of her tail. Just because she had better hearing, sharper senses than any other cat didn't seem to give her more strength. She needed to rest, eat, talk with Jayfeather and Lionblaze about the challenge that Sol had left them with, of hostile Clans that would be crushed by the Dark Forest if they tried to fight alone. *StarClan, light my path, please.*

"Come on," she meowed to Hollyleaf. "It's time we went home. Our Clanmates are waiting for us."

ERIN HUNTER

is inspired by a love of cats and a
fascination with the ferocity of the
natural world. As well as having great
respect for nature in all its forms,
Erin enjoys creating rich mythical
explanations for animal behavior. She
is also the author of the bestselling
Seekers and Survivors series.

Download the free Warriors app and
chat on Warriors message boards at
www.warriorcats.com.

WARRIORS
ADVENTURE GAME

Visit www.warriorcats.com
to download game rules, character sheets,
a practice mission, and more!

Written by **Stan!**   •   Art by **James L. Barry**

TRAINING DAY

Whatever previous adventure you played, consider that one moon has passed since then. Determine what age that makes all of the cat characters (including the one belonging to the person who will take the first turn as Narrator) and use the information found in the "Improving Your Cat" section of Chapter Four in the game rules to make the necessary improvements.

Unless you are the first person who will act as Narrator in this adventure, you should stop reading here. The information beginning in the next paragraph is for the Narrator only.

The Adventure Begins

Hello, Narrator! It's time to begin playing "Training Day." Make sure all the players have their character sheets, the correct number of chips, a piece of paper, and a pencil. For this adventure, you will also need a six-sided die (like those you find in most standard board games). Remember that the point of the game is to have fun, so don't be afraid to go slow, keep the players involved, and refer to the rules if you aren't sure exactly what should happen next.

When you're ready, begin with **1** below.

1. A Time to Teach

Special Note: Over the course of the previously published adventures, your cat characters have grown and improved—going from newly promoted apprentices to experienced warriors. The Clans are tight-knit groups that depend on older members to pass their knowledge down to the younger ones. Just as the players' cats had mentors and teachers who taught them the basics of life around the lake, in the opening scenes of "Training Day" the players' cats take their turn sharing the knowledge they've gained with a new generation of apprentices.

Read Aloud: "Usually, the training of apprentices is handled completely within their own Clans. However, in an effort to reduce suspicion and tension between Clans, the Clan leaders have decided to try an experiment. They want a group of warriors to spend a day working with apprentices from Clans other than their own, and your cats have been chosen to take part in this experiment."

Narrator Tips: Tell the players that their cats are each approached by the leaders of their individual Clans and told about this. The leaders feel that it is an important task and that the players' cats have been chosen because they seem to be good at working side by side with cats of varying backgrounds (as may happen every time you play the game, if the players' cats come from different Clans). Their job will be to teach basic warrior skills—patrolling a border, stalking an enemy, and hunting for fresh-kill—to show these apprentices that all cats are alike no matter what Clan they belong to.

Each cat will get a specific apprentice to work with. Have the players (including the Narrator) each roll the six-sided die and use the chart below to discover what Clan the apprentice comes from. If the result is the same Clan that the player's cat belongs to, reroll. Remember that what Clan a cat is from gives that cat an added boost in one skill (see Chapter Two of the game rules).

Die Result	Clan
1	ShadowClan
2–3	RiverClan
4–5	WindClan
6	ThunderClan

Then have the players (including the Narrator) each roll the six-sided die again, using the chart below to see what personality and skills their apprentice has. Have the players write down the game details for their new apprentices, listed below the chart. They'll need this information as the adventure progresses.

Die Result	Personality
1-2	Clever
3-4	Tough
5-6	Insightful

Clever Apprentice: A clever apprentice has the following Ability scores—Strength 1, Intelligence 3, Spirit 1. The apprentice has the following Skill levels—Jump 1, Ponder 1, Sneak 1.

Tough Apprentice: A tough apprentice has the following Ability scores—Strength 3, Intelligence 1, Spirit 1. The apprentice has the following Skill levels—Pounce 1, See 1, Swat 1.

Insightful Apprentice: An insightful apprentice has the following Ability scores—Strength 1, Intelligence 1, Spirit 3. The apprentice has the following Skill levels—Focus 1, Listen 1, Smell 1.

Finally, have the players (including the Narrator) each roll the six-sided die one more time. If the result is even, their apprentice is female. If it's odd, the apprentice is male. Once that is known, the apprentices need names. Rather than have the players choose the names themselves, have each player select the name for the apprentice belonging to the person on her or his right (keeping the apprentice's personality and Clan in mind).

With all the apprentices fully developed, the players' cats must decide in what order they want to teach the skills. Will they start with border patrol, stalking, or hunting practice?

Once that is decided, it is time to reveal the final

surprise—during this adventure they will sometimes be playing as their regular cats and sometimes be playing as the apprentices. Have each player set aside his or her cat's character sheets and focus on the game details of the new apprentices.

The big challenge will be that, when playing an apprentice, the players need to remember that the young cat does not know everything that the more advanced cat does. The Narrator may find it helpful to remind the players of what perspective and knowledge they are supposed to be using—the apprentice's or the mentor's—as that shifts during play.

What Happens Next: If the players' cats want to begin with border patrol practice, continue with **5**.

If the players' cats want to begin with stalking practice, continue with **7**.

If the players' cats want to begin with hunting practice, continue with **10**.

2. Hey, You!

Read Aloud: "That tall tree in the distance marks the border, you're sure of it. As you approach, though, you can tell that this isn't the tree you thought it was. In fact, you've never seen this tree before in your life because it's deep within ShadowClan territory."

Narrator Tips: The apprentices are more lost than ever. They've made a terrible error and wandered deep into ShadowClan territory. Ask the players what the apprentices want to do about it, but tell them to make a quick call—you never know who might have seen, heard, or smelled them.

In fact, a pair of ShadowClan warriors has caught scent of the apprentices and is padding over to find them. The apprentices must act quickly or they will be discovered. The Narrator should give the group a fair warning that danger could arrive at any moment. If the group continues to dawdle or is unable to decide on a plan of action, the aggressive older cats arrive.

If the apprentices try to make their way back to Thun-derClan territory, ask whether they want to do so quickly or quietly (they can't do both). If the answer is quickly, have all the apprentices make a Strength Check and tell them that any total lower than a 4 will be a failure. Before attempting that test, tell the group that any player whose regular cat has the Dash Knack may spend three Strength Chips to add them to the bonus pool. If any of the apprentices fails this Check, the ShadowClan cats catch the group.

If the apprentices try to escape quietly, tell the players that all the apprentices must make two separate Sneak Checks and that any total lower than 3 will count as a failure. Also tell them that any player whose regular cat has the Hide or Stalk Knack may add three Spirit Chips to the bonus pool. If any of the apprentices fails either of the Checks, the ShadowClan cats catch the group.

If the ShadowClan warriors catch the group, they will start a fight. (This fight uses all the usual rules as described in Chapter Five of the game.) They know that the apprentices are here by accident, but they believe swatting a young cat whenever it makes a mistake is the best way to encourage better behavior in the future. These cats each have Strength 5, Intelligence 3, and Spirit 3. Each round, each one of them will attack one of the apprentices. The Narrator can determine which one by any method she likes, or one of the apprentices can volunteer to receive the attack by throwing him- or herself in front of the attack. (A single apprentice can only jump in front of one attack per round.)

The ShadowClan warriors' plan is to make a show of force and frighten the apprentices. They expect that the young cats will run from a fight, proving that the cross-Clan training is a failure and will only weaken ShadowClan. These warriors will fight for three rounds. If all of the apprentices are still standing their ground and ready to continue the fight at the end of the third round, they have proven their strength and bravery to the ShadowClan warriors, who will leave them alone from now on.

Although the ShadowClan warriors only want to scare the apprentices, it is possible that one or more of the younger cats will be Knocked Out. The older cats will be ashamed of themselves but, after making sure that no permanent damage has been done, they will still use this turn of events as "proof" that the current training is making the apprentices weak.

What Happens Next: If the apprentices manage to sneak safely back to ThunderClan territory, or to beat the ShadowClan warriors in battle, the apprentices can try the test again. Go to **5**.

If the apprentices are seen running away from ShadowClan territory (and do not face down the ShadowClan warriors in battle) or if any of the apprentices is Knocked Out during the battle, continue with **13**.

3. Who's Stalking Who?

Read Aloud: "The scent of your foe is getting stronger. You can hear his movements nearby. You know—hey . . . wait . . . that's coming from the wrong direction!"

Narrator Tips: The apprentice has made such a mess of this attempt to stalk a pretend foe that the quarry was able to turn things around and stalk the apprentice instead.

Describe the end of the "hunt," where the apprentice thinks he or she is about to catch the target, but suddenly the pretend foe comes charging at the apprentice from an unexpected location and pounces on him or her instead. It should be a little embarrassing, but not actually painful.

Ask the players what suggestions their regular cat characters have for the apprentice. Where did things go wrong? How could he or she do better next time? What should a warrior do when he or she realizes that the situation has been reversed like that? Could the apprentice have done the same thing to turn the situation around again?

As Narrator, you should be keeping track of how many failures the apprentices get. This result was so bad that it counts as two failures instead of just one.

What Happens Next: If the apprentices have amassed a total of four or more failures in the stalking test, continue with **13**.

If the apprentices have not yet amassed four failures, return to scene **7** and let them try again. Note, though, that once an individual apprentice succeeds at this test, he or she does not have to perform it again.

4. Is It Dinner Yet?

Read Aloud: "None of the Clans is particularly large in number. You all easily know every member of your own Clan, and a good many of the cats in other Clans, too. But the size of a Clan suddenly seems much bigger when you look at your newly caught fresh-kill and realize that the hunters do not get any food until all the other Clan cats eat first."

Narrator Tips: If the adventure has reached this scene, the apprentices have not yet gathered enough fresh-kill. The Narrator should keep track of how many times the apprentices' efforts return them to this scene—it will determine what happens next.

Ask the players to discuss what they think went wrong. What advice would their cats offer to the apprentices to help them gather fresh-kill more quickly? Is it better to hunt small prey or large? Would things be better if the apprentices worked together in pairs or trios?

The Narrator should tell the players that the apprentices can work in teams using special rules. If a group of apprentices hunt the same creature, all of the apprentices may try each of the required Skill Checks, but only one apprentice needs to succeed in that Check in order to overcome the prey. In other words, no matter how many cats are hunting together, they only need a single success by any one of the apprentices for the whole team to succeed.

What Happens Next: If there is not enough fresh-kill and this was the fourth time that the adventure has reached this scene, continue with **13**.

If there was not enough fresh-kill but the adventure has reached this scene fewer than four times, the apprentices may continue hunting. Return to **10**.

5. On Patrol

Read Aloud: "Patrolling the borders of the Clan's territory is one of the most important jobs a warrior has. It's the best way for the Clan to keep an eye out for any new threats, and to find out if anything unusual is happening in a neighboring Clan's territory."

Narrator Tips: In this section, the older cats are teaching their new apprentices how to behave on border patrols. As a group, they've gone to an area where there is a complicated border separating ThunderClan territory, ShadowClan territory, and non-Clan forest territory.

Begin by asking the players what advice their cats would give to the apprentices. What should a cat do on patrol? How should they behave? Are there any particular tricks or dangers to look out for? Lead this as a discussion among the players to get them to role-play what their cats might say.

When the instructional part is over, it is time for the players to take control of the apprentices again. Let the apprentices refresh their chips, if they need to. Then have them try to walk the border without crossing into the other Clan's territory. To do this successfully, each apprentice must make one of the following Checks: Focus Check, Intelligence Check, Ponder Check, or See Check. Add together the results of these Checks to create a group total. If the group total is 12 or higher, the apprentices have successfully walked the patrol route. If the group total is lower than 12, the cats have crossed the border. **What Happens Next:** If the apprentices have successfully walked the patrol route, continue with **11**.

If this is the first or second time the apprentices crossed the border, continue with **8**.

If this is the third time the apprentices crossed the border, continue with **2**.

6. Waiting for Supper

Read Aloud: "It seemed certain that the apprentices were about to complete their task. You were sure they'd bring back enough fresh-kill to meet their goal, but you were wrong."

Narrator Tips: The Narrator should begin by telling the players to set aside the information about their apprentices and focus on the character sheets for their usual cat characters—the apprentices have failed to return from their hunting expeditions.

One of the interesting things about role-playing games like this is that the players will sometimes have access to different perspectives of the story and levels of ability. Over the last few scenes, the players have been able to see the actions both through the eyes of their regular cat characters and through the eyes of the apprentice cats. The more experienced cats could easily have succeeded on any and all of the tests being performed, but the apprentices often struggled to do so.

In this instance, the players know everything that happened to the apprentices up to a certain point, but not beyond. Now they must use the skills and abilities of their experienced cat characters to find the missing information and (hopefully) find the missing apprentices, too.

Ask the players what their cats are going to do about the situation. How will they go about trying to find the missing apprentices? Likely strategies include trying to follow the young cats' trail (either by sight or scent), trying to hear far-away sounds that might hint at where they've gone, or simply sitting down and using the cats' knowledge about the apprentices to puzzle out what could have happened. These activities can be represented by See, Smell, Listen, and Ponder Checks, but other possibilities exist, too. If a player's plan seems reasonable and likely to help, figure out which Skill or Knack is appropriate, and allow the player to use that.

Since what happened to the apprentices was sudden and unplanned, getting clues is difficult. Any cat that got a total of 12 or higher on the Checks above succeeds in that action and gets a bit of an idea. However, it will take the group as a whole to puzzle this out. Add up the number of successes the players' cats got as a group.

What Happens Next: If the players' cats as a group got five or more successes, continue with **18**.

If the total number of successes for the group was four or fewer, continue with **15**.

7. Finding Your Foe

Read Aloud: "Some will say that a warrior's most important assets are their sharp claws. But if you cannot find and follow your enemy, it doesn't matter how sharp your claws are—you'll never get close enough to use them."

Narrator Tips: In this section, the players' cats are teaching their new apprentices how to find, follow, and eventually catch a foe that is sneaking through the woods. Stalking an enemy is similar to hunting for fresh-kill, but other cats and wild predators are much more clever and dangerous than prey like rabbits and voles, and tracking them is a very complex task. On the other hand, clever foes can often be convinced to leave the territory simply by letting them know that their movements are being followed—a smart creature avoids unnecessary combat.

Begin by letting the apprentices refresh their chips, if they need to. Then ask the players what advice their cats would give to the apprentices. What Skills are most important when it comes to stalking? What Knacks can a cat learn to make this process easier? Are there any tricks that are useful when trying to chase down a clever foe? Lead this as a discussion among the players to get them to role-play the things their cats might say.

When the instructional part is over, it is time for the players to take control of the apprentices again and have them try to stalk a pretend foe. In this case, it will be one of the players' cats, though that cat will not use all of his or her sneakiness—these are just apprentices, after all. To succeed at this test, an apprentice must try all three of the following Checks and be successful at two of them: a Listen Check, a Smell Check, and a Sneak Check. These Checks must have a total of 5 or higher to succeed.

In most cases, even an apprentice who fails the overall test will succeed on at least one of the Checks. However, if any of the apprentices fail at all of the Checks in the test, it counts as a complete failure.

What Happens Next: If all of the apprentices succeed at this test, continue with **9**.

If some apprentices fail but none have a complete failure, continue with **12**.

If any of the apprentices had a complete failure, continue with **3**.

8. Learning the Land

Read Aloud: "At first it seems like following a marked border is easy, but after a while all the trees begin to look alike and there are many places where one scent overwhelms another. Despite your best efforts, you have wandered over the border into another Clan's territory."

Narrator Tips: The apprentices have failed at their attempt to patrol a border. This counts as one failure for determining the next step of the adventure (as described in Scene **5**).

Ask the players to discuss what they think went wrong. Why did the apprentices fail? What could they do differently to get a better result next time? What advice would their cats offer to the apprentices? Sometimes the best way to learn something is to try and fail, then try again. The apprentices have certainly learned something from this experience and now the players can allow them to make use of the advice that the players' cats are giving them.

The Narrator should create a bonus pool of Ability Chips. This pool should consist of one chip for each of the players' regular cat characters, and the chips should represent the Abilities in which the player's regular cats have the highest scores. If a cat's highest Ability score is Strength, then a Strength Chip is added to the pool. (If this is the second time the adventure has come to this scene, double the number of chips in the bonus pool.)

As the apprentices try again to patrol the border, they may use the bonus pool of Ability Chips to augment their efforts. Any apprentice may take a Chip from the bonus pool, but these Chips never refresh. Also, once the apprentices succeed in the border patrol test, this bonus pool may no longer be used—it is only useful for the test in Scene **5** and the action in Scene **2**.

What Happens Next: The apprentices may now try to patrol the border again, but this time with the advantage of the Ability Chip bonus pool. Return to **5**.

9. Gotcha!

Read Aloud: "It hardly seemed fair—apprentices trying to track down fully trained warriors—but with solid effort and a bit of luck, you succeeded. Well done!"

Narrator Tips: The apprentices have completed the stalking test, and they are to be congratulated. Since the players are taking the roles of the apprentices and may feel uncomfortable using the voices of their regular cat characters to basically praise themselves, it is important for the Narrator to do so. These apprentices have just proven that even when in a confrontation with a well-trained opponent, they have the ability to think, adapt, and find a path to success. Make sure that the moment is properly captured.

Once that's done, it is up to the players' regular cat characters to decide where to take their apprentices next—to practice border patrol skills or to practice hunting for fresh-kill. (Note that the apprentices can only go to each test section once.)

What Happens Next: If the players' cats want to continue with border patrol, this is the end of the chapter. Hand the adventure to the next Narrator and tell him or her to continue with **5**.

If the players' cats want to continue with hunting practice, this is the end of the chapter. Hand the adventure to the next Narrator and tell him or her to continue with **10**.

10. Finding Food

Read Aloud: "Hunting is not the most difficult task a warrior must perform, but it is one of the most important. The Clan counts on the warriors to bring back enough food to feed all of its members. Since the warriors eat last, there is always an incentive to make sure every empty belly has something to fill it."

Narrator Tips: In this section, the players' cats are teaching their new apprentices how to hunt, stalking small prey and catching it so that the Clan will have enough fresh-kill come day's end. As they become more proficient, the apprentices will learn that different types of prey require different strategies, but for now they must be introduced to the basics of this important activity. Stalking prey is similar to stalking an enemy, and oftentimes easier. But it must be combined with rougher physical skills of pouncing or biting to bring the prey to ground. Altogether, the combination is trickier to master than most new apprentices realize.

Begin by letting the apprentices refresh their chips, if they need to. Then ask the players what advice their cats would give to the apprentices. What Abilities and Skills are most important for a hunt? What Knacks do the best hunters use? Is it better to try to kill a single larger bit of prey (like a rabbit) or to gather a large collection of smaller prey (like voles)? Lead this as a discussion among the players to get them to role-play the things their cats might say.

When the instructional part is over, it is time for the players to take control of the apprentices again and have them try hunting on their own. Have each apprentice decide whether she or he is going to try to hunt rabbits or voles. Then let them try.

Hunting a rabbit requires a Sneak Check with a total of 5, a Pounce Check with a total of 6, and a Bite Check with a total of 5. If any of these Checks fails, the rabbit gets away. However, if all the Checks succeed, the rabbit is now fresh-kill that the apprentice can bring back at the end of the day.

Hunting a vole requires a Sneak Check with a total of 3, a Pounce Check with a total of 4, and a Bite Check with a total of 1. If any of these Checks fails, the vole gets away. However, if all the Checks succeed, the vole is now fresh-kill that the apprentice can bring back at the end of the day.

Each rabbit that the apprentices bring down can feed three cats. Each vole can feed one cat. The Narrator should keep a running tally of how many cats can be fed with what the apprentices have collected. In order to succeed at this test, the cats must gather enough fresh-kill to feed a number of cats equal to three times the number of players (not including the Narrator). So in a group of four players and a Narrator, the apprentices would have to gather enough fresh-kill to feed twelve cats.

What Happens Next: If the apprentices have gathered enough fresh-kill to succeed at this test, this is the end of the chapter. Hand the adventure to the next Narrator and tell him or her to continue with **6**.

If the apprentices have not gathered enough fresh-kill to succeed at this test, continue with **4**.

11. Walking the Line

Read Aloud: "The scents are muddled, the way twisting and ridiculous, but warriors and apprentices patrol this route every day—and now you have, too."

Narrator Tips: Despite the difficulty of the task, the apprentices have succeeded at border patrol. They are to be congratulated. Since the players are taking the roles of the apprentices and may feel uncomfortable using the voices of their regular cat characters to praise themselves, it is important for the Narrator to do so. These apprentices have just completed a difficult task. Make sure that the moment is properly captured.

Once that's done, it is up to the players' regular cat characters to decide where to take their apprentices next—to practice stalking foes through the forest, or to practice hunting for fresh-kill. (Remember that the group should not repeat a test they have already passed.)

What Happens Next: If the players' cats want to continue with stalking practice, this is the end of the chapter. Hand the adventure to the next Narrator and tell him or her to continue with **7**.

If the players' cats want to continue with hunting practice, this is the end of the chapter. Hand the adventure to the next Narrator and tell him or her to continue with **10**.

12. The Gold Trail

Read Aloud: "Until now, the only sights, scents, and sounds that the apprentices have been exposed to were those in their Clan camp. Out in the woods, there are an endless series of distractions. It's not surprising, then, that the young cats are having trouble finding and catching a skilled foe."

Narrator Tips: The apprentices have failed in their attempt to stalk a foe through the woods. Reaching this scene counts as one failure. Keep track of the total number of failures the group amasses while attempting this test.

Ask the players to use the perspective of their regular cat characters to discuss what they think went wrong. Why did the apprentices fail at this action? What could they do differently to get a better result next time? What advice would their cats offer to the apprentices? Sometimes the best way to learn something is to try and fail, then try again. The apprentices have certainly learned something from this experience and now can make good use of the advice that the players' cats are giving them.

The Narrator should create a bonus pool of Ability Chips. Each player whose apprentice has already succeeded at this test may add one Ability Chip of his or her choosing to the pool.

When the remaining apprentices try again to stalk a foe, they may use the bonus pool of Ability Chips to augment their efforts. Any apprentice may take a Chip from the bonus pool, but these Chips never refresh. Also, once all the apprentices succeed, this bonus pool may no longer be used—it is only useful for the stalking test in Scene 7.

What Happens Next: If the apprentices have amassed a total of four or more failures, continue with **13**.

If the apprentices have not yet amassed four failures, return to scene **7** and let them try again. Note, though, that once an individual apprentice succeeds at this test, he or she does not have to perform it again.

13. Flunking Out

Read Aloud: "Not every adventure ends successfully. Sometimes cats make mistakes, and sometimes they hit a patch of bad luck. The important thing for a Clan warrior is what happens next."

Narrator Tips: There are several reasons why the adventure may end up at this scene, but none of them are good. Either the apprentices failed one of their tests or the mentors lost their apprentices.

There isn't any crucial need for the apprentices to succeed at these particular tests immediately. And no matter how hard the players' cats want to work at it and be good mentors, eventually they may have to accept that the lessons are not going to be learned today.

The Clan leaders will thank the players' cats for their hard work, and congratulate the apprentices for being part of such a grand undertaking. But as sundown approaches, they decide to bring this experiment to an unsuccessful close. Maybe in the future they will try it again.

Alternatively, if the story ended up here because the players' cats lost their apprentices, tell them that another group of warriors (the ones they met in scene 15) managed to find the missing youngsters and bring them back to safety.

What Happens Next: Although no one did anything particularly wrong, arriving at this scene means that the apprentices did not learn quickly enough for the training experiment to count as a success—the adventure has ended badly. The players' cats do *not* get any Experience rewards for this adventure. The players' cats *can*, however, play the adventure again, hopefully finding ways to get better performances out of their apprentices.

14. Under the Old Oak Tree

Read Aloud: "The scent of young cats becomes overwhelmed by another, more dangerous smell—the powerful fumes of weasel musk. Dangerous creatures, weasels. If they have the apprentices, there could be real trouble."

Narrator Tips: The players' cats have arrived at a burrow that contains a weasel den. Unfortunately, it is the wrong weasel's den. The missing apprentices are not here, though the players may not realize it at first.

Describe for the players a scene where the scent trail they've been following takes them to a burrow entrance that leads into the ground below a large oak tree. There are signs of activity in the area, but only weasel tracks can be seen.

If the players' cats have not yet had a chance, allow them to make Ponder or Intelligence Checks to see what facts they may know about weasels. (This information can be found in scene **18**.)

Have each of the players' cats make Smell Checks. Anyone whose total is 8 or higher notices that all the scents around this burrow come from a single weasel—this is not a large family's den. Anyone whose total is 12 or higher notices that there is a complete lack of any scents related to the missing apprentices—not even faint, lingering scents.

The players will have to make a decision about what to do next. If enough of them had very good Smell Checks, they may think that it is very likely that they are following a false trail. Of course, the only way to be one hundred percent certain would be to explore the burrow, but doing that means likely running into the weasel. If the players decide to leave the burrow unexplored skip to the last paragraph of this scene.

Going into the weasel's den is difficult. The burrow is narrow and winding, and the cats must proceed in single file. Eventually, the lead cat will reach the burrow's end—a small chamber where the weasel is sleeping. The lead cat must make a Stealth Check with a total of 12 or higher, and all the other cats that are in the burrow must make Stealth Checks with totals of 8 or higher. If any of these Checks fail, the weasel awakens.

The weasel will immediately attack the lead cat using its claws and its teeth. The weasel has Strength 6, Intelligence 4, and Spirit 5. It also has 5 levels each of Jump, Pounce, and Sneak, and 3 levels each of Bite and Swat. It will fight until it has

taken 10 Chips worth of damage. If the players' cats manage to draw it out into the open, the weasel will give up the fight and run away if it sees that it is being attacked by three or more opponents.

Backing out of the burrow is also slow going. Once a fight begins, only one cat can make it out for every round. In other words, the lead cat must stay underground fighting the weasel for at least as many rounds as there are other cats currently in the burrow. Once there are no more cats behind him in the tunnel, the lead cat can back out the following round.

When the players' cats decide to start looking elsewhere for the missing apprentices, have each of them make a Scent Check. The goal of this Check is to get a total of 10. If half of the group or more fails that Check, the players' cats are following another false trail. Otherwise, they manage to pick up the apprentices' trail again.

What Happens Next: If the players' cats are following a false trail, continue with **13**.

If one or more of the players' cats were Knocked Out while fighting the weasel, continue with **17**.

If the players' cats pick up the missing apprentices' trail, this is the end of the chapter. Hand the adventure to the next Narrator and tell him or her to continue with **22**.

15. The Wrong Apprentices

Read Aloud: "Your temporary apprentices have been all over this area, so it's hard to find the most recent scent trail. But suddenly you hear a young cat call out in shocked surprise. Something's wrong!"

Narrator Tips: The players' cats have followed the wrong trail. Describe for them an exciting chase along a relatively short trail that ends with them bursting in on another group of warriors training a different group of apprentices. Like the players' cats, these warriors and apprentices are from a mixed group of Clans. They are engaged in the stalking test (as described in **3**), but the apprentices are doing much worse than the players' apprentices did (if they already played through that section).

The other warriors can explain that the players' cats must have followed the wrong trail, because they have been here for a while and have seen no sign of the missing apprentices. Normally, they would offer to help in the search immediately, but they have the safety of their own apprentices to worry about. They have to take the young cats back to their Clan camps before they can do anything else, particularly if there may be something dangerous lurking in the forest.

The players' cats may begin their search again with the same rules as before.

Ask the players how their cats will go about trying to find the missing apprentices and then allow them each to make appropriate Skill Checks. If a cat gets a total of 12 or higher on the Checks above, it counts as one success. However, it will take the group as a whole to puzzle this out. Add up the number of successes the players' cats got as a group.

What Happens Next: If the players' cats as a group got five or more successes, continue with **18**.

If the total number of successes for the group was four or fewer, continue with **13**.

16. Tight Squeeze

Read Aloud: "The farther underground you get, the darker it becomes. As the faint light from the surface dwindles to nothing, you find yourselves in complete darkness. You know nothing has changed. So why does it feel like the tunnel walls are starting to squeeze in around you?"

Narrator Tips: The players' cats have chosen to go down the wrong tunnel. This one is an incomplete weasel passageway, simply leading away, getting thinner and thinner until it simply reaches a dead end.

Describe to the players that as their cats go along, they really do feel the walls pressing in against them. They can only proceed in single file now. Soon they have to squeeze through to continue onward. At this or any of the future junctures, the cats may choose whether to back up or press on. If they want to press on, it requires a Strength Check with a total of 10 or higher. A little farther on, another juncture requires another Strength Check with a total of 12 or higher. Farther on still, a third juncture requires a Strength Check needing a total of 14 or higher. If the cats make it past this point, the one in the lead feels his or her nose bump into solid earth as they reach the tunnel's disappointing end. Now they have to back up and try a different tunnel.

Backing up through such a tight tunnel is difficult and (because of the rocks in the raw earth) sometimes painful. For each Strength Check that the cats made on the way into the tunnel they suffer 1 Chip worth of damage on the way out. So if they turned back immediately upon meeting earthy resistance, they suffer no damage. If they passed the first Check before turning back, the cats suffer 1 Chip worth of damage, etc.

What Happens Next: If any of the players' cats are Knocked Out from the damage taken getting out of the tunnel, continue with **17**.

If all of the cats got out safely, they can try going down the right-hand tunnel. Continue with **20**.

17. Knocked Out!

Read Aloud: "Sleep is usually a warm, comfortable thing that covers you like a queen wrapping her tail around her kits. What you're experiencing now is nothing like that—restless and disagreeable, even painful. When you open your eyes, you remember why."

Narrator Tips: The adventure reaches this scene when one or more of the players' cats were Knocked Out. Because of the multiple threats, the confused emotions of the apprentices, and the mission given to the cats to serve as an example for all warriors in every Clan, the loss of even one member of the team is enough to keep the adventure from finishing as a success.

As Narrator, you may want to make sure that the players keep in mind that there is a subtle but important difference between "not succeeding" and "failing." In a difficult situation like this, it is possible to do very well, and still not achieve full success. Any of the Clan leaders would certainly tell the cats this. The players' cats did many things right, and may have ended up here solely because of bad luck. That's how life can be sometimes, and every warrior knows that the only thing to do in these situations is dust yourself off and try again.

Describe a likely ending for the scenario—probably based around another set of warriors (like those in scene **15**) having come in and rescued the missing apprentices. Tragedy has been averted, but the players' cats are not the heroes of the day.

What Happens Next: The adventure is over. The players' cats do *not* get any Experience rewards for this adventure. The players' cats *can*, however, play the adventure again.

18. Found One!

Read Aloud: "The scent trail is getting clearer now, so you can begin to move more quickly. With that added speed, you almost go straight past a bush until you hear a weak, plaintive mew coming from beneath its leaves."

Narrator Tips: If the players' cats look under the bush described above, they find one of their apprentices. (Determine which one randomly.) Unfortunately, the youngster cannot provide answers about what happened because he or she is Knocked Out.

An Intelligence or Ponder Check with a total of 5 or higher will reveal that the apprentice is Knocked Out from sheer exhaustion, rather than any more serious injuries. (The Medicine Lore Knack may be used in this Check, if the player's cat has that option.) This means that the apprentice will make a full recovery, but not quickly enough to be of further help today. If the players are not able to determine that information, they find that the apprentice appears unharmed and they may continue to worry about the young cat's health, but they realize that they need to carry on and look for the others.

The players' cats must try to find the scent trail again. Have them all make Smell Checks. Any cat whose total is 8 or higher can find the trail, but any cat whose total is 12 or higher also notices another scent following the same trail. That scent doesn't belong to any of the apprentices; indeed, it doesn't belong to any cat at all. It is the smell of a weasel.

Any cat with the Animal Lore Knack automatically knows a few things about weasels. (Others can get this same information by making a Ponder Check with a total of 7 or higher.) Weasels are vicious, mean creatures with terrible tempers. Unlike most other beasts that the Clan cats might encounter, weasels actually like to fight. They will often attack another creature just for the "fun" of having a fight to the death. However, weasels are also bullies—they only attack in situations where they have a good chance to win. If a weasel is overpowered or severely outnumbered, it will flee if there is anywhere for it to go. When cornered, a weasel always puts up a ferocious fight.

What Happens Next: If more than half of the players' cats succeeded on the Smell Check, this is the end of the chapter. Hand the adventure to the next Narrator and tell him or her to continue with **22**.

If half or fewer of the players' cats succeeded on the Smell Check, continue with **14**.

19. Well Played

Read Aloud: "As the last weasel disappears deeper into the burrow, the apprentices rush over to show their thanks. It's unclear, though, whether they're more thankful for your arrival or impressed with the way you were able to beat the weasels without ever resorting to violence."

Narrator Tips: The players' cats have rescued the missing apprentices. They've also shown that it is not always necessary to use fighting to solve a tense and dangerous situation. A true warrior knows when it is time to attack, and when it is time to use his or her other strengths.

Describe scenes where the Clan leaders repeat this message at their camps, holding the players' cats up as examples of what is best in their Clan. In addition, the cross-Clan mentoring is considered a complete success, and the players' cats are given a good deal of credit for that. It seems likely that they will get to meet with and train these apprentices again in the future, and hopefully this will increase communication between the Clans.

What Happens Next: The players' cats should be proud of what they've done. This is a good ending—the apprentices have been rescued and taught a valuable lesson about the use of force. The members of all the Clans will speak about this day for many moons to come, and your actions will inspire others who want to bring all the Clans closer together in peace and harmony. The players' cats get all the rewards listed in the "Experience" section at the end of this adventure.

20. Den of Weasels

Read Aloud: "Pressing through a slight narrowing of the burrow, the earth opens up around you and you're standing in what must be the weasels' den. Ahead you see three of the beasts—nasty, snarling, and cruel. Behind them are the missing apprentices—pressed against the den wall in fear."

Narrator Tips: This is the climactic scene of the adventure. The missing apprentices are here, the enemy weasels are here, and the players' cats have one big decision to make before you can resolve the situation: Are they going to fight the weasels, or are they going to try to use a less violent strategy? Either could work.

Remind the players of the facts that their cats may have remembered about weasels—that they are vicious fighters who never give up once a fight has begun, but also that they will run away if they seem outmatched. If the group has not yet uncovered these facts, give them one more chance to do so with a Ponder Check that has a total of 7 or higher (any cat with the Animal Lore Knack knows the information automatically).

If the cats line up like they're going to fight, clearly indicating which weasel they mean to attack, they might scare the creatures off without a fight. Any weasel that has more than two cats aligned against it will automatically run away (scurrying through another tunnel that leads deeper into the burrow). A weasel that has two cats aligned against it will run away if those cats each make a Hiss or Arch Check and have a group total of 12 or higher. A weasel that faces just a single cat will fight unless the cat can scare it off by making a Hiss or Arch Check of 8 or higher.

If a weasel is not immediately scared off, it will start a fight. Each of the weasels has Strength 6, Intelligence 4, and Spirit 5. It also has 5 levels each of Jump, Pounce, and Sneak, and  3 levels each of Bite and Swat. A weasel will fight until it has taken 10 Chips worth of damage, then will run away.

Once a cat's weasel opponent has fled or been Knocked Out, that cat can join one of the other fights on the following round. Each round, the weasel will reassess its situation. If it is facing more than two opponents, it will break off the fight and run away.

What Happens Next: If any of the players' cats are Knocked Out during the fight, continue with **17**.

If the players' cats are able to scare off the weasels without a fight, continue with **19**.

If the players' cats get the apprentices back by winning a fight with the weasels, continue with **21**.

21. Take That!

Read Aloud: "The weasels have been routed and your cats stand proud and unbeaten. The apprentices rush forward to thank you for rescuing them, and almost immediately begin to mimic the fighting moves they saw your cats use during the battle."

Narrator Tips: The players' cats have rescued the missing apprentices. They've demonstrated the skill that warrior cats can wield, and the damage that they can inflict when claws are bared. The apprentices immediately start talking about ways they're going to make use of the fighting moves they've seen— applying it to hunting and fighting training they'll do with the rest of their Clan's apprentices.

Describe scenes where the Clan leaders make speeches at their camps, telling their Clans what great warriors your cat characters are. They point out that if all the apprentices and kits work hard, they too can learn to fight the way your cats do. This, however, makes it seem less wise to teach other Clans' young warriors the same lessons—after all, the next time the Clans square off in battle, it would be best to have a secret advantage. As Narrator, your challenge is to show that all the Clans are saying the same thing—each one thinking that their warriors were superior to all the others.

While your cats will get to see their temporary apprentices again in the future at Gatherings and other times when the Clans get together, they won't get to teach them again. And one day, it is possible that after those apprentices grow into warriors, they may have to fight against them in battle. Hopefully, though, the peace will be maintained.

What Happens Next: This is a good ending—the apprentices have been rescued and brought home; and all of the players' cats came through safely. The players' cats get all the rewards listed in the "Experience" section at the end of this adventure.

22. The Right Burrow

Read Aloud: "The overlapping scents of cat and weasel lead down a winding but distinct trail toward a patch of gorse shrubs, where you see a small, furry body on the ground. It doesn't appear to be moving at all."

Narrator Tips: Build a quick bit of tension about whether that's one of the apprentices and how hurt it might be, but quickly let the players' cats investigate. When they do, they'll find that it is another of the missing apprentices who, like the one they found previously, is Knocked Out because of sheer exhaustion. After a night's rest and perhaps some medicinal herbs, the apprentice will be fully healed and ready to resume training.

The scent of a weasel can clearly be smelled on the apprentice's fur, as if the creature had been nudging the small cat, but not actually attacking her.

If the players' cats look under the shrub near the unconscious apprentice, they can see the mouth of a large burrow (much larger than the one in scene **14**, if the cats' journey followed that route). Have any cat exploring this area make a Smell Check. If the Check has a total of 8 or higher, the cat knows that there are other cat scents here, but cannot be sure whether or not they belong to the missing apprentices. If the Check has a total of 12 or higher, the cat recognizes the scents of the other apprentices and is sure that they went down into the burrow. If the Check has a total of 15 or higher, the cat realizes that there are also scents for a handful of weasels, not just the one they smelled on the unconscious apprentice—this burrow is home to a group of the vicious creatures.

The only way for the players' cats to rescue the apprentices is to go down into the weasel burrow and get them. But as the Narrator, you should never force the players to make their cats do anything that dangerous—the players must make that decision for themselves. Your job as Narrator is simply to give the players the information they need to decide what their next course of action will be.

Describe the situation and the things that the cats know for certain. If the players' cats want to try different tactics to, perhaps, entice the weasels to come out of the burrow, let them—but they will not be successful. If the players' cats do anything that will let the apprentices know that they are there, the young cats will begin crying out for help. They can tell the players' cats that they are, indeed, in the burrow somewhere (though they can't say exactly where) and that the weasels are guarding them and looking at them hungrily.

When the cats finally decide to head into the burrow, tell them that the tunnel is wide enough for them to walk through one at a time, or squeeze through two at a time. After a twisting, turning path downward, the burrow forks in half. There are now two tunnels. The scents are confused and the sounds echo through the underground passageways. There is no way to be sure which way leads to the apprentices—the players' cats will just have to guess.

It's possible that the players will want their cats to split up and search both tunnels at the same time. If so, have them tell you which cats are going in which tunnels.

What Happens Next: If the players' cats want to follow the right-hand tunnel, continue with **20**.

If the players' cats want to follow the left-hand tunnel, continue with **16**.

If the players' cats want to split up and try both tunnels, role-play the left-hand tunnel first, then continue with **16**.

AFTER THE ADVENTURE

After the last scene of the adventure has been played, the game itself is not necessarily over. There still are a few things you can do if the players want to keep at it.

Play It Again

If the players' cats chose to make hunting the first thing they taught their temporary apprentices, you may want to go back and play again so that the group can experience the action to be had in the stalking and border patrol tests. Or perhaps you just want to go back and pick up the adventure again somewhere in the middle where it feels like things went wrong. In either case, your cat would be right back where he or she was and have another chance to try to find a more favorable outcome.

One of the great things about storytelling games is that you can always tell the story again. And, since there are many different ways the players' cats could choose to interact with their temporary apprentices, the story could unwind in a different way every time you play (particularly as different Narrators get to guide the storyline).

Experience

If the cats completed the adventure successfully, then they all get Experience rewards. It is important to note, though, that each cat can only get experience from this adventure *once*! If you play through and successfully finish the adventure several times, your cat only gains the rewards listed below after *first* time he or she completes the adventure.

If you use different cats each time, though, each one can get the experience rewards. The rule is *not* that a player can only get experience once, it's that a *cat* can.

Age: Although the action in this adventure clearly happens over the course of a single day, the presumption is that this is the most interesting and exciting thing that happens to your cat during the whole of that moon. Increase your cat's age by 1 moon and make any appropriate improvements described in Chapter Four of the game rules.

Skill: On top of the improvements your cat gets from aging, he or she also gains 1 level in one of the following skills: Listen, Ponder, or Smell.

Knack: If the players' cats rescued the missing apprentices without fighting the weasels (and your final scene was **21**), your cat also gains one level of the Clan Lore Knack.

More adventures can be found at the back of each novel in the Omen of the Stars series, and you can find extra information at www.warriorcats.com.

DON'T MISS

OMEN OF THE STARS

WARRIORS

BOOK SIX:
THE LAST HOPE

CHAPTER 1

Someone's bleeding!

Ivypool stiffened as the memory of Antpelt's death flooded her mind, just as it always did when the scent of blood hit her. She could still feel his flesh tearing beneath her claws, still see his final agonized spasm before he stopped moving forever. She'd been forced to kill the WindClan warrior to convince Tigerstar of her loyalty. It had earned her the grim honor of training Dark Forest warriors, but she knew she would never wash the scent of his blood from her paws.

"Stop!" she yowled.

Birchfall froze mid-lunge and stared at her. "What's wrong?"

"I smell blood," she snapped. "We're only training. I don't want any injuries."

Birchfall blinked at her, puzzled.

Redwillow scrambled up from underneath Birchfall's paws. "It's just a nick," the ShadowClan warrior meowed. He showed Ivypool his ear. Blood welled from a thin scratch at the tip.

"Just be careful," Ivypool cautioned.

"Be careful?" Hawkfrost's snarl made her spin around.

"There's a war coming and it won't be won with sheathed claws." Hawkfrost curled his lip and stared at Ivypool. "I thought you were helping to train our recruits to fight like real warriors, not soft Clan cats."

Birchfall bristled. "Clan cats aren't soft!"

"Then why do you come here?" Hawkfrost challenged.

Redwillow whisked his tail. "Our Clans need us to be the best warriors we can be. You told us that, remember?"

Hawkfrost nodded slowly. "And you can only learn the skills you need *here*." He flicked his nose toward Birchfall. "Attack Redwillow again," he ordered. "This time don't stop at the first scent of blood." He narrowed his eyes at Ivypool.

Ivypool swallowed, terrified she'd given herself away. No Dark Forest cat could ever know that she came here to spy for Dovewing, Jayfeather, and Lionblaze. Growling, she lifted her chin and barged past Birchfall. "Do it like this," she told him. With a hiss she hurled herself at Redwillow, ducking away from his claws, and grasped his forepaw between her jaws. Using his weight to unbalance him, she snapped her head around and twisted him deftly onto his back. He landed with a thump, which she knew sounded more painful than it felt. She'd hardly pierced his fur with her teeth and her jerk was so well-timed it had knocked him off his feet without wrenching his leg.

She glanced back at Hawkfrost, relieved to see approval glinting in his eyes. He'd only seen the flash of fur and claw and heard the smack of muscle against the slippery earth.

"Hawkfrost!"

Birchfall and Redwillow stared wide-eyed as Applefur

appeared from the mist. The ShadowClan she-cat's eyes were bright, her mottled brown pelt pulsing with heat from training. "Blossomfall and Hollowflight want to fight *Dark Forest* warriors."

Applefur's apprentices padded out of the shadows. "We can fight Clan cats anytime," Blossomfall complained.

Hollowflight nodded. "We come here to learn skills we can't learn anywhere else." The RiverClan tom's pelt was matted with blood. Clumps of fur stuck out along his spine.

Haven't you had enough? Ivypool glanced at Hawkfrost. "Are there any Dark Forest warriors close by?" she ventured, praying there weren't.

"Of course." Hawkfrost tasted the air.

The screech of fighting cats echoed through the mist. It had become like birdsong to Ivypool—filling the forest, so familiar that she only heard it when she listened for it. "Why aren't we training with them tonight?" she asked. Most nights, the Dark Forest warriors couldn't wait to share their cruel skills with the Clan cats.

Hawkfrost wove between Blossomfall and Applefur. "I want you to learn how other Clans fight."

Ivypool shivered.

"You may be fighting side by side one day," Hawkfrost went on.

Liar!

"You need to know your allies' moves so you can match them, claw for claw."

No, you're training them to destroy one another in the final battle.

FOLLOW THE ADVENTURES!

WARRIORS: THE PROPHECIES BEGIN

WARRIORS
INTO THE WILD

ERIN HUNTER
#1 *NEW YORK TIMES* BESTSELLING AUTHOR

 1

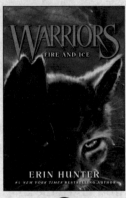

WARRIORS
FIRE AND ICE

ERIN HUNTER
#1 *NEW YORK TIMES* BESTSELLING AUTHOR

 2

WARRIORS
FOREST OF SECRETS

ERIN HUNTER
#1 *NEW YORK TIMES* BESTSELLING AUTHOR

 3

WARRIORS
RISING STORM

ERIN HUNTER
#1 *NEW YORK TIMES* BESTSELLING AUTHOR

 4

WARRIORS
A DANGEROUS PATH

ERIN HUNTER
#1 *NEW YORK TIMES* BESTSELLING AUTHOR

 5

WARRIORS
THE DARKEST HOUR

ERIN HUNTER
#1 *NEW YORK TIMES* BESTSELLING AUTHOR

 6

In the first series, sinister perils threaten the four warrior Clans.
Into the midst of this turmoil comes Rusty, an ordinary housecat,
who may just be the bravest of them all.

HARPER
An Imprint of HarperCollinsPublishers

www.warriorcats.com

WARRIORS : THE NEW PROPHECY

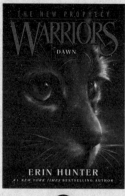

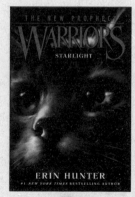

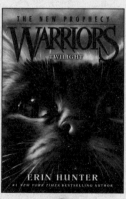

In the second series, follow the next generation of heroic cats as they set off on a quest to save the Clans from destruction.

HARPER
An Imprint of HarperCollinsPublishers

www.warriorcats.com

WARRIORS: POWER OF THREE

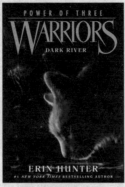

In the third series, Firestar's grandchildren begin their training as warrior cats. Prophecy foretells that they will hold more power than any cats before them.

HARPER
An Imprint of HarperCollinsPublishers

www.warriorcats.com

WARRIORS: OMEN OF THE STARS

1

2

3

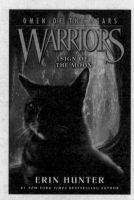

4

5

6

In the fourth series, find out which ThunderClan apprentice will complete the prophecy.

HARPER
An Imprint of HarperCollinsPublishers

www.warriorcats.com

WARRIORS: DAWN OF THE CLANS

1

2

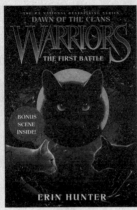

3

4

5

6

In this prequel series,
discover how the warrior Clans came to be.

New Look Coming Soon!

HARPER
An Imprint of HarperCollinsPublishers

www.warriorcats.com

WARRIORS: SUPER EDITIONS

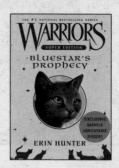

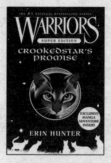

These extra-long, stand-alone adventures will take you deep inside each of the Clans with thrilling adventures featuring the most legendary warrior cats.

HARPER
An Imprint of HarperCollinsPublishers

www.warriorcats.com

WARRIORS : BONUS STORIES

Discover the untold stories of the warrior cats and Clans when you download the separate ebook novellas—or read them in two paperback bind-ups!

HARPER
An Imprint of HarperCollinsPublishers

www.warriorcats.com